WHEN SWORD ANSWERED
SPELL-STORM—

I felt it before I heard it: a thrumming, numbing, gut-deep tingle that rattled the bones of my elbows and threatened to shatter wrists. The power I sensed was sweet, seductive, oh so attractive. It knew me. It knew my song. I had quenched it, then requenched, and we were doubly bonded now.

And then the power changed. The essence surrounding me winked out, and I felt something else burst into flame to take its place. Something very strong. Something very *angry*.

It sheeted down from the sword, corruscating like heat lightning across the Punja's horizon. Black light. *Black* light. And yet it glowed. It flooded down the blade, tapped tentatively at my hands upon the grip, then flowed downward again, engulfing fingers, hands, wrists.

I swore. I said something very rude. Because I was, abruptly, more frightened than I had ever been before.

The light was touching me. . . .

SWORD-BREAKER

JENNIFER ROBERSON

DAW BOOKS, INC.
DONALD A. WOLLHEIM, FOUNDER
375 Hudson Street, New York, NY 10014

ELIZABETH R. WOLLHEIM
SHEILA E. GILBERT
PUBLISHERS

First Printing, July 1991

3 4 5 6 7 8 9

 DAW TRADEMARK REGISTERED
U.S. PAT. OFF. AND FOREIGN COUNTRIES
—MARCA REGISTRADA,
HECHO EN U.S.A.

PRINTED IN THE U.S.A.

*This book is dedicated to the memory of Jan Carpenter,
to her beloved Tootsie and Kizzy,
and to all the friends who miss her.*

Acknowledgments

Appreciation and gratitude to the following, for a variety of reasons: Russ Galen, agent extraordinaire; Alan Dean Foster and Raymond E. Feist, wise men both, for advice most sound in all respects; Betsy Wollheim and Sheila Gilbert, the Future of Fantasy (but next time let's stay in the suite and send out for pizza and beer!); Debby Burnett, for Kismet Cheysuli Wld Blu Yond'r, AKA "Pilot"; and Mark—for everything.

Lastly, to the men and women who understand sexism is a sword that cuts both ways and are working diligently to break it.

Prologue

There are things in life you just *know*, without having to think much about them.

Like *now*, for example.

I lurched to my feet in the darkness, staggered two steps through rocks, landed painfully on my knees. "Oh, hoolies," I muttered.

And promptly discarded my supper.

Supper such as it *was*; Del and I hadn't really had much chance to eat a proper meal the night before, being too tired, too twitchy, too tense. And, in my case, too dizzy.

Around me, insects fell silent. The only sounds I heard were the scraping of shod hooves in dirt—my bay stud, Del's blue roan, hobbled a few steps away— and my own rather undignified bleat that was half hiccup, half belch, and all disgruntlement.

From behind me, a sleep-blurred voice, and the scratch of pebbles and gritty dust displaced by a moving body. "Tiger?"

I hunched there on my knees, sweaty and cold and miserable. My head hurt too much to attempt a verbal answer, so I waved a limp, dismissive hand, swiping the air between us, and hoped it was enough.

Naturally, it wasn't. With her, it never is.

Blurriness evaporated. She wastes little time waking up. "Are you all right?"

My posture was unmistakable. "I'm praying," I mumbled sourly, wiping my mouth on a burnous sleeve; it was already filthy dirty. "Can't you tell?"

Sand gritted again. From behind she slung a bota, which landed next to me. The sloshing thwack of leather on stone was loud in the pallor of first light. The stud snorted a protest. "Here," Del said. "Water. I'll warm the kheshi."

Belly rebelled at the thought. My turn for a protest. "Hoolies, bascha—kheshi's the last thing I need!"

"You need *something* in your stomach, or you'll be spewing your guts up all day."

Nice way to start the morning. Glumly, carefully, I reached down and hooked the bota thong, shifting weight to ease aching knees. I was stiff and sore inside and out from the exertions of the sword-dance.

Well, no, not really a sword-dance; more like a sword-fight, which is an entirely different thing with entirely different rules; better yet, a sword-*war*. Del and I had won the battle, with a little help from luck, friends, and magic—not to mention mass confusion—but hostilities were not concluded.

I thought briefly about rising, then considered the state of head and belly and decided staying close to the ground in an attitude of prayer, regardless of true intention, was a posture worth practicing.

Squinting against my reasserted headache, I uncorked the bota, drank a little, discovered tipping my head back did nothing at all to still the hammer and anvil. With great care I leveled my head again and peered out at the pale morning, focusing fixedly on dimming stars to distract me from the discomfort in offended skull and belly.

Realizing, as I did so, something *besides* my belly desired emptying.

Which meant I had to get up anyway, if only to find a bush.

Hoolies, life was much easier before I joined up with a woman.

"Tiger?"

I twitched, then wished I hadn't. Even blinking hurt my head. "What?"

"We can't stay here. We'll have to ride on."

I grunted, thinking instead of ways to rid myself of the headache. Drinking aqivi might help, except we had none. "Eventually," I agreed. "First things *first*, bascha like finding out if I can walk."

"You don't have to walk. You have to ride." She paused: elaborate, sarcastic solicitude. "Do you think you can ride, Tiger?"

My back remained to her, so she didn't see the oath I mouthed against the dawn. "I'll manage."

She chose to ignore my irony. "You'll need to manage soon. They'll be coming after us."

Yes, so they would be. Every "they" they could muster. Tens and twenties of them; possibly even hundreds.

The sun began to crawl above the swordblade of the horizon. I squinted against the light. "Maybe I *should* pray," I muttered. "Aren't I the jhihadi?"

Del grunted skepticism. "You are no messiah, no matter what you say about Jamail pointing at you."

Injured innocence: "But I swore by my *sword*."

She said something of succinct, exquisite brevity in Northern, which is her native tongue, and which adapts itself as readily to swearing as my Southron one does.

"Hah," she said, more politely. "You forget, Tiger— I know better. I know *you*. What you are is a man who's been kicked in the head, and drunk on top of it."

Well, she had the first part right: I *had* been kicked in the head, and, of all the indignities, by my own horse. But the second part was wrong. "I'm not drunk."

"You were yesterday. *And* last night."

"That was yesterday—and last night. And most of *that* was the kick in the head . . . besides, I don't notice it kept me from rescuing you."

"You didn't rescue me."

"Oh, no?" With meticulous effort, I got off my knees and onto my feet, turning slowly to face her. Movement hurt like hoolies. Sweetly, I inquired, "And who *was* it who held back an angry mob of people intent on ripping you to pieces for killing the jhihadi?"

Del's tone, surprisingly, was perfectly matter-of-fact. "He wasn't the jhihadi. He was Ajani. Bandit. Murderer. Rapist." She looked through thready smoke seeping upward from the handful of coals masquerading as a fire. Lumpy, bone-gray kheshi dripped from a battered cup as she scooped up a generous serving and held it out to me. "Breakfast is ready."

The stud chose that moment to flood the dirt. Which reminded me of something.

"Wait—" I blurted intently.

And staggered off to the nearest bush to pay tribute to the gods.

One

I hooked my foot into the stirrup as I caught reins and pommel—and stopped moving altogether. Which left me sort of *suspended,* weight distributed unevenly throughout sore legs stretched painfully between stirrup and ground. Since the stirrup was attached to saddle—which was, in turn, attached to a horse, however temporarily by dint of a cinch—I realized it was not the most advantageous of positions if the horse decided to move. But for the moment, it was the best I could manage.

"Uck," I commented. "Whose idea was this?"

The stud swung his head around and eyed me consideringly with one dark eye, promising much with nothing discernible. Except I know how to read him.

I exhibited a fist. "Better not, cumfa-bait."

Del, from atop her roan, with some asperity: "Tiger."

"Oh, keep your tunic tied." With an upward heave that did nothing at all to ease the ache in my head—or the rebellion in my belly—I swung up. "Of course, in *your* case, I'd just as soon you *un*tied the tunic." I I cast her a toothy leer that was, I knew in my heart of hearts, but a shadow of the one I am capable of

displaying. But a battered body and too much liquor—
and a kick in the head—will do that for you.

One pale brow arched. "That is not what you said
last night."

"Last night I had a headache." I gathered loose rein
as I settled my rump in the leather hummock some
people call a saddle. "I *still* have a headache."

Del nodded. "It often comes of a man who believes
himself a person of repute. The head swells . . ." She
gestured idle implication.

"That's a panjandrum. I never claimed I was a panjandrum—although I suppose I am, being the Sandtiger." I ribbed a gritty, sun-dazzled eye. "No, what
I am is a jhihadi; even the Oracle said so." I displayed
teeth again. "Will you call your brother a liar?"

She gazed at me steadily. "Before yesterday, I
would have called my brother *dead*. You told me he
was."

I opened my mouth to explain all over again that
the Vashni had told me Jamail was dead; I'd had no
reason not to believe the warrior since the tribe is so
meticulous about honor. Telling a falsehood is not a
Vashni habit, even though no one in his right mind
would even suggest such a thing. I hadn't, certainly.
Nor had I thought it.

No, Del's brother wasn't dead, no matter what the
Vashni had told me. Because Jamail—supposedly
dead, *mute* Jamail—had pointed across a milling
throng in the midst of a violent sword fight between
his older sister and the man who had murdered his
kin—and proclaimed me the messiah.

Me, not Ajani, who had gone to great pains to convince everyone he was the jhihadi. Although no one,
including Del (*still*), believed Jamail had pointed at
me.

Which had a little something to do with our present predicament.

I stared blearily eastward beyond Del, raising a shielding hand to block the brilliance of the sun. "Is that dust?"

She looked. Like me, she squinted, lifting a flattened palm. Against the new day she was a darker silhouette: one-quarter profile, mostly fair hair; a shoulder, an elbow, the turn of hip and the line of thigh beneath the drapery of Southron silk.

And the slash of a scabbarded sword, slanting diagonally across her back to thrust an imperious hilt above one taut-muscled shoulder.

"Out of Iskandar," she said quietly of the gauzy haze. "I would not waste a copper on a wager that it could be anything else."

Which made a decision imperative.

"North across the border into your territory," I suggested, "but, under the terms of your exile, that's not exactly an option—"

"—or south," she interposed, "into the Punja again, *your* territory, which will surely kill us both if we give it the opportunity."

"Then again," I continued, "there is Harquhal. Half a day, maybe—"

"—where they will surely come, all of them, knowing it is the only place to buy supplies, and we with little to spare."

Which was true. Our sudden and unanticipated departure—better yet, *flight*—from Iskandar had given us little time to pack our horses. We had a set of saddle-pouches each, thanks to a friend, but food was limited. So was our water, something we *had* to have if we were to cross the Punja. While I knew of many oases, cisterns, and settlements—I'd grown up in the

Punja—the desert is a transitory and unforgiving beast. The only certain thing is death, if you don't play the game right.

I spat out a succinct oath along with acrid dust as I lifted eloquent reins, putting the stud on notice. "Doesn't seem to me as if we have much choice. Unless, of course, you can magick us out of here with your sword."

"No more than you with yours." Unsmiling, as always. But the glint in blue eyes was plain.

The weight of the weapon in my harness was suddenly increased tenfold, just by the mention of it. And the implications.

"You sure know how to ruin a perfectly good morning," I muttered, swinging the stud.

"And you a beautiful night." Del turned her roan toward Harquhal, half a day's ride from the border. "Perhaps if you shut your mouth, the snoring would not be so bad."

I didn't bother to answer. The thundering of the stud's hooves drowned out anything I might say.

The thunder in my skull drowned out the desire to even *try*.

We hadn't done much, Del and I. Not when you really think about it. We'd just gone south through the Punja hunting a missing brother, stolen by Southron slavers. To Julah, the city near the sea, where we had, with little choice, killed a tanzeer. That sort of offense is punishable by death, as might be expected when you knock off a powerful desert prince; except Del and I had gotten clean away from Julah and her freshly-murdered tanzeer. And gone on into the mountains at the rim of the ocean-sea, where we'd encountered Vashni. The tribe that held her brother.

Except he wasn't really being *held;* not any more. Mute and castrated, he'd nonetheless managed to make a life for himself. Del's plans for rescue were undone by Jamail himself, who clearly had no desire to leave the tribe that had delivered him from a life-time of slavery. While not precisely a Vashni—they don't take kindly to half-bloods, let alone foreigners—neither was he suitable for sacrifice. He'd made his place.

So we'd left him, and ridden north, across the border to Del's homeland. Where she had taken me to Staal-Ysta, the island in black water, and delivered me as ransom to buy her daughter back.

Well, not *exactly*—but close enough. Close enough that I'd discovered just how single-minded she could be; to the point that nothing else in the world mattered, only the task she'd set herself: to find and kill Ajani, the man who'd murdered her family, raped a fifteen-year-old girl, and sold a ten-year-old boy into Southron slavery.

To find Ajani, she needed to be free of the blood-debt, which she owed to the Place of Swords, high in Northern mountains. Where she'd left her infant daughter to find and kill the daughter's father.

And, eventually, where she'd offered my services, me all unknowing, to pay part of her blood-debt.

My services . . . without even asking me.

Now, I've always known women are capable of doing just about anything they set their minds to, once they've made a decision. Getting *to* that decision isn't always the easiest thing, or the most logical, but even-tually they get there. And, when pressed to it, they make promises they have to, no matter what it takes.

For Del, it took me. And very nearly our deaths.

Oh, we'd survived. But not before I wound up with

a Northern sword, a magical *jivatma* as dangerous as Del's—only I didn't know how to key it, and it damn near keyed *me*.

And then, of course, there had been that thrice-cursed dragon, which wasn't a dragon at all, and the sorcerer called Chosa Dei.

A man no longer a man. A *spirit*, I guess you'd call him, who now lived in my sword.

Ahead of me, riding hard, Del twisted in the saddle. Horse-born wind snatched at white-blonde locks, tearing them free of burnous. Pale, glorious silk masquerading as hair . . . and the flawless face it framed, now turned in my direction.

I have never failed, not once, to marvel at her beauty.

"Hurry up," she said.

Of course, then there's her *mouth*.

"One of these days," I muttered, "I'm going to pin you down—*sit* on you, if I have to—and pour as much wine as I can buy down that soft, self-righteous gullet, so you'll know what my head feels like."

I didn't say it where she could hear it. But of course she *did*.

"Even a fool knows better than to drink after being kicked in the head," she commented over the noise of our horses. "So what does that make you?"

I shifted on the fly, finding a more comfortable position over the humping spine of my galloping horse. "You left me," I reminded her, raising my voice. "You left me lying there on the ground with my broken, bloodied head. If you'd stayed, I probably wouldn't have drunk anything."

"Oh, so it's *my* fault."

"Instead, you went flouncing off to fight Abbu Bensir—*my* dance, I might add—"

"You were in no shape to dance."

"That's beside the point—"

"That *is* the point." Del reined her roan around a dribble of rocks, then tossed hair out of her face as she twisted to look at me again. "I took your place in the circle because someone had to. You had been hired to dance against Abbu . . . had I not taken your place, you would have forfeited the dance. Do you want to consider the consequences?"

Not really. I knew what they were. The dance was more than merely a sword-dance: it was binding arbitration between two factions of tanzeers, powerful, ruthless despots who, whenever they could, chopped the South into little pieces among themselves and passed out the remains as rewards.

A reward *I* had been promised, if I won.

Except I didn't win, because the stud kicked me in the head, and Alric got me drunk.

My belly was, I thought unhappily, riding somewhere in the vicinity of my breastbone, jounced and bounced and compressed within the cage of my ribs. Knees, bent by shortened stirrups, reminded me whenever they could that I was gaining in age, while losing in flexibility. And then there was my head, which shall go unremarked so as not to give it ideas.

Hoolies, this sort of thing is enough to give a man pause. To remind him, rather emphatically, there are better ways than this of making a living.

Except I don't know of any.

The stud's misstep threatened to rearrange a portion of my body I was rather fond of. I bit out a curse, lifted weight off formed leather, and thought rather wistfully of other fleshly saddles.

"You're falling behind," she said.

"Just wait," I muttered. "There will come a day—"

"I don't think so," Del said, and bent lower over her roan.

Harquhal is . . . well, Harquhal. A border settlement. The kind of town no one *means* to build, really, because if it had been planned from the beginning, everyone contributing would have done the job right.

Oh, it was good *enough,* but not the sort of place I'd want to raise a family.

Then again, I didn't have a family, nor did I intend to start one, which meant the kind of town Harquhal was was good enough for me.

Del and I rode in at a long-trot, having dropped out of a gallop sometime back, then from lope to trot as we approached the wall-girded town. The stud, who has an adequate gallop and a soft, level long-*walk,* does not, most emphatically, know how to trot very well. He just isn't built for it, any more than I am built for low doorways and short beds.

A long-trot, trotted by a horse who does not possess the ability to offer this gait in anything approaching comfort, is nothing short of torture. Particularly if you are male. Particularly if you are male, and your head has been abused by aqivi and the kick of the horse you're riding.

So why trot at all? Because if I dropped to a walk I surrendered the advantage to Del, except I suppose it wasn't really an advantage, since we weren't actually racing. But she can be so cursed patronizing at times . . . especially when she thinks I'm in the wrong, or have done something stupid. And while I suppose there *have* been times I haven't been right, or I've behaved in such a way as to cast doubt upon my intelligence, this wasn't one of them. It hadn't been my fault the stud had kicked me. Nor my decision to suck

down so much aqivi. And anyway, I *had* still managed
to save her.

No matter what she said.

We reached the first sprawl of adobe wall encircling
Harquhal. I eased the stud to a walk, breathing impre-
cations as he took most of the change of gait on his
front legs, instead of distributed through his body. It
makes a man sit up and take notice, in more ways
than one.

Del cast a glance at me over a shoulder. "We
shouldn't stay long. Only to buy supplies—"

"—and get a drink," I appended. "Hoolies, but I
need a drink."

She opened her verbal dance pedantically, in the glacial way she has that ages her three decades. "We will
not waste time on such things as wine or aqivi—"

I reined the stud next to her roan, hooking a knee
just under the inner bend of her own. It is a technique, when fully employed, that can unhorse an
enemy. And while Del and I were not precisely *enemies*, we were most distinctly at odds. "If I don't get
a drink, I'll never make it through the day. In this
case, it's *medicinal* . . . hoolies, bascha, haven't you
ever heard of biting the dog back?"

Del disentangled her leg by easing the roan over.
Her expression was wondrously blank. "Biting the
dog? What dog? You were not bitten. You were
kicked."

"No, no, not like that." I scrubbed at a stubbled,
grimy face. "It's a Southron saying. It has to do with
having too much to drink. If you have a taste of whatever it was that made you sick, it makes you feel
better."

Blonde brows knitted. "That makes no sense at all.

If something makes you sick, how can it make you feel better?"

A thought occurred to me. I eyed her consideringly. "In all the time I've known you, I've never seen you drunk."

"Of course not."

"But you do drink. I've seen you drink, bascha."

Her tone was eloquent. "It is possible to drink and not get drunk. If one employs *restraint*—"

"Restraint is not always desirable," I pointed out. "Why employ restraint when you *want* to get drunk?"

"But why get drunk at all?"

"Because it makes you feel good."

Lines appeared in her brow. "But you have just now said spirits can make you sick. As you were sick this morning."

"Yes, well . . . that's different." I scowled. "Drinking spirits, as you call them, is not a good idea after you've been kicked in the head."

"It is not a good idea to drink so much at *any* time, Tiger. Especially for a sword-dancer." She tucked a strand of hair back. "It was a thing I learned on Staal-Ysta: never surrender will or skill to strong spirits, or you may defeat yourself."

I scratched my sandtiger scars idly. "I don't lose much, strong spirits or no. Matter of fact, I haven't *ever* lost, not when it counted—"

Del's tone was level as she cut in. "Because you and I have never danced for real."

The riposte was too easy. "Oh, *yes* we did, bascha. And it nearly got us killed."

It shut her up altogether, which is what I'd meant it to. It's how you win a dance: find the weakness, then exploit it. It is a strategy that carries over even to life outside of the circle, in every single respect.

Del knew it well. Del knew how to do it. Del knew how to win.

Except this time she didn't.

And this time she knew she couldn't.

Two

Under the eye of the morning sun, Del and I dismounted in an elbow-bend of a narrow, dust-choked street. She headed in one direction, leading her roan gelding, I in the other with the stud, until we realized what had happened and turned back, each of us, speaking at the same time. Telling one another which way was the proper direction.

I pointed my way. She pointed hers.

I pointed a bit more firmly. "Cantina's down there."

"Supplies are down *here*."

"Bascha, we don't have time to argue—"

"We don't have time to do anything more than reprovision and leave."

"Getting something to drink *is* reprovisioning."

"For *some*, perhaps." Nothing more. She obviously believed it enough. Del is very good at saying much with little. It's a woman's thing, I think: they get more out of a tone of voice than a man out of a knife.

Of course, some men might argue a woman's tongue is sharper.

"Or," I continued, overriding what she would undoubtedly refer to as common good sense, "we

could hole up in one of the cantinas. Rent us a room."
Which *I* thought was good sense; we'd have plenty of
provisions, plus a roof over our heads.

One hand perched itself on a burnous-swathed hip.
A jutting elbow cut the air, eloquent even in silence.
"And do what, Tiger? Wait for them to come find
us?"

I ground teeth. "They *might* assume we'd ridden
on."

"Or they might realize we'd need provisions and
rest, and search all the rooms. Each and every one."
She paused. "Then again, I think there would be no
need for such trouble. Do you truly believe there is
a soul alive in Harquhal who would not sell us to
them?"

Maybe one or two. Maybe three or four.

But all it took was one.

We glared at one another, neither of us giving an
inch. The roan slobbered on Del's left shoulder; with
a grimace of distaste, she shook off the glop of green-
ish grass-slime. Meanwhile the stud dug a hole, raising
gritty Southron dust that insinuated itself between my
sandaled toes.

Which put me in mind of a bath; I'm as clean as I
can be, mostly, though the desert makes it hard. The
sun makes you sweat. Dust sticks to sweat. Pretty
soon you're caked.

I hadn't had a bath in days. *During* those days I'd
gotten real sweaty, drunk, and bloody, not to mention
dust-crusty. I needed a bath badly. And if we had a
room, I could *have* a bath.

But.

"How many do you think?" I asked finally, ignoring
the dispute altogether.

She shrugged, avoiding it also; thinking, as I did,

of other considerations. "We killed the jhihadi—at least, the man they *believe* was jhihadi. It is all to pieces, now—the prophecy, the Oracle, the promises of change. Many will not come, but the zealots will not give up."

"Unless your brother has managed to talk some sense into them. Convince them Ajani wasn't their man at all." And that I *was*, but that I doubt they'd believe. To everyone in the South—well, at least to the people who knew me, which wasn't *quite* the whole South (if I do say so myself)—I was the Sand-tiger. Sword-dancer. Not messiah. Not the person who was supposed to, somehow, change the sand to grass.

Del raised an illustrative finger intended, I knew, to put me in my place by pointing out lapses in logic. She likes to think she can. She likes to think she can *tell*. "If my brother *can* talk. You say he can. You say he *did*—"

"He did. I heard him. So did a lot of others. The only reason *you* missed it was because you were danc-ing with Ajani."

"It wasn't a dance," she countered instantly. (Trust a woman to change the subject in mid-discussion.) "Dances have honor attached. That was an exe-cution."

"Yes, well . . ." It had been, but I didn't feel like debating it just now, under the circumstances. "Look, I don't know what those religious fools are going to do, and neither do you. They could still be back in Iskandar—"

"Then what was all that dust we saw earlier?"

Sometimes she has a point.

I sighed. "Go get the provisions, bascha. I'll go get us some wine."

"*And* water."

"Yes. Water."

And aqivi as well. But I didn't tell her that.

Eventually, she came looking. I'd known she would, because women always do. They make you wait forever when *you* want to go somewhere, but when *they* want to leave they don't give you even a moment. I'd barely swallowed my aqivi.

My *second* cup, that is, but I wouldn't tell Del that.

The cantina was dim, because cantinas in border towns—in any desert town, for that matter—always lack for light except for what the sun provides. Here in the South, a little sun goes a long way; hence, windows are nearly nonexistent, and usually cut in the eastern wall because the sun's morning eye is coolest. Which means that by midday the sun's altered angle cuts off much of the light that would otherwise slant through a window and illuminate the room. By late afternoon, it starts to get downright gloomy. But at least it's not so hot.

Del pulled aside the door sacking hung to cut the dust, and stepped into the cantina. One swift glance assessed the place easily: tiny, grimy, squalid. A barely breathing body sprawled on the dirt floor in a corner near the door, far gone in huva dreams. A second, more lively body hunched on a stool by one of the eastside windows. As Del entered, it murmured and sat up. I'd gotten used to that. I wondered if Del had.

For just that suspended moment, I saw her as others did; as *I* had, so often, the first few times I'd laid eyes on her. She was—and *is*—spectacular: tall, long-limbed, graceful, with a powerful elegance. Not feminine, but *female,* in all the vast subtleties of the word.

Even swathed in a white burnous the body was glorious. The flawless face was better still.

Something flared deep in my guts. Something more than desire: the knowledge and the wonder that what other men might dream about was freely shared with me.

A brief, warm moment. I lifted my cup in tribute. "May the sun shine on your head."

Del eyed me in speculation. "Are you ready yet?"

I grinned fatuously, still oddly touched by the moment. "A swallow, but a swallow . . ." I downed the last of my drink.

Blue eyes narrowed beneath down-slanting, dubious brows. "How many have you had?"

The moment was over. Reality intruded. I sighed. "Only as many as I had time for in the very brief moment of freedom allowed while you purchased provisions." I inspected the interior of the cup, but the aqivi was gone.

"The way *you* gulp wine, you might have had an entire bota." She scowled at the numerous suspect botas hanging over both shoulders. "Can you ride?"

I resettled bota thongs. "I was born on the back of a horse."

"Then I feel sorry for your mother." Del angled a shoulder, reaching toward the sacking. "Are you coming?"

"Already halfway there." I strode past her rapidly, pausing long enough to bestow upon her outstretched arm five sloshing botas.

Del, muttering as she struggled to untangle thongs, followed me out of doors. "I am not carrying your foul-tasting aqivi."

"I have the aqivi. *You* have the water."

She glared up at me as I mounted the stud. "Equitable arrangement. I have more botas than you."

"Extra water," I agreed. "I thought at some point in time you might want to wash your face."

I swung the stud as she mounted, grinning to myself as she rubbed surreptitiously at her face. She is not a woman for vanity, though the gods have blessed her threefold, but I've never yet known a woman not to fall for the implication.

We all have our petty revenge.

Riding. Again. Only this time my head was better. This time I could see straight. Biting the dog back does wonders for the soul.

Del reined her horse in beside me as we left Harquhal behind and took the straightest road. "So," she said, "where?"

I planted a heel into the stud's shoulder as he reached to bite the roan. "Give it a rest, flea-bag. . . . Well, since we're already heading south, I thought it was sort of decided."

"We *discussed* it last night. Nothing was decided."

I vaguely remembered our conversation. Bits and pieces of it. Something to do with finding someone.

Realization pinched my belly. "Shaka Obre," I blurted.

Del unstuck a strand of hair from her bottom lip. "And again, I say it will be difficult. If not impossible."

I shifted in my saddle. The nape of my neck crawled: hairs standing up. Even my forearms tingled. "Hoolies, bascha, now you've brought it all up again."

She slapped aside the stud's questing nose as it lingered near her left knee. "One of us had better."

I worked my shoulders, trying to shake off the crawly feeling. I'd spent all morning mostly concerned with abolishing my headache and the discontent of my belly. While neither was completely cured, both were much improved—which left me with the time to think about something else. Something downright confusing, as well as unsettling.

"I don't like it," I muttered.

"It was your idea to seek out Shaka Obre."

"That's what it was: an *idea*. Not everyone acts on them."

Del nodded sagely. "So, we are merely running, then? Not seeking?"

"It might make things easier. I know enough places in the South. We could find a spot and hole up until all the furor dies down."

Del nodded again. "There is that. Given time, even a holy war will pass."

I didn't think much of her tone of voice: too guileless. "Wait." I dug under my burnous and caught hold of my coin-pouch. Years of experience had taught me to count by weight. "How much coin do you have?"

Del didn't bother to check. "A few coppers, nothing more. I spent most on the provisions."

I tugged the burnous back into place, pulling it free of harness straps. "Well, we'll just have to rustle up a few dances here and there. Fatten the purses a little. Then go into hiding." I sighed. "Hiding always takes coin."

Pale brows arched. "You are suggesting we accept sword-dances to make money?"

I scowled. "It *is* how we make our livings."

"But only when people are willing to pay to see the match, or to hire us to dance for some other reason. Why would they pay us to dance now, in hopes of winning a few wagers, when all they need do is take us prisoner? Surely the price on our heads outweighs any profit in a dance."

"I'm not so sure there's a price on our heads—" The stud tripped over a rock. "Pick your feet up, lop-ear, before you fall on your nose."

"We—*I*—killed the jhihadi. What do you think?"

I leaned down from the saddle and spat grit out of my mouth. "What do I think? I think they'll be like the hounds of hoolies, tracking us to ground. I don't necessarily think there's a price on our heads . . . I think they'll want to kill us just for the doing of it, because we stole their dreams."

"And such folk will pay to find us. Even a rumor of our direction will earn a copper or two."

"Maybe. Maybe not." I sighed and scratched stubbled scars. "All right. I agree it might be best if we didn't go looking for dances. But there are other occupations . . . we could hire on with a caravan. Holy war or no holy war, there will be caravans trying to cross the Punja through borjuni-infested areas. They'll need us."

"There is that," she agreed. "Except that a holy war disrupts trade, and therefore the caravan traffic may not be quite what it was, for a while. And if you were a caravan-serai, would you hire on the two people who killed the messiah?"

"He wouldn't have to know who we were."

Del perused me intently. Her expression was exquisitely bland, which meant I was in trouble. "How many *other* Southron sword-dancers are there who are a head taller than other men, two shades lighter at least, without being Northerner-pale, who bears sand-tiger scars on his face—not to mention the *green* eyes—and who carries a Northern *jivatma*?"

I scowled. "Probably about as many of them as

there are six-feet-tall, blonde, blue-eyed, mouthy Northern baschas who *also* carry a sword. And a magical one, at that."

Del's tone was sanguine. "The price a panjandrum must pay."

"Yes, well . . ." I aimed the stud monotonously southerly, suggesting he rediscover his soft-stepping long-walk. "We have to do something. We're running out of money. Life on the run costs."

"There is another option."

"Oh?"

"We could steal."

In shock, I stared at her. *"Steal?"*

Del's Northern accent and word choice colors all her speech, but she managed a decent mimicry of my Southron drawl. "In all your vastly honorable life, have you never heard of such a thing?"

I thought it unworthy of an answer. "But *you.* This is *you* suggesting theft? I mean, isn't it against Staal-Ysta's code of ethics, or something? You're always nattering on about how much emphasis you Northerners place on honor." I stared at her more intently. "Have you ever stolen anything in your whole entire Northern life?"

"Have you?"

"I asked you first. And anyway, I'm not Northern. It doesn't count."

"It does count. Of you I would expect it . . . you yourself have said, time and again, you would do anything for survival."

"A certain amount of ruthlessness does help in my line of work."

"Well, then, as my line of work and yours are the same, regardless of gender, it would seem logical to assume I understood the concept of stealing."

"Understanding and *doing* are two different things," I reminded her. "Have you ever stolen? You, personally? You, the Northern sword-dancer, master of a *jivatma*? Trained in all the ancient and binding honor codes of Staal-Ysta?"

Del's turn to scowl. Except hers is prettier. "Why is it impossible for you to believe I might have stolen? Have I not killed men? Have you not seen me kill men?"

"Only those who wanted to kill you. There's a bit of difference between self-defense and stealing, bascha." I grinned. "And the 'might have stolen' phrase is a dead giveaway."

Del sighed. "No, I have not personally ever stolen. But it does not mean I can't. Before Ajani murdered my family, I had never killed, either. And now it is my trade."

A discomfiting chill touched the base of my spine. "It isn't your trade, bascha. You have killed, yes— but it isn't your *trade*. You're a sword-dancer. Not all of us kill. When some of us do, it's because we have to. When our own lives are in danger."

The line of her jaw was tight. "The last seven years of my life, I have done little *but* kill."

"Ajani's dead," I told her. "That part of your life is over."

"Is it?" Her voice was grim.

"Of course it is. The blood-debt is paid. What is left for you to do?"

"Live," she bit out. "I have nearly twenty-three years. How many are left to me? Twenty more? Thirty? Perhaps even forty—"

"Occasionally," I agreed, trying to lighten the mood.

"And what am I to do with *forty more years?*"

A man my age—thirty-six? Thirty-seven?—would love to have forty more years. Meanwhile, Del made the length of time sound obscene. Which didn't sit real well.

"Hoolies, bascha—*live* them! What else is there to do?"

"I am a sword-dancer," she said tightly. "I have made myself such on purpose. But now you say that purpose is finished, because Ajani is dead."

"Del, in the name of valhail—"

Naturally, she did not allow me to finish. "Think, Tiger. You say that part of my life is over. The killing part; the part where I compromised my humanity in the name of my obsession." Something glittered in her eyes: anger, and frustration. "If that is true, what is left to me? What is left to a woman?"

"Not *that* again—"

"Shall I retire to a tanzeer's harem? Surely I would bring a fair price. I am exiled from the North—should I therefore marry a Southron farmer, or a Southron caravan-serai, or a Southron tavern-keeper?" She lifted an explanatory finger. "Remember, I am now barren. There can never be any children to repopulate the name." The hand slapped down. "Of what use am I, then?"

I grinned wryly, a little amused, a lot self-conscious, because the answer was so easy. The answer was *too* easy; Del had taught me to see it. Nonetheless, it was true. "In your case, some men—a *lot* of men!—might argue children are not necessary in order to maintain interest."

A wave of color washed through her face. Then Del gritted teeth. "If I am beautiful now, enough to 'maintain interest,' of what use will I be when the beauty has all faded? What do I *do*, Tiger? What is left to me?"

"Well, I hadn't really thought in terms of you going off to marry some Southron farmer—"

"Do I become a cantina girl? *You* appear to like them."

"Now, Del—"

"Or do I try to catch the eye of Julah's tanzeer?"

"Julah's tanzeer is a woman."

She shot me a glare. "You know what I mean."

"Julah's tanzeer would also like to kill us, remember? Especially you. You killed her father."

"*Killing*," Del said vehemently, "is what I do best."

"You don't like it? Then change it," I declared. "You've been spouting off to me for the last—what, almost two years?—about how a woman has to fight to make her way in a man's world. You've fought, and you've won. But expecting me to give you your answers is devaluing what you've accomplished. You became what you had to be for a specific purpose. That purpose is finished. So now find another one."

Del watched me. What she thought I couldn't tell; she is, even for me, difficult to read. But she had lost the burning intensity of her anger moments before. Her tone was much less strident. "As you have found a purpose?"

I shrugged. "I don't have a purpose. I just *am*."

Del smiled at last. The last trace of tension flowed out of her face. "The Sandtiger," she murmured. "Ah, yes, more than enough. A veritable panjandrum."

"Speaking of which," I said, "we still haven't made a decision."

"About what?"

"Where we're going."

"South."

"I've got that part. *Where* in the South?"

Irritated, she scowled. "How in hoolies should I know?"

Which pretty much summed up the way I felt, too.

Three

The oasis was little more than a tumble of squarish, yellow-pink boulders stacked haphazardly against the southerly encroachment of wind and sand, and a few sparse palm trees with straggly gray-green fronds. Not much shade to speak of, except the north-side blanket's-width of curving line at the foot of the boulder "wall," but not much is better than none. And besides, we weren't truly into the South by much; the border between the two lands is considerably cooler, and lacking in Punja crystals.

The water itself, captured in a natural stone basin rimmed by hand-mortared stones, was little more than wrist-deep, and therefore suspect as a sufficient supply—except that deep in the earth, buried beneath sand, soil, pebbles, and webby, red-throated grass, there was a natural spring. While it was simple enough to drain the basin within a matter of minutes—a horse could do it faster—it refilled itself rapidly. The resource appeared undiminished, but no one in the South took any chances. The hand-mortared rim of rocks kept the basin from being fouled by wind-blown sand; the crude lettering cut into each stone suppos-

edly protected the oasis from anyone—or any*thing*—
that sought to destroy its bounty.

I swung off the stud and gave him rein, letting him
suck the basin dry. The sand-colored stone briefly glistened wetly, then hid itself beneath water as the spring
refilled the basin. I let the stud drink half again, then
pulled him away.

Del, still atop her roan, frowned as I began to undo
knots in pouches and cinch. "You don't mean for us
to stay here. . . ?"

"It's getting on toward sundown."

"But this is so exposed . . . would we not do better
to go elsewhere? Somewhere less obvious?"

"Probably," I agreed. "Except there's water here.
You know as well as I that in the South, you don't
pass up water."

"No, but we could refill the botas, let the horses
cool, and then ride on."

"Ride on where?" I dropped the pouches to the
ground. "The next closest water is a good day's ride
from here. It would be foolish to leave now with night-
fall coming on. There's no moon tonight . . . do you
really want to chance getting lost in the darkness?"

Del sighed, absently battling her roan with
restraining reins. The gelding snorted wetly. "I
thought you told me once you knew the South like
the back of your hand."

"I do. Better than most. But that doesn't mean I'm
stupid." I undid the saddle, peeled it and the sweaty
blanket-pad off, dropped everything atop the pouches.
The stud's back was wet and rumpled. "We haven't
been through here in some time, bascha. For all I
know there've been twenty sandstorms since then. I'd
just as soon discover the changes in landscape when I
can *see* them."

"I understand," she said patiently. "But if we stay here, it makes it easy for others to find us."

I pointed toward the basin. "See those carvings? In addition to protection for the water, it gives sanctuary to desert travelers."

Her chin rose a notch. "Even to travelers accused of murdering a messiah?"

I gritted teeth. "Yes." I didn't know any such thing, but I wasn't disposed to argue.

She grunted skepticism. "Will they respect it?"

"It all depends on who shows up." I braced and stood my ground as the stud planted his head against my arm and began to rub exuberantly, scratching heat- and dust-born itches. "The tribes have always honored the traveler's truce. They're nomads, bascha . . . such places as this carry meaning. Those are tribal devices carved into the stone, promising protection to water and traveler. I don't think they'd break that custom, even *if* they caught up. And that's not a certainty."

"What if it's someone else? Someone who *doesn't* honor this custom?"

The stud rubbed even harder, nearly upsetting my balance. I pushed the intrusive head away. "Then we'll just have to deal with it. Sooner or later. Tonight, or tomorrow." I squinted up at her. "Don't you think it's time you gave that horse a drink? He's been pulling rein since we got here."

He had. The roan, inhaling water-scent, had been stomping hooves and swishing tail, trying to edge toward the basin. Del had kept him on a taut rein, fighting his head.

She grimaced and unhooked from the stirrups, swinging a long, burnous-swathed leg over as she slid off the roan. She let him water as I had, cursorily attending amount—you don't let a hot horse drink too much right away—but still knitted pale brows in a faint, annoyed frown. But the expression faded as she pulled the roan away and tended to the untacking. Work smoothed her face, banishing the tautness of jaw and the creases between her brows. It made her young again.

And gloriously beautiful, in a deadly, *edged* way, like a sword blade newly honed.

Ordinarily I'd have slipped the stud's bridle and left him haltered and hobbled. But current circumstances called for a bit more care and preparation. We needed the ability to mount and ride instantly; a hobbled, unbridled horse makes for too much delay. So the stud I left bitted with the reins trapped beneath a flat stone, although he was not much for wandering when water was near. Desert-born and bred, he knew better than to leave a known supply.

I stacked saddle and pad against the boulder wall, hair-side up to dry, and made my own arrangements with blankets, botas, pouches. All in all I was feeling pretty cheerful. My head had stopped throbbing, although a whisper of discomfort remained, and my belly no longer rebelled. I was human once again: I cast Del a grin.

She eyed me askance and tended the roan, rock-tying him as I had the stud, and stripped him free of saddle and pouches. He was a good enough horse, if tall—but then I'm used to my short-legged, compact, hard-as-rock stud, not a rangy, hairy Northern gelding with too much fat beneath his hide. Then again, in the North it was cold, and the extra layer of fat undoubtedly kept him warmer, along with the extra coat. As it was, the roan was shedding; Del, grimacing, stripped a few handfuls of damp blue-speckled hair and let them drift down through still air.

With the roan tended to, Del turned to me. "So, we are staying here the night."

I considered her a moment. "I thought we'd settled that."

She nodded once, decisively, then turned her back on me and stalked off through the grass and dirt and pebbles to a spot facing north. There she unsheathed her sword.

"Not again," I murmured.

Del lifted the naked weapon above her head, balancing blade and pommel across the flat of both bare palms, and sang. A small, quiet song. But its quietude had nothing to do with power, or the quality thereof; she summoned so easily, then dealt with what she wrought: a shimmer of salmon-silver, a spark of blinding white, the blue of a deep-winter storm. All ran the length of the blade, then purled down as banshee breath to bathe her lifted arms.

She held the posture. I could not see her face, only the arch of spine beneath burnous, the spill of hair down her back. Still, it was enough; deep inside of me, painfully, Del stirred emotions I could not fully acknowledge. More than simple lust, though there is always that; less than adoration, because she is not perfection. But all the things in between. Good and bad, black and white, male and female. Two halves make a whole. Del was my other half.

She sang. Then she brought the sword down, slicing through the breath of frost, and plunged the blade into the earth.

I sighed. "Yes: again."

Another soft little song. Undoubtedly she meant me not to hear it; then again, maybe she didn't care. She'd made her feelings known. This little ritual, so

infinitely *Northern*, was undoubtedly meant as much
for me as for the gods she petitioned.

Abruptly, I sniggered. If I really *was* this jhihadi,
she might as well pray to me. At least I was Southron.

Then, unexpectedly, a doubt crawled out of darkness to assail me in the daylight. A quiet, unsettling
doubt, ancient in its spirit, but wearing newer, younger
clothing.

Was I Southron? Or something else entirely?

I hitched a shoulder, scowling, trying to ward away
the unsettling doubt. There was no room for it here,
no place in my spirit for such things; I was home again
after too many months away: warm, whole and contented by life, feeling comfortable again. Familiar.

Home.

Del sang her Northern song, secure in heritage, kin-
ships, customs. I lacked all three.

Irritably, I scowled. Hoolies, what was the use? I
was "home," no matter how odd it felt once I thought
about it. I mean, even if I *weren't* fully Southron, I'd
been born here. Raised here.

Enslaved here.

Del jerked the blade from the soil and turned back
toward me. Her face was smooth and solemn, hiding
thoughts and emotion.

With effort, I hid mine. "All better?" I asked.

She hunched a single silk-swathed shoulder. "It is
for them to decide. If they choose to offer protection,
we will be doubly blessed."

"*Doubly* blessed?"

Del waved a hand briefly toward the rock-ringed
basin. "Southron gods. Northern gods. Nothing is
wrong with asking the favor of both."

I managed a grin. "I suppose not. Doubly blessed,
eh?" I caught up my sheath and drew my own sword,

sliding it free of scabbard. "I'm not much for little songs, as you know, but this ought to be enou—*hoolies!*"

Del frowned. "What?"

Thoroughly disgusted, I inspected the cut on my right hand. "Oh, not much—just a slip . . ." I scowled, sucking the shallow but painful slice in the webbing between thumb and forefinger. "Stings like hoolies, though." I removed the flesh from my mouth and inspected the cut again. "Ah, well, too far from my heart to kill me."

Del, thus reassured, sat down on her own blanket, spread next to mine. "Getting careless in your old age."

I scowled as she, all innocence, turned her attention to cleaning her blade, soiled with gritty dust and sticky grass juices.

As for my own, I'd intended much the same. I'd unpacked oil, whetstone, cloth. Such care was required if the steel was to stay unblemished and strong, and it was nothing I considered a chore. It was as much a part of me as breathing; you *do* it, you don't think about it.

Cross-legged, I settled the sword across both thighs. In dying light it glowed, except for the blackened tip. About a hand's-width of darkness, soiling beautiful steel as it climbed toward the hilt; as always, I swore beneath my breath. Once upon a time the blade had been pure, unblemished silver, clean and sweet and new. But circumstances—and a sorcerer—had conspired to alter things. Had conspired to alter *me*.

"Thrice-cursed son of a goat," I muttered. "Why'd you pick *my* sword?"

It was an old question. No one bothered to answer.

I put one hand around the grip, settling callused

flesh against taut leather wrappings knotted tightly around the steel. I felt warmth, welcome, wonder: the sword was a *jivatma*, blessed by Northern gods because I'd troubled to ask them, "made"—in the Northern way—by a Southron-born sword-dancer who wanted no part of it. I'd blooded it improperly by killing a snow lion instead of a man; later, knowing just enough to get myself into serious trouble, I'd requenched the thing in Chosa Dei, a sorcerer out of legend who turned out to be all too real. In requenching I'd finally keyed it. The sword was alive now, and magical—as Northern beliefs had it—only I'd perverted that life and magic by requenching in Chosa Dei.

That I hadn't had much choice didn't seem to matter. My *jivatma*, Samiel, hosted a sorcerer's soul.

An *angry* sorcerer's soul.

"Tell me again," Del said.

Distracted, I barely glanced at her. "What?"

"Tell me again. About Jamail. About how he *spoke*."

Frowning, I stared at blemished steel. "He just did. The crowd separated, leaving him in the open, and I heard him. He prophesied. He was, after all, the Oracle—or so everyone said." I shrugged. "It fits, in an odd sort of way. Rumor had it the Oracle was neither man nor woman . . . don't you remember the old man in Ysaa-den? He said something about—" I frowned, trying to recall. "—'a man who was not a man, but neither was he a woman.' " I nodded. "That's what he said."

Del's tone was troubled. "And you believe he meant Jamail."

"*I* don't know what he meant. All I know is Jamail

showed up at the sword-dance and pointed me out as the jhihadi. *After* he spoke."

"But his tongue was *cut out*, Tiger! Aladar did it, remember?" Del's face was pale and taut. Words hissed in her throat. "He made him a mute, and *castrate—*"

"And maybe an Oracle." I shrugged, wiping soft cloth the length of the blade. "I don't know, bascha. I have no answers. All I can tell you is he did point at me."

"Jhihadi," she said. The single word was couched in a welter of emotions: disbelief, bafflement, frustration. And a vast, abiding confusion no weaker than my own.

"I don't know," I said again. "I can't explain any of it. And besides, I don't know that it really matters. I mean, right now all anyone wants to do is *kill* me, not worship me. That doesn't sound much like a true messiah to me."

Del sighed and slid her sword back into its sheath. "I wish—" She broke off, then began again. "I wish I could have spoken to him. *Seen* him. I wish I could have found out the truth."

"We had to leave, bascha. They'd have killed us, otherwise."

"I know." She glanced northward. "I just wish—" Then, more urgently: *"Dust."*

Hoolies. So there was.

I climbed to my feet even as Del unsheathed her sword. "We could run," I suggested. "The horses are rested."

"So am I," Del said, assuming a ready posture. She made no motion to mount the roan.

Two steps and I was beside her. "After this, I could use some dinner."

Del shrugged. "Your turn to cook."

"*My* turn!"

"I fixed breakfast."

"That glop we ate wasn't my idea of breakfast."

"Does it matter? You were spewing it anyway."

Trust her to remember that.

Trust her to *say* it.

Four

The dust, dyed orange by the sunset, resolved itself into a single rider. A man, with thick reddish-blond hair and great drooping red mustaches waving below his chin. He was too far yet to see his eye color, but I knew what it was: blue. I even knew *him*: Rhashad, a Borderer, half Southron, half Northern, who made his living as I did.

A rich blue burnous billowed in horse-born wind as he galloped up to the oasis. I saw big teeth bared in a grin half hidden in mustaches, the hand lifted in friendly greeting. He halted the sorrel before us, furrowing dirt and sand and grass, as multiple botas sloshed. Peeping over his shoulder glinted the pommel-knot of his sword, worn in Southron-style harness.

Teeth again: for Del. Blue eyes glinted against sun-creased, sunburned skin. "Hoolies, but you're a woman made for a man like me! I *saw* what you did against Ajani . . ." Rhashad laughed joyously, slewing a sly glance in my direction. "No, Sandtiger, no need to unsheathe your claws—*yet*. I don't steal women from friends."

I grunted. "As if you could."

"Oh, I could—I *have*. Just not from my friends."

He arched ruddy, suggestive brows and aimed a bold stare in Del's direction. "What do you say, bascha— once you grow tired of the Sandtiger, shall you come ride with me?"

I recalled that for some strange reason, Rhashad's swaggering manner did not offend or irritate Del. In fact, she seemed to enjoy it, which I found somewhat puzzling. *Other* men, behaving in much the same way, met with a colder reception.

I had, once. A very long time ago.

And sometimes not so long. It all depended on her mood.

Del didn't even flick an eyelash. "Would your mother approve?"

Rhashad's braying laugh rang out. He slapped a thick thigh, then reined in the pawing sorrel. "Oh, I think so. She's a woman much like you . . . how *else* do you think she got me?"

I lowered my sword and stood hip-shot. "Have you come for a *reason,* or just to trade gibes with me?"

"Gibes with you, pleasantries with her." But even as he spoke, some of the gaiety faded. Rhashad unhooked a leg and slung it across a saddle well-hung with plump botas. He jumped down easily, raising dust, which he waved away absently. "Yes, I came for a reason. I thought you might need some help." He led his sorrel to the basin and gave it leave to drink, doling out rein. "Like I said, I saw what she did. Now, *we* all know Ajani was no jhihadi, but all the tribes thought he was; at least, they're all sure that Oracle fellow pointed straight at him. Which means now they all think Del killed the jhihadi when she lopped off Ajani's head."

"Yes," I agreed patiently. "We had that part fig-ured out."

He was unperturbed by my irony. "And *that* means now they all want to kill you." Rhashad shrugged wide shoulders; the Borderer is bigger than I. "For now, at any rate."

Del, who still wore her harness beneath burnous, sheathed her sword easily, making most of it disappear under shelter of slick white silk. As always, it was impressive; I saw the appreciative flicker in Rhashad's eyes. "For now?" she echoed.

"Eventually they'll stop," he declared. "After all, they can't chase you all over the South. Not forever. Even if they *are* nomads. One of these days this little mistake will get all straightened out, and you two will no longer be hunted."

" 'This little mistake,' " I muttered.

"Meanwhile," she said lightly, "they might yet catch us, and kill us."

"Well, yes, they could." Rhashad pulled his sorrel from the basin, dripping water. "If you're stupid enough to be caught."

I nodded. "We'd sort of hoped to avoid that."

"That's why *I'm* here." Rhashad looked past Del and me to the horses. "I rode out before dawn, hoping to catch you. The tribes were still in disarray. After all, they're none of them accustomed to cooperating, being solitary sorts." He shrugged. "But that won't last. By now they'll have banded together for one purpose: to kill the jhihadi's murderer. So, I decided to do what I could to help." He jerked his chin to indicate our horses. "I've come to take one of your mounts."

I blinked. "You've what?"

"Come to take one of your mounts."

"Details," Del suggested, waggling fingers in invitation. "I'm rather fond of details."

"A pretty little thing like you?" Rhashad grinned at her. He was big, bold, uninhibited; not at all Del's type. (I think.) "This is men's business, bascha . . . Tiger and I will attend to details."

In the spirit of the moment, Del offered cool smile and arched brows. "Is that what you tell your mother?"

He laughed. "Hoolies, *no*—I know better. She'd have both my balls." The smile slid into crooked consideration. "Of course, then there'd be no one to carry on the line . . . no, I think she'd settle for an ear instead, which would then destroy my good looks." Blue eyes twinkled beneath heavy brows. "Which do *you* want, bascha? Balls, or an ear?"

If he meant to shock, he failed. Again the cool smile. Only I saw the glint in *her* eye; no one else knew her as I. "And do you think I could take neither?"

Rhashad's grin wavered in the depths of red-blond mustaches. He frowned, thinking about the promise implicit in Del's tone, but only for a moment; the expression cleared quickly. His manner was bluff as he shifted in the sand, but I could tell her implication had gone home. Rhashad liked what he saw. It was easy to think only of that, and forget what she could do. "Well, I think that's a question that will have to be settled another time. Right now we'd best attend to those details." He looked at me. "They'll be tracking *two* horses. Why don't you switch to one?" He glanced again at our mounts. "I'd take the roan. He's bigger, more suited to carrying two, and neither of you is little—"

I shook my head, cutting him off. "He'd never last if we went into the Punja. He's Northerner-bred . . . the stud's smaller, but he's tough. He won't give up."

Rhashad shrugged. "Whatever you like. Give me

one of them—I'll ride off in the other direction and lead them a pretty chase."

"If they catch you—" Del began.

"If they do, I'm just a Borderer. My hands—*and* face—are clean." He cast a glance at the scars in my cheek. "I'm not the Sandtiger. I'm not his woman, either. I think they'll let me go."

I spoke up hastily, before Del could light into Rhashad for daring to suggest she was my woman. Even if she was, in Southron parlance; Northerners are like that. (Or maybe just *Del* is like that.) "*Meanwhile*, it's given us time to put some miles between them and us." I nodded. "A good plan, Rhashad."

He lifted a single big shoulder off-handedly. "Even my mother would like it." He inspected our tiny camp, then glanced at the horizon as it swallowed the sun. "No moon tonight. You can get a few hours' sleep, then ride out just before dawn. Meanwhile, I'll take the other horse now. They might as well think you're that far ahead of them; it'll make them all the more willing to overextend their own mounts."

"Why?" Del asked. "Why are you doing this?"

Rhashad smiled, chewing mustache. "Tiger and I are old friends. He's taught me a trick or two for the circle, tricks that saved my life. I just figure I owe him. As for you, well . . ." The Borderer grinned. "My mother wouldn't mind if I brought home a bold bascha like you. But since I can't do that, I'll settle for helping you escape. It would be such a waste if they killed you." Rhashad shot me a glance. "Though not so much of one if they killed *him*."

"Ha-ha," I said dutifully, and turned back to lean my sword against the wind- and sandbreak. "Can you stay for food? Del's just about to cook it."

"Del is just about to do nothing of the sort," she

retorted. "Don't try to trick me into it simply because Rhashad is here. I have no skills, remember? No devotion to womanly duty." Del smiled sweetly. "I have no manners at *all*—I'm a sword-dancer, am I not?"

I ignored the implication. "He's a *guest*," I explained.

"No, he's not," she countered. "He's just one of us."

Rhashad, laughing, waved a hand. "No, no, I can't stay. I'm going to ride out now. But—there is one more thing."

The humor was gone from his eyes. Del and I waited.

The Borderer turned to his horse and mounted. "You remember what I told you about how things are in Julah? About how Aladar's daughter succeeded to the tanzeership?"

"Yes," I answered. "And at the time we also discussed the fact she probably won't be tanzeer for long. This is the South. She's a woman. Someone will take it away."

"Maybe," Rhashad said. "And maybe not. She's got the gold mines, remember? She may be a woman, but she's a very *rich* woman. Money buys men. Money also buys loyalty. If she pays them enough, they might not care if she's a woman."

I knew very well she had gold mines. Her father had held them before her; it's where he'd made me a slave.

I suppressed an involuntary shudder. Even now, I dreamed about it. "Anyway, what's this got to do with us? Del and I aren't necessarily heading to Julah."

"Doesn't matter," Rhashad declared. "She's coming after *you*."

Del glanced at me, inspecting my expression. "Does she know, then? Or is it merely convenient to blame the so-called jhihadi's murderers for every drop of blood spilled from this day forward?"

Rhashad shrugged slightly. "Probably. Except Sabra has a very good idea exactly who killed her father. I told you that before: there were rumors about a big Southron sword-dancer with clawmarks on his face, and a magnificent Northern bascha who was living in Aladar's harem."

"Not my choice," Del snapped. "As for his death, he deserved it."

"Undoubtedly," Rhashad nodded, "but his daughter doesn't agree. She's put a price on your head."

"Oh?" I brightened. "How much are we worth?"

Rhashad's expression was solemn. "Enough to buy sword-dancers."

I sighed. "Anything else?"

Rhashad nodded. "Late last night, after you and Del rode out, I had a few drinks with Abbu Bensir."

I shrugged. "So?"

"So, he said Sabra had sent for him."

Del frowned. "But—he would not . . ." She glanced at me. "Would he? He is your friend. Like Rhashad."

"Not like Rhashad," I countered. "And not properly a *friend;* Abbu and I were—and are—rivals." I shook it off with a twitch of shoulders. "It makes no difference. If he hires on, it becomes a matter of money. And a contract."

"Did he not take oaths to honor the code of the dance?" she asked sharply.

"Southron circle oaths have nothing whatsoever to do with not killing specific people," I told her. "We're free to hire on however we will . . . even if it means dancing to the death against someone we know rather well." I exchanged a glance with Rhashad. "Are you sure about all of this?"

He nodded. "Iskandar was full of it, *and* Harquhal, when I stopped for water . . . you were named, and Del, although mostly they just call her the Northern bascha." He grimaced briefly. "And other less flattering things."

"It doesn't matter." Del's brows were puckered. "If she has hired Abbu Bensir—and *other* sword-dancers—the situation changes."

"A little," I agreed. "We've got tribes after us for murdering the jhihadi, and assorted sword-dancers—maybe even Abbu Bensir—hunting us to complete a tanzeer's contract. *If* Abbu hired on; we don't know that."

"If he has, he is dangerous." Del's tone was deadly. "He is very, very good. I danced against him, remember?"

"So did I," I sighed, "a very long time ago."

Rhashad, smiling, touched his throat. "He makes no secret of it. Other men might be ashamed, but not Abbu Bensir. The ruined throat is a battle scar gained while in the circle against an honorable opponent."

I hissed another oath. "I was seventeen," I muttered. "Does he say that, too?"

Rhashad laughed. "No, not that. Your name is more than enough. Let the others think what they will."

Del removed a few things from her saddle-pouches, transferred them to mine, then saddled the roan. Slowly, she led him over to Rhashad. "What will you do with him?"

"Take him southeasterly for a few days, just to throw them off, then head back toward the border. My mother can use a good horse."

She nodded. "He is that." She slapped a blue-speckled rump. "May the sun shine on your head."

Rhashad displayed big teeth. "Not much chance it won't." He swung his sorrel aside and pulled the roan up close as he looked at me. "It may work for a while. The tribes are too worked up right now to think things through, which means they'll make mistakes, and I doubt many of the established sword-dancers will hire on, since you're one of their own—and she's a woman, after all. I'd say it'd mostly be the younger ones trying to make a name. Capturing the Sandtiger would really mean something, in which case they might get careless in the rush to track you down." He chewed one of his mustaches. "But if *Abbu* has hired on . . ." The Borderer shrugged. "You know Abbu. He's not a stupid man."

"It does change things," I agreed. Then, seriously, "I owe *you*, Rhashad."

He shrugged. "One day." And headed out at a lope with the Northern roan at the end of taut reins.

I turned abruptly. "Let's pack."

She was startled. "Now?"

"We'll do as he's doing: ride out now and get a few hours' head start. Hopefully, it'll give us an edge in addition to leaving tracks for only one horse." I bent down to pick up my sword. "It was a good idea. I should have thought of it my—*hoo*lies—"

"What now?" Del asked.

I stared down at the fallen sword. I had put out my hand, closed fingers around the grip, lifted—and the thing had pulled free of my grasp. Once free, it had fallen. It now lay across my right foot.

I'm a Southroner: I wear sandals. There's not a whole lot of protection against a falling sword when you wear sandals—but then you don't ordinarily figure you'll drop one, either. Not if you're a sword-dancer, and you know how to handle a sword.

I was. I did. I hadn't dropped the sword. The thing had pulled *free*.

"Hoolies," I murmured, very softly.

Blood began to flow.

"Tiger!" Del stood next to me, staring down at the mess. "Tiger—" She reached for the sword, then drew back. "I can't touch it; you know that. I may know the name, but there is still Chosa Dei."

"I don't expect you to touch it," I muttered, pulling my foot from beneath the blade. I let the weapon lie there.

"You're bleeding . . . here—" She knelt down and began to unlace my sandal. "I'm beginning to think you *are* getting careless . . . first you cut your hand, now this—"

I pulled my foot away. "Leave it alone. You don't have to do that." I rested the ball of my still-sandaled foot against the sandbreak wall and took up where Del had left off, untying leather knots. "Pack up whatever we need and saddle the stud . . . I'll be with you in a moment."

She turned away, gathering gear and saddle-pouches, and said nothing more about carelessness, teasing or otherwise. As for me, I slipped off a sandal no longer worth very much; the blade had cut through leather straps before slicing into flesh.

I used the hem of my burnous to sop up the blood. The cut was not very deep and the blood stopped quickly enough. It wouldn't bother me much, although the sandal required repairing. We didn't have the time; for now I'd simply ride barefoot.

I stripped off the good sandal and toed through pockets of sand and webby grass patches to the stud.

I tucked the sandals into one of the pouches, then turned back to stare at the sword. It lay naked in the dirt: four feet of deadly *jivatma*.

Del, making a last inspection sweep of the tiny oasis, glanced at me sidelong. "Do you intend to leave it there?"

"In a minute," I declared. "If I could. But you've convinced me it would not be a wise thing to do. Look what it's doing to me—if someone *else* got a hold of it . . ." I shook my head. "I remember all too clearly what Chosa Dei, in that sword, did to Nabir. How it unmade Nabir's *feet*—" I shook off a sudden chill. "Imagine what it—*he*—might do if he got control of a weaker man."

"You're saying *Chosa*—?" Del let it trail off, staring at the sword. "The tip is still black."

"And will be, I'm beginning to think, until it's fully discharged. And you know what *that* means."

"Shaka Obre," she breathed.

"Shaka Obre," I echoed, "and the strength to destroy Chosa Dei before he destroys me."

Five

We rode for maybe an hour, heading due south. A straight line would take us into the heart of the Punja. I had no plans at that particular moment to actually *enter* the Punja, but then the beast is often perverse; thanks to frequent sandstorms, called simooms, the Punja is rarely where you expect it to be. Wind-powered, scouring, it moves. Anything in its way, including something so trivial as a boundary—or a city, or a tanzeer's entire domain—is swallowed by acres of sand. Which means sometimes no matter how hard you try to avoid it, the Punja gets in your way.

We stopped riding because I knew if we kept going we'd stand a very good chance of getting lost. Getting lost in the South is ridiculously easy, especially if you're stupid enough to ask for it by riding too far on a night with no moon, and only stars to see by. Stars make it easy to choose a general direction, but they're not so great at providing light enough to ride by.

So we stopped, and Del asked why, and I explained. Somewhat testily, I'll admit; I was not particularly happy about life, and when I am not happy I can be surly. Sometimes downright unpleasant. But not very often; I am, by nature, a particularly good-natured, even-tempered individual.

"Enough already," I growled. "Get off, bascha—you're sitting over his kidneys. And you're not what I'd call light."

Del, who was seated behind me, stiffened. But, for once, did as she was told: she slid backward over the stud's rump and then down his tail.

"Well?" she said after a moment. "You outweigh *me*—are *you* not going to dismount?"

Engaged in untangling my harness straps from bota thongs fastened in front of my knee—not being a fool, I had *not* put the harness back on where the sword might next decide to try for my neck—I did not immediately answer. The stud, for his part, snorted noisily. Then he shook himself. Violently. From head to tail.

"Oh, *hoolies*—" A horse, shaking himself, spares no thought for the rider on his back. He simply shakes, like a big, wet dog, only with much more enthusiasm.

Botas sloshed. Bridle ornaments clashed. Assorted gear rattled. As for me, every joint protested. As did my innards.

"Jug-headed, flea-bitten *goat*—" I climbed down painfully, dragging harness and sword with me, and made sure my head was attached. Just when it had begun to feel better. . . .

"Well?" Del asked.

"Well *what*?"

"What are we doing?"

"What does it look like we're doing?"

She considered it seriously. "Stopping?"

"Good guess!" I said heartily, then stomped off into the darkness.

Del caught the stud before he could follow. "Where are you going?"

Did she have to know everything? "Something I have to do."

"Are you sick again?"

"No."

"Then what—oh. Never mind."

"Not that, either," I muttered. "First things first."

Or last things last, depending on who you are, and what you intend to do.

With a sword.

My sword.

Whose true name was Samiel: hot desert wind, with the strength of storm behind it.

Whose name had been perverted by a man known as Chosa Dei, a sorcerer out of legend whose gift, when he could use it, was to *collect* powerful magic. Duly collected, its original form was unmade, and Chose Dei reshaped it to serve his own purposes.

He had unmade many things, including much of the South. He had unmade human beings.

And now he wanted me.

I stripped out of burnous, clad now only in suede dhoti and the necklet of sandtiger claws. Not even sandals adorned my feet; grit lodged itself beneath toenails. For a long time I just stood there in the desert darkness, holding harnessed sword. The mere *thought* of pulling the blade free of the rune-scribed scabbard and summoning life to it set my bones to itching. Magic does that to me: it eats its way into my bones, making even my teeth ache, and sets up housekeeping. A belly sick on magic is worse than the biting dog who lives in a wine bota.

Futility welled up. My voice was thick with it.

"Gods-cursed, hoolies-begotten sword . . . why couldn't those Northerners let me *borrow* a blade, instead of making me take—instead of making me '*make*'—this thrice-cursed thing called a *jivatma*?"

Sweat ran down my temples; down the scarred corrugations of ribs encased in muscle and flesh. Like I said, I hadn't had a bath in too long. I smelled me, I smelled sweat, I smelled fear. And the acrid tang of magic that coated even my teeth.

I jerked Samiel free. In starlight, the steelglow was muted. A flash, a sheen, a shimmer. And the blackness of Chosa Dei climbing a third of the way up the blade.

I leaned. Spat. Wished for wine, aqivi, water. For something to cut the taste. Something to settle my belly. Something to still the itching that ached inside my bones.

A brief shudder wracked me. Hairs writhed on arms and thighs. The back of my neck prickled.

"I know you're there," I whispered tightly. "I know you're in there, Chosa. And you know I'm out *here*."

A rolling drop of sweat threatened one eye. I wiped the salty dampness away impatiently with a brusque, thick forearm, scrubbing wrist against itching eyebrow. And clenched my jaws tightly shut as I let the memories flow in prelude to the dance.

I recalled what I had done, in the depths of the Dragon's gullet. How I had, pushed to the farthest extremes of strength and will and *need,* somehow managed to defeat Chosa Dei within the walls of his prison, deep in Dragon Mountain. By calling on all my reserves and banishing all my beliefs in things other than magic; in powers of the flesh, not of gods or sorcery. I had, because I'd *had* to, set aside skepticism and welcomed the Northern magic deeply seated

within the steel. I'd used it, bending it this way and
that, *singing* it, in Northern fashion; forcing it to serve
me—until I was no better than Chosa, unmaking and
then *re*making . . . requenching at my need. Keying
when I shouldn't, on the brink of the gates of hoolies,
and knowing why, how, how much. Knowing exactly
what I did, and the woman for whom I did it.

Did I blame her? No. She'd have done the same
for me. Months before we'd met in combat to deter-
mine her fate, and mine; we'd both of us lost, but
neither had surrendered. And when it came down to
it, we'd each of us do it again. But at that moment in
Chosa's cave, in the heart of Dragon Mountain, I'd
called up all the power and remade my Northern
jivatma into something more than sword. Something
more than magic.

And something *less* than good.

I let the harness fall from my left hand. Now I held
only the sword, as a sword is always held: firmly, by
the grip, fingers wrapped around knotted leather;
twenty-year-old palm calluses settling into familiar
patterns of flesh and leather and steel. Into patterns
of soul and spirit, and the thing that makes a man
whatever the man is supposed to be.

Nearly half my sword was black, charred as if by
fire. But the flame was cold as death, and lived *inside*
the steel. Coexisting unpleasantly with what the sword
should be: a *jivatma* named Samiel, progenitor of
storms much as Del's own Boreal. *Her* storms were
Northern-cold. Mine were Southron-hot.

But Chosa lived there, too. Chosa filled every
strand of the magic laced throughout the blade. The
invisible net pulsed, turgid in its poison. If Chosa were
not destroyed, if the blade were not discharged, Samiel would die. And Chosa, breaking free, would

require the nearest body in order to house himself. The sword-dancer known as Sandtiger would simply cease to exist. In his place would be Chosa Dei, aged six-hundred and forty-two years.

Or was it forty-*three?*

Hoolies, but time flies.

I lifted the sword and plunged it deep into Southron sand, sinking it halfway down. I heard the hiss of grit displaced; the entry of steel through soil. Then I knelt and encased the leather-wrapped grip in a hard, callused prison. Another prison for Chosa.

One he'd already begun to destroy.

Six

The roar broke free of my throat. For the moment I didn't care; it was enough merely to shout, to scrape my throat hoarse with will and strength expended in an effort to beat Chosa.

But the roar died almost instantly, and so did comprehension. I knew only I held the sword, or it held me, and that was the whole of it.

He was strong, was Chosa Dei. And so very, very angry. He hated being entrapped within a prison of Northern steel. He hated the sword itself, for daring to hold him. And he hated me as well, much deeper and far stronger, with a cold, abiding strength. *I* was the one. *I* was the man. I was the enemy who had stolen away his soul and lodged it in a sword.

The thin slice in the webbing of thumb and forefinger stung. So did the cut across my foot. And I knew, with perfect certainty, that such clumsy "accidents" wouldn't stop. If anything, they'd get worse. Eventually, even deadly. Chosa had learned a little something of Samiel. Now he exerted himself, stretching the boundaries, doing whatever he could to harm me. To make the sword as dangerous to me as to my enemies.

So now it was up to me to show him who was boss.

Easier said than done. In addition to smelling so bad, magic also *hurts*.

I clung to the grip with all my strength, hands locked around steel and leather. I shook, and the sword shook with me, cutting down through Southron sand. I felt the strain envelop wrists, forearms, then shoulders, setting muscles into knots. Tendons, like taut ropes, stood up all over my body. I gritted teeth and hissed violent Salset curses, spewing all the invective the tribe had bestowed upon me as I labored in Southron bondage, too big in body to break, too small in spirit to fight.

Now I fought. The Salset had merely beaten me. Chosa Dei would *unmake* me.

Sweat ran down my face, dripping onto a dusty chest. Unencumbered by sandals, toes dug spasmodically into sand. I itched all over. Bile tickled my throat, leaving behind its acrid taste.

"—not—" I said. "—NOT—"

It was all I could manage.

Starlight flickered. Or was it my eyes? Speckles of white and black, altering vision into a patchwork curtain of pitch-soaked darkness and blinding, frenzied light.

I smelled the stink of magic; of power so raw and wild only a fool would try to control it. Only a fool would summon it.

A fool, or a madman. A man like Chosa Dei.

Or a fool like me?

Hoolies, but I hurt. The dull headache flared anew, pounding behind wide-stretched eyes. I felt the labored repetition of my heart, squirming behind my breastbone; the annoying tickle of fine hair stirring on arms and thighs and groin; the deep, hollow cramping of a belly soured by fear.

A hissing, breathy rasp: in and out, in and out, forcing lungs to work. Trying to clear a befogged head battered by a hoof as well as the presence of alien magic, and the promise of Chosa's power.

If I could just *prove* to him that mine was the stronger soul—

Inwardly, I laughed. Scornful and derisive, clogged with self-contempt. Who in hoolies was *I*? An aimless, aging man with aching knees and much-scarred hide who sold his sword for a living, honoring only the skill sheer desperation had forged, and the need to be someone better—someone *more*—than a nameless Southron slave deserted as an infant by a mother too jaded to care.

Uncertainty flickered briefly. Del had said once there was no proof. That perhaps the Salset had lied. That maybe I *hadn't* been left to die, at least not intentionally.

But I could never know. The only link to my past willing to speak of it had died but days before, ridiculed by her people because a jealous old magician, stripped of fading power, had said she deserved punishment for succoring me. And though no one had actually killed her, the disease had been as much of the spirit as of the flesh.

Sula. Who had, without fail, *always* believed in me.

Self-contempt melted away.

I drew in a guts-deep breath and gave myself over to the power gathering in answer to my summons. In answer to Chosa Dei. Both of us wanted it. Both of us needed it. But only one could wield it. Only one could win.

Into my head came a song. A tiny, quiet song. I snatched at its edges, fraying with every moment, and wove it back together. Tied all the ties, knotted all the knots. Then made it whole again. Made it *mine* again.

A breeze began to blow. Sand kissed my cheek greedily, lodged in my teeth, forced tears to wide-open eyes. But I didn't give up my song.

The world turned white. I stared, blinked, stared again. I could see nothing. Nothing but all the white.

Steel trembled in my hands. It warmed, softening, until I felt it flowing freely, squeezing its way between leather wrappings and the unsealed grasp of rigid fingers. I clutched more tightly, trying to push the steel back in, but it continued to flow. It dripped from fisted hands, spotting the star-washed sand.

If Chosa unmade the sword—

"—*not*—" I said again.

The breeze blew harder, but I could see none of it. Only white, nothing but *white*—

And then, abruptly, red. The red of an enemy's blood; the red of eyes bleeding inside from the strain of staring too hard. Of trying so fiercely to conquer.

The sword trembled. Runes flared brass-bright, then blazed briefly blood-red before fading once again into silver. Where the blade met the sand, I saw an ashy bubble burst. And then the quiet explosion of dust and grit and soil; the silver-gilt bloom of crystals from deep beneath the surface.

Translucent Punja crystals, deadly in Southron sunlight.

Sand bubbled away until most of the blade was naked, baring its charred black stain. It had climbed a finger's-width higher.

"Can't go down," I muttered. "—have to come *up*, to me—"

But of course, I wouldn't let him.

I clung to the song, wrapping myself in its power.

Del says I can't sing, that mostly I croak discordantly, not knowing how to shape notes or melody, but that didn't matter to me. Samiel doesn't care about *skill*, only about focus, and the strength to sing the magic before Chosa unmade it all.

Noiselessly, a thin line fractured the pan of sand. I watched it trickle outward from the blade tip, then spread. The silence of it was eerie. A fissure here, a fissure there, until I knelt in the center of a webwork tracery spreading in every direction, black in the light of the stars.

It did not, as you might expect, fold in upon itself, sucking sand this way and that. It held, flat as glass: a complex netting of fracture lines spilling out into the desert.

"Can't unmake it," I gritted. "—can't unmake *me*—"

I clenched my hands more tightly. Sang my song more strongly, if tucked away inside my head. And felt the power wax.

Smoke. A puff at first, a wisp, like warm breath on a cold Northern morning. Expelled from the fracture lines.

Smoke, followed by fire.

But only a little bit.

The air grew warmer. On the horizon, stretching before me, sheet lightning crackled. The air stank with it. Hair rose on my body. The back of my neck prickled. Flesh jerked, then stilled; breathing was harder yet.

The breeze became a wind. It came to visit me, bringing gritty, unwelcome company and throwing it in my face. It hissed as it flung itself against rune-scribed blade. As it scraped against my flesh, finding creases and folds and scars, leaving sand to mark its passing. Stripping hair away from my face so the scouring was surer.

I spat. Squinted. Gripped the sword harder still. No longer did it leak liquefied steel through rigid, cramping fingers. What I held now was whole.

"—hear me, Chosa? *Mine*—"

Wind blew flames out. Carried smoke away.

"Mine," I mouthed again.

Wind died quietly. Sand settled itself. The world was the world again, and I still myself within it.

A thought occurred: Was I? Myself?

What *was* I?

What in hoolies had I just done?

Summoned—and fought—Chosa Dei.

A chill rippled flesh. I knew why, and what I had done. I didn't question the need. Didn't question that it was real.

Just questioned who had done it: Me? Me? *Me?*

A handful of months before I'd have laughed at the possibility. Laughed at the *idea*, that a man could do such a thing. Would have scoured myself with self-contempt, for allowing the thought to occur.

Knowing to think of such things, such victories of the spirit, opens the door to anguish and pain.

With the Salset, I hadn't dared.

But with Chosa Dei, I did. Not only dared, but *did*.

Was I stronger because of the magic? The Northern sword? Or just more willing to take risks with things I didn't understand?

Inside me, the voice was cruel: *You're a fool, chula. You are what you've made yourself—what you can make yourself, using whatever tools lie at hand. If you turn your back on magic, you turn your back on yourself.*

I swore. Laughed softly. Called myself names. Put

my mind to the task at hand: dealing with what had happened.

Spasmodic breathing slowed. I swallowed and wished I hadn't; grit and harsh breath had scoured my throat. A shudder ran through my body as tension melted away, leaving in its place a twitching, itching body well-caked with dust and powder.

The stink of magic was gone. What rode the air now was the tang of human effort expended.

When at last I could move, I unlocked aching hands. The sword fell away. As it landed, something cracked.

For a moment I could not move. I could only kneel, too stiff to shift my weight, until at last muscles loosened and I climbed awkwardly to my feet. All around me more cracking, and a shower of silvery powder.

Hoolies, but I itched. Sand, grit, and powder clung to sweat-damp skin like a shroud, burrowing into joints and flesh-creases to mimic Punja-mites. I shook myself head to toe, freeing myself from one layer of debris, and heard the tiny chiming.

I glanced down. Like oracle bones, thrown, tiny bits of glass were strewn across my feet. Stretching in all directions was a near-perfect circle, slick and flat and glossy.

Somehow, I had made glass. Conjured of sand, birthed in fire, I'd created a circle of glass.

Glass which broke, I might add, if I even so much as twitched.

And me without my sandals.

I thought of asking how and why, but didn't waste my breath. There wouldn't be an answer.

The sword was whole. The leakage I'd sworn was real was nothing more than illusion. Samiel lay silently in a puddle of shattered glass, birthing fractures in all

directions that sparkled and glinted in starglow. I bent
and picked him up.

Then turned, and saw Del.

She stood at the perimeter of the glass circle, Boreal
unsheathed in her hands. The sword was a slash of
star-lighted steel diagonally bisecting her chest. She
had shed the white burnous. She wore only the Northern tunic of soft, creamy leather, which bared all of
smooth, lithe arms and most of magnificent legs;
bared also determination. It sang throughout her body
in tensed, defined muscles and the watchful tilt of her
head. In the hard readiness of her eyes.

But also something else. Something that shocked
me.

Del was afraid.

She is a woman who kills, but not out of whim. Not
out of irritation, or a perverse desire to harm. She
kills when she must, when circumstances push her to
it; if she is a woman who, by her strength of will and
dedication, puts herself *into* those circumstances in the
name of murdered kin, it does not make the accomplishment less valid, nor the ability less dangerous.
She has honed her skills, her talent, her mind, shaping
the woman into a weapon. She knows how, and when,
to kill. She even knows why.

One of Del's strengths is a remarkable *control:* the
ability to do what needs to be done without expending
anything more, in strength, breath, and state of mind,
than the moment absolutely requires.

Fear destroys that control. In anyone, that is frightening. In Del, it is lethal.

I did not lift Samiel. I did not so much as blink.

Del waited. Lids lowered minutely as she glanced
quickly at the tip of the blade, measuring discolor-

ation; then back at me, *weighing* me, until at last the assessment was done.

Almost imperceptibly, the posture relaxed. But not the awareness of what had taken place, or what I had accomplished in my "discussion" with Chosa Dei.

I decided now was not the time to resort to irony. *"Sulhaya,"* I said quietly, using her own tongue. "It's what I'd have wanted, too, had I lost the fight to Chosa."

Still Del waited. Measuring and weighing, if at a quieter intensity. Clearly, the initial danger had passed; she weighed me differently, now.

Eventually, she smiled. "Your accent is atrocious."

Relief was overwhelming; I did not want to deal with Del's fears just yet, because they magnified my own. "Yes, well . . . you don't say thanks very often, so how am I to know?"

Lips twitched. She took down the sword, easing the tilt of the blade. "Are you all right?"

Now I could be the me I knew better. "Stiff. Sore. A little shaky." I shrugged. "More in need of a bath than ever before. . . ." I raked a hand across my belly. "Hoolies, this stuff *itches*—"

Del squatted, picked up a sliver, inspected it. In starlight, it glittered like ice. "Interesting," she murmured.

All of ten feet separated us. Del knelt in sand. Before me gleamed a fractured sheet of glinting, magicked glass. "Do me a favor," I said. "Go get me my sandals?"

In the desert, at night, it is cool, belying the heat of the day. I lay on spread blankets, wrapped in underrobe and burnous, and tried to go to sleep. We had, at best, three hours before the sun climbed into the sky. Only a fool would waste them.

I shifted minutely, trying not to wake Del, who is a light sleeper, but also trying to settle myself yet again. For a moment the position felt just fine—then the impulse renewed itself, as it had so many times, and I scratched abraded flesh.

A finger poked my spine. "Sit up," she said. Then, "Sit *up*. Do you think I intend to lie here all night while you scratch yourself raw?"

She sounded uncommonly like many mothers I had heard chastising children. Which made me feel worse. "I can't help it. All the dust and grit and glass powder is driving me sandsick."

The finger poked again. "Then sit up, and I'll tend to it."

I rolled and levered myself up on one elbow as Del knelt beside me. "What are you doing?"

She motioned impatiently as she dug a cloth from the pouches and reached for a bota. "Strip out of everything. We should have done this sooner."

"I can't *bathe*, Del . . . we can't waste the water."

"To me, the choice is simple: we wash off as much of the powder as we can, here and now, or spend the rest of the night awake, with you scratching and complaining."

"I haven't said a *word*."

"You say more than most without even opening your mouth." Del pressed folded cloth against the lip of the bota and squeezed. "Strip down, Tiger. You'll thank me when I'm done."

Since once Del has her mind set on a thing there's no arguing with her, I did as ordered and shed everything but the dhoti. A glance at arms and legs, lighted by stars, displayed the powdering of glass and sand adhering to skin and hair.

Del clucked her tongue. "Look at you. You've

scratched so much you've got raw patches. And *stripes*—"

"Never mind," I growled. "Just do what you want to do."

Unexpectedly, Del laughed. "Quite an invitation . . ." But she let the comment die and set to work on legs and arms, taking great care with the creases at the backs of knees and elbows. She was right: I was raw. Abraded flesh stung.

So did my pride. "I *could* do this myself."

"What? You? Do you mean you don't like having a woman kneeling at your feet, tending you carefully?" Del grinned briefly, arching eloquent brows. "Not the Sandtiger I met all those months ago in that filthy, stinking cantina."

"*Give* me that." I bent, snatched the damp cloth away, began to swab my ribs. "We all change, bascha. None of us stays the same. It's the way life works."

She stood before me now, one hand resting on the taut-muscled border between narrow waist and curving hip. The starlight was kind to her; but then, it's hard to be cruel when the bones and flesh are so good. "Admit it," she suggested. "You're a better man now than you were when I met you."

I scrubbed at gritty flesh. "And is that supposed to mean you're taking credit for the improvement?"

A slow, languorous shrug of a single sinewy shoulder. Her answer was implicit: had I *not* met her, I'd not be the kind of man she believed me to be now.

Whatever man that *was;* who knows what a woman thinks?

The glint in her eyes faded. Her expression now was pensive. She put out a hand and gently traced the knurled scar cut so deeply along my ribs. The ruined flesh was still livid, requiring more time before purple would alter to pink, and later to silvery-white.

Where she touched, flesh quivered. Tension tightened my belly, and deeper. Del looked at me.

"What do you expect?" I growled. "I've never made a secret of what you do for me."

Del's mouth flattened. "Do for? Or do *to?*" She pulled her hand away from the scar. "I would have done it, Tiger. The killing. Had it been necessary."

"Which one?" I countered. "The one on Staal-Ysta? Or the one earlier tonight?"

"Either. Both." Briefly, her face convulsed. "You don't know what it was like that time . . . that time I touched your sword, and felt Chosa's power. Felt the violence of his *need.*" Del, uncharacteristically, shuddered. "Given the chance, he will take me, with a sword made of steel. *Or* a sword made of flesh."

She had been raped by Ajani, and very nearly, later, by demons known as loki. Such violence takes its toll. I could see it in her eyes; most, craving her body, wouldn't even bother to look.

I inhaled deeply, oddly light-headed. "So you really would have killed me earlier, thinking I was Chosa."

Del's face was taut. White. Stark. "There may come a time when you are."

Oddly, it didn't hurt. I'd acknowledged it myself, on the sand with Chosa Dei.

I gave her back the cloth. "And there may come a time when you have to."

Seven

"**H**unh," I commented; I thought it was enough.

"*Look* at it," Del urged. "Do you see what you did?"

I shrugged. "Does it matter? I didn't really *mean* to; and anyway, I don't know that it's worth getting into an uproar over. I mean, what can you do with it?"

"Very rich men put it in windows."

"That?"

"It's glass, Tiger."

"I *know* what it is." I scowled at the shattered circle. Dead center was a downward spiraling funnel of pale sand, hemmed by a swollen rim resembling the lip of a bowl. Radiating outward, stretching in all directions, was a complex network of hairline cracks. A brittle, perfect circle, but hazardous to a sword-dancer foolish enough to go barefoot. (Not me; I'd repaired my sandal.) "But every window *I've* ever seen—" (which weren't very many: one) "—had regular *sheets* of glass. Thick glass, maybe, hard to see through—but not little bits and pieces no bigger than my thumb."

"You broke it up last night," she pointed out. "You

did a lot of things last night, not the least of which was making the glass in the first place."

I shifted weight irritably, still stiff from the night before. "With the magic I summoned."

"With *some*thing, Tiger—I don't think it was your good looks." Del smiled sweetly.

I eyed her in annoyance. "Are we not happy this morning?"

"Happy?" Pale brows arched. "Happy *enough;* what more is there to be with assassins on our trail?"

I glanced northerly. "Speaking of which, we really ought to be moving."

"Don't you want a keepsake?"

"Of that? No. Why would I? It's just *glass,* bascha!"

Del shrugged almost defensively. "In the sunrise, it's very pretty. All the creams and pinks and silvers. Almost like thousands of jewels."

I grunted, turning. "Come on, Delilah. No sense in burning daylight."

She glared after me as I shuffled through sand and soil toward the waiting stud. "You have *no* imagination at all."

I gathered hanging reins. "Last time I looked, neither did you."

"Me!" Outraged, Del followed.

"Hoolies, woman, all you ever thought about for six whole years of your life was revenging yourself on Ajani. That sort of obsession doesn't require imagination. What it requires is a *lack* of it." I snugged a sandaled foot into the stirrup and pulled myself aboard. "I'm not taking you to task for it, mind—you did what you set out to do. The son of a goat is dead—but now there's us."

Del waited for me to kick free of the stirrup so she could put it to use. "Us?"

"Lots of other people with no imagination are coming after us. Do you really think we have time to gather up bits of pretty glass?"

Del gritted her teeth and mounted. "I only meant you might want a keepsake of the magic you worked last night. I'm sorry I said anything."

I leaned into the right stirrup to counteract her weight, keeping the saddle steady. I waited until she was settled, arranging legs, pouches, and harness, then turned the stud southward. "That's the trouble with women. Too sentimental."

"Imaginative," she muttered. "And a lot of other things."

"I'll drink to *that*." I shook out the reins and kneed him forward. "Let's go, old son . . . we've got a ways to travel."

The "ways to travel" turned out to be farther than anticipated. And in a different direction. But first things first.

Like—swearing.

It was now late midday. Not hot, but hardly cool; not even *close* to cold. It lingered somewhere in between, except the farther south we rode, the hotter it would become. And anticipation always makes it seem worse, even when it's not.

For now, it was warm enough. Beneath burnous and underrobe, sweat stippled my flesh. It stung in the scratchy patches of powder-scoured scrapes.

Del brushed a damp upper lip with the edge of her hand. Fair braid hung listlessly, flopping across one shoulder. "It was cooler back home."

I didn't bother to answer such an inane, if true, comment; Del generally knows better, but I suppose everyone can have lapses. I *could* have pointed out that "home" wasn't home to me, because I, after all, was Southron; then again, "home" wasn't home to *her* anymore, either, since she'd been formally exiled from it. Which she knew as well as I, but wasn't thinking about; probably because she was hot, and the truth hadn't quite sunk in all the way yet.

I wasn't about to remind her. Instead, what I did was swear. Which probably wasn't of any more use than Del's unnecessary comment, but made me feel better.

Briefly.

But only a little.

I stood beside the marker: a mortared pile of nine mottled, gray-green stones chipped to fit snugly together. The top stone was graven with arrows pointing out directions, and the familiar blessing (or bless*ed*, depending on your botas) sign for water: a crude teardrop shape often corroded by wind and sand and time, but eloquent nonetheless. Cairns such as this one dotted much of the South to indicate water.

In this case, the marker lied.

"Well?" Del asked.

I blew out a noisy breath of weary, dusty disgust. "The Punja's been here."

She waited a moment. "Meaning?"

"Meaning it's filled in the well. See how flat it is here? How settled?" I scraped a sandal across a hard-packed platform of fine, bone-colored sand, dislodging a feathering of dust, but nothing of any substance. "It's fairly well packed, which means the simoom came through some time back. The sand has had time to form a hardpan . . . it means there's no hope of digging deeply enough to reach the water." I paused. "Even if we had the means."

"But . . ." Del gestured. "Ten paces that way there

is dirt and grass and vegetation. Could we not dig there?"

"It's a *well,* bascha, not an underground stream. A well is a hole in the ground." I gestured with a stiffened finger. "Straight down, like a sword blade . . . there's nothing else, bascha. No chance of water here."

"Then why is there a well at all?"

"Tanzeers and caravan-serais used to have them dug for the trade routes. There are wells scattered all over, though some of them have dried up. You just have to know where they are."

She nodded pensively. "But—we are not far enough into the South to reach the Punja. Not yet." She frowned. "Are we?"

"Ordinarily, I'd say no; the Punja *ought* to be days ahead of us yet, holding to this line." I flapped a hand straight ahead. "But that's why it's the Punja. It goes where it will, forsaking all the rules." I shrugged dismissively. "Maps most times aren't worth much here, unless you know the weather patterns. The boundaries always change."

Del stared pensively at the hard layer of packed sand full of glittering Punja crystals. "So we go elsewhere."

I nodded. "We'll have to. For now, we're all right . . . we can last until tonight, but we'll need water before morning. Let's see . . ." Into my head I called the map I'd carried for so many years. If you don't learn the markers, if you don't learn the wells, if you don't learn the oases, you might as well be dead.

And even *if* you learn them, you might die anyway.

"So?" she asked finally.

I squinted toward the east. "That way's closest. *If*

it's still there. Sometimes, you can't know . . . you just go, and take your chances."

Del, still mounted, hefted flaccid botas. Dwindling water sloshed. "Most for the stud," she murmured.

"Since he's the one carrying double." I moved toward his head. "Time for walking, bascha. We'll give the old man a rest."

The sunset glowed lurid orange, glinting off horse brasses sewn the length of the stud's headstall. Also off the bits and pieces of metal gear—*and* weapons—still a ways distant, but suddenly too near.

"Uh-oh," I murmured, reining the stud to a halt.

Del, slouched behind, straightened into alertness. "What is it?"

"Company at the oasis."

"Is that where we're going? An oasis?" She leaned to one side to peer around my body. The stud spread his legs to adjust to the redistribution of weight. "Surely you don't think *everyone* in the South is looking for us!"

"Maybe. Maybe not." I scowled over a shoulder. "Sit straight, or get off altogether. The poor old man is tired."

Del slid off, unhooking legs from a tangle of pouch thongs and dangling botas, not to mention other gear. "He isn't an old man, he's a horse. He was bred to do such work. But the way you persist in talking to him—*and* about him—like a person, I'll begin to believe you *are* sentimental."

"He wasn't bred to haul around *two* giants like us. One is more than enough. One is what he's used to." I peered toward the oasis. A thin thread of smoke wafted on the air, swallowed by the sunset. Could be a cookfire; could be something else. "I can't see well enough to count how many there are . . . or to see *who* they are. It could be a caravan, or a tribe—"

"—or sword-dancers hired to kill us?" Del resettled her harness, yanking burnous folds into less binding positions. "And what do you mean, 'giants like us'? In the North, you are not so very tall."

No, I hadn't been. I'd been sort of average, which was quite a change for me, as well as a bit annoying. In the South I *was* a giant, standing a full head taller than most Southron men, while towering over the women. I'd grown used to ducking under low lintels, adept at avoiding drooping lath roofs. I'd also grown accustomed to using the advantage in the circle: I am tall, but well proportioned, with balanced arms and legs. My reach is greater than most, as is my stride. I am big, but I am quick; no lumbering behemoth, I. And many Southron men had learned it to their dismay.

Then, of course, there was Del. Whose fair-haired, blue-eyed beauty set her apart from everyone else in a land of swart-skinned, black-haired peoples; whose lithe, long-limbed grace disguised nothing of her power, or the strength she would not hide no matter the proprieties of the South, which she found an abomination.

Ah, yes: Delilah. Who had absolutely no idea what she could do to—or *for*—a man.

I raked her with a glance. Then turned pointedly away. "If you like, bascha."

Which, of course, prompted the response I expected. "If I like? If I like what? What do you mean?"

"If it pleases you to think of yourself as a delicate, feminine woman . . ." I let it trail off.

"What? You won't disabuse me of the notion?" Del strode past the stud to stand beside me. Flat-footed, in sandals, she was nearly as tall as me; I am a full four inches above six feet. "I have no desire to be a simpering, wilting female—"

I grinned, breaking in. "Just as well, bascha. You don't exactly have the talent."

"Nor do I want it." Del's turn to look me up and down. "But if we were to discuss *softness*—"

I overrode her. "We're here to discuss water, and whether we want to risk ourselves trying to get it."

She stared past me at the distant oasis, sheltered by fan-fronded palms. We could hear the sound of shouting, but could not distinguish words. It could be a celebration. It might be something else.

Del's mouth twisted. "The botas are nearly empty."

"Meaning it's worth the risk."

"Everything's worth the risk." A twitch of shoulders tested the weight of Northern *jivatma* snugged diagonally across her back. "We are what we are, Tiger. One day we will die. It is my fervent hope a sword will be in my hands when I do."

"Really?" I grinned. "I'd always kind of hoped I'd die in bed with a hot little Southron bascha all a-pant in my arms, in the midst of ambitious physical labor . . ."

"You would," she muttered.

"—or maybe a *Northern* bascha."

Del didn't crack a smile; she's very good at that. "Let's go get the water."

Eight

By the time we reached the oasis, all the shouting had died down. So had all the living.

"Stupid," I muttered tightly. "Stupid, foolish, ignorant *idiots*—"

"Tiger."

"They never learn, these people . . . they just load everything up and go traipsing off into the middle of the desert without even *thinking*—"

"Tiger." Very soft, but steadfast.

"—that valhail only knows awaits them! Don't they ever learn? Don't they ever stop and think—?"

"Tiger." Boreal was still unsheathed, though the threat was well past. "Let it go, Tiger. What they need now is a deathsong."

My face twisted. "You and your songs . . ." I waved a rigid hand. "Do what you want, bascha. If it makes you feel better." I turned and strode away, slamming home the Northern *jivatma*. Walking until I stopped and stood stiff-spined with my back to the tiny oasis, hands clenching hips. I leaned, spat grit disgustedly, wanted nothing better than to wash the taste of anger and futility from my mouth. But nothing we had would do it: nei-

ther water, wine, nor aqivi. Nothing at all would
do it.

"Stupid fools," I muttered. And felt no better for
it.

It wasn't the bodies. It wasn't even that one was
male, one female, one the remains of an infant whose
gender was now undetermined. What it was, was the
waste. The incredible senselessness and *stupidity*—

The familiar *Southronness* of it.

Recognition was painful. It washed up out of
nowhere and sank a fist into my belly, making me
want to spew out anger and frustration and helplessness. What I said was true: they had been senseless
and stupid, ignorant and foolish, because they had
mistakenly believed they could cross the desert safely.
That their homeland offered no threat.

I knew they had been stupid. I could call them idiots
and ignorant fools, because I knew why it was so
senseless: no one, crossing the desert, was safe from
anyone. It was the nature of the South. If the sun
doesn't get you; if the Punja doesn't get you; if lack
of water doesn't get you; if the tribes don't get you;
if greedy tanzeers don't get you; if the *sandtigers* don't
get you . . .

Hoolies. *The South.* Harsh and cruel and deadly,
and abruptly alien. Even to me.

Especially to me: I began to wonder if I was a true
son of the South, in spirit if not in flesh.

It was my home. Known. Familiar. Comforting in
its customs, in the cultures, in the harshness, because
it was all I knew.

But does knowing a deadly enemy make him easier
to like? Harder to destroy?

Behind me I heard the stud snuffling at the rock-
rimmed, rune-carved basin, the need for water far

greater than the fear of death. And I heard Del, very quietly, singing her Northern song.

My jaws locked. Between my teeth, I muttered, "Stupid, ignorant *fools*—"

Two adults, alone. And one tiny baby. Easy prey for borjuni.

I swung. "If they'd only hired a sword-dancer . . ." But I let it trail off. Del knelt in the sand, sword sheathed, carefully wrapping the remains of the infant in her only spare burnous. Very softly, she sang.

I thought at once of Kalle, the five-year-old girl Del had left on Staal-Ysta. She had borne the girl, then given her up, too obsessed with revenge to make time for a baby. Del was, I had learned, capable of anything in the patterns of her behavior. It was why she had offered me in trade for her daughter's company for the space of one year. She knew it was all she could get. She knew I was all she had to offer in exchange, and counted it worth the cost.

The cost had come high: we'd both nearly died.

But obsession and compulsion didn't strip her of guilt. Nor of a deep and abiding pain; I slept with the woman: I knew. We each, for different reasons, battled our demons in dreams.

Watching her tend the body, I wondered if she, too, thought of Kalle. If she wished the exile ended, her future secure in the North with a blue-eyed, fair-haired daughter very much like the mother who had given her up; who had been *forced* to give her up, to satisfy a compulsion far greater than was normal.

Now Ajani was dead. So was the compulsion, leaving her with—what?

Del looked up at me, cradling the bloody burnous. "Could you dig her a grave, Tiger?"

Her. I wondered how Del could tell.

Futility nearly choked me. I wanted to tell her this wasn't the South, not *really* the South. That it had changed since we'd gone up into the North. That something terrible had happened.

But it wasn't true. It would be a lie. The South hadn't changed. The South was exactly the same.

I stared hard at the bundle Del cradled in her arms. We didn't have a shovel. But hanging from the ends of my arms was a pair of perfectly good, strong hands with nothing else to do, since there were no borjuni present for me to decapitate.

At dawn, they came back. It wasn't typical—borjuni generally strike quickly and ride on after other prey— but who cares about typical when you're outnumbered eight to two?

Del and I heard them come without much trouble just at dawn, since we'd slept very lightly in view of the circumstances, and we had more than enough time to unsheathe blades from harnesses kept close at hand, and move to the ready. Now we stood facing them, perfectly prepared, backs to the screen of palm tree trunks huddling vertically near the rock basin.

"I thought you said something about those runes protecting the traveler," Del murmured. "So much for desert courtesy."

"Against tribes, yes. Not much of anything protects anybody against scavengers like borjuni—unless you want to count on a sword." I stared at the eight gathered men mounted on stocky Punja-bred horses. They were all typically Southron: black-haired, dark-eyed, swart-skinned, robed against the rising sun, aglitter with knives and stickers and swords. "A camp," I muttered thoughtfully. "There must be a camp nearby. . . ."

Del, from beside me, "Do you want to pay a visit?"

I grinned. "Maybe later. *After* we're done with these."

It was said for their benefit in clear, precise Desert, though Del's was accented. Not that it mattered: language skill was the last thing the eight mounted borjuni considered while staring down at the Northern woman so different from their own.

Which really was all right, when you looked at the scheme of things. It meant they didn't notice—or didn't *care*—that a sword was in her hands.

More likely, didn't care. It's hard not to notice Boreal.

Deep inside, I laughed. I had a *jivatma,* too.

"Well?" I invited.

One of the men stirred. His dark face was pocked by childhood disease. Long hair, greased back, glistened with too much oil. The curling ends stained grimy gray-brown the shoulders of his dusty cream-colored burnous. He challenged me with a stare. "Sword-dancer?" he asked.

I altered the tilt of my blade minutely, just enough to catch the newborn sunlight and throw it back into his eyes. Answer enough, I thought; you don't mess around with borjuni, or consider subtleties of feelings. You go straight to the point; in this case, it was *my* point, blackened by Chosa Dei.

The borjuni swore, squinted, thrust up a forearm to ward away the light. Behind him, his men muttered, but a single sibilant word held them in their places. He brought down his arm, settled a hand on his knife-hilt, glared down the length of his pocked, bony nose. He didn't look at Del. But then, he didn't need to. He'd seen all he needed to see, to know how much he wanted.

The other hand he took from the reins and waved

in a fluid gesture of encompassing possession: seven
mounted men, all dangerously ruthless. Their worth
was already proven, if you counted the bodies we'd
buried.

The hand settled once more. He waited expectantly.

"I'm not impressed," I told him.

Dark eyes narrowed. He flicked a glance at Del,
eyed the bared blade a moment, then looked back at
me. "The woman," he growled, "and you go free."

A bargain, yet. *Very* unlike a borjuni. Being a
sword-dancer has its uses—except in this case I wasn't
so sure of things. Eight to two were not good odds,
even if the borjuni, in their ignorance, believed it
eight to one. I am big, yes, and quick, and I've culti-
vated a tough appearance, but I'm not *that* big or
quick or mean.

Still, I was willing to play up the chance.

I displayed a cheerful, toothy grin. "I go free anyway. Do you think you can take the Sandtiger?"

Del, trained according to the exquisite honor codes
of Staal-Ysta, no doubt considered it unnecessary
braggadocio, but it's the way things are in the South.
With borjuni, you need every edge. If they were at
all concerned about me and the dangers of trying my
skill, all the better. It could tip the balance in our
favor.

Black eyes flickered. The borjuni leader tried a different approach. "Why has the woman a sword?"

"Because she, too, is a sword-dancer." I didn't see
the sense in lying; besides, he wouldn't believe me.
"And she has magic," I added casually. "Powerful
Northern magic."

He squinted, assessing Del. Looking for magic, no
doubt. Except he wouldn't see any, not so obviously,
other than the magic of a leggy Northern beauty with

a thick plait of white-blonde silk falling over one muscled shoulder bared by the almost sleeveless leather
tunic. It didn't occur to him to consider the sword
seriously, or what it was capable of.

Then again, who would? Boreal is very good at
keeping secrets. Almost as good as Del.

A subtle flick of fingers. The seven men behind him
began to spread apart. Del and I, without speaking,
shifted stance at once, moving to stand back-to-back.
I balanced very precisely, feeling familiar tension in
thighs and calves, the tightening of abdomen. Behind
me, Del hummed. Prelude to the song. Prologue to
the dance.

The leader did not move. "Sandtiger," he said, as
if to be very sure.

It occurred to me then, and only then, that even
borjuni might find it opportune to listen to the
rumors. Maybe I hadn't been so smart in giving him
my name. Maybe I'd been downright *stupid*, handing
him the truth to lend credence to the tales. If what
Rhashad had said were true—and I had no reason to
doubt him—gold had been set on our heads.

Very softly, I swore.

Del's song gained in volume just as the borjuni
charged.

Nine

One of the easiest—and most violent—ways of taking out a mounted enemy is by cutting down his horse. It isn't clean, it isn't nice; what it is, is quick. It also has the occasional benefit of doing the whole job for you; I have known opponents killed by falling horses, or by the fall alone. It saves time and energy. And while you can't always hope for that, you do hope for the shock alone to drop the mounted man into your path. Then you finish the work.

When I fight, whether within the confines of the circle or outside in the codeless world, I experience an odd sort of slowing in time. While nothing is really still, it *is* nonetheless slowed so that my vision is unobscured by motion too fast to follow.

Once I'd thought it was the way everyone viewed fight or dance, until I'd mentioned it in passing to my shodo. The next day he had kicked me up a training level and handed me over to a well-known, established sword-dancer by the name of Abbu Bensir in order to test my claim. Whom I had not only beaten, but had also marked for life by nearly crushing his throat.

I'd explained to my shodo, once I'd gotten over the shock of actually winning the sparring dance, that

91

Abbu's patterns had been relatively easy to block, because he'd been lazy and complacent, but mostly because I'd seen the path-within-the-path: the angles and sweeps and snaps *before* Abbu carried through. It was simply a matter of seeing the possibilities, prob- abilities, and alternatives, and selecting the action judged by my opponent as most likely to succeed. It required snap judgments of his technique, a rapid assessment of his style, and an immediate counter move.

I thought everybody did it. How else is the dance won?

Eventually I was told no, that *not* everyone had the ability to see motion before it happened, or to select the likeliest course for the opponent to follow, and then fashion a counter measure before the action occured. Such anticipation and countering ability was, my shodo explained, the truest gift a sword-dancer could ever hope for. And that I, more gifted than most, would reap the reward for a very long time, *years*, even—if I didn't throw the gift away by growing lazy, or too complacent.

Arrogant, always. Robustly confident. But never, ever complacent.

The mounted borjuni came on. Everything dutifully slowed, so I could see all the possibilities, and the path-within-the-path. Patiently I waited, sword at the ready, and watched him come riding at me, keening a promise of death.

Oh, it was promised, all right. But it wasn't *my* death.

I cut the horse out from under him, then spitted him on the way down.

One gone: seven to go. Of course, some of them would be Del's.

I spun in place even as the horse thrashed and screamed, briefly sorry about the waste, but knowing that survival requires many distasteful things. Later, if I lived, I'd dispatch the horse completely, but for now—

Senses thrummed. My ears focused on the sussuration of hooves digging through sand; the clatter of bridle brasses; the thick snort of a horse reined up short. I ducked, darted a false cut at the forelegs, let the borjuni jerk his horse aside as he swooped down with glinting blade. I caught it on my own, steel screeching; hooked, twisted, counter-rotated; snapped free, flowed aside, ducked a second time. Yet again the dart at the forelegs; yet again the sideways jerk: he valued his mount too well. It split his concentration.

I snap-chopped with a leveled blade, cut deeply into his calf-booted leg, heard him scream in shock and rage. The pain would follow quickly enough—except I didn't wait for it. As he slopped sideways in the saddle, clutching impotently at the nearly severed leg, I reached up, caught an arm, jerked him down from the horse. Sliced fragile throat effortlessly.

Two.

The rune-worked blade ran wet with bright new blood. In my head I heard a song, a whispered murmur of song, creeping into my bones. This was what it was for, my gods-blessed *jivatma*. This was its special task, to spill the blood of the enemy. This was its special talent: to part the flesh from bone, sundering even that, and *unmake* the enemy—

Rage and power and need.

Dimly I recognized none was born of me, but of something—some*one*—else.

The song wouldn't go away.

I spun, lunged, sliced. Horses everywhere, crowding

the tiny oasis, compressing my personal circle. I heard
Del's harsh breathing, the snatches of Northern song,
the muttered self-exhortations spilled on choppy, blurted
breath. Horses *everywhere,* snorting and stomping and
squealing and thrashing—

—teeth snapping, hooves slashing—

—wild, rolling eyes—

—shouted Southron curses and threats of dis-
memberment—

—the thick hot scent of blood commingling with the
sand—

—Del weaving sunlight with a shuttle of magicked
steel—

—*rage*—and *power*—and *NEED*—

Chosa Dei wanted free.

The daylight around me exploded.

The enemy was shouting. I couldn't understand,
couldn't decipher the words; knew only the enemy
was required to be unmade—

"Tiger—Tiger, *no*—"

Trapped at the end of the blade; transfixed by dis-
coloration: all I had to do was cut into the enemy's
neck, barely slit the fragile flesh, and the enemy was
unmade.

"Tiger—don't make me *do* this—"

It whispered in my head. A tiny, perfect song.
Take her now, it sang. *Take her NOW, and set me
free.*

So many horses destroyed. So many enemies—

The swearing, now, was in Northern. For a moment
it nonplussed me . . . then the song swelled in my
head.

"—unmake—" I muttered aloud.

I had only to touch her throat with the blackened tip of the blade—

"You thrice-cursed son of a goat!" she cried. "What kind of an idiot are you? Do you *want* this dance, you fool? Do you really want us to do to each other what no one else can do?"

No one else?

Rage.

And power.

And *need*.

Blood dripped from the blade. A droplet ran down the sweep of Northern-fair collar bone and beneath the ivory tunic.

Del lifted her weapon. In her eyes I saw frantic appeal replaced by grim determination.

Something occurred to me.

I leapt, even as she snapped the blade aside in preparation of engagement. I leapt, lunged, dropped, and rolled, scraping through blood-soaked sand. Somehow got rid of the sword and came up empty-handed—

—to kiss turgid Northern steel as it lingered on my mouth.

I hung there on my knees, sucking air, trying very hard not to twitch or itch or blink, while Del gazed down at me out of angry banshee-storm eyes.

She looked at me, measuring. Looked at the sword, lying ten feet away. Stared hard at me again.

After a long, tense moment, Del gritted teeth. "How in hoolies am I to know when it's you, and when it's not?"

Because I could, because I knew her name, I put a finger on Boreal's edge and moved her slightly away from my mouth. "You could *ask*," I suggested mildly.

"Ask! *Ask!* In the midst of hostilities, not knowing

if I am to be spitted by a borjuni blade—*or on yours*—
I am to *ask* if I can trust the man supposedly my
partner?" Blue eyes blazed as she shaped a sarcastic
tone. " 'Excuse me, Sandtiger, are you feeling friendly
today, or not?' " Del shook her head. "What kind of
a fool are you?"

"Bad joke," I murmured. "Either that, or you have
no sense of humor."

"I find very little humorous about what just happened." Del scowled blackly. "Do you even *know*
what happened?"

"I think I killed some people." I glanced around
briefly, absently noting bodies. I counted eight of
them. "Do you mind if I stand up?"

"You may piss rocks for all I care, so long as you
do not go near that sword."

My, but she *was* perturbed. I sucked in a breath
and got myself to my feet, marking aches and pains
and twinges and tweaks, all epilogue to the battle.

I took a step. "Del, I'm not—" I broke if off on a
throttled oath of discovery. Then sat down awkwardly
on the sand.

"What is it?" Del asked suspiciously.

I was too busy swearing to answer. With great care
I stretched out my right leg, felt the grinding pop
within, then bent over it in supplication to the gods
of ruined knees.

"Hoolies—not my knee—*please* not my knee—" I
sucked in a ragged breath, sweat stinging scrapes and
cuts. "I don't need this—I *really* don't need this . . .
oh, hoolies, not my *knee*—"

Del's tone sounded more normal. "Are you all
right?"

"*No,* I'm not all right—do I look all right? Do I

sound all right?" I glared up at her, trying to will away the pain. "If you hadn't made me lunge and roll just now—"

"*My* fault! My fault? You son of a goat—that was *my* throat at the end of your sword!"

"I know—I know—I'm sorry . . ." I was, too, but couldn't deal with it just then; it was too big, too threatening—besides, my knee was killing me, and it was easier to focus on that rather than on what I'd done—or nearly done—to Del. "Oh, hoolies, let it be all right—not something permanent—"

"What have you done?" she asked.

"Twisted it," I blurted. "Oh, hoolies, I hate knees . . . all they do is give out just when you need them most, or keep you awake at night . . ." I scrubbed sweat away from eyes. "I suppose you're just *fine.* You with your twenty-one years."

"Twenty-two," she corrected.

"Twenty-one, twenty-two—who cares? You can do anything you want, ask anything of your body, and it does it without fanfare . . ." I probed gently at the knee, checking for things that shouldn't be there, wincing at the pain. "I wish I were your age again. . . ."

"No, you don't," she said briskly, finally sheathing her sword to squat down beside me, examining my knee. "I don't know a soul who would trade the wisdom he's gained for a younger, more ignorant body." She paused. "Of course, that's if he *has* any wisdom."

I saw blood on arms and legs, staining the ivory tunic. Her braid was sticky with it. "Are *you* all right?"

"One of us has to be, and you are already damaged." Her palm was cool on my knee. "Will you be able to ride?"

"Not if I have a choice."

Del's mouth quirked. "That depends," she said, "on whether you want to wait and see if their fellow borjuni come out to discover what's keeping the rest from the midday meal."

I glanced again at the bodies. Eight of them, as before. Also a handful of dead and dying horses. My stud was where I'd left him, tied to a palm tree. He was not particularly happy, surrounded by so much death.

I frowned. "Four are missing."

"They galloped off. If there *is* a camp, that is where they will go."

"Thereby carrying word." I stretched the leg again, testing the knee. "You're right: there is no choice. Find me something to bind this with, and we'll be on our way. We don't dare stay long enough even to tend the bodies—we'll let the other borjuni do that." And as she walked away, "Don't forget to refill the botas."

Del shot me an eloquent glance that said she knew very well what was to be done before we departed, but she checked it without saying a word. Grimly she went to the nearest body, cut a portion of burnous, came back ripping it. She dropped the pieces down to me. "There. I will see to the botas. You tend your knee—and then you will tend that sword."

That sword.

As she walked away I looked, and saw the suspect sword. Lying quietly in the sand, stained red and black and silver.

The sword with which I had killed a handful of borjuni, who without question deserved it . . . and had also tried to kill Del?

Hoolies, I was *afraid*. But I didn't dare let her see

it, because then she would realize how precarious was my control.

I rubbed wearily at my face. Then bound up my aching knee.

Ten

I waited. I watched her unsaddle the stud and stake him out, doing my work for me in deference to my knee, and then I watched her settle us in for the night. It wasn't precisely night *yet,* but close enough; besides, the stud was extra tired because I hadn't been able to do my share of walking in order to rest him.

We had no shelter to speak of, just a scattered cluster of spare, scrubby trees with next to no foliage on knotty branches, and a fringe of sparse, sere desert grass. A few rocks and a little kindling served as a fire cairn. A sad, shabby encampment, but adequate to our needs.

Whatever those needs might be, under the circumstances.

I waited. I watched her spread blankets, build the tiny fire, portion out food and water. She didn't say much. Didn't look at me much. Just did what needed doing, then settled down on her blanket.

Across the fire from me.

Foreboding flickered, but I ignored it, seeking a restoration to normality by falling back on familiar banter. "It's only a knee," I told her. "Not exactly catching."

Del's frown was brief, but significant. There is a look she gets in her eyes no matter how hard she tries to hide it. She masks herself to the world—and still to me, sometimes—but I can read her better now than when we first met. Which is to be expected.

With effort, I maintained a light tone. "Ah," I nodded, "it isn't the knee at all. That must mean it's *me*."

Del's mouth flattened minutely. She flicked me a glance, chewed briefly and thoughtfully on her bottom lip, then twisted it into a crooked grimace of futility.

"Well?" I prodded. "I know it's been a long time since I had a proper bath, but that goes for you, too. And that never stopped *me*."

"Because you have no self-control. Most men do not." But the rejoinder was halfhearted; no sting underlay the tone.

I gave up on normality. "All right, bascha—say what you have to say."

Del was clearly unhappy. "Trust," she said softly.

I put my hand upon the sheathed sword lying next to me. "This."

"It is abomination. The soul of the sword is black. Chosa Dei has perverted the *jivatma,* perverted the honor codes—"

"—and you're afraid he's perverted me."

Del didn't answer at once. Color bloomed in her face, then drained away as quickly. "It shames me," she said finally. "To trust, and then not trust. To question the truth of the loyalty . . ." She gestured emptily, as if lacking the proper words. "We have done much, you and I, in the name of honor, and other things. Trust was never questioned, as is proper in the circle, whether drawn or merely believed." Her accent was thicker, twisting the Southron words. "But now, there is question. Now there must be question."

I sighed heavily. My bound knee ached unremittingly, but so did everything else. "I suppose I should ask you what it was I did. Just to understand. I don't remember much after the second borjuni."

"You killed them," Del said simply. "And then you tried to kill me."

"Tried? Or merely *appeared*—" I let the irony go. The shield fashioned of bluster and sarcasm was not required. The imagery was too lurid; the truth too painful. "Bascha—"

"I am sure," she forestalled. "I know it wasn't you, not *really* you—but does that matter? Chosa Dei wants me. Chosa Dei wants *you* . . . and for a time today, he had you." Del picked violently at her blanket, shredding a fraying corner. "The song you sang was—not right. It wasn't a song of your making. It was a song of *his*—"

The first stirrings of comprehension made me itchy, shifting on the blanket. It was easier to dismiss her fears than consider them. "I can control him, Del. It's just a matter of being stronger."

"*He* is growing stronger. Tiger, don't you see? If you give in to violence, it lends the power to him. Once he collects enough, he will use the sword as a bridge to *you*, then use you for his body." Distaste briefly warped her expression. "I saw it today, Tiger. I saw *him* today, as I saw him inside the dragon."

Denial was swift. Was easy. "I don't think—"

She didn't let me finish. "Chosa Dei looked out of your eyes. Chosa Dei was in your soul."

The tiniest flicker of fear lighted itself in my belly. "I beat him," I blurted urgently. "Last night, and again today. I'll *go on* beating him."

The setting sun was gone. Firelight overlay her face. "Until he grows too strong."

Desperation combined with impotent anger. The explosion was potent. "What do you *expect?* I can't get rid of this sword the way any sane man would—you said it's too dangerous to sell, give away, or cast off, because then he'd have his body. And I can't *destroy* the sword—you said it would free his spirit. So what does that leave me? What in hoolies am I to do?"

Del's voice was steady. "Two choices," she said quietly. "One you already know: find a way to discharge the sword. The other is harder yet."

I swore creatively. "What in hoolies is harder than tracking down a sorcerer out of legend—Chosa's *brother*, no less!—who may not even exist?"

"Dying," she answered softly.

It was a punch in the gut, but I didn't let her see it. "Dying's easy," I retorted. "Look at what I do for a living."

Del didn't answer.

"And besides, Chosa—in this sword—already tried to kill me once. Remember? So how would dying serve any purpose?"

Her mouth twisted. "I doubt he wanted to kill you. More like he wanted to *wound* you; seriously, yes, because then you would be weakened. Then he could swallow the sword . . . and eventually swallow you. But if you were to die . . ." She let it trail off. No more was necessary.

Trying not to jar my knee, I flopped spine-down on my blanket and stared up at the darkening sky. As always in the desert, the air at night was cool, counterpoint to the heat of day. "So, as I understand it—" I frowned "—all I have to do is stay alive—and in one piece—long enough to find Shaka Obre, who can help me discharge this thrice-cursed sword . . . or avoid all kinds of violence so as not to give him power . . . or not turn my back on you."

It startled her. "On *me!*"

I rolled my head to look at her. "Sure. So you won't start thinking of ways to defeat Chosa—through me—without benefit of discharging."

Stunned, Del gaped. It was almost comical.

I managed a halfhearted grin. "That's a joke, bascha. But then I keep forgetting: you don't have a sense of humor."

"I would not—I *could* not—I would never . . ." She broke it off angrily, giving up on coherency.

"I *said* it was a joke!" I rolled over onto a hip, easing my sore knee, and leaned upon an elbow. "See what I mean about no sense of humor?"

"There is nothing amusing about loss of honor, of *self*—"

Abruptly very tired, I smeared a palm across my face. "Forget it. Forget I said anything. Forget I'm even here."

"I can't. You *are* here . . . and so is that sword."

"That sword," again. I sighed heavily, aware of a weary depression, and lay down again on my blanket. "Go to sleep," I suggested. "It'll be better in the morning. Everything's better in the morning—it's why they invented it."

"Who?"

"The gods, I guess." I shrugged. "How in hoolies should I know? I'm only a jhihadi."

Del didn't lie down. She sat there on her blanket, staring pensively at me.

"Go to *sleep*," I said.

A dismissive shrug. "I will sit up for a while. To guard."

I also shrugged, accepting it readily enough; it was a

common enough occurrence. I snugged down carefully
beneath a blanket, swearing softly at the taut bindings
that made it hard to settle my knee comfortably, then
stopped moving entirely.

Something new occurred. Something I didn't like,
but knew was possible. More likely *probable*.

"Guarding, are you?" I growled. "Guarding me
against danger—or guarding against *me?*"

Del's voice was even. "Whatever is necessary."

Eleven

I woke up surly, which I do sometimes. Not very often, on the whole; like I've said before, I'm generally a good-natured soul. But occasionally, it catches up to the best of us.

Usually it's after a night of too much aqivi (and, once upon a time, too many women, but it seems like everything changes as you get older); in this case, it was after a night of too-active sleep, and a sore knee less than pleased about having to move.

Del, one of those perfectly disgusting people who wakens with relative ease and no disgruntlement that the sun has reappeared, watched me untangle the blanket, muttering beneath my breath as I did so, and then, equally silently, watched me try to lever myself up. Sitting was easy enough. Standing was not. Walking was worse.

I hobbled off, tended my business, hobbled back. I was stiff, itchy from healing sand scrapes, smelly from lack of bath, stubbled on cheeks and chin. My knee hurt like hoolies. So did a few other things: namely, my pride.

"You talked," Del mentioned, neatly folding her blanket aside.

It was, I thought, basically inconsequential. But since she'd brought it up . . . "Talked?"

"Last night. In your sleep." Kneeling, she set about stirring life into the coals of the cairn. "I almost woke you, but—I was . . . well . . ."

"Afraid?" I bit it out between gritted teeth. "Did you think I'd snatch the sword out of my sheath and have at you with it in the middle of the night?"

Del said nothing.

Which hurt most of all: it meant there was a chance my sarcastic question was more accurate than I liked.

Explosively, I challenged her. "Hoolies, bascha, this is going to have to be settled once and for all. If you really are afraid of me—"

"*For* you," she said quietly.

"For me? Why? *For* me?"

She bent, blew on the coals, looked through ash grit and smoke at me. "I am afraid of what he will do to you. What he would make of you, once you were *un*made."

"I'll admit it: it was unsettling. "Yes, well . . . I don't think he'd get very far, with me. I'm sort of stubborn about things like sorcerers trying to make me over into some sort of *thing*, like those men-turned-hounds." A grimace of distaste warped my mouth. "Hoolies, what a way to die . . ." I let it go, forcibly thinking about something else as I sat down awkwardly. "What was it I said, in my sleep?"

"Patterns," Del answered, tossing a bota to me. "Lines and patterns and furrows."

I stared. *"That's* what I talked about?"

"Some of it. Some I could not understand. Drawings in the sand, you said." She pointed. "See?"

I looked. Beside my blanket, near to hand, was a "pattern" of four straight lines, with the hint of a curve at the bottom. As if someone had taken a stick and sketched one line after another.

I frowned. "I did that?"

She nodded, digging through saddle-pouches. "You muttered something about patterns and lines. Then you stuck all four fingers in the dirt and drew that." She touched her cheek. "It looks like you."

"You" meant my own cheek, beneath the stubble: four slashed lines, very straight, to the bottom of the jaw. Where the sandtiger had at last been persuaded to take his claws out of my face.

The lines in the dirt *did* look very much like claw marks. A "pattern," I guess you could say.

I grunted, unimpressed. "Who knows? I don't even remember dreaming." I sucked down water, then replugged the bota. "Our best bet is to head toward Quumi. It's a trade settlement on the edge of the Punja—that is, *usually* it's on the edge. Depending on what the Punja feels like."

Del nodded absently, staring beyond me toward the horizon. She squinted, frowning; the expression didn't inspire trust.

I was instantly alert. "What?"

"Dust. I think. In thin light, it's hard . . . no, it is. Dust." She rose, dropping the pouch, and bent swiftly to retrieve the salmon-silver blade from its rune-worked sheath. "If it is borjuni—"

"—then we may as well offer them breakfast," I finished. "I'm not exactly mobile . . ." But I tried anyway, levering myself up and dragging my own sword from its sheath.

Wishing I could trust it.

Wishing I could trust *me*.

Not borjuni. Sword-dancer. A young, Southron

male, spare in frame but not arrogance; he stared down at me from atop a sand-colored horse and put his imperious desert-bladed nose into the air.

He wore a pale, bleached yellow burnous, and the hilt of a properly harnessed sword peeked over the set of his shoulder. "Sandtiger?" he asked.

It is not easy to put a considerable amount of contempt into a single word—into a single *name*, for that matter—without overdoing it when you're eighteen or nineteen, but he managed. It takes practice; I wondered if he was as attentive to his dancing. The tone was mostly contempt, and a few other things—namely stupidity; did he really think I would start quivering in my sandals because he knew my name?

"If I said no," I began mildly, "would it convince you to leave us alone and ride straight on into the Punja? With nearly empty botas, no less?"

Dark eyes glittered. His mount fidgeted. He stilled it with an impatient snatch at reins. "My botas are as they are because I chose to ride harder and faster than the others, so as to keep the honor for myself."

The "honor" meant challenging me to a dance, no doubt. The reference to *"others,"* however—that bothered me.

"Pretty stupid, aren't you?" I asked affably. "How will you get back on so little water?"

"You will forfeit your botas to me when I have won." His eyes flicked briefly to Del, then back. "Botas—and your woman."

"And my *woman*," I echoed. "Well, let me give you a hint—you might want to ask her, first. She *prefers* being asked, generally . . . although I doubt you'd get very far. Del sort of does her own choosing when it comes to bedpartners."

Idly, Del tilted her blade. It flashed in new light.

He glared down his nose at her, clearly affronted to see a sword in the hands of a woman, *any* woman, but particularly a foreign one; then looked back at me. "My name is Nezbet. By all the honor codes of the Southron sword-dance, I challenge you to step into the circle, where we may settle the contention."

"What *is* the contention?" I asked. "That I killed the jhihadi?" I smiled, shaking my head. "But I didn't. I *am* the jhihadi. And I, most obviously, am not dead, so there is no need to dance at all."

It worked about as well as expected. "I am Nezbet. I am a third-level sword-dancer. I have been hired to bring you back to Iskandar."

"*Third*-level?" I grunted, leaned sideways, deliberately spat. "I'm seventh-level, boy. Haven't they told you that?"

Elegant nostrils flared. "I know who—*and* what— you are. Will you step into the circle?"

I assessed him openly, provocatively, letting him see what I did. Then I lifted one shoulder in a lazy, eloquent shrug. "Not worth it," I answered idly.

Dark color stained his face. "I need not be of your level to challenge you. *Any* level may challenge—that is a tenet contained in the honor codes—"

"I *know* what is and is not contained in the honor codes, boy. I learned them before you were born." I altered my stance slightly, to take some of the weight off my sore knee. "I know many things Nezbet, in his youth, has yet to learn."

Youthful Nezbet was disturbed. "Then, if you know them, you know also that if you refuse to dance against me after formal challenge has been laid— according to the codes—you can be proscribed."

"*Any* man can refuse a dance," I reminded him. "It's not good for his reputation, and in the long run he'd lose any chance at making a living because people would stop hiring him, but he can still refuse."

"This is *formal* challenge," he stressed, and then uttered one of the long-winded, twisty phrases I'd labored so hard to learn myself, back when I was his age.

I bit out an oath short and sweet and succinct. Del glanced the question, as what the boy had said was in a Southron dialect only rarely spoken. A Northerner would not know it, not even one as well-traveled— and well-taught—as Del. The language of the circle, it was called in Desert; the more formal name is nearly unpronounceable.

"Shodo's Challenge," I told her, explaining the shortened—and comprehensible—idiomatic form. "Seems this boy and I learned from the same school, so to speak . . . my shodo is long dead, but he had apprentices. And one of them apparently trained this Punjamite of a boy." I smiled up at him insincerely, though I still spoke to Del. "It means I *am* required to dance against him, or forfeit my status. Which means I become little more than a borjuni, since no one will hire me." I glanced at her. "Remember how up north they said you were a blade without a name, stripped of honor and rights? Well, it's sort of the same thing."

"But—" she began, and stopped.

"But," I agreed. I looked back at the Southron boy, whose pride in place was so evident. Had I ever been that cocky?

Rephrase that. Had I ever been that cocky so *young?*

"I can't accept," I told him. "Shodo's Challenge or no. A true challenge is predicated on equality in health, if not rank—" another gibe; often, they work, "—and I have a very sore knee. See?" I pointed to the wrapping. "I'd just *love* to open up your guts with this sword, Nezbet, but I'm a bit hampered at the moment. And an injury forfeit is not a true forfeit, since we are not yet in the circle."

His jaw worked. The beardless flesh was stretched tight over distinctly desert bones. He was, as are nearly all Southroners, swarthy of coloring. His age and attitude reminded me a little of Nabir, the Vashni halfling who had wanted my Chosa Dei-ridden sword. And had died for it. Horribly.

"I will wait," he said at last. "I will follow you and wait, until your knee is whole."

"You want me *that* bad?"

"Defeating you and taking you back will earn me another level. Possibly *two*."

So that was it. More important than coin. It touched on pride, on status; on the name that would shape the boy, as mine had shaped me.

I swore. "You stupid little Punja-mite—the only true way of earning a level is by staying with your shodo! For however long it takes! There are no *tasks* to be done, no *quests* assigned and undertaken. It's *work*, Nezbet, nothing more. Years and years of discipline, until the shodo declares you have reached the level for which you are judged the worthiest—" I broke it off, because I was too angry. Why is it so many young sword-dancers want to take shortcuts? Don't they know their lives could depend on the extra training a year or two—or *three*—offers?

No. They don't. Or they just don't care.

Stupid Punja-mite.

Now I wished my knee *was* sound. So I could teach him a lesson.

"There is me," Del offered.

I frowned. Nezbet said nothing, not comprehending what she meant; he wouldn't: she's a woman.

"There is me," she repeated. "I will stand proxy for him."

Nezbet stared at her. Then looked back at me. "I will wait. I will follow."

Del moved forward a step. "And if the Sandtiger *allows* me to stand proxy for him? According to your codes?"

"You are a woman," Nezbet said.

Del's smile was cool. "And this is a sword."

"And if it *matters* so much to you," I interjected, "why are you working for a woman?"

"I am not."

I frowned. "*Why* have you been hired to bring me back to Iskandar?"

"You murdered the tanzeer of Julah."

Del scowled. She was never proud of killing, but undoubtedly she was weary of me getting credit for all of her doings. I didn't really blame her.

"I didn't," I said mildly, "but at the moment it doesn't really matter. Who hired you?"

"The new tanzeer of Julah."

"She's a *woman*, Nezbet! Or are you too young to notice things like that?"

Color stained his face. "I did not speak with the tanzeer himself."

"Ah," I said. "I see. So you're going to persist in believing the tanzeer's a man, because you didn't really *meet* the tanzeer. And it couldn't possibly be a woman."

Dark eyes glittered. "I have laid formal challenge."

"Would you unlay it if you believed the tanzeer was a woman?" I asked curiously.

Del stirred. "You can't prove it," she murmured. "He's never going to believe you."

No. He wasn't. Any more than he'd believe Del was a sword-dancer.

Which brought us once more to the challenge.

"She's my proxy," I said, "formally designated." I grinned cheerfully at Nezbet, leaning upon my planted weapon. "Too bad there aren't enough people to lay a wager on this."

Nezbet glared. "You would allow a *woman*—"

"Try her and find out." I shrugged. "Might as well, you know. Find out what she's like in the circle before you find out what she's like in bed."

Del winced. Indelicate, maybe. But it did the job.

Nezbet's nose went up. "If she is proxy, it is done according to the proper codes. A loss equals a forfeit. If she loses, *you* lose . . . and will become my prisoner."

"If," I agreed, and bent to draw the circle.

Twelve

A farce. Pure and simple. The boy was young, strong, nimble, and trained. Del was that, and more. Del was simply herself: exquisite, elegant excellence. A potent, lethal enemy, more skilled than any he knew, regardless of the gender.

It didn't take her long. She didn't even bother to sing, which helps her focus. Del is not arrogant, nor is she interested in the games I like to play, designed to unbalance an opponent. She wastes no time at all, thinking merely of the dance and the ways to force a win. It doesn't matter to her if it is exhibition, or to the death. She takes either equally seriously because, she'd told me once, a woman in any employment considered a man's will be ignored unless she forces the issue, no matter what the game.

It was illuminating. It also taught me a lot about dispensing with entertainment and getting right to business. Wasted effort, she said, was wasted energy; she had no time for either.

Now that I was older, with aches and stiffness becoming a factor, I needed every edge. And Del was not a fool.

Nor was she one now. She caught and trapped Nezbet's blade even as the dance opened, disallowing disengagement, and backed him easily to the thin curving line of the circle. There she stripped him of his sword, tossed it wheeling out of the circle, and pinned him at the perimeter with the faintest of Boreal's kisses.

"How many?" she asked. "Who? And how far away?"

Nezbet's already dark eyes glazed black with shock. Empty hands clutched air; the mouth gaped inelegantly. But he dared not leave the circle for fear Boreal would object. Her touch is never sanguine, nor lacking in promises. He knew as well as I that a single wayward step could result in his death. Del had won the right.

"A day or two," he rasped, answering the last first. "Sword-dancers and warriors. The sword-dancers want the Sandtiger. The warriors want the jhihadi-killer."

"Me," she said tightly. "I killed them both: Aladar and Ajani."

I saw the look in his eyes: masculine disbelief, underscored by a trace of doubt. The beginnings of comprehension, tempered by the overwhelming power of Southron beliefs. She would not convince him, not even here and now. But she had planted the seed of doubt. The seed of *possibility*.

"The jhihadi isn't dead," I told him, knowing the tribes offered more threat. Religion makes fools of people. "That man's name was Ajani. He was a Northerner, and borjuni, riding both sides of the border. He *told* people he was the jhihadi, but none of it was true. The tribes are caught up in prophecy, not in the truth of things . . . they have only to ask the Oracle." Who was Del's brother.

Nezbet shrugged carefully. "They want to execute

you. They saw you, in the city . . . they saw you summon fire from the sky with your sword."

"That's magic," I said, having no time to marvel at my matter-of-factness. "Not perverted truth, just magic. Ajani was borjuni. Rapist and murderer. He sold this woman's brother to slavers—he'd have sold her, too, but she got away from him. And became a sword-dancer." I didn't bother to smile; I didn't care if he believed me. "He wasn't the jhihadi. I am the jhihadi."

Nezbet managed to spit. "You were a sword-dancer held up as an example. And now you come to *this:* liar and murderer."

"I have lied," I agreed. "And certainly I have murdered, if you count enemies trying to kill *me.* But in this I am neither." I drew in a breath, changing topics. "As for Aladar's death, all I can say is he deserved it. It was personal. I'll accept challenges as I have to, even if it *was* Del who killed him." I flicked a glance at her, then looked back at Nezbet. "But no matter what you believe, you *are* working for a woman. She used a man to hire you, knowing how you would feel. Which means she hired you on a falsehood. The coin you accepted is tainted."

"There is no payment until you are delivered!" he snapped.

"Really?" I arched brows. "Then you're even stupider than I thought."

"Tiger," Del said; her way of asking a question.

I shrugged. "He's lost. The dance is over. And unless he turns borjuni, sacrificing his status and pride, he won't bother us again." I gestured. "Let him go. Send him back to the others. He can tell them what we've said." As she lowered Boreal, I caught his gaze with my own. "Hear me, Nezbet: one sword-dancer to another. I swear on my shodo's name what they have told you is false. Tell the warriors that."

Nostrils flared. The mouth, suddenly old, was a grim, flat line. "Then you are disgraced," he spat, "and your shodo's name dishonored."

I waved dismissal at him. "Get out of here, Punjamite. You're too stupid to live, but I won't be the one to kill you. My sword likes the taste of men."

Nezbet scooped up his blade and snapped it back into the diagonal sheath. He cast me a final withering stare, then turned and mounted his sand-colored horse. Dust showered us as he jerked his mount around and rode off at a hard gallop.

I sighed heavily. "Short on water," I said, "and now he runs his horse. He'll be lucky to *reach* the others; we may yet be safe."

"No," Del said.

"No," I agreed. "Time we rode on, too."

"Tiger?"

"What?"

"Why didn't you take his horse? The others are coming, he says . . . they could have picked him up."

I thought about it. Scowled. Looked at Del. "Guess we're just not cut out to be thieves, after all."

Del grinned. "Guess not."

It began imperceptibly, as the worst of them usually do. The tiniest of breezes, lifting a ruffle of sand; a wisp of wind swirling down to ripple silken burnous; the pressure of air against face, stripping hair from brow and eyes. Sand kicked up by the stud was caught, trapped, blown free, stinging ankles and eyes. Del and I, riding double, retreated beneath drawn hoods, until I yanked mine off my head and reined the stud to a halt.

"Samiel," I said; meaning the wind, not my sword.

It took Del a moment. Then she stiffened against me. "Are you sure?"

"I can smell it." I squinted. The sun still blinded the eye, unobscured by rising sand, but if the wind grew much stronger the samiel would transform itself into simoom. A hot wind was bad enough. A sandstorm was worse. "Our best bet would be to find some sort of shelter, like a sandwall at an oasis—" I shook my head, blocking sun and sand with a shielding hand. "We're too far. The best we can do is a sandrill blown against the scrub."

Del shivered. "I recall the simoom. . . ." She let it trail off.

I recalled it, too. We'd barely met, and Del was still most distinctly unobtainable. . . .

I smiled crookedly, recalling those days. And the long, dark nights of frustration.

Del poked me in the spine. "Do we ride on? Or stay here?"

"*One* of us needs to walk. Give the stud a rest."

Delicate irony: "Oh, let me be the one. . . ." She slid off, patting the stud's brown rump, and moved to his head. "There are bushes just ahead."

I shrugged. "Might as well. Much as I hate to stop, with the new hounds of hoolies on our trail . . ." I twisted, squinting back the way we had come. "If they're as close as Nezbet said they were, it won't take long before they catch up. Some of them. We're slowed like this. Much too much."

"What else is there to do? If we stop and wait for them, they will surely outnumber us."

"Eventually," I agreed. "Let's just hope if any more show up soon, it's because they did what Nezbet did: rode ahead of the larger contingent."

Del's face was grim. "I like not the idea that so many sword-dancers have been hired to hunt down two of their own."

I turned back. "Sword-dancers we can handle. We're two of the best, remember? If not *the* best." I gave her the benefit of the doubt by saying "we," figuring she'd earned it. "And besides, they won't converge upon us—that's not the way of the circle. They'd take us one by one. No, I'm more concerned with the tribes."

Del was stuck on the sword-dancers. "And how many can *you* defeat, even in single combat, injured as you are?"

"Me? Hoolies, bascha—I can plead sore knee for a very long time." I grinned. "Maybe until they get tired of waiting and give up."

"Did you ever give up when hired to do a job?"

"Once. The man got real sick . . . he was dying, so I let him go. Didn't pick up the second half of my hire fee, either, which should restore some of your faith in me."

"Some," she agreed. "But you should have returned the first half, since you did not complete your contract."

"Yes, well . . ." I blinked against stinging sand. "Let's get to those bushes. And hope this blows itself out before it becomes a full-fledged simoom."

A little while later, as we huddled amid the bushes, Del stated the obvious: "It's not stopping."

"No."

"If anything, it is worse."

"Yes."

"Then it *will* become a simoom."

"Seems like." I shifted my knee, swearing absently,

and sat up judiciously. She was right. It wasn't stopping. It was worse. And it was just on the verge of becoming—

No. It *was*.

"Hoolies," I murmured.

Del, hunkered down against the scrubby bush, twisted. And saw what I saw: ocher-dark cloud of sand and debris rolling across the horizon.

The stud whickered uneasily and pawed, adding to the mess. I got up, hobbled the two steps to him, passed a soothing hand down his neck. "Easy, old son. You know the dance. Lie down for me, shut your eyes . . ." I put my hand on his headstall, intending to urge him down.

A thought blossomed into idea.

Frowning, I scowled out at the roiling mass of sand as it blew across the horizon. At the moment it was still samiel, not simoom, in our location, but in a matter of minutes the true strength and fury of the sandstorm would swallow us. It was not impossible that we could die from it, although unlikely; we had water and blankets and food, so even if the simoom lasted days—

No. Let's not think about that.

Think about something else. Like magic.

Nezbet had said it: I had called fire from the sky with my sword. I had also made glass but a day or two before. Twice I had created something out of nothing, by using the magic in Samiel and enforcing my will upon it. In Iskandar I had created a controllable firestorm to ease our flight. The circle of glass had been unintentional, and only vaguely interesting—to me—but it did indicate I could do strange and wondrous things with Samiel, given the motivation, the need, the wherewithal.

And the control.

The jhihadi, the tribes believed, could do impossible things, like changing the sand to grass. So why didn't they believe *I* was the jhihadi since I called fire out of the sky?

Because the Sandtiger was a only sword-dancer who once had been a chula. Ajani—huge, powerful, clever Ajani, whose burning, as Bellin the Cat had put it, was very bright indeed—had swayed them in his direction. With lengthy, meticulous care.

The only way I could ever prove to them their Oracle had pointed at *me* was to show them what I could do.

In properly jhihadi-ish ways.

Which meant, of course, magic.

The stud nodded unhappiness, then swung his head to plant a forehead against my chest and rub very hard. It destroyed my already precarious balance; I stayed upright only by clutching at the saddle, swearing as my sore knee blared a protest.

The song of the wind altered.

"Tiger—"

I quit swearing and looked. Night was engulfing day.

No more time.

Purposely, I untied the stud from the bush he could easily have uprooted, but didn't, because it hadn't occurred to him that he was considerably stronger—and smarter—than the bush. Horses are like that. I looped the reins up over his neck and hooked them to the saddle. If he needed to run, as I feared, I wanted him unencumbered. A dangling rein usually breaks when stepped upon. But I'd seen a runaway once plunge a foreleg into a loop of loose rein, snug himself tight, and fall. He'd broken his neck on landing.

"Stay down," I told Del. "Lie down, if you like. You might even cover your eyes, or hide under a blanket. I don't really know what might happen."

Del sat bolt upright. "What are you . . . *Ti*ger!"

I unsheathed the sword. "Long as I've got the thing, I may as well see what I can do with it."

"And what it can do to *you!*"

"Yes, well . . ." I squinted against the sand, spat grit, shrugged. "Chance I'll have to take. Look at it this way, bascha—it might slow down our hounds."

"It might *kill* you!"

"Nah," I scoffed. "That will be for *you* to do, if Chosa Dei gets too uppity."

It silenced her instantly.

Sort of the way I planned it; I wasn't any happier about what I was about to do than Del.

And a whole lot more at risk.

I think.

Hoolies, but I hate magic.

Thirteen

I thought of a song. Just a silly little thing; I'm not much good at singing (Del would say I'm not *any* good), and therefore I always feel a trifle stupid standing in the middle of the desert thinking up a song, let alone *singing* it, but it seemed to be required. At least, it had been all the other times.

The Northerners on Staal-Ysta had explained it thoroughly to me, the rite of singing to focus the sword, to focus the dancer, and to summon whatever power there was in the ritual- and rune-bathed *jivatma*. Left to my own devices, singing a focus was about the last thing I'd do. I'd been taught the inner path, the way to summon the soul within a soul, as you prepare to enter the dance. There are mental preparations—

Ah, hoolies, it *all* sounds silly, when you think about it; and even stupider if you say it out loud. So let me make it easy: I look at myself as a weapon, and the sword an extension of me. So that when I think about *me* cutting in a certain direction, or twisting a specific way *just so*, the sword does it, too.

Singlestroke had been perfect for me, before he'd broken in combat against a Northern sword-dancer who'd requenched his *jivatma*. Together we'd carved

out a piece of the South as our domain, though unac-
knowledged by the tanzeers who *really* ruled; but in
the way of the sword-dancer, who rules the South by
fighting skills and a willingness to kill for pay, Singlestroke and I had been perceived as the best.

Of course, Abbu Bensir might object, claiming *himself* the best, but Abbu and I had only rarely crossed
paths. He had his portion of the South, I had mine.
We respected one another.

Whether he still respected me, I couldn't say. Probably. That he'd hired on to track us down didn't mean
he respected us any less, just that we were worth
money. After all, it was Abbu who'd tossed me his
sword in the midst of the confusion in Iskandar, when
I'd briefly lost mine.

Of course, that was before I was worth money.

Now he wouldn't toss me a sword to replace the
one I'd lost. He'd *take* mine, if he could get it . . .
which brought me around to Samiel—and Chosa
Dei—once again.

Wind and sand buffeted my ears. I heard a low-
pitched growling, the complaint of a sandstorm trying
to satisfy an insatiable appetite. I'd heard the noise
before, and felt the power. If I didn't do something
very soon, it might be the last thing I heard—and felt.

I flicked a glance over my shoulder at Del. She was
huddled down against the sandrill—a mound of sand
created by wind blowing it into a lopsided pile against
some kind of obstruction—with burnous hood pulled
up and a blanket swaddled around her body. I thought
momentarily of that body, recalling long limbs entan-
gled with my own, the scent of white-silk hair, the
taste of Northern flesh. I did not want to lose it—or
the spirit that went with it—to a simoom.

Nor to untamed magic.

Hoolies.

Nothing for it, then, but to prove I was the master.

"All right," I muttered into the wind, "let's have a little talk, you and I, about the merits of blowing in *this* patch of desert—or in the patch holding all those sword-dancers after our hides . . . and the money that comes with it, of course."

The simoom growled on, whining and hissing and roaring. Even with my eyes squinted nearly closed, sand and grit stung them. My lashes were fouled and crusty, my nostrils halfway obstructed, my mouth stiff and caked. Sand grated in my teeth, scouring gums and throat. But if I turned my back to the wind, I gave precedence to the simoom.

From behind me, the stud made verbal protest. I was faintly surprised he hadn't gone yet. But, then, likely he thought he was still tied . . . I should have whopped him on the rump and sent him off.

Two-handed, I gripped the hilt and lifted the sword into the air. Wind whined against steel, screeching and shrieking as the edge bit in. Around me the world howled. Hair was stripped from my face, blown back almost painfully. I spread and braced both legs as best I could, hampered by my sore right knee, and dug supporting hollows for sandaled feet, ridding myself of precarious underpinning. I raised both hands high above my head, slicing vertically through the storm, until arms—and blade—were outstretched.

It is the classic pose of the conqueror; the barbaric swordsman counting coup, or singing his own praises with posture rather than voice. *"I am master,"* it says. *"I am the lord. You who would have my place must first remove me from it."*

I thought it rather fitting, in light of the situation.

"Mine," I said aloud.

The storm was unabated.

"Mine," I said more forcefully.

The simoom sang on, scouring at wind-bared legs and arms. And then more than legs and arms; it ripped the burnous and underrobe from my body, shredding them like rotted gauze, and left me bare on all counts, save for sandtiger necklet, which rattled; the suede dhoti anchored too firmly around my hips; Southron sandals cross-gartered to my knees; and the Northern harness hugging ribs and spine and shoulders.

Barbarian, indeed.

"MINE," I roared, and the song in my head rose up to deafen me.

Samiel answered simoom. I felt it before I heard it: a thrumming, numbing, gut-deep tingle that rattled the bones of my elbows and threatened to shatter wrists. I clamped down every muscle I owned, locking joints into position. The power I sensed was sweet, seductive, oh so attractive. It knew me. It knew my song. I had quenched it, then requenched. We were doubly bonded, Samiel and I.

And then the power changed. The essence of Samiel winked out, like a spark caught in a maelstrom, and I felt something else burst into flame to take his place. Something very strong. Something very *angry*.

It sheeted down from the sword, corruscating like heat lightning across the Punja's horizon. Black light. *Black* light. Not true illumination, because it wasn't sunlight or moonlight or firelight. It was black. And yet it glowed.

Sweat broke out on my flesh. Sand adhered at once. Every hollow, crease, and furrow began to itch.

Hoolies. Here we go again.

Black light, radiating. It flooded down the blade, tapped tentatively at my hands upon the grip, then flowed downward again, engulfing fingers, hands, wrists.

I swore. I said something very rude. Because I was, abruptly, more frightened than I had ever been before.

The light was *touching* me—

Black, radiant light, coating flesh in darkness.

"Hoolies," I croaked.

Not magic. I knew it. *Not* magic. Something worse. Something more powerful. Something infinitely more dangerous.

The sword had been partly black. The discoloring had waxed and waned, like the moon, dependent upon Chosa Dei. Dependent upon me, and the strength of will I employed to drive the sorcerer down.

The entire blade was black. The hilt. The hands upon it.

Black-braceleted wrists.

He had been waiting for this.

I shouted. Tried to let go. Tried to cast off the blackened sword, to throw it arcing far into the wind, where the simoom would swallow it. But I could not let go of the weapon that imprisoned Chosa Dei.

Who now imprisoned me.

I felt him, then. A feather-touch. Caress. The merest whisper of breath across my soul. Blackness spread.

"Del," I croaked. "Del, do it *now*—"

But Del didn't—or couldn't—hear me.

I thought, *If I turn this on myself*— wondering if my death would indeed destroy Chosa; remembering belatedly that by giving up my life I also gave up my body. Chosa had already proved himself capable of unmaking and remaking things he found suitable to his needs. A dying body would hardly stop him. Even mine.

The simoom howled on. It stopped up eyes, and ears; took residence in my soul. I felt Chosa's fingertip—or *something*—touch my right forearm. Then my left. Blackness welled coyly, flirting, then swallowed another portion of my flesh.

The hairs stood up on my flesh. My belly twisted and cramped, threatening to spew everything I'd eaten.

Oh, hoolies, what have I done?

Blackness.

So much blackness.

Eating me inch by inch.

Deep inside, bones ached.

Was he trying to unmake them?

Fear and sand had scoured my mouth dry. I swallowed painfully, wishing for water; for wine. For the strength and courage I needed so desperately.

I gripped the sword more tightly, squeezing leather wrappings until my knuckles complained. Toes curled against leather soles, cracking noisily. Even my good knee ached; I flexed muscle, reset, locked everything down once again.

One last try.

"Mine," I mouthed soundlessly. "This sword, this body, this *soul*—"

Abruptly my eyes snapped open. Staring sightlessly into the storm, unheeding of sand and grit and wind, I knew. I *knew*.

There were things Chosa didn't understand. About the spirit. He knew magic and flesh and bone; he knew *nothing* about the spirit.

Nothing about the obsessive compulsion of a young Southron chula sentenced to life as a beast of burden

. . . and finally being given something no one else knew about. Something secret. Something he could keep. Something he could touch, and stroke, and talk to, speaking of dreams of someday; of spells to destroy his demons, living and dead.

Something of his *own*.

I grinned grittily into simoom.

"Mine," I whispered triumphantly, with a powerful, peculiar virulence born of a chula's childhood; of the man-sized boy branded foreign, and strange, and stupid.

Who believed everything he was told.

"Mine," I said again.

This time Chosa heard me.

Pain.

It drove me to my knees.

Ground me into sand.

Fragmented wits and awareness and sense of self, stripping me of everything but fear and comprehension.

Chosa Dei was no legend. The story of his imprisonment at the hands of his brother-sorcerer, Shaka Obre, was truth, not a tale-spinner's unfounded maundering. Chosa Dei was everything they said he was.

Chosa Dei was *more*.

In my hands, the sword turned. The blackened tip— *no*. Not black. The tip was *silver*. Like steel. Clean, unblemished steel, tempered in Northern fires, cooled in Northern water, blessed by Northern gods.

Samiel?

Black light corruscated. Chosa Dei lashed out, swallowed another piece of me, climbed higher on my forearms. Halfway to my elbows.

The sword was aimed downward, twisting in my grip. Another sliver of Samiel showed his true colors.

And then I understood.

Chosa Dei was leaving. Chosa was deserting. Chosa was trading a Northern-made *jivatma* for a Southron-bred sword-dancer.

Freeing Samiel.

If the sword was empty of Chosa . . .

If.

But emptying Samiel would mean filling me.

With Chosa Dei.

If.

If I took him. If I let him come. If I let him have the body, forsaking the sword, would the sword then be strong enough to defeat him?

But with no one able to wield it.

Hoolies.

Guts cramped. Teeth ground. Eyes bulged and refused to close.

Black up to the elbows.

Muscles contracted. Down through the air, slicing wind and wailing. Black light flashed. Clean steel glittered. Shoulders locked as I thrust the sword tip into the sand. Then deeper. Driving it down, down. Scouring steel flesh.

Kneeling, I clutched the sword. Hung there, transfixed. Powerless before the sword. The sorcerer. Nothing more than the shell he wanted to fill.

"No," I mouthed.

Vision flickered. Went out. Blindly, I stared wide-eyed into the scouring wind.

"Tiger—" I husked. "Wizard's wooden tiger . . ."

The memory was distant. A small wooden sand-tiger, shaped to catch the eye. It had been mine. Only mine. And I had petitioned it, begging it for power. For the means to escape.

Sandtiger, I had called it. Sandtiger I had made it.

In flesh: deliverance.

Children and men, eaten. More killed in the attempt. Then *I* had tracked it down. *I* had found its lair. *I* had leveled the spear and plunged it into the belly.

Screaming from shock and pain as the claws raked cheek. As the poison filled the body.

I had killed the sandtiger. He had nearly killed me.

Chosa was killing me.

The flesh would go on living, but the spirit, the soul, would not.

Vision flickered. Died.

Inside me, something laughed.

The inner eye opened. And Saw.

"Del!" I screamed. "Del—*Delilah*—Del— Do it! Do it! Don't let—don't *let*— Del— *Do what you have to do*—"

The inner eye *Saw*.

"Del—" I croaked.

Sandaled feet. Wind-whipped burnous. The glint of a Northern sword.

I couldn't see her expression. Maybe it was best. "Do it, Del—*do* it!"

Wind stripped her face of hair, leaving it stark and bleached and anguished. In her hands, *jivatma* trembled.

"—have to—" I managed. "You said—you could . . . you said . . . like Ajani—"

Del flinched. The wind screamed around us, hiding her face again.

Hoolies, bascha. Do it.

Deep inside, something laughed.

Chosa was *amused*.

"Like Ajani," I husked. "Quick. Clean. No risk to you— *Del*—"

Why was she taking so long?

The Northern sword glinted. It cut through the simoom's howling and sang its own song. Of nightsky curtains of color; of the hue of a banshee-storm, screaming through Northern mountains.

Too cold for me.

I was Southron-born.

My storm was the samiel.

From the sand I ripped the sword. Blackness glistened.

"Too late," I mouthed. *"—left it too late—"*

The wind stripped hair away. I saw her face once more: the architecture of bones framed in precise perfection; the smooth, flawless flesh; the contours of nose, of cheekbones; the symmetry of the jaw.

The warped line of her mouth, parting to open.

Delilah began to sing. Deathsong. Lifesong. The song of a sword-dancer's life. Of a Southron chula's passing from the world of free men he had tried to make his own.

Don't wait, bascha.

A new determination came into Del's expression. She cut off her song in mid-note and raised the deadly *jivatma*, whose name was Boreal.

Even as I raised mine.

As Chosa made me do it.

"Samiel," she said.

But it was lost in the wail of wind.

Fourteen

—With his brother upon the pinnacle, staring across the vast expanse of the land they have created; marveling that they could, because they are sorcerers, not gods—

He frowns.

—or is it possible, he wonders, that gods are merely constructs of magic? A magic so deep and abiding and dangerous no one else has dared try it, before now; to summon it, collect it, wield it, shaping something out of nothing—

—unmaking what had been, to make what now exists.

He smiles.

—I have done this

He pauses. Rephrases.

WE have done this. Shaka and I.

He glances at his brother. Chosa Dei and Shaka Obre, twin-born, inseparable, indistinguishable from one another. Matched in will, in strength, in power. In so very many things, offering two halves of a whole; the balance of dark and light.

Matched in everything save ambition.

"What we have done—" Chosa begins.

Shaka smiles, completing it: "—is truly remarkable. A gift for the people."

Chosa frowns, distracted from triumph. "Gift?"

"Surely you do not expect them to PAY for this," Shaka says, laughing. *"They did not ask it, did not request—"*

"—except in petitions to gods."

Laughter dying, Shaka shrugs. "Men petition for many things."

"But this time WE answered. We gave them what they wanted."

"And now you want payment?" Shaka shakes his head. *"How is it we are so alike, but so different? The power we have wielded is compensation enough."* Shaka thrusts out an illustrative hand, encompassing the grasslands below. *"Don't you see? We've made the land lush. We've made the land fertile. In place of sand there is grass."*

Chosa's expression is grim. "We have answered their worthless petitions. Now they must compensate us."

Shaka sighs deeply. "With what? Coin? Goats? Daughters? Useless gems and domains?" He puts his hand upon his brother's stiffened shoulder. *"Look again, Chosa. Behold what we have wrought. We have remade the world."*

Chosa's face spasms. "I'm not so benevolent."

Shaka removes his hand from his brother's shoulder. "No. You've always been impatient. You've always wanted more."

Chosa stares down across the vast expanse of grass that had once been sand. He speaks a truth no one has ever before considered, but he has long suspected: "We are two different people."

Shaka's eyes widen. "But we want the same thing!"

"No," Chosa says bitterly. "No. You want THAT."
And points to the grass.

"Chosa—don't you?"

Chosa shrugs. "I don't know what I want. Just—
more. MORE. I am bored . . . look what we've done,
Shaka. As YOU said: Look what we have wrought.
What is there left to do?"

Shaka laughs. "We will think of something."

His brother scowls blackly. "We are very young,
Shaka. There is so much time, so MUCH time. . . ."

"We will find ways to fill it." Shaka gazes at the
grasslands below, nodding satisfaction. "We have given
a dying people the gift of life, Chosa . . . I think I want
to watch how they use it."

Chosa makes a dismissive, contemptuous gesture.
"Watch all you like, then. I have better ways to spend
my time."

"Oh? How?"

Chosa Dei smiles. "I have acquired a taste for
magic."

Shaka's expression alters from indulgence to alert
awareness. "We have always had magic, Chosa. What
do you mean to do?"

"Collect it," Chosa says. "Find more, and collect it.
Because if it was this easy to MAKE this, it will be
more entertaining to destroy it." He sees the shock in
Shaka's eyes, and shrugs offhandedly. "Oh, not at
once. I'll let you play with it a while. I'll even let you
keep part of it, if you like; exactly half, as always."
Chosa laughs. "After all, everything we've ever had has
been divided precisely in two. Why not the land we've
just created?"

"No," Shaka says.

Chosa's eyes widen ingenuously. "But it's the way
we've ALWAYS done it. Half for you, half for me."

"No," Shaka says. "This involves people."

Chosa leans close to his brother and speaks in a pointed whisper. "If any of them get broken, we'll simply make MORE."

Shaka Obre recoils. "We will do no such thing. They are PEOPLE, Chosa—not things. You are to leave them be."

"Half of them are mine."

"Chosa—"

"It's the way we DO it, Shaka! Half and half. Remember?"

Shaka glares. "Over my dead body."

Chosa considers it. "That might be fun," he says finally. "We've never done that before."

Now Shaka is suspicious. "Done what?"

"Tried to kill one another before. Do you suppose we could? Really die, I mean?" Excitement blossoms in Chosa's face. "We have all those wards and spells . . . do you think we should try to counteract them, just to see if we really could?"

"Go away," Shaka says. "I don't like you like this."

Chosa persists. "But wouldn't it be FUN?"

Shaka shakes his head.

Frustration appears in Chosa's eyes. "Why do you always have to be such a spoilsport, Shaka?"

"Because I have more sense. I understand responsibility." Shaka nods toward the grasslands. "We created this for people in need, Chosa. We sowed the field. Now we ought to tend the crop."

Chosa makes a derisive sound. "YOU tend the crop. I'm going collecting."

Shaka watches him turn away. "Don't you do anything! Don't you hurt those people, Chosa!"

Chosa pauses. "Not yet. I'll let you play with your toy. For a while. Until I can't think of anything else to do.

By then, centuries will have passed, and you'll be tired of it, too. Ready for something NEW." He smiles. "Yes?"

Sound. No sight: I can't open my eyes. Sound only, no more; flesh and bone won't answer my need.

"Curse you," she whispered. "I hate you for this."

It was not what I might have expected.

"I *hate* you for this!" A warped, throttled sound, breaking free of a too-taut throat. "I hate you for what you have done; for what you have become, in spite and *because* of this sorcerer—" She broke it off abruptly, then continued in a more controlled, but no less telling tone. "What am I to do? Let him have you? What am I to do? Turn my back? Walk away? Refuse to acknowledge the worth of the doing, the worth of the man, because it is easier *not* to do?"

I had no answers for her. But then, she didn't want them from me. Had she known I could hear her, she wouldn't have said a thing . . . except maybe those words designed to draw blood. Even now, she tried to do that. All unknowing. Which more than anything underscored the strength of her anguish.

"If you could see what he has done . . ." Despair crept into the tone. "If I could kill him, I would. If I could cut off his head as I cut off Ajani's, I would. If I could use magic or whatever else it might take to free you, *I would*—" Then, on a rush, expelling words and emotions, "There are things I would say to you, could I do it, could I say them . . . but we are neither of us the kind to admit weaknesses, or failures, because to admit them opens the door to more. I know it. I understand it. But now, when I *need* to know who and what you are . . . you offer me nothing—and I can't ask. I lack the courage for it."

Deep inside, I struggled. But no words were emitted. Eyelids did not lift.

"What am I to do?" she rasped. "I am weak. I am *afraid*. I am not the person I need to be to vanquish this enemy. I am not the Sandtiger."

And then a spate of muttered uplander, all sibilant syllables of twisty, foreign words strung together into a litany made to ward off that fear.

Silence. A hard, shattered silence. I wanted to fill it badly.

"You have warped my song," she declared. "You have reshaped all the words, and altered all the music."

Oh, bascha, I'm sorry.

"Please," Del said. "I have been so many things and sung so many songs, to make myself hard enough. To make myself strong enough. I am what I am. I am—not like others. I can't *be* like others, because there is weakness in it. But you gave me something more . . . you *make* me something more. You don't make me less than I am—less than I have had to be and *still* have to be . . . you make me more."

I wanted badly to answer, to tell her I made her nothing at all, but that she made *me* something; something better. Something *more*—

The tone was raw. "What am I to do? Kill you for your own good?"

Not what I had in mind.

Nor Chosa Dei, either.

Who stood once more on the overlook beside Shaka Obre.

Again, sound. The hissing sibilance of edged steel pulled from lined sheath. The sluff and grate of Southron sandals. The subtle beat of a soft-stepping horse approaching across the sand.

"So," she murmured quietly. "He comes to us after all."

Metallic clatter: bridle brasses, bit shanks; the creak of Southron saddle. A horse, protesting vaguely, reined to a halt.

"Come down," she invited. "I give the honor to you: you may draw the circle."

The answering voice was male, catching oddly on broken syllables. "Why do I want a circle?"

"Have you not come to challenge him?"

He didn't answer at once. Then, "He seems a bit indisposed."

"For the moment," she agreed. "But there is always me."

"I didn't come for you. At least—not to meet in the circle. Beds are much softer."

"A circle is the only place we *will* meet."

"Unless I beat you. If bedsport were the prize." Creaking leather again. "But that's not why I came."

"She sent you."

A trace of surprise underlay his tone. "You know about her?"

"More, perhaps, than she would like."

"Well." He cleared his throat, but the huskiness remained. "What has befallen him? Certainly not Nezbet . . . unless the Sandtiger has grown so old and careless even boys may defeat him."

Contempt laced her tone. "Nezbet didn't beat him. This was—" She stopped. "You wouldn't understand."

Bridle brasses clattered as the horse shook its head. "What I understand is that he hasn't been himself for some time. There are rumors in Iskandar, and even

in Harquhal . . . tales that make good telling when
men gather to drink and dice."

"*You* are undoubtedly the subject of such tales.
How often are they truthful?"

He laughed huskily. "Ah, but even I have seen he's
not the same. And he *isn't*, Del . . . but then, you
never saw him in his prime."

"His *prime*." She was angry. "In his prime he was—
is—three times the man you are."

"*Three* times." He was amused. "And as for being
a man—as a woman judges a man—only you can say.
I've never slept with him."

"Three times the man," she said coolly, "in bed—
and in the circle."

The broken voice was dangerously mild. "And I've
never slept with *you*."

"Nor will you," she retorted.

"Unless I win it from you."

The answering tone turned equally lethal. "Just like
a man," she said, "to make a woman's body the issue
instead of the woman's skill."

He dismounted, jangling brasses. "I know you have
the skill. We danced together, remember? I was, however briefly, shodo to—" he paused. "—the *an-
ishtoya?*"

"You served a purpose," she answered, avoiding
the question. "That is all, Abbu."

Steps sloughed through sand. Paused beside my
head. "Is he dead?"

"Of course not. Do you think I'm keeping vigil?"

The voice was very close. "I don't know what you
might be doing. You're Northern, not Southron—*and*
you're a woman. Women do odd things."

"He's exhausted. He's resting."

"He's *unconscious*, bascha. Do you think I can't tell?" He paused. "What's wrong with him?"

"Nothing."

"Is that why he looks half dead?"

"He's not."

The tone was speculative. "I was in Iskandar, remember? I was in the middle of the fury just like everyone else. Only I'm not a man for religious ecstasy." He paused. "Does the condition he's in have something to do with magic?"

Reluctantly: "Yes."

"I thought so," he said. "And it begins to make me wonder."

"Wonder what?" she snapped.

"The tribes think Ajani was the jhihadi."

"Yes. Because Ajani took pains to make it appear he was."

"But the Sandtiger took no pains at all, at anything, because it isn't his way. He just *does*." A single step nearer; the body knelt at my side. "What I'm wondering—now—is exactly how *much* he can do."

"Tiger is Tiger," she said. "He isn't the jhihadi, no matter what he says."

"*He* says he's the jhihadi?"

Silence.

Dryly: "Of course, he could be saying it just to try and impress you."

"No." Grudgingly. "He says my brother pointed at him."

"Your brother? What in hoolies does your brother have to do with any of this?"

"He's the Oracle."

Silence. Then, ironically. "Do I seem that gullible to you? Or is this a game you and the Sandtiger have cooked up?" He snorted. "If it is, I don't think it's working. Right now you have dozens of *very* angry warriors on your trail, not to mention ten or so sword-dancers hired by Aladar's daughter."

"Believe what you wish to believe." Sand grated as she shifted her position. "Will you draw the circle?"

"Not now." A husky chuckle. "You've frightened me badly, bascha. I don't dare a dance with you."

She said something in eloquent uplander. I opened my mouth to answer.

Fifteen

Chosa Dei nods. "You'll grow tired, Shaka. You'll grow bored, like me. And there won't be anything else to do, except start all over again."

In counterpoint, Shaka Obre shakes his head. "I won't let you hurt those people."

"Puny, fragile toys."

Shaka, angry, lashes out. "Then go make your own! If you're so good at it, go make your own. Somewhere ELSE, Chosa. Leave my world alone."

"Your world! YOUR world? We made this together, Shaka."

"It doesn't matter. You don't want it anymore. I do."

Contempt warps Chosa's expression. "You don't know what you want."

"Neither do you, Chosa. That's part of your problem."

"I don't HAVE a problem. And if I do, it's you!"

Shaka Obre sighs. "Just go away. You're cluttering up my world."

"You'll miss me, if I do."

Shaka shrugs. "I know how to keep myself busy."

Abbu again. "What exactly did you *do* to him, Del?"

"You wouldn't understand."

"Tell me anyway."

"The story is very long."

"Tell me anyway. We have time."

"The others will come, and then where will we be? I can't dance against them all, and you *won't*."

He was amused. "Of course not. You think I'm one of them, after all."

"Aren't you? Why else would you come?"

"Curiosity."

"Greed, more like. Did she offer you enough?"

"She offered me a very great deal. I am something of a legend, after all."

"Panjandrum," she muttered.

"That, too," he agreed. "Now, as for the Sand-tiger—"

Ice descended abruptly. "You would have to dance against me *first*."

"I know that, bascha. You've made that very clear." He shifted. "What did you do to him? And what did *he* do to make you risk his life?"

I struggled to open my eyes. Tried to speak. Tried to do *something* that told them I was alive, awake, aware.

Nothing worked.

—Chosa Dei on the pinnacle, overlooking the grassy valley cradled by forested hills; sunlight glinting off lakes—

"I made this," he says. "I could UNmake this—"

Back.

"Hoolies," Abbu remarked. "You did all this by taking his *sword* away from him?"

"Not—precisely." Del's tone was a mixture of

things: weariness, worry, reticence. "As I have said, there is much more to it. A long story."

"As *I* have said, bascha, we have time."

Del sighed. "I don't understand why you're doing this."

"Healing instead of hindering?" He laughed in his broken, husky voice; I'd given him that. "Because maybe I didn't hire on to catch him. Did you ever think of that? And even if I *did*, it's no challenge to capture a man in his present condition. Does nothing for the reputation. This is the *Sandtiger*, after all . . ." Abbu paused. "At least—it *was*."

"And will be again." A cool hand touched my forehead, smoothing back sweat- and sand-crusted hair. "It begins with his sword," she said finally. "A Northern sword. *Jivatma*."

Abbu grunted. "I know about them. And I've seen yours, remember? When we danced."

The fingers tightened briefly against my brow. I realized my eyes were held forcibly closed with a damp cloth binding. "There is more," Del said quietly. "A sorcerer. Chosa Dei."

Abbu's tone was incredulous. "Chosa Dei? But he's only a *story!*"

"Wards!" Chosa shrieks. "You put wards upon the land!"

"Of course I did," Shaka says quietly. "I didn't want you showing up one day, sick to death of boredom, and deciding—out of spite—to destroy what I made."

"YOU made!" Chosa bares his teeth. "WE made, you mean. It was both of us, Shaka—and you know it!"

"But only one of us wants to destroy it."

"Not destroy. Unmake," Chosa explains. "And if

*you like, we can REmake it once we're done." He
grins, reaching out to clasp his brother's shoulder. "It
would be fun, yes? To unmake what we made, then
remake it all over again. Only better—"*

"I will not release the wards."

*Chosa's fingers tighten rigidly, digging into Shaka's
shoulder. "You will. You have to. Because if you
don't. . . ."*

The implication is clear. But Shaka shakes his head.

*They stand again upon the pinnacle, overlooking the
lush green grasslands they had, centuries before, made
out of barren wasteland. Five generations have labored
on the land, knowing fertile soil, water in plenty, abun-
dant crops. Shaka's benevolent blessing has allowed
them the freedom to blossom and grow, knowing little
hardship.*

*And now Chosa Dei wants to unmake it. Out of
boredom.*

"No," Shaka says. "The land stays as it is."

*"Divide it," Chosa counters. "Half is mine, after all;
you couldn't have done any of it without my portion
of the power."*

*Shaka's expression is distasteful. "I've heard all
about you, Chosa. You do destroy. You kill. You—"*

*"I unmake," Chosa clarified. "And remake, yes?"
He smiles. "We learn from our mistakes. Each generation is an improvement upon the last; don't you think
we might do better this time?"*

Shaka shakes his head.

*Rage contorts Chosa's features. "Lift the wards,
Shaka. Enough of this folly. Lift the wards or I will
unmake them, and then I'll unmake YOU."*

Shaka laughs. "I think you're forgetting something."

"What am I forgetting?"

"I have magic, too."

"Not like mine," Chosa whispers. *"Oh, not like mine. Trust me, brother. Test me, thwart me, and you will suffer for it."*

Shaka assesses his brother. He shakes his head very sadly. *"You weren't always like this. As a child, you were cheerful and kind and generous. What happened? Where did you go wrong?"*

Chosa Dei laughs. *"I acquired a taste for magic."*

"Then magic will be your bedmate." Shaka no longer smiles nor assesses; his decision is made. *"Try my wards, Chosa, and you will find out how powerful they are. And how powerful I am."*

Chosa scoffed. *"You have been here for two hundred and fifty years, stagnating. While I have been in the world, collecting all the magic."* He pauses. *"Have you any idea AT ALL how powerful I've become?"*

Shaka smiles sadly. *"Yes. I think I do. And that's why I can't let you 'unmake' what I have labored to protect."*

"You must share," Chosa appeals beguilingly. *"The way we've always shared."*

"Not in this."

Rage convulses Chosa's features. *"Then you will see what I am, yes? You will see what I can do!"*

"Probably," Shaka agrees. *"Since I can't change your mind."*

"And you will suffer for it!"

Shaka looks down upon the lush grasslands. *"Someone will,"* he says sadly. *"You. Or I. Or them."*

"THEM!" Contempt is explicit. *"What do I care for them? I can make as many of them as I need."* He bares his teeth. *"But I don't need them, yes?"*

"Yes," Shaka says. *"You do. Though you haven't the wit to see it."*

Chosa Dei raises one hand. "Then let the testing begin."

Shaka Obre sighs. "It already has. But you haven't the wit to see THAT, either."

One finger stabs toward the valley below. "I will remake it into hoolies!"

Shaka shrugs. "And I will restore it. One day."

"Not if you're destroyed. Not if YOU'RE unmade!"

"Someone will," Shaka says. "If not me, someone else will. Hoolies can't last forever."

"I'll make it last," Chosa threatens.

Shaka merely smiles. "Do try," he suggests. "You're ruining a perfectly beautiful day with your danjac's braying."

Chosa's expression is malignant. "You'll see," he says. "You'll SEE what I can do."

Shaka Obre strokes a languid hand through dark hair. "I'm still waiting."

Chosa stares. "You mean it," he says finally.

"Yes."

"But you're my brother."

"You're not mine. My brother would never have done this. BECOME this." Shaka's dark-eyed stare is harsh. "You must have unmade your brain when you were playing all your games."

"I'll send you to hoolies!" Chosa shrieks.

Shaka's smile is wintry. "After I send you."

"Shaka!" I screamed. "*Shaka—*"

Hands closed over my wrists, clamped down, forced me back against the blanket.

"Shaka!" I cried. My voice was a mockery.

Another set of hands joined the first. "Hoolies," Abbu breathed.

"Do you see?" Del pressed spread fingers against

my chest, speaking quietly. "Lie still, Tiger. Shaka isn't here. Shaka's never been here."

"The wards," I rasped. "Don't you see? Chosa destroyed them. He *did*. Shaka's magic didn't hold—Chosa was too powerful—" A bone-deep shudder wracked my body. "He unmade the *wards*—"

"And thereby imprisoned himself; remember?" Del asked. "That's how the story goes."

Breathing was difficult. My lungs felt constricted. Abdomen contracted as I labored to draw in breath, then expell it. "I don't know the story. I only know the truth. I was *there*—"

"There!" Del's fingers tightened.

"—bascha . . . gods, *Del*—" I tasted blood in my mouth.

"He's delirious," Abbu commented. "Remember how he was when his horse kicked him in the head?"

"—bascha, I can't see."

"You will," she promised. "You're not blind. But too much sand got into your eyes . . . they need to heal, that is all."

"I have to see . . ." I tried to pull my hands from Abbu's grip, and could not. "Let go. Abbu—take your paws off me!"

He did. I dragged the cloth from my eyes and realized what Del meant at once. My eyes were gritty, itchy, and very sore. Sunlight made them water.

But I forgot about my eyes. What I wanted was my hands.

Flat on my back, I thrust them into the air and inspected every inch of them. Then expelled a gusty breath of relief. "He's gone," I murmured dully. And then to myself, bewildered, afraid to say it aloud: *No, he's not. He's IN me. I can feel him.*

I sprang up, hurling myself against their arms; fell

back as my knee collapsed. I was weak, trembling, undone. "Hoolies," I choked. "Am I him?"

A thin line of moisture dotted Del's upper lip. She scraped it away with a forearm. "But you said he was gone." She exchanged a glance with Abbu Bensir. "Do you believe me now?"

His face was ashen. "Sandtiger . . ." But he let it trail off, as if not knowing what to say.

"Am I him?" I repeated. And then: "Where's my sword?"

Del pointed. "There."

I looked. "There" was not so far. Unsheathed, it lay in the sand. Sunlight bathed charred steel.

"Black," I blurted in relief. "Half of it, now . . . but that's better than none of it. Better than—" I let it go, slumping back against the blanket, and stared again at my arms and hands, lifting them against the sun. Turned them this way and that. "*Not* black," I murmured.

No. Pallid white. Like they'd been left too long in the snow. But the hair was all burned off, and the flesh was flaky and scaled. From elbows to fingertips. The nails were all discolored, as if they'd been frozen.

Del drew in a deep breath. "You asked me to kill you," she said. "You *begged* me to kill you."

I stared at my hands, working blue-nailed fingers in distracted fascination. "Something tells me you didn't do it."

"No. I did something else. I knew it might kill you, but since that was what you wanted anyway . . ." Wearily, she scrubbed hair back from her face. Tension had drained her of color, of life. "I sang a song, and then I knocked your sword away. Chosa hadn't taken all of you yet, just some. I thought it worth the risk."

I frowned, chewing my lip. "And by separating me from the sword . . ."

Del nodded. "I hoped that because part of Chosa remained in the steel, he would have to let you go."

I avoided the truth by denying it aloud. "It could have gone the other way. Chosa could have jumped to me."

"Yes," she agreed. "And had I judged that accomplished, I'd have done to you what you begged me to do."

Memories were not clear; at least, not *my* memories. They were all jumbled up with Chosa's. "What was it?" I asked warily. "What was it I asked you to do?"

"Cut off your head," she answered. "Like I did with Ajani."

"Hoolies." Abbu again.

Which distracted me. "What are you doing here?" I asked. "Making time with Del?" It hadn't been beneath him before.

Fleetingly, he grinned. "No, but now that you mention it—" He waved it away. "Nezbet appeared at my campfire, mouthing nonsense about a white-haired woman sword-dancer." He shrugged. "I knew right away who he meant. And since I was well ahead of the others, I sent him on his way and came on myself."

"Doesn't Nezbet have any idea who I am?" Del asked. "You'd think Tiger was the only one involved, the way that boy talked."

"That boy" was probably all of two or three years younger than Del.

Which made me feel all the older.

"Nezbet's a fool." Abbu rubbed a hand through gray-frosted black hair. "Like most Southroners, he bears little respect for women—except as bedpartners.

Then again, neither do I." He grinned at Del; she'd changed a lot of his opinions, but he wasn't about to admit it. "So if he heard anything about a woman being involved, he dismissed it as unimportant." He shrugged. "So Tiger's taking the blame for Ajani's murder."

"People *saw* me," she declared. "Have they all gone sandsick? Hundreds of them saw me cut off his head!"

"Ah, but there's a story going around that you're a Northern afreet conjured by Tiger to distract the jhi-hadi's attention long enough for Tiger to kill him." He laughed. "I told you about the stories."

"Afreet!" Del was astounded. "*I'm* not a spirit!"

Abbu leered pointedly. "I know *that.*"

It made me irritable. I shifted against the blanket, aware of aches and itches; the protests of a body driven beyond its final reserves. "Bascha—"

But what I'd intended to say wisped into nothingness.

"Tiger?" she asked.

No, bascha.

Chosa.

Sixteen

Dawn. Three of us gathered as the sun broke over the horizon. Two of them would watch. I would do more than that.

Del's frown was clearly worried, drawing pale brows together. Boreal glinted in her hands, as Abbu's blade in his. Only *I* lacked a weapon; mine lay on the ground.

"You don't—" But she broke it off.

"Yes, I do," I told her.

"Why?" Abbu asked in his half-throttled, broken voice. "If it's that dangerous . . ." His tone was a mixture of disbelief and disgust, that he could give any of it credence. Underscored by reluctant acknowledgment: he, like so many others, had seen me call fire from the sky.

"Because I can't just leave it here," I told him. "Believe me, if I could I would . . . but Del's told me time and time again that it's too much of a risk to take. If someone *else* wound up with this sword . . . someone innocent . . ." I shrugged, suppressing a shiver born of morning chill. I still wore only a dhoti, wishing I'd pulled my other burnous from the saddle-

154

pouches. But there had been other things to concern us.

"Or someone Chosa Dei could unmake, then *re*-make for his own uses," Del added. "But—I wish . . ." She sighed, raking loose hair from her eyes. She had yet to confine it in a tightly woven plait. It spilled across her shoulders, tumbled down her spine, lingered at her breasts. Snagged on the rune-broidered leather tunic that bared so much arm and leg.

Chosa Dei had seen her. Deep in Dragon Mountain, when he'd asked her for the sword that could break imprisoning wards set by Shaka Obre. Chosa *remembered* her.

With effort, I shut him out. "You know what to do," I said harshly. "Don't wait for me to invite you . . . I can't—I don't think—" I stopped, sucked air, tried to speak more evenly. "I don't have the strength to hold him off. Not this time." But I couldn't tell her why.

"Tiger—" But she bit her lip on the rest.

I flicked a glance at Abbu. "If she can't—or won't—you'll have to be the one."

His dark Southron face, older than mine, was oddly gaunt and tight. Silently, he nodded.

I bared my teeth in a grin. "Look at it this way, Abbu—you'll finally be able to say you really are the best."

He raised his Southron sword. He managed a ghost of a smile. "Any way it comes."

I didn't look at Del. I bent and picked up the sword.
—nothing—

"Tiger?" she ventured, and I realized I'd been standing there for gods' knew how long, waiting for something to happen.

I considered things. "My knee hurts," I said. "My

eyes itch like hoolies. I'm still in need of a bath." I arched eyebrows. "Nothing seems to have changed.

"Is he—in there?"

I looked down at the sword in my hands. Samiel was blackened to the halfway point of the blade. My hands on the grip were blue-nailed, pallid white, still cracked and scaly, but not a drop of blackness touched them.

Nothing on the outside. How much was on the *inside?*

"He's in there," I confirmed, offering part of the truth. "But—I think he's hurt."

"Hurt?" Abbu blurted. "First you expect me to believe there's a sorcerer *in your sword*, and now you say he's *hurt?*" He snapped his own back into its sheath, harnessed diagonally. "I think you've made this up. I think there's no truth in this at all, and you are *using* it to keep from dancing against me. Because you know you will lose."

"Oh, I'd lose," I agreed. "I've only got one knee."

He scowled. "And how long will you use that as a crutch, Sandtiger?"

"It's true," Del said quietly. "What would you have me swear on, that you will believe me?"

Abbu grinned. "Oh, bascha—"

"Never mind *that*," I interjected. "Like I said, I think he's hurt." I scowled down at the sword. "I can't tell you why. It just feels different. Sort of—*bruised*." I glared at both of them, knowing how it sounded. "It feels a lot like I do: a horse ridden hard and put away wet."

"Poetic," Abbu said dryly. He rubbed idly at the scarred flesh of his throat, where my wooden sword had nearly killed him so many years before. "So, is this how we leave it? You on one knee, with a *bruised* magical sword . . ." He let it go, laughing. "I should challenge you anyway."

Del stiffened. We both knew what she intended to say, except Abbu cut her off with a raised hand.

He eyed her thoughtfully as he lowered it. "We never finished the dance we began in Iskandar."

"And you won't," I snapped. "Knee or no knee, *I'll* dance. I'm tired of you taking on Del in my place."

The smile was as expected; his unspoken rejoinder was implicit.

"Well?" Del asked curtly, wise to the ways—and thoughts—of men. "How is this to be settled?"

Abbu and I stared meaningfully at one another for a long moment. Then he ended the contest. "Hoolies," he said affably, "there's nothing in this for me. Not enough coin, anyway." He patted the coin-pouch hanging from his belt. "The shodo always said money couldn't buy friendship—or rivalry. When the Sandtiger and I dance our final dance, it will be for another reason."

"*More* money?" I gibed.

"Undoubtedly," he drawled, turning away toward his horse. "If I were you, either of you, I would not go to Julah."

"Why?" Del asked. "If there is a need—"

He overrode her. "There is a need *not* to." All pretense was dismissed; Abbu was no longer amused. "Yes, I was asked to track both of you, catch you, and bring you back to Iskandar. Because Sabra knows exactly who killed her father. Unlike all the tribes, she doesn't care about the jhihadi. She just wants revenge."

"And you're working for her," I said.

"Me work for a woman?" He grinned. "What do you think, Sandtiger? You were a Southroner, once."

It got to me, as he intended. *"Once?"*

Abbu swung up into the saddle and turned his horse to face us. "Before you crossed the border, so to speak." He gestured negligently, indicating Del and Samiel. "Northern sword. Northern woman." His grin was sly and crooked. "But one might be worth the trouble."

I scowled at him. "Get the hoolies out of here."

"Wait," Del said.

He reined in his horse, eyebrows arched.

"Are you working for her?" Del asked quietly.

"You should know the answer," he told her. He hooked his head in my direction. "Tiger knows. Ask *him."*

Del waited till he was gone. "Well?"

"No," I answered.

Her eyes narrowed. "How can you be certain? You yourself have said you are not friends, and so has he. How do you know he isn't lying?"

"He isn't working for her. Because if he were, he'd do exactly what he'd hired on to do: invite me into a circle, beat the hoolies out of me, then haul me back to Iskandar."

Del's expression was odd. "Do you think he can beat you?"

"Right now, with this knee, Rhashad's *mother* can beat me." I hefted the sword. "Believe me, if he'd hired on—woman tanzeer or no—he'd finish the job. Abbu Bensir always finishes what he starts."

Del watched me maneuver my knee, extending it to pop it, then bending it back again, testing flexibility. "How are you? How are you *really?"*

It had nothing to do with my knee. The woman knows me well, but not well enough.

I expelled a breathy half grunt, half laugh. "How

am I? I don't know. Sore. Tired. Itchy. Smelly. Beat to death inside and out." I turned gingerly, hobbling back toward my blanket spread next to the tiny cairn. "Pretty well bored with the whole situation."

Del followed, offering no assistance as I levered myself awkwardly down to sit. Without thinking I set the sword aside—it was, at the moment, quiescent—and began to untie knee wrappings.

She had not yet resheathed. "What you said . . . what you asked. Before." She sounded half ashamed, half concerned. "You asked if you were him."

I shrugged negligently, unwinding ragged fabric that had once clothed a borjuni. "Just a little confused." With wrappings gone, the knee was fully displayed. I prodded it carefully with a forefinger, checking for puffiness and pain. "Not so bad," I observed. "Should be mostly healed in a day or two. Then Abbu, when he comes calling, can have the dance he wants."

Del sighed and squatted, finally sheathing her sword. "You would be foolhardy to undertake it. Better or not, your knee will not support you in a true dance . . . and why are you so certain he will come back? He could have challenged you now, and had a better chance. Why do it later, when you are a tougher opponent?"

"Because he will. I would." I cast her a glance, smiling. "This has nothing to do with woman tanzeers. This has to do with something that's lain unsettled between us for years."

"His throat." She touched her own.

"That's part of it. But so's pride. So's reputation." I smiled. "The South isn't big enough for *two* sworddancers like us."

"So one of you will kill the other."

"Only if one of us insists. Myself, I think I could

stand it if he beat the hoolies out of me and made me yield . . . I don't see much good in dying in the name of pride. *Dancing,* yes; it's been a long time coming. As for Abbu?" I shrugged. "I don't know. I just know he'll be back. He only gave up for now because he *wasn't* working for Sabra, and because he doesn't want anyone to think he won the dance because I wasn't in proper condition."

"*You* think."

"I know. These things are important, Del . . . Abbu Bensir and I have spent most of our respective careers hearing stories about one another. And since *he* was here before I was, it grates on him harder. Nobody who's been the premier sword-dancer in the South wants to give up any part of that honor . . . then I came along." I arched my brows. "Of course, he had full warning. When I nearly crushed his throat with a wooden sword."

Del's smile was wry. "Will it be like that for you?"

"You mean, will I be annoyed when someone younger and better comes along?" I shrugged. "By the time that happens, I'll be an old man. It won't matter any more."

Del laughed aloud. "Old man," she jeered, "it has *already* happened."

"Ah, but you'll never be acknowledged," I countered, "not that I'm admitting you're better. *Good,* yes—but better?" I shrugged. "Anyway, you're a woman. No Southron sword-dancer will ever acknowledge you."

"You do. Abbu does." She frowned. "I think. Either that, or he's only saying he does because he thinks sweet words will win my regard and make me want to share his bed." She tucked hair behind one ear. "Men do that."

"Because it works." I grinned as she glared, then began to rewrap my knee. "Too bad he didn't leave us his horse."

It startled her. "Did you think he would?"

"Maybe. If the other sword-dancers are still only a day behind, he could have waited for them, then gone on back to Iskandar."

"They are not a day behind. Sword-dancers *or* tribes. They are perhaps *two* days, because of the simoom." Del frowned. "Don't you remember?"

"Remember what?" I asked warily.

She stroked hair out of an eye. "You turned the simoom. You stopped the wind, stopped the sand . . . then sent it on around us."

"But—I thought . . ." I frowned, trying to remember. I recalled *wanting* to do all of that, but I couldn't remember accomplishing it. There had been too much of Chosa Dei clamoring at my soul. "Well, good," I said finally. "It'll help us get ahead a little, if the simoom has set them back."

"Besides, had Abbu left us his horse, it would have made him a fool."

That caught my attention. "You think Abbu Bensir could never be a fool?"

Del assessed me a moment. Her face was masked, but something—was it amusement?—lurked in her eyes. "I suppose he could be," she said finally, with careful solemnity. "You and he are much alike."

"Now, bascha—"

She expressed overly elaborate surprise. "But you are. He is older, of course—though how much I couldn't say—" Hoolies, she *was* amused! "—and he is undoubtedly wiser, because of experience . . . but there are remarkable similarities." She caught up her hair and began to divide it into three sections. "But probably only because you were trained by the same shodo."

"I'm not anything like Abbu! You heard what he said: 'Me work for a woman?'—as if it might contaminate him." I glared at her wide-eyed expression. "He'd like nothing better than to get you into bed, because that's all he thinks you're good for. Like most Southroners."

Del continued braiding. "Like you were, once."

I scowled. "I'm still a Southroner. Just because I went traipsing off across the border to help you out . . ." I frowned at my knee. "Maybe there are some things different about me now, thanks to you, but I'm still a Southroner. What else would I be?"

Del's tone was soft as she tied off her braid. "You don't know, remember? The Salset never told you."

Vigorously, I knotted the wrapping on my knee. Changing the subject. "Our best bet is to go on to Quumi and buy another horse. Then we can head on down to Julah."

"Julah! But Abbu just said—"

"Abbu doesn't know what I know." I moved off my blanket, began to roll it up. "Nobody knows what we—what *I*—know."

"We?" Del rose, resettling harness straps. "If you mean *me*, enlighten me . . . I don't know what you're talking about."

The "we" hadn't meant Del. But I couldn't tell her that.

"Let's get going," I said. "We're burning daylight again."

Seventeen

"It isn't much, is it?" Del rode double behind me, which was hot in the warmth of the day. "When you said a trade settlement, I thought you meant something significant."

"It used to be." I aimed the stud toward the lath gate attached precariously to the shattered adobe wall. "Quumi was once one of the largest settlements in the South, bursting at the seams with caravans and merchants. But the Punja came along and swallowed it, and the caravans began going another way. Soon most of the merchants left. Quumi never recovered."

"But this isn't the Punja."

"Close enough." I waved a hand in a southerly direction. "Half a day that way. Anyway, everyone got so used to the alternate route that Quumi was mostly forgotten. It's never been what it was."

It never would be, either. What once had been a thriving settlement was now a shadow. Lath instead of adobe. Powdered dirt in place of brick. The narrow streets were clogged with windblown drifts of sand, and most of the buildings had surrendered to decades of the scouring desert wind. Quumi was tumbled together like ancient oracle bones, spills of brickwork

163

here and there, drifts of powdery dust, slump-shouldered dwellings with all the edges rubbed off. Quumi's profile was round and soft: bone-colored, sun-baked adobe chewed through like a loaf full of weevils.

We approached from the north, paused at the broken city gate to flip the so-called guard a copper, then rode through.

Del was horrified that we had to pay to enter. "The wall is broken," she said. "But five paces down the way anyone can *walk* through . . . why pay to ride through a dilapidated gate?"

"Because you just do." I thought it answer enough. Anyone who knew what Quumi had been ignored its disrepair. It was a game everyone played.

Through the broken gate into the city itself: the stud scuffed across scoured hardpack, rattling pebbles, and into the labyrinth. Quumi was a warren of tumbled buildings, but I knew my way around. I headed straight for Cantina Row.

"It's sort of—gray," Del observed, as we passed into the sand-choked narrow street.

"We're at the edge of the Punja."

"But even the sky is gray."

"That's dust," I told her. "Punja dust mixed with dirt. It's very fine, like powder . . . if you breathe, it blows. See?" I pointed at the powdery dust rising from the stud's hoofprints.

"It looks like ash," she said. "Like a fire cairn gone to ash . . . or a funeral pyre."

The sun-bleached, wind-tattered awnings drooping from flimsy lattices and framing poles above deep-cut windows and doors lent but a trace of tired color to the overall gray-beige of the city. They fluttered faintly in a halfhearted breeze. Sunlight striped pale walls, making blocky, patched patterns against lopsided brickwork. With the hand-smoothed outer coating of adobe scoured away, drifted tufts of long-dead grass were exposed. The stud tried to grab a mouthful on the way by.

"So long as we can find a horse—and a bath—I don't care what it looks like."

"Does this place have water?"

"Yes. But we'll have to pay for it."

"We already paid at the gate."

"That was the entry toll. There's also a water toll in Quumi. It's how the place survives."

"But—to charge for *water!* What if you have no coin?"

The stud tangled a hoof in a fallen awning, stumbling and snorting. Sun-rotted cloth tore, freeing him. I dragged his head up. "You make shift where you can."

"It is abysmal," she declared.

"Undoubtedly," I agreed, looking ahead to my favorite cantina.

Del figured it out as soon as I halted the stud. The building was much like the others: the outer shell of the adobe egg had cracked, baring the yolk of lopsided bricks. A bleached, patched orange-brown awning dangled from the sole remaining pole, obscuring most of the doorway. The aroma of wine, aqivi, and other liquors drifted into the street.

She frowned, reining in. "What are we doing *here?*"

"I know the owner."

"He or she?"

"He, of course. This is the South." I waited. "Are you getting off? Or do I have to climb down the hard way?"

"Once you explain just why we have to stop *first* at a cantina, before buying water or a horse."

"There is a room for rent."

"How long are we staying?"

"Overnight, at least. I want a bath, a good meal, a bed. You may join me, if you like." I thought it only polite to extend an invitation; Del hates to be taken for granted.

She slid off the stud. "I thought you wanted to buy a horse."

"First a drink. And a bath. Then food. Then a bed. In the morning comes the horse." I kicked free of the stirrup and hoisted my fragile knee across the saddle. "What I want most to do is sit quietly for a while in the shade, out of the sun, musing contentedly over aqivi—or wine, if there's no aqivi—and then I'll tend to the rest."

Del smiled as I somewhat gingerly allowed the street to take my weight. Everything I owned ached. "Go in," she said kindly as I bit my lip on an oath. "I will see to the stud."

I wasn't about to remonstrate, even if her behavior was out of the ordinary. Usually she argues against stops at cantinas. "Around there." I flopped a hand in the proper direction. "It isn't much of a stable, but there's shade and water."

Del took the reins. "Will I have to pay for it?"

"I told you: I know the owner." I paused. "He only charges me half."

"Half," Del muttered, and led the stud around the corner.

When she came back, I was sitting on a rickety three-legged stool in the rickety cantina, slumped forward over the rickety table with my chin in blue-nailed hand, elbow planted so as to prop me up. In my other hand was a bone-beige, unglazed clay cup of aqivi, mostly drunk. Altogether I was feeling rather rickety myself, in a numb, groggy, twitchy sort of way.

There was no one else in the cantina. Del, fighting her way through tattered awning, stopped short upon seeing me—and no one else—and stared musingly around the room.

"Well," she said finally, "I knew you needed a bath, but maybe I've just gotten used to you and it's worse than I thought."

"You know," I opined, "you're not particularly good at that."

Pale brows arched. "Good at what?"

"Making up jokes." I hoisted the clay up to my mouth, swallowed more aqivi, set it down again. "But then, that's never been a quality I looked for in a woman."

Pale brows came back down. And knitted. "How much have you had?" She moved carefully through a thicket of rickety stools and tables. "I haven't been gone *that* long."

I considered it. "Long enough," I told her eventually. "Long enough for me to find out Akbar's dead."

She paused at my—our?—table. "Akbar was your friend the owner?"

"Yes." I drank more aqivi.

"I'm sorry," she said inadequately.

"Yes." The cup was empty. I put it down, picked up the ceramic jug—the lip was chipped and cracked—and splashed liquor in the general vicinity of the cup. The pungent tang of very young aqivi filled my nose. "Have some aqivi, bascha."

She glanced around. "Water will be fine . . . is there anyone here?"

"Water costs three coppers a cup. Aqivi's cheaper."

"I don't *like* aqivi." Still she looked around, peering into the gloom. "Are we alone here?"

"Akbar's cousin is somewhere in back." I waved a hand.

"Is he that borjuni who charged me ten coppers to stable the stud, then five more for water?"

"I told you aqivi's cheaper."

"You can hardly give aqivi to a horse." She hooked a stool with a foot and dragged it out. "Of course, with his temperament, you might as well." She eyed my jug. "Are you going to drink all of that?"

"Unless you want to help me."

Del assessed me a moment. "Are you all right?"

"I'm tired," I told her. "Tired of finding out my friends are dying. Wondering if I'm next."

A brief smile curved her mouth, then died away. "I'm sorry your friend is dead. But I think *you're* in no danger."

"Oh? Why not? My line of work is rather risky, upon occasion."

She picked at the splintered table with a fingernail cut short for bladework. "Because you are much like your horse: too stubborn to give up."

"Right now I'm not stubborn. Just a little drunk." I swallowed more aqivi. "You'll say I should have eaten first, and be right. You'll say I should quit now, and be right. You'll say I'll feel better in the morning after a good night's sleep, and be right." I stared balefully at her over the thumb-printed rim of the clay cup. "Is there anything you're ever *wrong* about?"

Del stopped picking splinters. "I was wrong about offering your services to Staal-Ysta."

I brightened. "So you were."

"And wrong about you, period." She eyed the cup

darkly, but said nothing about aqivi souring my temper. Of course, she didn't have to. "When we first met, I disliked you intensely. And you deserved it. You *were* everything I thought you were. A typical Southron male." Her mouth quirked. "But you improved with time. You're much more bearable now."

"Thank you."

"Mmm." She glanced around again. "If Akbar's cousin does not arrive very soon, I'm going to help myself to the water. For free."

She wouldn't. She'd leave the money. "Here." I held out the cup. "It'll wet your throat."

"I don't want it."

"Have you ever had it?"

"I tried it once."

"A whole cup? Or just a swallow?"

"One swallow was enough."

"You didn't like me either, at first. You just said so."

Del sighed, scratching wearily at a shoulder. "Sit here and drink, if you like . . . I think I will gather the botas and fill them."

I waved a hand. "There's a big well in the market square. That way. They'll charge you."

"Three coppers a cup?" Del rose, kicking back her stool. "And how much for a bota?"

I thought about it. "Don't know. Prices fluctuate. Depends on how good you are at dickering." I eyed her: tall, lean, lovely. And incredibly lethal. "If you went about it right, you could probably save yourself a few coppers."

"Probably," she said dryly. "But I don't think submerging my dignity for a few coppers' worth of discount is a fair exchange."

I filled my mouth with aqivi as Del walked out of the cantina.

Because I had no answer.

Sundown. And no candles, lamps, or torches because you had to pay for them. At the moment, I saw no need; orange-pink-purple sunset tinged the lath-screened cantina pale violet.

The hand was on my shoulder. "Come on," she said calmly. "Time you were in bed."

I looked blearily up from my plate of inedible mush masquerading as mutton stew. "Can I finish my dinner first?"

"I think it would finish *you*." The hand changed shoulders from left to right. Now each resided in a strong, unfeminine grasp that cut through burnous, underrobe, harness straps, and flesh to the sore muscles beneath. It felt wonderful. "You can eat more in the morning, once you have killed the dog."

A bizarre image. "What dog?"

"The one biting you. Or are you biting *it?*"

Oh. Now I understood. "—gods, bascha—don't stop—"

"This?" She kneaded more firmly. "You are tight as wire."

"—hoolies . . . *that feels good*—"

"I have left our things in the hideously expensive room that will probably fall down on our heads before sunrise. The bedding is ready. Shall we put you in it?"

"Right now I just want to sit here while you do that."

Her right hand moved to my neck. Cool fingers squeezed sore tendons, biting through rigidity. "Up," she said only.

I stood up unsteadily, felt her slip beneath an arm,

let her take the weight my knee didn't want to carry. "I'm terribly drunk, bascha. Incredibly, horrifically drunk."

"I know that. Here. This way . . . please don't fall down. Your dead weight would be more substantial than most."

"Dead weight . . ." I echoed. "Like Akbar."

Del didn't say another word. She just walked me into the tiny little, hideously expensive room that probably *would* fall down on our heads before sunrise, and helped lever me down onto bedding. It smelled of horse and sweat and human flesh in dire need of a bath.

I didn't lie down. I hitched myself up against the wall and stared blearily through the violet gloom of sunset to the pale-haired Northern woman who knelt before me. In silence I unhooked awkwardly from harness straps, then set aside the sheathed sword.

"He was a good friend," I told her. "When I left the Salset, Quumi was one of the first places I came. I was sixteen years old, with hands and feet too big for the rest of me. I'd been a chula for all of my life. I didn't know how to be free."

Del said nothing.

"I didn't even know how to talk to people. Oh, I knew the *language*—I mean, I didn't know how to speak to them. I'd been taught to say nothing, and answer only if an answer was required." I grimaced. "I went into four cantinas before this one, hoping to find some kind of work so I could buy a meal . . . in all four I just stood there inside the door, saying nothing, hoping someone would speak to me, because I couldn't speak first. If I did, I'd be beaten . . ." I shifted against the wall. "No one said anything to me. Oh, they talked *about* me—insults, jokes, you know—

but no one spoke to me. So I couldn't ask for work.
Couldn't ask for food."

Del's face was taut.

"So when I came here to this cantina, the fifth, I
expected much the same. Without understanding why.
And I got it. Until Akbar spoke to me." I smiled a
little, recalling. "He asked me if I wanted a drink. I
thought he meant water: I nodded yes. Instead, he
gave me aqivi."

Del's eyes were strangely bright.

"I'd never had it before. Only water. But I was
thirsty. And free to drink what I wanted. So I drank
it *all*. As fast as I could." I rubbed a hand across
tired, grit-scored eyes. "I was drunk almost immediately. Akbar saw it, but instead of throwing me out
into the street, he took me to a room. He let me
sleep it off." I flopped a hand on the bedding. "This
room."

Del swallowed tightly.

"Every time I came here, he put me up. At half
price. And gave me all the aqivi I wanted." I sighed,
peering up at the woven lath roof trailing strips of
bark and dried desert grass. Through the cracks and
gaps I could see the purpling night. "One time I came,
he said he had a horse. A stallion. No one could ride
him, he said. He tried to kill everyone who climbed
into the saddle. No one wanted to buy him. Akbar
didn't want to feed a horse who couldn't be used. So
he said if I wanted him, I could have him." I smiled
lopsidedly. "He said I was hard-headed enough to
beat the flea-bitten, jug-headed, lop-eared Punja-mite
of a horse at his own game."

Silence.

"He threw me off four times. Then he gave in. I

guess he decided anyone stupid enough to keep trying wasn't worth the effort."

Del smiled. Her voice was husky. "But he still makes the effort. Occasionally."

"And sometimes he even wins. Except I climb back on again." I sighed and scrubbed muzzily at a stubbled, grimy face. "I'm tired. I'm drunk. I need to sleep . . . but I don't think I can."

"Lie down," she said quietly.

"Bascha—"

"Facedown," she said, cutting off an unnecessary protestation of too much aqivi for bedsport. Which was just as well; who wants to admit such a thing? "You're tight as wire, Tiger. And much too close to snapping. Let's see if I can loosen the tension a little."

Facedown, as ordered. Head resting on interlaced hands. It felt good just to be still.

Even better when she touched me.

Neck. Shoulders. Shoulder blades. The layers of rigid muscle knotted much too tight for comfort. Then up and down the spine, pressing and popping carefully, thumbing the tension away. At the bottom of the spine, deep in the small of the back. Then up again to the neck, tucking just behind the ears.

She laughed as I growled contentment, murmuring incoherent thanks.

But the laughter died. So did the vigor of her efforts. She smoothed the wavy brown hair left too long on the back of my neck. "I'm sorry," she said softly. "It is never easy to lose those who are special to you."

Especially when there are so very few to start with. Sula. Akbar. My shodo, twelve years dead. Even Singlestroke, a sword, who had nonetheless been very special.

All dead. Even the sword.

The only one left was Del.

Eighteen

I awoke to familiar, repeated noise: the metallic, ringing scrape of whetstone against blade. I smelled oil, stone, steel.

And Del.

I rolled over, cursing tangled bedding, and peered squinty-eyed through morning. Not dawn; beyond it. The sun was well and truly up, striking slatted patterns of mote-fogged light and shadow through the lath roof.

Which reminded me of something. "It's still up," I observed. "The roof."

Del didn't look. "Yes," she agreed tightly, working the whetstone in intense concentration.

Combed damp hair was loose on her shoulders. The creamy tunic beneath was water-marked, but drying. "You bathed," I observed.

"Yes." Scrape. Slide. Ring. Hiss. "Earlier, I went to the bathhouse."

"Akbar would bring—" I broke it off abruptly. Del flicked a glance at me, then returned her attention to her work. "I feel better," I told her, stripping off bedding. "You worked all the kinks out of my neck and shoulders. Of course, there's still my head . . ." I let it go. She wasn't listening. "What's the matter?"

Scrape. Slide. Hiss. "Nothing."

"It's not 'nothing.' What is it?"

She shook her head.

"If it's because I got drunk yesterday—"

"No."

I thought it over. "Something I said? I mean, when I passed out. . . ?"

"You didn't pass out. You just went to sleep. I know the difference. And, no, it's nothing you said; you talked, yes, but I could understand none of it, so I can't accuse you of impropriety."

Progress. I'd gotten more than a shrug or a single sentence. "Then what's bothering you?"

She stopped working the steel. Displayed the blade. "There."

I looked. In morning light, it glinted. Salmon-silver steel, warded by tangled runes indecipherable to anyone but Del. "Bascha—"

"There," she repeated. And put her fingertip on the blade, profaning it with skin oil, but I knew she'd wipe it clean.

I saw it then. A smudge. A blemish. A patch of darkness. "I don't understand—"

"I knocked your sword from your grasp with mine," she said evenly. "I struck aside your infested blade with my *jivatma*. And this is the result."

Infested. Interesting term.

Appropriate, too.

I pursed lips, then chewed one. "It could be something else."

"No." She began to work the steel again. "No, it is not 'something else.' It is Chosa Dei's handiwork. He has tainted my *jivatma*."

"You don't know—"

"I know." Her eyes were icy as she glared at me

over the blade. "Do you think I can't tell? Look at your fingernails, Tiger. Look at your hands and arms. Then tell me again it could be 'something else.' "

I looked, as she suggested. My nails had darkened from blue to black. Not Chosa Dei's black, though he had caused it, but the blackening of deep bruising. Of nails peeling up from fingers, readying to fall off. The hairless flesh of hands and forearms was still scaly and flaky. Still an odd corpse-white.

I shivered, then sat up rigidly, throwing aside bedding. Squinted at the light. The headache was not so bad after all . . . but I needed to bite the dog back. At least on the end of his nose. "I don't know what to tell you. How long have you been working the whetstone?"

"Long enough to know it isn't doing any good." She gazed at me in despair. "Tiger—my *blooding-blade*—"

"I know." I did. More than she believed. "Bascha, I don't know what to tell you. Can a spell take it off? Maybe a song?"

Mutely, she shook her head. Damp hair fell over her shoulders. The fine locks next to her face were mostly dry. Such pale, lustrous silk . . . and so alien to the South.

I cleared my throat. "You can't be certain it won't go of its own accord."

"I have told you. Chosa Dei wants this sword. He has always wanted this sword. It is the key to his power. If he had it—if he tapped into this sword—he would have all the power he needs to overcome you and break free. Do you see?"

I saw. I also felt. I knew very well why Chosa Dei wanted—and needed—Boreal.

"Then we had best be on our way." I got up carefully, favoring my knee, and limped with slightly more

steadiness into the common room. "I need a cup to
start the day, and a bath—" I stopped and turned
back. "Can you wait long enough for me to take a
bath and get a shave?"

Del had risen also. She stood in the doorway, one
hand holding aside the thin gauze curtain. The other
held her sword. "For that," she said gravely, "I will
wait through the day and all of the night."

"Thank you very much," I said sourly. "I don't
think it will take me *that* long."

"Perhaps not," she agreed politely. "But you are
very dirty."

So I was. But I didn't bother to fashion a properly
biting retort. If Del could tease me, however lamely,
about needing a bath, she wasn't as upset as I feared.

Then again, maybe it was just that I *was* that filthy.

Bath first. Then the aqivi.

The dog would have to wait.

The price for bath and shave was, of course, exorbi-
tant, like everything else in Quumi. But worth it,
which is why they can ask for the moon. Even though
it nearly emptied my coin-pouch, I felt very much the
new man as I walked out into the street again, stroking freshly shaved jaw approvingly, and resettled the
fit of the harness. Now all I needed was a cup, and
I'd be ready to go.

Except for one thing.

She sat atop a dark bay mare, holding the stud's
reins. She wore a white burnous; pale hair was braided
back. In harness. With pouches loaded and attached
to respective saddles.

I nearly gaped. "A *mare?*"

Del shrugged. "It was all there was."

"In all of Quumi, there are no geldings for sale?"

"None. I asked. I *looked.*"

"Did you explain about the stud?"

"The stud's behavior is no concern of mine. That is for you to control." She smiled sweetly. "Surely you understand how a male might learn to curb his appetites."

"Hoolies, bascha—"

"She's not in season."

I swore. "Are you sure?"

Del glared. "Do you see him mounting her?"

A point. "But if she comes in, he'll lose his mind."

"Had he one to lose." She shifted in the saddle. "Will you come along?"

I snatched the stud's reins. "Come along *where?* Do you even know where we're going?"

She frowned. "You said something about Julah."

"Yes. Julah. Aladar's daughter's domain."

"But she's in Iskandar. At least, she was. We can stay ahead of her—and out of danger—if we leave *soon.*"

"I thought you said you'd wait all of the day and all of the night so I could have my bath."

"You've had it. I can tell. My *nose* can tell." Del grinned briefly as I scowled. "Shall we go?"

I flipped reins over the stud's neck and climbed aboard. "Why are you in such a hurry?"

"If finding Shaka Obre will rid my sword of Chosa Dei's taint, I would prefer to do it today rather than tomorrow."

"You don't even know where he is."

"Neither do you." She paused. "Do you?"

I aimed the stud toward the southern gate, hidden by slumping, sloppy gray-beige buildings, and flapped a hand. "Somewhere out there."

Del made a sound of derision. "*That's* promising."

"Then suppose you lead."

In grave silence, she reined her bay mare around in front of the stud. Who noticed. As was intended. "Like so?" Del asked innocently.

"Never mind," I muttered.

The stud was less than happy when I made him take the lead once again. I had a brief but firm discussion with him, and convinced him to let *me* be the guide.

I didn't think we could go all the way to Julah walking backward.

Around midday, we stopped. In silence we stared grimly at the expanse of crystal-flecked desert before us. The border was subtle, but clearly defined. This side, we were safe. Cross it, and we were at risk.

But we'd been at risk before.

Del's mare bobbed her head. The stud answered with a rumbling, deep-chested nicker that threatened to rise to a squeal. I kicked him high on the shoulder. "She's not interested," I said.

Del merely smiled. Then lifted her chin toward the Punja. "How many days to Julah?"

"Depends on the Punja."

"I know that. How many did it take us before?"

"I don't know. Who can remember back that far?" I slapped the stud's thick neck and reined him aside. "Besides, we met with a few delays, remember? Like the Hanjii and their Sun Sacrifice . . . that ate up a few days. Recovery even more."

"And Elamain," Del recalled. Naturally, she would. "We rescued Elamain's caravan from borjuni. Then we took her to that tanzeer—"

"Hashi."

"—who wanted to make you into a eunuch." Del glanced sidelong at me. "I remember that."

So did certain parts of *me*. "Then we stopped in Rusali—"

"—and met Alric and Lena and the girls." Del paused. "Only two, then. But she was expecting what became the third—"

"—and the last time we saw them—all of four days ago—she was expecting *another* child."

Del's mouth pulled sideways. "I hope this one's a boy. Maybe then she can rest."

"Seems to me Lena didn't much mind having Alric's babies." I prodded the stud's questing nose with a sandaled toe. "Don't even think about it."

"And there was Theron," Del recalled.

Whom I had killed in the circle.

"And Jamail," I countered.

Del's face tautened. "And Jamail," she echoed. Then she looked at me. "Are you *really* this jhihadi?"

"How in hoolies should *I* know?"

She stared at me. "But you said Jamail pointed at you. You swore on your *jivatma*."

"He did. I did. I'm not making it up."

"Then maybe . . ." She frowned. "No. It can't be. It is impossible."

"What? That I might be a messiah?" I grinned. "I can't think of a single man better suited to the job."

Her look was withering.

"All right. I know it all sounds silly. But it's true, Del—he really did point at me."

"So when are you going to change the sand to grass?"

I snickered. "As if I could."

"The jhihadi supposedly can."

"Maybe he can."

"And you *did*—" Del stopped short. Her face went

red, then white. She turned to stare wide-eyed at me. Her expression was particularly unnerving.

"What?" I asked sharply. *"What?"*

She swallowed tightly. Her voice was mostly a whisper. "You changed the sand to *glass.*"

Del and I spent several moments staring at one another, trying to deal with new thoughts and implications. Then I managed a laugh. It wasn't my usual one, but enough to get by with. "Hoolies, bascha—wouldn't it be funny if it turned out this desert prophet got the word wrong?"

Even her lips were white. "What do you mean?"

"That this jhihadi won't restore the South to lushness, but change it instead to *glass.*"

"But . . ." Del frowned. "What good would glass be?"

"It means everyone can afford to put it in their windows." I grinned. "Glass, grass—who can say? I think it's all a bunch of nonsense."

"But—" She chewed a lip, then gave it up, sighing. "I think it would indeed be a foolish thing if you were the man."

It stung. "Why?"

She eyed me thoughtfully. "Because you are a sword-dancer. Why should you be more?"

"You don't think I'm good enough? You don't think I could do it?"

"Be a messiah? No."

"Why not?"

"You lack a certain amount of delicacy. Diplomacy." She smiled. "Your idea of dispensing wisdom is to invite someone into a circle."

"The sword is a very *good* dispenser of wisdom."

"But jhihadis aren't sword-dancers."

"How do you know? You didn't even know what one was until I explained it to you."

"Because—I just know."

"Not good enough." I whopped the stud between the ears. "Not now, flea-brain . . . no, bascha, really—I want an answer."

She shrugged. "You're just—you. You have your good points. A few here and there, tucked in behind all the bluster. But a jhihadi? No. Jhihadis are *special*, Tiger." She watched me pop the stud again as he tried to sidle into the mare. "Jhihadis don't have trouble dealing with horses."

"How do you know? Iskandar himself got kicked in the head, remember?"

"And died ten days later, or so you told me." Del eyed me speculatively. "How many days ago was it that *you* got kicked in the head?"

"See? That's proof—I got kicked, too."

"No," Del countered. "*Real* proof would be if you died because of it."

I scowled. "What kind of jhihadi would I be if I died before I could do anything?"

"Well, if you really were supposed to change the sand to *glass,* rather than grass . . ." Del's expression was guileless. "How many days again?"

I kneed the stud into motion. "Never mind that. Let's just go."

"Four?" Del fell in behind. "That leaves six days to go."

"And I suppose you're going to *count!*"

Her tone was exquisitely tranquil. "I like to be prepared."

Hoolies. What a woman.

Depending on your perspective.

Nineteen

"It makes my skin hurt," Del said.

Eventually, I roused. "What?"

We rode mostly abreast. She glanced across at me. "Are you asleep?"

"No."

"*Were* you asleep?"

"No. Just thinking."

"Ah." She nodded sagely. "Your version of deep thought resembles sleep in others. Forgive me."

We were still horseback. Still riding south out of Quumi. It was mid- to late afternoon. We'd eaten on the move but an hour or so before, and I'd washed mine down with wine. The motion of the stud, walking monotonously onward, combined with food, wine, and the warmth of the day—not to mention boredom— had proved overwhelming.

Which meant I *had* been asleep, if only briefly; actually, it was more like a momentary nap caught between one blink and the next. When you spend as much time as I do atop the back of a horse, you learn to sleep however—and whenever—you can.

But you don't admit it to Del.

I scowled. "*What* makes your skin hurt?"

"The South. The Sun. The Punja." Del twitched her sword-weighted shoulders. "I remember what it was like, before. When the sun was so bad, and I got so sick." She rubbed a cupped hand down one burnous-sleeved arm. "I remember very clearly."

So did I. Del had nearly died. So, for that matter, had I, but the sun hadn't been quite so ruthless to my copper-hued Southron hide. Oh, it had tried its hardest to burn me to bits, but I'd survived. Del very nearly hadn't.

"Well, we don't have to worry about it this time," I observed comfortably.

She arched one brow. "Why not? We could come across the Hanjii again, could we not? And they could turn us loose once again in the desert with no mounts or water."

Comfort evaporated. I grunted disagreement. "More likely this time we'd wind up in the cookpot."

"Oh. I'd forgotten that." Del, squinting, peered across the sand. "It all looks exactly the same."

"It's hot. Dry. Sandy." I nodded. "Pretty much the same."

"But *we're* not." She glanced sidelong at me. "We're both a little more experienced than the last time."

I knew what that meant. "And older?" I showed her my teeth in an insincere grin. "Believe me, bascha, now that we're back where it's warm, I feel a whole *lot* younger."

Her assessive expression very plainly suggested I didn't *look* younger. The problem was, I couldn't tell how much of it was part of the gibing, and how much was unfeigned.

"Thirty-six is not so old," I growled.

Del's smile was too sanguine, and therefore suspect. "Not if you're thirty-seven."

"To *you*, maybe, it's old—you're not long out of infancy. But to *me*—"

"In sword-dancer years, it is." She had dropped the bantering. "You are of an age now that many never see, if they live their lives in the circle." Her tone was very solemn. "You should seriously consider becoming an *an-kaidin*, a—" she frowned, breaking off. "What is the Southron word?"

"Shodo," I said sourly. "I don't think I'm ready for that."

"You have been a professional for many years. You have learned from the best. Even on Staal-Ysta, they honored your skill—"

"No, they didn't. They just wanted another body." I reined the stud away from the mare. "I'm not made for that, Del. Being a shodo takes a lot more patience than I have."

"I think if you had a student, you would find patience in abundance. If you knew that what you taught the *ishtoya* could mean survival or death, you would come to know how much you had to offer."

"Nothing," I said grimly. "What kind of shodo would I make with Chosa Dei in my sword?"

"After it was discharged—"

"No, bascha. I'm a sword-dancer. I just do it, I don't teach it."

"You have taught *me*," she said. "You have taught me very much."

"I nearly killed you, too. What did you learn from that?"

"That you are a man with immense strength of will."

I stared. "You're serious!"

"Of course I am."

"Bascha, I nearly *killed* you. Once on Staal-Ysta, and once at the oasis, after I slaughtered all the borjuni."

"But each time you held back." She shrugged. "On Staal-Ysta, you denied a newly awakened *jivatma*, freshly keyed and wild for the taste of blood, the chance to make a first kill. At the oasis, you denied Chosa Dei. A weaker man with a lesser will would have lost himself on either count. And I would no longer live."

"Yes, well . . ." I shrugged uncomfortably. "That doesn't make me a shodo."

"I do not insist," she said quietly. "I only point out you have another choice."

Something pinched my belly from the inside. "Or is it that you've accomplished your goal of killing Ajani, and now you're looking ahead to a different way of life?" And different people in it?

Del's mouth tightened. "We spoke of this before. There is nothing else for me. I am exiled from the North, and I could never be a shodo here. Who would come to a woman for teaching?"

I shrugged. "Other women might."

Blue eyes were smoky. "How many Southron men would allow their women that freedom?"

"Maybe it would be women who had no men to placate."

Del made a sound of derision. "There are no women in the South willing to risk losing a man, or the chance of winning a man's interest, by apprenticing to me."

No. Probably not.

"Which leaves us," I said, "right where we started

out. Why don't we just accept what we are, and not worry about the future?"

Del stared into the distance.

I waited. "Well?"

"There." She pointed. "Is that something moving?"

I followed her finger and saw what she meant. A dark blotch against the horizon. "I don't—wait. Yes, I think you're right . . ." I stood up in my stirrups, peering over the stud's ears. "It looks like a person."

"On foot," Del declared. "Who in his right mind would *walk* through the Punja?"

"We did," I said. "Of course, you were sandsick, so you weren't *in* your right mind—"

"Never mind that," she snapped. "Let's not waste any more time talking about it. He—or she—might not have any to spare."

Del sent her mare loping across the desert, kicking dust into the air. The stud snorted loudly, then went after her.

There was nothing better to do. So I let him go.

It turned out to be a he, not a she. And Del had been right: he didn't have any time to spare. By the time I reached him, Del was off her mare and kneeling beside the man, helping him suck down water from one of her botas.

She glanced at me over one dusty, burnous-clad shoulder. She said nothing; she didn't have to. Del has a considerable vocabulary in simple body motions, let alone expressions. All in all I thought censure uncalled for—I'd gotten there not long after she had, if without her haste—and scowled back at her to tell her the silent reprimand was unappreciated.

Whether she cared was entirely up to her.

The man wore a plain burnous of tattered, saffron-hued gauze, and a matching underrobe. No sword. He was perhaps in his early twenties, but dust caked his face, so it was hard to tell. Sweat—and maybe tears?—had formed disfiguring runnels.

Now, as he sucked at the bota with eyes closed in the pure physical bliss of a great need fulfilled, water spilled down his chin. It splashed onto his grimy, threadbare burnous, drying quickly; before Del could say a word, he thrust a hand up to cup his chin and catch the runaway water.

A Southroner born and bred in habits as well as color.

The desperate thirst initially slaked, he opened his eyes for the first time and peered over the bota at Del. Brown eyes dilated as he acknowledged several things, among them her gender.

He sat bolt upright. Then saw me beyond her. He stared again at her, disbelievingly. And back again to me. He husked a single word: "Afreet?"

I snickered. Del glanced over her shoulder at me, frowned bafflement at my amusement, then turned back. That she didn't understand the tongue was clear; she'd have said something, otherwise. But then I hadn't expected her to. The language he spoke was an archaic Desert dialect, unknown to anyone outside the Punja. I hadn't heard it for years.

I briefly debated the merits of lying. It would be amusing to tell him she *was* a Southron spirit, but I decided against it. The poor man was dry as bone, nearly delirious; the last thing he needed was me convincing him he was dead—or near death—by agreeing with him.

"No," I told him. "Northerner."

He sat very still, staring at her, drinking in Del as if she were sweeter than bota water.

Which amused me briefly, until I thought about how that amusement could be considered an insult of sorts. Del was worth staring at. Del was worth dreaming about. Del was even worth looking upon as salvation: she *had* given him water.

I grinned. "You've impressed him."

Del hitched a self-conscious shoulder; she's never been one for trading on her looks, or talking much about them. Down South, for the most part, those looks got her in trouble, because too many Southron men wanted a piece of her for themselves.

"More?" she asked briefly, offering the bota again.

He took it by rote, still staring. And drank by rote, since the first thirst had been satisfied; now he drank for pleasure instead of need.

And, I suspected, because her actions suggested it.

The stud bent his neck, trying to reach the mare Del had left groundtied a pace or two away. He snorted gustily, then rumbled deep in his chest. Tail lifted. The upper lip curled, displaying massive teeth—*and* his interest in getting to know the mare better.

The last thing I needed—the last thing *anyone* needed—was the stud developing an attachment to Del's mare. And since a stallion outweighs a man by a considerable amount, it takes firm methods in dissuading him of such interest. Before someone got hurt.

I punched him in the nose.

Bridle brasses clanked as the head shot skyward. I took a tight grip on the reins, managed to retain them, managed to retain *him*—and avoided placing sandaled feet beneath the stomping hooves.

Del, of course, cast me a disapproving glance across one shoulder. But she wasn't on the end of an uncut horse taking decided interest in a mare; *her* mare, I might add. If she'd bought a gelding in Quumi, we'd all be a lot better off.

Meanwhile, the bay mare nickered coy invitation.

Also meanwhile, the young man on the ground was getting up from it. At least, partway: he knelt, then placed one spread-fingered hand over his heart, and bowed. All the while gabbling something in a dialect even *I* didn't know.

And then he stopped gabbling, stopped kneeling; stood up. He pointed westerly. "Caravan," he declared, switching back to deep-Punja Desert.

I squinted. "How far?"

He told me.

I translated for Del, who frowned bafflement. Then I invited him to be more eloquent.

He was. When finished, I scratched at brown hair and muttered a halfhearted curse.

"What?" Del asked.

"They were bound for Iskandar," I told her. "Him and a few others. They hired a couple of guides to see them across the Punja. These so-called guides brought them out here, and left them."

"Left them," she echoed.

I waved a hand. "Out there a ways. They didn't hurt anyone. Just brought them out here, took all their coin and water, and left." I shrugged. "Why waste time on killing when the Punja will do it for you?"

Del's eyes narrowed. "Had he no mount?"

"Danjac. He was thrown, and the danjac deserted." I grinned. "They do that a lot."

Del looked at the young man. "So, *he* came looking for help."

"He figured out pretty quickly they'd been led a merry dance. Off known tracks, far from any markers . . ." I shrugged. "He just wanted to find some help, someone who knew the way to a settlement, or an oasis. He's hoping to trade for a mount and botas." Again, I shrugged. "Meanwhile, the others are with the wagons."

Del glanced skyward, squinting against the glare. "No water," she murmured thoughtfully. Then glanced assessively back at the young man, scrutinizing him.

I knew what was coming.

I also knew not to protest; she wasn't really wrong. I sighed gustily, putting up a forestalling hand. "I know. *I* know. You want to go out there. You want to take him back to his caravan, then lead them all to Quumi."

"It's the closest settlement."

"So it is." I stared into the west. "Might as well, I suppose. I mean, the Salset picked *us* up out of the desert and saw to it we recovered."

"Don't sound so ungrateful."

"I'm not ungrateful. Just thinking about how much time this will eat up. *And* what we may find once we get back to Quumi."

Del frowned. "What?"

"Sword-dancers," I answered. "And, for all that, religious fools like this one."

Eyes widened. "Why do you call him a religious fool? Just because he believes in something you do not—"

I cut her off, forestalling a lengthy discussion on the merits of religion. "He *is* a fool," I declared, "and I have every right in the world to say so."

She bristled. "Why? *What* gives you the right—"

"Because any man who worships me has *got* to be a fool."

That stopped her in her tracks. "You?" she ventured finally. "Why do you say that?"

"I'm the one he and the others are going to Iskandar to see."

She blinked. "What *for?*"

"Seems they heard the Oracle's stories about the jhihadi." I shrugged. "They packed up their lives and headed north."

Del's mouth opened to protest. But she said nothing. She stared at the religious fool a long moment, weighing what I'd said against the man himself, and eventually sighed, rubbing a hand across her brow.

"See what I mean?" I asked. "You think he's a fool, too."

Her mouth twisted. "I will admit that opinions can be led astray, but that doesn't make him a fool for believing in a man whose coming is supposed to improve his homeland."

"Right," I agreed. "Which means the least I can do is get him and his people to Quumi. It seems like a properly jhihadi-ish thing to do, wouldn't you say?"

"Will you tell him?" she ventured.

I grinned. "What—that I'm a fraud?"

Del's expression was sour. "He would probably figure that out for himself."

"I thought you'd see it my way." I patted the stud's neck. "Well, old son, looks like we'll be carrying double again."

Del hitched a harness strap. "Why not put him with me? Together he and I weigh less than *you* and he."

I looked at the religious fool who gazed at Del raptly. "Yes," I agreed sourly. "He'd probably like that."

Del frowned.

"Never mind," I muttered. "Let's just get going."

Twenty

His name was Mehmet. Mehmet was a pain in the rump.

He didn't start out that way. He was what he was: an exhausted, thirsty young man badly in need of help. Trouble was, we'd offered that help, and he'd taken us up on it.

Now, I'm not really as ungracious as I might seem, some of the time. I admit I sound that way upon occasion, but the truth of the matter is, I'm soft-hearted enough to get myself in trouble. So here we were, helping Mehmet, who wanted to help his companions.

Who wanted to help them *now*.

Trouble was, now meant now, the way he looked at things; while Del and I looked on it as an in-the-morning thing, since the sun had disappeared, and we saw no great benefit from riding through the night.

Mehmet, however, did.

Del, busily unrolling a blanket beneath a dusky sky, frowned across at me as I did the same with mine. "What's he saying *now*?"

"What he said a minute ago. That we can't wait till morning while his aketni is in need."

"His what?"

"Aketni. I'm not exactly sure what it means, but I think it has something to do with the people he's traveling with. Sort of like a family, I think . . . or maybe just a group of people who believe in the same thing."

"A religious sect." Del nodded. "Like those ridiculous *khemi* zealots who shun women."

"They carry things a bit far. Mehmet doesn't seem to feel that way." I glanced at him, standing expectantly between us with hands clutching the front of his grimy burnous. "Matter of fact, about the *last* thing Mehmet would shun is women, I think—he's staring at you again."

Del scowled blackly.

We didn't bother with a fire, since there was no wood on the crystal sands, and the charcoal we carried with us was for emergencies. We had plenty of supplies for a trip across the Punja, and while we were not enthusiastic about travelers' tedious fare, we knew it would get us where we were going. So Del and I settled in for the evening. The sun was down, the twilight cool; what we wanted now was to eat and sleep.

Mehmet, seeing this, started in yet again on how we should not stop, but ride on to his aketni. Where, he announced, we would be well recompensed for our services.

"How's that?" I asked dryly. "You said the guides stole all your money."

His chin developed a stubborn set. "You will be paid," he declared, "in something much better than coin."

"I've heard *that* before." I unrolled my blanket the rest of the way, shaking out folds and wrinkles. "Look, Mehmet, I know you're worried about them, but the best thing to do is get some sleep. We'll start

out again at first light, and reach them by midday. *If*
you remember your distance right." I shot him a bale-
ful glare. "You do remember it right, don't you,
Mehmet?"

"That way." He pointed. "If we left *right now*, we
would be there before morning."

"We're not leaving *right now*," I told him. "*Right
now*, I'm going to eat something, digest it in calm,
quiet dignity, then go to sleep."

He was offended. "How can you go to sleep when
my aketni is in need?"

I sighed and scratched at claw scars. "Because," I
said patiently. "I'm not part of your aketni, whatever
the hoolies it is."

Mehmet drew himself up. He was a slender, dried
out stick of a young man, with very little fat beneath
his flesh, which made his desert features sharper than
ever. Punja-born, all right—he had the prominent
nose that reminded me of a hawk, but his brown eyes
lacked the predator's piercing impact.

He stood rigidly between Del and me, glaring down
at us both. He was young and full of himself, if in a
more subtle way; Mehmet wasn't as obnoxious as a
cocky young sword-dancer trying to earn a reputation,
such as Nezbet, but he had that mile-wide streak of
youthful stubbornness that eclipsed the wisdom of
experience and age. To him, Del and I were simply
being selfish—well, maybe only me; I don't think he
looked on Del as anything other than a wonder, and
wonders aren't selfish—and purposely difficult.

Behind him, the night sky unrolled its own version
of blanket bedding, spangled with glittering stars. A
sliver of new crescent moon glowed overhead.

And Mehmet continued to glare, although I noticed
he stared with more virulence at me. Trust Del to

escape the wrath of a male firmly smitten by her beauty.

"It is an *aketni!*" he hissed. "A *complete* aketni!"

Del heard his tone, even if she missed the context. "What's he so upset about?"

"Nothing new," I explained. "He's singing the same old song." I sat down on the blanket, automatically settling my knee in the position least likely to stress it, then looked up at Mehmet. "I don't know what a complete aketni *is,* let alone what it means. So why don't you just spread out that spare blanket, settle in for the night, and worry about it in the morning?"

He stood so rigidly I thought he might break. But he didn't. He wavered eventually, then collapsed to his knees, bowed his head as he spread one hand over his heart, and began mumbling in the dialect even I didn't understand.

"That again," I muttered.

Mehmet stopped mumbling. He appeared to be applying tremendous self-control. "Then may I borrow a horse?" he asked quietly. "And water? *I* will go now; you may come in the morning."

It crossed my mind that if we let him take a horse and water, *we* wouldn't need to go. But that gained us nothing we hadn't encountered before: two people on one horse, with less water than ever. "No." I dug through pouches to flat, tough loaves of traveler's bread, and two twisted sticks of dried cumfa meat. "Just bide your time."

Abruptly, Mehmet turned to Del, who, arrested by his fervor, stared warily at him as he spewed out an explanation to her, along with a request for her mare and some water.

"She doesn't understand," I told him. "She doesn't speak your language."

He considered it a moment. Then began again in dialect-riddled Desert.

Del glanced at me. "If I say no, he won't try to steal her, will he?" She as much as I wanted nothing to do with riding double and walking again.

Smiling, I repeated Del's question to Mehmet, who was horrified. He leapt to his feet, then fell down to knees again, clutching his tattered burnous as if he meant to rend it, and gabbled on in something akin to a reproachful dialogue, except parts of it were addressed equally to Del, to me, and the sky.

"I don't know." *Before* Del could ask. "But I'm guessing we've offended him."

"Oh." She sighed and reached into the pouch to dig out her share of the evening meal. "I'm sorry for that, but if he's so horrified, he probably won't try for the mare."

"Better the mare than the stud." I chewed tough bread while Mehmet muttered prayers. "Do you think he'll do that all night?"

Del's expression was perplexed as she stared at him. "If he is *so* worried—"

"No."

"If they are in danger—"

"They aren't. They're probably pretty thirsty, but they'll survive the night. These are deep-Punja people, bascha . . . going without water for a day or two won't kill them. They know how to adapt. Believe me, if you know the tricks—"

"Mehmet is afraid—"

"Mehmet just thinks he'll get in trouble for taking so long." I stuffed too much dried cumfa into my mouth, and chewed for a very long time.

Del clicked her tongue in disgust.

Bulge-mouthed, I grinned.

"Jamail used to do that," she remarked. "Of course, he was considerably younger, and didn't know any better."

"See there?" I glanced at Mehmet, who glumly unrolled the spare blanket. "Just like a woman— always trying to remake a man. The thing *I* can't understand is, if she liked him in the first place, why does she want to change him?"

"I didn't like you," Del answered coolly, as Mehmet stared at me in blank-faced incomprehension; was he really *that* young? Or just slow to assert himself in the way of a man with a woman?

I chewed thoughtfully. "You've done your share of trying to change me, bascha."

"In some things, I've even succeeded." Del bit off a small piece of cumfa from her own dried stick and ate it elegantly.

I indicated her with air-jabs of my stick. "See there?" I said again to Mehmet. "What kind of women do you have in your aketni?"

Mehmet gazed at Del. "Old ones," he answered. "And my mother." Which said quite a lot, I thought.

I hefted a bota. "And I suppose they've done their best to change *you*, too."

He shrugged. "In the aketni, one does as one is told. Whatever is cast in the sands—" He broke it off. "I have said too much."

"Sacred stuff, huh?" I nodded. "Women'll do that to you. They twist things all around, make it ritual, because how else can they convince anyone to do some of the things they want? Old, young—doesn't matter." I slanted a glance at Del. "Even Northern ones."

Del chewed in stolid silence.

I looked back at Mehmet. "About this recompense
. . . anything worthwhile?"

Mehmet pulled cumfa from the pouch. "Very
valuable."

I arched a skeptical brow. "If it's so valuable, how
come the 'guides' didn't relieve you of it?"

"They were blind." Mehmet shrugged. "Their souls
have shutters on them."

"And mine doesn't?" I beat Del to it. "Given that
I have one, that is?"

Mehmet chewed cumfa. "You are here." Which
also said something.

I shifted irritably, rearranging my knee, and sucked
down more wine. "Well, we'll see to it you get to
Quumi. It won't take long—you're not that far off the
track. Maybe your guides didn't really mean for you
to die."

Mehmet shrugged again. "It doesn't matter. Their
futures have been cast."

I quirked an eyebrow. "Oh?"

But Mehmet was done talking. He ate his cumfa in
silence, washed it down with water, lay down on his
back on the blanket, and stared up into the sky.

Murmuring again. As if the stars—or gods—could
hear.

I kinked my head back and stared up into darkness.
Wondering if anyone did.

I roused when the stud squealed and stomped. I was
on my feet and moving before I remembered my knee,
but by then it was too late. Swearing inventively, I
hobbled toward the stud.

Mehmet turned as I arrived. He held the saddle
pad. When he saw my expression—and the bared
sword—he fell back a step. "I meant only to help,"

he protested. "Not to steal, to *help*. By readying him
for you." He placed a hand across his heart. "First
light, you said."

It *was* first light, but just barely. More like false
dawn. But I was willing to give him the benefit of the
doubt; if he'd really meant to steal a horse and ride
out quietly, he'd have taken the mare. He knew that
already, having ridden with us the day before.

Del, too, was up, folding her blanket. Pale braid
was loose and tousled, flopping against one shoulder.
"We can eat on the way."

I scrubbed grit from eyes and face, turning back
toward the bedraggled encampment. The blade glinted
dull black in the weak light of a new dawn. A little
more sleep would have been very welcome; dreams
had awakened me on and off all night.

"Come away from him," I told Mehmet. "He's
surly in the morning."

Del snickered softly, but forbore to comment.

Mehmet came away with alacrity, glancing over a
shoulder at the thoroughly wakened stud, and knelt
to refold his blanket. I bent, picked up harness, slid
the sword into scabbard. And cursed as a fingernail
caught on the leather lip and tore.

It didn't hurt so much as implied it. Blackened nail
loosed itself from cuticle and peeled away entirely,
vacating my finger. It left behind the knurled bed of
pinkish undergrowth.

I wavered on my feet.

Del came over, inspected the "injury," looked into
my rigid face. "It's a *fingernail*."

"It's—ugly."

"Ugly?" She stared, then laughed a short, breathy
laugh of disbelief. "After all the wounds you've had—

not to mention the gutting I nearly gave you on Staal-Ysta—*this* bothers you?"

"It's ugly," I said again, knowing how it sounded.

Del caught my wrist and pushed the back of my hand into my range of vision. "A fingernail," she repeated. "I think you've done worse shaving!"

"You're enjoying this," I accused.

Del let my hand go. A smile stole the sting. "Yes, I think I am. I find it very amusing."

I rubbed the ball of my thumb across the ruined bed of index fingernail, and suppressed a shudder. I don't know why, but it made my bones squirm. Also weak in the knees—and since one was *already* weak, I didn't need the help.

"Let's go," I said crossly. "Mehmet's aketni is waiting."

Del snickered again as I turned away. "*Now* he wants to move swiftly."

"Never mind," I grumbled, and knelt to roll my blanket.

Del went back to her own, laughing quietly to herself.

I hate it when women do that. They take their small revenges in the most frustrating ways.

Twenty-one

By midday, I'd lost the nail off my right thumb and two other fingers, and very nearly my breakfast. But we'd found Mehmet's aketni.

Five small wagons, huddled together against the sun, with domed canopies of once-blue canvas now sunbleached bone-gray, stretched tautly on curving frames. Unhitched danjacs hobbled but paces away in a bedraggled little herd brayed a greeting as we rode up. I wondered if Mehmet's bad-tempered one had come back to join the others.

As expected, everyone was excited to see Mehmet again, but more excited to learn he'd brought water. Del and I handed down botas as Mehmet jumped off the mare and quickly doled them out, answering excited questions with enthusiasm of his own in the deep-Punja dialect I'd yet to decipher. Dark eyes shone with joy and relief and browned hands stroked the botas.

But no one drank. They accepted the botas with fervent thanks, yet stood aside as Mehmet turned to Del and me. We still sat atop our mounts, staring down in bafflement.

"It's yours," I told him in Desert. "We've kept

enough back to get us all to Quumi—go ahead and drink."

Mehmet shook his head even as the others murmured. I counted five at a glance, heads wrapped in turbans, dark faces half-hidden by sand-crusted gauze veils. I couldn't see much of anyone beneath voluminous burnouses, just enough to know the five were considerably older than Mehmet, judging by veined, spotted hands and sinewy wrists. But then, he'd told us that.

"What is it?" Del asked.

I shrugged, reining in the stud, who wanted to visit the danjacs to show them who was in charge. Horses hate danjacs; the ill-regard is returned. "Nobody's thirsty."

Mehmet took a single step forward. "We owe you our thanks, sword-bearers. The gratitude of the aketni, for bringing water and aid to us."

I started to shrug it away, but broke it off, stilling, as Mehmet and his companions dropped to knees and bowed heads deeply, then tucked sandaled feet beneath buttocks and rocked forward to press foreheads against knees. Deep, formal obeisance; much more than we warranted. Five of them turbaned, with narrow, gray-black braids dangling beneath the neck-flap meant to shield flesh against the sun. All women? I wondered. Who could tell with so much burnous swaddling and veiling?

Mehmet intoned something in singsong fashion, and was answered instantly by a five-part nasal echo. They all slapped the flat of a hand against the sand, raising dust, then traced a line across their brows beneath turban rims, leaving powdery smudges of crystalline sand to glitter as they raised their heads.

Four women, I decided, and one old man. Six pairs of dark desert eyes locked onto blue and green ones.

I felt abruptly alien. Don't ask me why; I just did. I realized, staring back, there was nothing of me in these people. Nothing of them in me. Whatever blood ran through my veins was not of Mehmet's aketni.

I shifted in the saddle. Del said nothing. I wondered what she was thinking, so far away from home.

"You will come," Mehmet said quietly, "for the bestowing of the water."

"The bestowing—?" I exchanged a puzzled glance with Del.

"You will come," Mehmet repeated, and the others all nodded vehemently and gestured invitation.

They seemed a harmless lot. No weapons were in sight, not even a cooking knife. Del and I, after another glance exchanged, dropped off respective horses. I led the stud to the nearest wagon and tied him to a wheel. Del took her mare around the other side and tied her to the back.

Mehmet and his aketni gathered around us, but with great deference. We were herded respectfully to the very last wagon and gestured to wait. Then Mehmet and the other male drew back folds of fabric and climbed up into the wagon, murmuring politely to the interior. The wagon eventually disgorged an odd cargo: an ancient, withered man swathed in a gray-blue burnous draped over a gauzy white underrobe.

Mehmet and his fellow very carefully lifted the old man down from the wagon, underscoring his fragility with their attentiveness, even as the others gathered cushions, a palm-frond fan, and makeshift sunshades. The old man was settled on the cushions as the others stretched above his turban the gauzy fabric that cut out much of the sun. Then Mehmet knelt down with one of the botas, murmuring quietly to the old man.

I've met my share of shukars, shodos and priestlings, not to mention aged tanzeers. But never in my life have I seen anyone so old. Nor with such life in his eyes.

The hairs on my neck rose. My bones began to itch.

Mehmet continued murmuring, occasionally gesturing to Del and me. I didn't know the lingo, but it was fairly obvious Mehmet was giving an account of his adventures since leaving the caravan. I thought back on my unwillingness to ride through the night. I'd had my reasons. But now, faced with the bright black eyes of the ancient man, guilt rose up to smite me.

I shifted weight, easing my knee, and exchanged a glance with Del. Neither of us were blind to the old man's acuity as he weighed each of us against the truth of Mehmet's story. If Mehmet had only *said*—

No.

Mehmet *had* said. I'd chosen not to hear.

Like the others, he was turbaned. The facecloth was loosened, looped to dangle beneath a chin and throat nearly as wattled. The dark desert face was quilted like crushed silk, with a sunken look around the mouth that denoted a lack of teeth. He hunched on his cushion, weighing Del and me, and listened to the man so many decades younger than he.

Grandfather? I wondered. Maybe *great*-grandfather.

Mehmet ran down eventually. And then, bowing deeply, offered the old man the bota.

The bestowing of the water. Around us the others knelt. Del and I, noting it, very nearly followed. But we were strangers to the aketni, and both of us knew very well that even well-meant courtesy can be the wrong thing to offer. It can get you in serious trouble.

We waited. And then the old man put a gnarled, palsied hand on the belly of Mehmet's bota and murmured something softly. A blessing, I thought. Or maybe merely thanks.

Mehmet poured a small portion of water into the trembling, cupped hand. The old man cracked his fingers to let the water spill through, watching it splatter, then slapped his palm downward against wet sand, as if he spanked a child.

I don't know what he said. But all the others listened raptly, then sighed as he drew a damp sandy line across an age-runneled brow.

It was nothing. But I stared. At the runnels. The furrows. The lines. Carved deeply into his flesh; now drawn in wet sand.

"Tiger?" Del whispered.

I stared at the old man. Pallid forearms crawled, as if trying to raise the Chair Chosa Dei had burned away. My scalp itched of a sudden. Something cold sheathed my bowels.

I should get out of here—

Lines and runnels and furrows.

Del again: "Tiger?"

I should leave this place, before this old man unmasks me—

I lifted my hand to my face, tracing sandtiger scars. Lines and furrows and runnels. Not to mention deep-seated stripes carving rivulets into my cheek.

The old one smiled. And then he began to laugh.

Dusk. We sat in a circle with the old man atop his cushion. Facecloths were loosened and looped, displaying at last a collection of very similar blade-nosed, sharp tribal faces leeched of water fat. What I'd told Del was the truth: these Punja-bred people were more accustomed to limited water, and didn't require as much as others. The bodies reflected that.

We'd passed around the bota, each of us taking a swallow, and passed around the cumfa and bread, each of us taking a bite. Ritual duly completed, the others began to talk quietly among themselves.

They were, Mehmet explained, close kin all. Aketni were like that, he said—founded in blood and beliefs. He was the youngest of all, the last born of his aketni, and unless he found a woman to wife there'd be no more kin of the old hustapha.

The hu-*what?* I'd asked.

Mehmet had been patient. The hustapha, he explained, was the tribal elder. The aketni's father. Each aketni had one, but theirs was very special.

Uh-*huh.* They always were.

Their hustapha, he went on, had sired three girls and two boys on a woman who now was dead. They had, in their turn, sired other children, but none remained in the aketni. Two had died in fever season; three others had fallen away.

Del and I looked at each other.

Fallen away, Mehmet repeated. They had deserted their aketni to seek out a tainted life.

Ah, yes. Any life outside of the aketni—or outside of any belief system, for that matter—always had to be tainted. It was easier to explain.

Hoolies, but I hate religion.

The aketni was very small. Seven people, no more, and only one young enough to sire more. Mehmet needed a wife.

I looked at Del. Mehmet looked at Del. Everyone in the circle looked at Del.

The recipient of such rapt attention abruptly tensed

like wire. Even without the language, Del knew something had occurred. The air vibrated with it.

"He wants a wife," I told her, enjoying the moment.

Del stared at Mehmet. I have been in warmer banshee-storms.

But Mehmet wasn't stupid. He lifted a limp hand. "O white-haired afreet of the North, I am too humble for you."

It was, I thought, a deft way of escaping her wrath, and of killing off the aketni's instantly burgeoning hopes without being too rude. No doubt it had crossed Mehmet's mind on more than one occasion during the ride back that he'd like Del in his bed—only a dead man wouldn't, and even then she might resurrect him—but he knew better. A woman such as Del was not for the likes of him.

He had to content himself with bringing back help and water. Enough for a start, I thought sourly. He shouldn't be so greedy.

Del settled slowly, like a dog unsure of surroundings. Her hackles barely showed, but I knew how to see them underneath the outward demeanor.

Mehmet went on explaining things, telling us how even they, deep in the Punja, heard word of the jhihadi, and what he was meant to do.

I perked up. That was *me* he was talking about.

Of course, it had long been expected by their hustapha, that such a one would come. It was why their aketni existed.

I frowned. Mehmet saw it. Voluble as he was, he explained it thoroughly.

When he was done, I nodded. But Del didn't. He'd couched most of it in the dialect she didn't understand.

"What?" she prompted.

"An aketni is what we thought it was: a group of

people who have developed their own religion. This sort of thing happens a lot in the Punja . . . tribes break up into little pieces whenever the auspices are bad, or when they lose a battle, or when sickness invades, the 'magic' weakens, and so on. Sometimes whole families do it, which is what this one seems to be. They just go off from the tribe and live their own lives, working out their own rules and religion." I shrugged. "I never paid much attention, except when I had to."

"Then *khemi* are an aketni?"

I twisted my mouth. "The *khemi* are different. That group got entrenched early, spreading taproots into the Punja. Then someone dug up some scrolls from a ruined city, and decided to worship them."

"The Hamidaa'n," she said sourly, "that claims women are abomination?"

"Never mind that," I said hastily, before she got carried away. "The thing is, Mehmet's aketni dates way back. This old man—the hustapha—is grandson of the founder. Which means it's been around for awhile, as time exists in the Punja." I shrugged at her frown. "Groups—tribes—die out. Sometimes within a single generation. Borjuni, simooms, drought, disease . . . this one's lasted five. That's a long-lived aketni."

She glanced at the old man. "This—hustapha. What is he?"

"Holy man," I answered. "Seer, if you will. It's what the word basically means, as far as I can tell." I shrugged. "Each aketni develops its own language hand-in-hand with a religion. I can only catch half of what Mehmet says, and translations can't be trusted."

"Why are they here?" Del asked. "Why have they come so far?"

"Bound for Iskandar," I explained gravely, "to witness the jhihadi's arrival."

Del recoiled. "No."

I lifted a chastening finger. This one still had a nail; for how long, I couldn't say. "Now, now—you're viewing it in terms of what you know about me. *These* people know only what they've heard . . . and what the hustapha's told them."

"You can't tell me they've left their *home*—"

"Others did," I declared. "Alric and Lena, Elamain and Esnat, not to mention all those tanzeers, and the tribes."

She stared at me. "But you say *you're* the jhihadi—"

"*Someone* has to be!" I scowled, switching to Northern in mid-spate so the aketni wouldn't understand. "Look, I don't know what's going on, or why your brother pointed at me—"

"—if he didn't point at Ajani—"

"—and I don't know what's expected of me—" I glared balefully, "—but I *do* know one thing: you can't tell them who I am."

Del blinked. "What?"

"You can't tell them I'm the jhihadi. Even if *you* don't think so."

She frowned. "Why not? If they've come to see the jhihadi, shouldn't they be allowed to?"

I glanced at the old hustapha, at Mehmet, at the rest of the aketni. And was glad I could speak Northern, so they couldn't understand.

"Because," I gritted through tight-clenched teeth, "if you'd based your life on a lie, would you want to find out?"

"On a *lie?*"

"These people worship the jhihadi. According to

Jamail, that's me; would *you* worship me?" I continued before she could answer, since I knew what she would say. "They also worship that silly prophecy about changing the sand to grass." I scowled, recalling Del's discovery of word similarity. "Grass or glass, whatever; it's what they live by. That's what this gesture is all about—" I slapped sand, then traced a gritty stripe across my brow. "It means the sand will one day be grass again, as it was at the Making. When the jhihadi comes."

"Making," Del murmured. "You mean—like a *jivatma?*"

"They're talking about the *world,* Del—not a magicked sword."

"So," she said finally, having digested that, "they want to get to Iskandar to see the jhihadi." She flicked a glance at the old man. "Are you going to tell him the truth? *Your* version, that is?"

"No. I told you that already."

"You'll just let them go on believing as they have for five generations; that the jhihadi's coming."

"It won't hurt anything."

She arched pale brows consideringly. "It might save old bones a long, wearing journey."

I looked at the hustapha. Saw the glint in eyes so dark pupils were indistinct. Measured the old man's power. I could smell the stink of it. No one, Mehmet or anyone, had to tell me he was special. I could *taste* the truth.

"Tiger?"

Hair rose on the nape of my neck. My belly clenched painfully. "No," I said thickly, knowing it wasn't enough.

Del's mouth tightened. "Do you want your reward so much?"

Without thinking, I answered in Southron. "I don't care about the reward. These people don't have anything."

Mehmet stiffened. "But we *do*," he insisted, "and we intend to reward you."

I waved a hand, sighing. "No, no—it's not necessary—"

Mehmet ignored me, speaking quickly to the old man. The hustapha smiled, fingered his mouth, said something in return. His grandson turned back. "The hustapha agrees."

"Agrees to what?" I asked warily.

"He will cast the sand for you."

Something writhed in my belly. Sweat dampened my brow. Even the words were powerful. "Cast . . ." I let it trail off in dull surprise. Something was pressing me down. A huge, encompassing hand. "You mean—" I thought about something he'd said the day before, about the man who'd stolen food, water, coin. "You said their futures had been cast."

Mehmet nodded. "Of course."

"Then . . ." I looked at the old man. Black eyes wreathed in ancient folds glittered blackly at me.

"What is it?" Del asked. "What is he saying, Tiger?"

Mehmet looked at her. "He is a sandcaster."

"A sandcaster . . ." Blue eyes slewed to me, asking explanation.

My chest felt tight. Breathing was difficult. "Sandcaster," I said dully. "He can foretell the future."

Del's brows arched. "But you don't believe that nonsense—or so you've always said."

Feeling sick, I licked dry lips and gazed across the circle at the old man. "You don't understand."

"He tells the future," she said lightly. "There are

many who do that. At *kymri,* at bazaars, even in the
streets—"

"This is different," I snapped. Something stirred
deep within. "I don't want to know. Not today, not
tomorrow—not next month. I just don't want to
know."

Del laughed. "Do you think he would tell you a
bad fortune, after what you have done to help them?"

"He tells the *truth!*" I hissed. "Good or bad doesn't
matter. What he shows you is what will happen, no
matter what you do."

Del shrugged. She just didn't understand.

Neither did I, really.

But Chosa Dei did.

Twenty-two

The ritual was meticulous. A designated plot of bone-white Punja sand was tended carefully by each aketni member save the old hustapha. He sat on his cushion, overseeing the work being performed directly in front of him.

Each member took turns employing a short-handled wooden rake to rid the plot of impurities. Then a finer rake, combing the selfsame plot. And finally a slender straight-edge to smooth the plot very flat. Both rakes and the straight-edge were of blood-veined, age-dyed wood daubed with ocher squiggles. I assumed the squiggles were runes, but I didn't recognize them.

I shivered. Sweat ran down my temple. I scrubbed it away with a hairless, scaly forearm, then let the limb fall away. The old man was staring at me.

Dusk had faded to night. Mehmet and another had removed two staff-torches from the hustapha's wagon, planted one on either side of the old man, then set the oil-soaked wrappings afire. The torches cast eerie sharp-edged shadows across the tended plot, limning its perfect smoothness.

Mehmet brought seven small pouches to the hustapha, setting three on each side, and the seventh

directly in front of the old man's cushion. The pouches
were of pale, soft leather, closed with beaded draw-
strings. Mehmet carefully opened each one, taking
care not to slip a finger inside or spill the sacred contents, then withdrew to join the semicircle of burnous-
swathed, veiled aketni hunched behind the turbaned
hustapha.

Del and I sat side by side. Between us and the
hustapha stretched a flat rectangle of silk-smooth
sand, and an acre of reluctance.

On my part, that is.

Sweat dribbled, scribing a runelike squiggle down
my right temple, until it was caught in sandtiger welts
and channeled to my chin.

Of their own accord, fingertips rose to trace the
dampened scars, following the pattern of lines excavated in my face.

Del gathered herself. I knew she meant to rise, to
leave me by myself. But I reached out and caught a
wrist. "Stay," I hissed.

"But—this is for *you*—"

"*Stay*," I repeated.

Only an instant's hesitation. Then she settled again
at my side.

I swallowed painfully, nearly choking on a closed
throat. The back of my neck itched. Layers of sinew
tautened, threatening to burst crawling flesh.

The hustapha closed his eyes. For a moment I
thought crazily he had merely fallen asleep, until I saw
the stuttering of wrinkled eyelids and the twitching of
his lips. Gnarled hands curled limply over bent knees.

The aketni made no sound.

The torches tore in a breeze that, an instant before,
had not existed. Smoke shredded in silence, like sun-
rotted, ancient gauze.

The old hustapha murmured. Then the eyes snapped open.

He was blind, I realized. Swallowed by his trance, he saw nothing of the night. Nothing of the sand. Nothing of the unsettled sword-dancer who sat in front of him, with the baby's butt of Punja shining pure and pristine before him.

Blind, he reached unerringly for the first pouch. Poured a measure of sand into one hand. A fine, bronze, burnished sand. He cast it across the tended surface, shaking it from his hand as he chanted unknown things, letting it fall as it would.

Six times he did this. Six measures of sand: bronze, vermilion, ocher, carnelian, sienna, slate-blue. Each cast against the ground.

There was no artistry to it. No attempt to blend hue, or juxtapose color for contrast. He merely cast and let it fall.

One last pouch. He reached into his voluminous burnous, removed an object from it, and held it up to the light. A small wooden spoonlike thing, hollow, with a square of gauze stretched across the bottom, bound on with brass wire. He placed the flat of one palm against the gauze, sealing it against spillage, then poured a measure of sand from the last pouch. Perfectly transparent Punja crystals glittered in the torchlight, like a shower of Northern snow.

He removed the sealing hand from the bottom of the spoonlike object. He began to shake it smoothly, slowly, with methodical precision. Punja crystals sifted through the gauze, powdering the colored drifts. All hue was muted by an almost translucent layer of glittering icelike crystal.

The sifter was hidden away once more. The pouch was closed and set aside. The hustapha, no longer blind, leaned forward over the rectangular window of randomly cast sands.

He blew. A single whuffing exhalation that barely ruffled the crystals, not much more than a baby's breath. Then he drew back and gestured for me to do the same.

I choked on the stench of magic. The contents of my belly crawled halfway up my gullet.

The old hustapha waited.

I gritted teeth. Bent. Blew a single perfunctory breath, getting the silliness over with.

Black eyes glittered. He lifted palsied hands, clapped them together once, then crossed one over the other and flattened palms against thin chest.

Torches whispered of wind.

A breeze only. It caressed eyelids, brushed lips, teased at sweaty flesh. Then settled on the palette of crystal-clothed colored sands.

I watched it. The breeze tugged at Punja crystals, shifted some, stole others, teased away grain by grain. As each gauzy layer was lifted, a new color was born. The random casts of sands began to form a pattern. And a pattern within the pattern.

"Behold," the hustapha invited.

The breeze died, allowing the sands to still. The hustapha waited patiently, letting me look upon the casting. The aketni behind him said nothing, nor made any movement. Beside me, Del was as still.

I was, abruptly, alone. I looked, as I was meant to. Read what was written there, in sand-conjured images still writhing like knots of worms. Bronze, ocher, ash. Others. All the colors of magicked casting, dependent upon the subject.

I stared at the threefold future wind- and breath-scribed in the sands.

What could be. Might be. Would be.
What I did not want to be.

Del's voice was soft in the star-glimmered darkness.
"You're not asleep."

Sleep? How could I sleep?

"What's the matter?" she asked. Her breath stirred
the sweat-stiffened hair on the back of my neck.

I sat bolt upright, scrubbing frenziedly at my nape.
"Don't *do* that!"

She levered herself up on one elbow. We slept apart
from the wagons, well-distanced from the aketni, but
it was still much too close as far as my comfort was
concerned. She brushed hair out of her face. "Why
are you so jumpy?"

I stared hard through the darkness. I knew the hustapha and the others had raked the sandcast patterns
into nothingness, dispersing the magic, but still I
looked for them. Still I smelled the odor. Still I
searched for images squirming in the sand, hoping
they might change.

I drew in a deep, uneven breath. "I Hate. Magic."

Del's soft laugh was inoffensive. If anything, it was
relieved. "Then you may as well hate yourself. You
have your own share of it."

Ice caressed my spine. "Not like that," I blurted.
"Not like that old man."

Del said nothing.

I twisted my head, looking at her. Asking it at last.
"You saw, didn't you? What the sands foretold?"

A muscle twitched in her jaw.

"You saw," I said.

"No."

It stopped me. "No?"

"No, Tiger. It was a private thing."

I frowned. "Are you saying you *saw* nothing? Or that by saying nothing about it, you create that privacy?"

"I saw nothing." She tucked hair behind an ear. "Nothing but sand, Tiger. Little drifts of wind-blown sand."

"Then—you didn't see. . . ?" But I let it go. As I unclenched my fists, another fingernail peeled off. "Then if no one else saw, maybe it won't happen. Maybe I can make it not happen."

Del's face was pale in starlight. Her voice was a thready whisper. "Was it so very bad?"

I frowned into darkness. "I'm not sure."

She thrust herself upright, sitting atop her blanket. "Then if you're not *sure,* how can it be so bad?"

I stared into the night.

"Tiger?"

I twitched. Traced the sandtiger scars. "I'm not sure," I repeated. Then I looked at her. "We have to go to Julah."

Del frowned. "You said something of that before. You gave no reason, just said we had to go. Why? That is Sabra's domain. She won't remain in Iskandar forever. It is not the destination *I* would choose."

"If you *had* a choice."

Del narrowed blue eyes. "Have you no choice?"

"We."

"We?"

"Have *we* no choice."

Pale brows hooked together. "What are you saying?"

"That of all the futures I saw, yours was the most potent."

"*My* future!" Del's spine snapped straight. "You saw *my* future in the casting?"

I reached out and caught a lock of white-silk hair.

Wound it around a callused finger, wishing I could feel it. Then slipped the hand behind her neck and pulled her close, so very close, holding her very tightly against my left shoulder. Losing the threefold future in the curtain of her hair.

Wanting to hold her so hard I cracked all her bones.

Before Chosa Dei did it for me.

Twenty-three

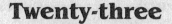

My eyes snapped open. I roused instantly and without fanfare: one moment asleep, the next completely awake, with no residual grogginess, or a desire to curse the inner sense that jerked me out of oblivion.

I lay perfectly still in my blanket, rolled up in a sausage casing of Southron-loomed, nubby weaving dyed gray and bloody and brown. Del slept beside me, pale hair hooded by blanket, except where one stray lock had escaped the others and ribboned across the skyward shoulder.

Something crawled from the pit of my belly. Trembling beset my limbs.

Fear? No. Just—trembling. *Tingling.* A quake of bone and muscle no longer willing to be quiescent.

I gritted teeth. Squeezed shut eyes. Willed myself back to sleep. But the tingling increased.

Feet twitched. A knee jumped. A palsy swallowed my hands, then spat them out again. From head to toe, my skin *itched.* But scratching didn't help.

I peeled back the blanket. Thrust myself up. Gathered scabbarded sword and walked deliberately away from Del, danjacs, wagons, aketni. But not away from the stud. I went straight to him, untied hempen hobbles, threw reins onto his neck. I didn't take time for saddle or pad, just swung up bareback, clamping legs around silk-smooth barrel; hooking bare heels into the hollows behind the border of shoulder and foreleg.

He snorted. Pawed. Stomped twice, raising dust. And then settled, waiting alertly.

"Toward the sun," I told him, doing nothing to give him guidance.

He turned at once, eastward, and walked away from the wagons. No saddle, stirrups, pad. Just the suede dhoti between us, allowing flesh and muscle to speak in the language of horse and rider.

He walked until I stopped him, speaking a single word. I swung a leg across sloping withers, dropped off, walked four steps away. Unsheathed the discolored *jivatma* and let the dawn inspect its taint.

A question occurred: *Why am I here?*

Was washed away in a shudder.

I set the tip into the sand and drew a perfect circle, slicing through the top layer of dust and sand to the lifeblood beneath, glinting with crystallized ice.

Yet another question: *What am I doing?*

A twitch of shoulders dismissed it.

When the circle was finished, I stepped across it, entered, sat down. Set the sword across my lap, resting blade and hilt on crossed legs. Steel was cool and sweet against the Southron (Southron?) flesh too light in color for many tribes, too dark for a Northerner-born.

Something in between. Something not of either. Something that didn't fit. Something—some*one*—different. Shaped by an alien song he didn't know how to hear.

I placed my palms across the blade. Shut my eyes to shut out the day. Shut out *everything* save the bone-deep, irritant itch that set muscles and flesh to twitching.

And a third: *What is happen—*

Unfinished.

The inner eye opened. It Saw far too much.

Would he unmake me? I wondered. *Or did he need me too much?*

The blade grew warm in my palms.

Eyes snapped open. I lurched up, spilling sword, staggered two steps toward the perimeter of the circle, then fell to my knees. Belly writhed as gorge rose. But there was nothing to spew.

I gagged. Coughed. Poured sweat.

Hoolies, what have I—

Limbs abruptly buckled. I sprawled facedown in the sand, laboring to breathe.

Digging fruitlessly with fingers that had shed each blackened nail. And was now replaced with new.

The urge that had brought me here died away into nothingness. The inner eye closed.

I rolled over onto my back, arms and legs awry. Breathed air unclogged with sand. Stared up at the changing sky as stars were swallowed by light. Heard the stud whicker softly, unsettled by the workings of a power he didn't know, and couldn't understand.

He hates magic as much as I do.

But he doesn't know the need seeping out of the darkened places into the light of day, lapping at a soul. He doesn't know what it can do. He doesn't know what it *is*.

He doesn't know what *I* know: there is bliss in ignorance.

I stared at the sky and laughed, because laughing is better than crying.

Hoolies, but I'm a fool.
Hoolies, but I'm *scared*.

Danjacs were hitched to wagons. The aketni sat on the seats. Del waited quietly atop her bay mare. Her face was taut and pale.

I halted, slid off, bent to gather gear and saddled the stud quickly, arranging botas and pouches. Grabbed one squirt of water, then remounted the stud. The language now was muted; saddle and pad interfered.

"Let's go," I said briefly.

Mehmet, driving the lead wagon, called out the departure order to the dun-colored danjac hitched to his wagon. Then lifted the stick from his lap and tapped the bristled rump. The danjac moved out, jingling harness brasses and gear. The wagon jolted into motion. Others followed suit.

Del brought her mare in close as I tapped heels to the stud, urging him to move, and planted herself in my way. I swore, reeled in rein, jerked the stud's head aside before he could bite Del, or go after the mare. "What in hoolies—"

"Where were you?" she asked curtly, cutting through my irritation.

"Out there." I thought it enough.

"Doing what?"

"Whatever I felt like," I snapped. "Hoolies, bascha— how many times have you gone off by yourself to sing your little songs?"

It opened the door to doubt. Del frowned faintly. "Is that what you were doing?"

"What I was doing is none of your business."

"You took that." "That" was my sword.

"And you take *that*." This "that" meant *her* sword. More doubt. A deeper frown. A twitch of jaw muscle. "I'm sorry," she said quietly, then turned the mare after the wagons.

I followed. Feeling guilty.

We might have made Quumi in a day and a half. With the wagons, it took two. At sundown on the second day we reached the gray-beige settlement, and Mehmet called me over.

"There is the toll," he said.

I nodded.

The dark face grew darker. "The others took our coin."

Yes. So they had. "Do you want me to find them? Get the money back?" I paused, seeing his startled expression. "They're probably here, Mehmet. Quumi's the only settlement in these parts where a man can buy food, liquor, women . . . where else would they go after stealing all your coin?"

Mehmet glanced toward the last wagon, where Del brought up the rear. The hustapha rode inside. Then doubt turned to decision. "No." He shook his head. "We have no business hiring a sword-dancer to right a wrong done us. It makes us no better."

"But it's *your* money."

He shrugged. "Let them keep it. There will be other coin, once the city knows we have a sandcaster with us."

I twitched. Then shrugged it away. "And how do you know they won't steal your coin again?"

"The hustapha has cast their futures."

Deep in my belly, something clutched. "He doesn't . . ." I let it trail off, intending to dismiss it, but the idea wouldn't die. "I mean, he can't, can he? Shape his casting to suit a whim?"

Dark arched brows knitted themselves above a

Punja nose. "Do you mean purposely shape a future? For personal pleasure, or retribution?"

"If he thought it was necessary."

Brows unraveled. Mehmet smiled faintly. "*You* cast your future in the sands last night. The hustapha cast possibilities."

"*I* cast . . ." I glanced back at the last wagon. "You mean, all of that rigamarole we went through—"

"Ritual. Ritual is required."

I waved it away. "Yes, yes, the ritual . . . Mehmet, why is it necessary if *I'm* responsible? Why all the sacred secrecy?"

"He is holy," Mehmet said simply. "Holy men are different. The hustapha is a seer. Father of the aketni, which waits for the jhihadi."

I forbore to consider the jhihadi, even though that more than anything convinced me this was all foolishness. My mind was on the hustapha. "He's a wizard," I snapped. "I could smell the stink of it, with or without the wind and a contrived future-casting."

Mehmet's dark eyes focused on the sword hilt peeking above my left shoulder. "All men with power *are* power: the name doesn't matter."

Obscure, I thought. And out of character for Mehmet. It made me wonder how much *had* been divulged in the casting the night before. Del said she'd seen nothing. But that was *Del,* not the others, who understood better than I what a casting was all about. "Are you trying to say something, Mehmet? Something about me?"

The young man smiled. "A man with a knife has power. A man with a sword has power. A man with knife *and* sword has more power yet."

"I'm not talking about knives and swords."

"Neither was the hustapha."

I gritted teeth. "That's not what—" But I broke it off, disgusted. "Oh, hoolies, I've had enough. . . ." I rode on ahead of the caravan to the broken gates of Quumi, and paid the aketni's toll. Which is all Mehmet had asked in the first place.

It was me who'd wanted more.

It was me who *needed* more, to learn what I could do to avoid the threefold future.

Because it *might* be true.

The threefold future: Could be. Might be. Would be.

Up to me to choose.

Twenty-four

Dust from the caravan drifted, working its way toward the street. Del and I sat on horseback at Quumi's battered gate. Sunset stained gray-beige adobe a sickly, washed out copper, tinged with lavender.

"Why did you come?" she asked.

"Why did I *come*?" I scowled. "I was under the impression I was helping the aketni. Which was *your* suggestion."

My sarcasm had no affect. "You might have stopped once Quumi was in sight. There was no need to come in all the way."

I arched brows. "Little thing called water."

Del raised one shoulder in an eloquent, negligent shrug. "You could have asked Mehmet to bring the water out."

"Could have," I agreed. "But why? Since we're this close, we may as well spend the night under a roof again."

Her gaze was steady. "You said you were concerned about sword-dancers and borjuni. That they could be here by now, to try and catch us both."

"Could be. Might be—" I bit it off abruptly, suppressing the sudden shiver prompted by unexpectedly familiar words. "Let's just go, bascha. We can take care of ourselves."

We made our way to Akbar's cantina as the sun fell behind the horizon. A crescent moon hung in the sky, urging the stars from hiding. They glittered like Punja crystals on a sandcaster's raked rectangle.

Feeling twitchy, surly, grouchy, I took the stud around the back and put him in the stable, in one of the tiny partitioned slots masquerading as a stall. Del wisely put the mare in one at the other end of Akbar's shabby stable, and pulled off gear and supplies. Bridle brasses clattered. I heard her speaking softly in uplander to the mare.

The language was still strange on my own tongue, but I spoke enough of it to survive, and understood a bit more. Yet it wasn't the words that spoke, but the tone underlying them. Del was worried about something.

I tended the stud, stripping him of tack and supplies as Del had stripped the mare, gave him fodder and water, walked back up the way to Del. Both of us carried pouches and botas, not risking them to others.

"Hungry?" I asked brightly, in an attempt to lighten the air.

Del shook her head.

"Thirsty, then."

All I got was a shrug.

"Maybe a bath, in the morning?"

A crooked twist of Northern mouth, indicating nothing.

Patience fled entirely. "Then what *do* you want?"

In the gloom, blue eyes were pale. "*That* discharged."

"That" again. My sword. "Hoolies, bascha—you're

making too much of it. I admit it's not comfortable, and I'd as soon dump it here as carry it to Julah, but I don't seem to have much choice." I walked past her and out of the stable. "Let's get rid of this stuff. I want food and aqivi."

Del followed, sighing. "That, at least, is unchanged."

We divested ourselves of burdens in short order, buying ourselves a bed, and retired to the taproom, already full of patrons. Huva weed drifted in beamwork. Spilled wine made the floor sticky. Rancid candles shed sickly light. The place reeked of young liquor, old food, older whores, and unbathed, sweaty bodies.

The way a cantina *should* smell.

If you have no nose, that is.

Del muttered something beneath her breath. I indicated a tiny lopsided table in a corner of the room, headed through the human stockyard, hooked a toe around a stool leg and dragged it from under the table.

"Aqivi!" I called to a plump cantina girl already laden with cups, and a jug of something. "And two bowls of mutton stew, with danjac cheese on the side!"

Del paused at the table, glancing around in silence. Her distaste is never blatant, but I read her easily.

"Sit down," I said curtly. "Do you expect it to be any better?"

Del's head snapped around. She studied me a long moment, then sat down on the other stool. The table was tucked into a tight corner, away from the raucousness; the stool I left to Del would ward her back and two sides. I *had* made an effort. She just chose not to see it.

The cantina girl arrived with the things I had

ordered. A jug, two cups, two steaming bowls with spoons. I opened my mouth to ask for water, counting coppers in advance, but Del cut me off. "I will drink aqivi."

I very nearly gaped. But hid it instantly, merely raising an eyebrow. "Heady stuff, bascha."

"It seems to agree with you." She reached for the jug, poured both cups full. The pungent aroma was so thick I thought a sword could cut it in half.

I flipped the cantina girl an extra copper, then waved her on her way. I had other concerns to tend. "Look, bascha, I know I've said in the past that you have no call to chide me for drinking so much of something you don't approve of, but—"

"You are right," she said quietly, and lifted the cup to her mouth.

"You don't *have* to, bascha!"

"Drink your own," she said coolly, and took a decent swig.

I have no subtlety: I laughed into her face. "Oh, gods, Del—if you could see your face!"

She managed to swallow the mouthful with elaborate dignity. Then took another one.

"Bascha—enough! You have nothing to prove."

Blue eyes were steady. She managed this swallow better, and the expression afterward. "One cannot judge a man until one has tried his vices."

I blinked. "Who told you *that?*"

"My *an-kaidin,* on Staal-Ysta."

I grunted. "Northerners. All pompousness and wind."

"Did your shodo not teach you something similar?"

"My shodo taught me seven levels of swordwork. That was all that mattered."

"Ah." A third swallow. "Southroners. All sweat and buttock blossoms."

Always in the middle of a swallow . . . I sputtered, choked, wiped my face. "What's *that* supposed to mean?"

Del considered a moment. "Something you do in your sleep, after too much cheese."

"After—oh. *Oh.*" I scowled. "I can think of better topics."

Del smiled sweetly. Drank more aqivi.

"Be careful," I warned uneasily. "I told you what happened to me. One cup of that too fast, and I was falling-down drunk."

She pulled her braid free of burnous, letting it dangle against one shoulder. "There are things I do better than you. This may be one of them."

"Drinking? I doubt it. I've had years more practice. Besides, I'm a man."

"Ah. That explains it." Del nodded, swallowed. "It is part of a man's pride, then, to drink more than a woman."

I thought back on contests to establish that very thing, though always among men. Women were not included, except as the reward.

Warmth stole up my belly, blossomed at my neck, traced its way into my face. Del, seeing it, smiled; my answer was implicit.

Which made me a bit touchy. "Men do a lot of things better than women. Men do things better than other men, too. There's nothing wrong with that. There's nothing wrong with pride. And there's nothing wrong with a competition to see who is best."

"Out-drinking one man is a way of proving yourself?"

"In some cases, yes." I could remember many.

"Pissing contests, too?"

"How do you know about that?"

"I had lots of brothers."

I grunted. "I don't make a habit of it. But I won't deny it's happened."

"What about women?"

"What?"

"Have you competed for a woman?"

I scowled. "What is this about? Are you angry with me about something? What have I done *now?*"

Del smiled, and drank aqivi. "I am merely trying to understand what makes a man a man."

I swore. "There's more to being a man than drinking and pissing—and whoring."

Del rested chin in hand. "And there's more to being a woman than baking bread and having babies."

"Hoolies, don't I know it? Haven't you made it clear?" I splashed more aqivi into my cup. "Do *you* want more?"

Del smiled. "Please."

"Eat your stew," I muttered, digging into my own.

"The cheese is green," she remarked.

So was the mutton, a little. "Eat around it, then. You won't find any better."

She excavated in her stew. "No wonder Quumi faded. How many survive its food?"

I found a chunk of meat-colored meat. "There's cumfa in our pouches."

Del grimaced. I grinned.

"Eat," I advised kindly. "So you'll have something to throw up."

Twenty-five

She drank more than expected. Ate less than I'd hoped. But one thing I've learned is, you can't tell a woman anything. Especially a drunk Delilah.

Except, I wasn't sure she *was*. A little maybe. A bit on the warm side, with a glitter in blue eyes and pale rose blooming in her cheeks. But mostly, she was happy.

Now, you might argue being generally happy is not a bad thing for a man. A happy woman is even better. A happy Del might be best of all—except I didn't know what to do with her.

Well, yes, I did. But she was in no condition.

Or was she?

But it was a bad idea. She'd only argue that I'd taken advantage of her, and I suppose she'd be half right. And saying half is a big concession; we *were* bed partners. How do you take advantage of someone who shares your bed anyway?

By letting her get herself drunk, then taking her off for a coupling she wouldn't remember anyway in the thumping of her head and the upheaval in her belly.

I like to think I leave a woman with a better memory than that.

Left, more like. I hadn't had a woman other than Del for—oh, I can't remember.

Which worried me, a little.

Shouldn't I remember?

Shouldn't I *want* to remember?

Hoolies, it wasn't worth it. I poured more aqivi.

Del saw him before I did, which wasn't really surprising since she sat with her back to the wall, and I sat with mine to the room. Which meant that when the man arrived, Del was already watching every move he made with intent, almost avid eyes.

Hands hung at his sides. Rings glinted in poor light. Gauzy saffron underrobe, embroidered with golden thread; copper-dyed burnous of exquisite cut and fabric; a wide leather belt studded with agate and jade. "I have coin," he said. "How much will you sell her for?"

For only an instant it caught me off-guard. And then I remembered: this was the South. I'd been north for long enough to forget some of the customs, such as buying and selling people whenever the urge struck.

I looked at Del. Saw the illusory blandness that was prelude to attack.

I beat her to it. "Who? Her?" A flick of a newborn fingernail indicated the subject. "You don't want to buy *her.*"

"I want her. How much?"

I didn't look up at him. Didn't have to. I knew he had the coin. He wore too much of it. "Not for sale," I said, and drank more aqivi.

"Name your price."

Inwardly, I sighed. "How do you know she's worth it?"

"I buy—differences." The word was oddly inflected.

"I judge differently than other men . . . worth is what I make it."

Carefully, I set down the cup. Swiveled slightly on my stool and looked up at the man. Contained my surprise: he was about my age, and very fair of feature. A Southroner, no question, but crossed with something else. The sharp tribal edge was blunted, softening his angles. The aqivi-pale eyes were intelligent, and very, very patient.

This could be trouble.

"No," I said briefly.

"What do you want?" he asked softly. "I have more than merely coin—"

"No." I glanced at Del, expecting a comment. She waited mutely, leaning indolently against the wall, which is not to suggest she was unprepared; then again, she was drunk. "She's not mine to sell."

"Ah." Enlightenment flickered in nearly colorless eyes, and I realized I had demoted myself without intending to. Now he thought me a bodyguard, or some other kind of hireling. "Then whom do I see regarding her purchase?"

"Me," Del answered.

Dark brown eyebrows arched slightly, expressing mild surprise. "You?"

"Me." She smiled her glorious smile; I snapped out of aqivi-induced relaxation into taut wariness. When Del smiles like *that*. . . .

"You?" This time he was amused. "And how would you price yourself?"

White teeth glinted briefly. "More than you would be willing to pay."

Pale eyes were amused. "Ah, but you have no idea how much I have to spend."

"And *you* have no idea how much it would cost you."

"All right," I said, "enough. This serves no purpose. Let's just end it right here, right now, and let all of us go on about our business." I started to rise. "I think it's time—"

"Sit *down,* Tiger," she said.

"Bascha, this has gone too far—"

"He has taken it this far. As I am the reason for it, it will be my decision." Her voice was cool, but color suffused her face. Blue eyes glittered. "I want to find out *exactly* how much he will pay."

I managed not to shout. "And if he pays it? What then?"

"Why, then he will have bought me." Del languidly pulled the leather thong confining her braid, shook loose pale hair, sectioned it again.

"Enough," I hissed. "If you think I'm going to sit here and let you bargain yourself into slavery—"

"Not a slave," the man interjected. "I don't purchase slaves. I purchase—differences."

"Who cares?" I snapped. "You can't buy her."

Del rebraided her hair. "Don't you trust me, Tiger?"

I stared back at her, grinding teeth. "You're *drunk,*" I accused. "Drunk and stupid and foolish—"

"As you have been often enough." The smile was perfectly bland. "Have I ever stopped you from doing exactly as you wished?"

"This is *different*—"

"No, it isn't." She smiled at the man. "You will assume responsibility for paying my price?"

Pupils dilated. He thought she was his already. "I have said I will pay it."

"No matter what it is."

"Yes." Rings glittered as fingers twitched. "Name your price."

Del nodded once, tying off her hair. Pushed her stool back and rose. Unbelted her burnous, unhooked the split seam from her sword hilt, slid soft silk to the floor. The harness bisected breasts, accentuating her body. It snugged her tunic tight.

Bare arms were pale in burnished, malodorous light. Silver hilt glinted pale salmon. "Choose a man," she said.

"A—man—?" For the first time, he was nonplussed.

"For the dance. Choose."

I stirred. "Now, Del—"

"Choose," she repeated. Then blonde brows rose. "Unless you mean to dance yourself?"

"Dance?" He looked at me. "What is she talking about?"

Resignation outweighed annoyance. "Ask her, why don't you? She's the one you want."

"My price," Del said. And drew Boreal, setting tip into tabletop. The sword jutted upright, braced against falling over by a single long-fingered hand wrapped loosely around the grip. Softly, she said, "I *love* to dance."

She's drunk, I told myself. She's drunk, and on the prod—what in hoolies do I do?

Could I do anything?

No one had ever stopped me.

He protested instantly. "I am not a sword-dancer—"

"*I* am." She smiled. "Choose another, then."

"You are not—" He stopped. One had only to look at her. And then he looked at me. "She is not."

"Tell you what," I said lightly, "why don't we wager on it?"

"But—she is a woman—"

"I did sort of think you had that part figured out."
I warmed to the verbal skirmish, beginning to feel
relieved. Del didn't mean to dance. She was playing
games with him. "I don't know a soul who could miss
that fact."

"Choose," Del said. "If I lose, you have won."

By now, of course, everyone else in the cantina had
discovered our discussion. Silence filled the taproom,
along with all the stink.

Which reminded me of something. "What in hoolies
are *you* doing here?" I asked him. "You don't seem
the type to spend much time in Akbar's place.
Another, better cantina, maybe . . ." I shrugged.
"You're sadly out of place."

"I have informants. One came with word of a
woman worth the trouble of putting myself out of
place." He smiled faintly, turning my words back on
me. "I will have to give him a bonus."

"She's a Northerner," I declared. "She isn't for
sale. They don't *do* that, there."

"Here. There. It makes no difference. Most of the
things I own were never for sale. But I bought them
anyway." He shrugged delicately. "One way—or
another."

A man pushed out of the throng. Young. Southron.
Eager. A scabbarded sword hung from his hip, which
meant he wasn't a dancer. He just *wanted* to be one.
This was probably the closest he would ever come.
"*I'll* dance against her."

Del's eyes narrowed. She assessed him carefully.

The rich man smiled. "I will pay you, of course."

"How much?" the young man asked.

"That can be arranged later. I promise, I will be

generous; I see no point in shortchanging you, if you win the dance."

Now I did stand. "This has gone far enough—"

"Tiger—*sit down*."

"Del, don't be ridiculous—"

She said a single word in clipped, icy Northern. I reflected silently she knew **more** of gutter language than I'd given her credit for.

"Fine," I said agreeably.

Then overset the table and walloped her one on the jaw.

Twenty-six

Del folded, dropping her sword. I caught her, missed the sword, dumped her ungently into the corner, then spun to face the others.

Samiel was in my hands.

"My name is the Sandtiger," I said. "Anyone who wants to dance can take it up with me."

A ripple ran through the room. But nobody said a word.

"No?" I flicked the sword, throwing a bi-colored flash across the cantina: silver and black. "No one? No one *at all?*" I glanced at the man who had wanted to buy Del. "How about you?"

His mouth was set tautly, but he said nothing, also.

"No? You're sure?" Another glance around the cantina. "Last chance," I warned. Then I locked gazes with the young man who had offered to dance against Del. "What about *you?* You were awfully eager. Would I satisfy you?"

Nervously, he licked his lips. "I didn't know it was you. I didn't know she was yours."

"Not *mine*," I said clearly. I looked around the room yet again. "I ought to challenge every one of you to a true dance. I'm bored, and I need the work."

"Sandtiger." The young man again. "No one here would stand a chance against you."

I smiled thinly. "I'm glad you realize that."

Behind me, Del stirred.

"Stay put," I snapped, not even bothering to look. I stuck a toe against Boreal, slid her toward the corner. I doubted anyone would try, but I didn't want to take the chance. He would thank me for it. "So," I said, "why doesn't everybody go back to whatever it was they were doing?" I turned toward Del's "purchaser," lowering my voice. "Because unless *you* want to dance, the entertainment's over."

Aqivi-pale eyes glinted. Rings glittered as fingers stiffened. But he shook his head in silence.

"Then go home," I suggested. "Go back where you belong."

He inclined his head briefly in elegant acknowledgment, then turned and walked out of Akbar's.

That much done. Now for the rest.

"Show's *over*," I declared.

They all agreed hastily.

When I judged the cantina sufficiently settled, though not quite itself again, I sheathed my sword and turned to Del. She had gathered up Boreal and sat against the corner, cradling her sword.

"Here." I reached for Boreal. "Let me put her away before you cut off a leg."

Deftly, Del flipped the grip into both hands and angled the sword upward. I discovered the tip threatening intimate knowledge of my suddenly sucked-in belly. Unexpectedly, the blade was rock steady.

"Back away," she said.

"Bascha—"

"Back *away*, Tiger."

I took a sharper look at her eyes. Then backed. Del

watched me every step, judged the distance between us sufficient, pushed herself up the wall as she scooped up dropped burnous. The misleading brightness of eyes and cheeks was banished, betraying the truth I'd missed: Del was not drunk. Del had *never* been drunk.

"What in hoolies—"

"To the room. Now."

I debated arguing it with her. But when a man's at the end of a sword—the sharp end, that is—he usually does as he's told. I did as she suggested.

The room was tiny, a rectangular sliver tucked away on the northern side, with a lopsided window block cut through chipped and flaking adobe letting in muted, lopsided light. The wall between the room and the next was of heat-brittle lath and paste-stiffened, bug-eaten cloth. Not the room I'd rented from Akbar, or the one we'd shared before. It was, I thought somewhat inconsequently, not so much better than the stall housing the stud. Possibly smaller.

Two paces into the sliver, I turned to face Del. "All right, what do you think—"

"A test," she said calmly, jerking closed the fraying curtain to lend us tissue-fine privacy.

"Test? What kind of test? What are you talking about?"

"Sit down, Tiger."

I was getting sick and tired of being told to sit down. I displayed teeth, giving her the full benefit of my green-eyed sandtiger's glare. "Make me."

She blinked. "*Make* you?"

"You heard me."

She thought it over. Then snapped the sword sideways, out of the way; rotated on one hip; caught me flush very high on the right thigh with one well-placed foot.

It wasn't what I was expecting. The day before I'd have gone down. But now I took the foot, the power, let it carry on through as I rolled my hip to the right to channel the blow past, then snapped back into position.

Del's smile died.

I waggled beckoning fingers. "Care to try again?"

She narrowed suddenly wary eyes. "Your knee . . ."

I shrugged. "Good as ever."

"I thought it would buckle . . . I *planned* for it to buckle."

"Dirty trick, bascha."

"No dirtier than the trick you pulled this morning, disappearing for so long." The sword glimmered between us; once more the tip teased my belly. "Why do you think I did this?"

"I have no idea why you did '*this*.' Idiocy, maybe?" Her turn to show teeth, but she wasn't smiling. "You're different. *Different*, Tiger! First you say little of what the sandcasting told you, as if it doesn't concern me, and then you disappear with nothing but that sword. Why do you *think* I did this?"

"A test, you said. But of what, I don't know—what do you expect from me?"

Del's face was taut and pinched. "I tell myself it is the strain, the constant knowledge of Chosa Dei's presence . . . and that you are as you are because you fight so hard to win. And sometimes I think you *are* winning . . . other times, I don't know."

"So you decided to play drunk to see what I would do?"

"I did not 'play drunk'—I merely let you believe what you wanted to believe: that a woman drinking so much aqivi would *have* to be drunk. And then you would become careless, thinking me fair game." Del's chin rose. "A test, Tiger: if you were Chosa Dei, you would not hesitate to take my sword—*or me*. He wants both of us."

I recalled thinking about hauling her off to bed. Guilt flared briefly, then died away as quickly. What I'd thought wasn't any different from what any man might consider, looking on a softened, relaxed Delilah. It wasn't a sign of possessiveness. Just typical maleness.

Which was not, I thought sourly, adequate grounds for sticking me with a sword.

I pulled myself back to the matter at hand. "But since I didn't try to take your sword—or you—I can't be Chosa Dei. Is that it?"

Del's mouth twisted. "It was a way of getting an answer."

I pointed. "Why not put her away?"

Del looked at the *jivatma*. A crease puckered her brow. Something briefly warped her expression: I recognized despair. "Because—I am afraid."

It hurt. "Of me?"

"Of what you could be."

"But I thought we just settled this!"

Her eyes sought mine, and locked. "Don't you see? You rode out this morning with no word to me. I don't ask you to tell me everything—I understand privacy, even for a song . . . but what was I to think? Last night your future was cast—and you told me *I* was in it."

I managed a small smile, thinking of other women who had grown a little possessive. "Don't you want to be in my future?"

"Not if it's Chosa Dei's." She stabbed a hand toward my knee. "And now—*this*. Your knee is suddenly healed. What am I to think?"

"And my arms." I lifted hands, waggled fingers. "New fingernails, too."

"*Tiger*—"

"Bascha—wait . . . Del . . ." I sighed heavily and put up placating hands. "I understand. I think I know how you feel. And believe me, I'm as confused—"

It cut to the heart of the matter. "Are you Chosa Dei?"

I didn't even hesitate. "Part of me is." I shrugged. "I won't lie, Del—you saw what he did to the sword. He left it—*part* of him did . . . and put a little in me. But I'm not wholly him. That much I promise, bascha."

She was intent. "But part of you *is*."

"Part of me is."

Del's eyes were glazed with something I thought might be tears. But I decided I was mistaken. "Which part of you healed yourself? Which part *remade* yourself?"

I drew in a very deep breath. "I tapped him. I used him."

"*Used* him! Him?"

"I went out there on purpose, summoned him, and used him. I borrowed Chosa's magic."

The sword wavered. "*How* could you do that?"

"Painfully." I grimaced. "I just—*tried*. There's a bit of him in me, bascha. I told you. And it gives me certain—strengths. But there's more of *me* in me."

"You bent him to your will? Chosa?"

"A little." I shrugged. "You once said yourself—and not so long ago—that I am a man of immense strength of will." Del said nothing. Self-conscious, I shrugged defensively. "Well—I thought I'd test *that*. To see if you were right."

Her lips barely moved. "If you had been wrong . . ."

"I addressed that. I drew a binding circle."

"What?"

"A binding circle. To keep Chosa trapped." I shifted weight, uneasy. I thoroughly disliked magic, and using it myself irritated me. It made me what I detested, and I hated admitting it. "Sam—my *jivatma* isn't dead, or empty. There's still *that* power available, if I remember how to key it; work my way past Chosa's taint. And I have the means to use it, if I feel like it. If I can." I scratched a shoulder. "I'm not very good at it. I nearly made myself sick."

"Magic does that to you, remember?" Del's brow puckered. "Then you healed yourself on your own. Remade yourself. Using Chosa's power."

"Some of it. I made it do what *I* wanted." I sighed. "I was getting awfully sick of aches and pains."

"Why didn't you try before? You might have saved yourself some trouble." Eyes glinted briefly. "Saved your knee some pain."

"Might have. But before, I didn't think I could do it. When it first occurred to me . . ." I shook my head. "It's not my way to use or depend on magic. It's a *crutch*, like religion."

Blue eyes narrowed. "What changed your mind?"

I sighed. "The threefold future."

"*What?*"

"What could be. Might be. Would be." I shook my head bleakly. "I never wanted this . . . *none* of this nonsense. But Staal-Ysta gave me a lump of iron and forced me to Make it. To blood and key a *jivatma*—"

"But not *re*quench in Chosa Dei! No one made you do that!"

I smiled sadly. "You did, bascha. I'd have lost, otherwise. And Chosa would have had you."

She knew it as well as I. Trapped in Dragon Mountain, penned by the hounds of hoolies, Del had stood no chance. He would have taken her sword, and her, then augmented his own growing power to destroy Shaka Obre's wards.

Del lowered her blade slightly. Progress. "What is to happen next? What of this threefold future?"

I shrugged. "Images. I saw death, and life. Beginnings and endings. Bits. Pieces. Fragments. Shattered dreams, and broken *jivatmas*."

"Do we die?"

"In one future. In another, we both survive. In yet another, one of us dies. In another, the other does."

"That's four," she said sharply. "Four futures, Tiger. You called it *three*fold."

"Multiple futures," I clarified. "Only three possibilities for any of them: it could be, it might be, it will be." I spread hands in futility, knowing how it sounded. "But each future shifts constantly, altering itself the instant I look at it—even *think* about it. If you look straight at it, it changes. It's only if you let it slide away and look at the edges . . ." Hoolies, it was worse when I tried to explain it! "Anyway, that's what happened last night, when the hustapha cast the sands." I smoothed tangled hair on the back of my neck, rubbing away tension. "I saw everything. It moved, everchanging. Squirmed, like a bowl of worms." I tried to find the words, the ones that would make her see, so she could explain it to me. "I saw everything there was, wasn't, will be. And you and I smack in the middle."

Del's face was pale. She seemed as overwhelmed as I.

"I don't *like* it!" I snapped. "I don't like it at all— I'd just as soon not have anything to do with any of this . . . but what am I to do? I'm stuck with this sword, and *it's* stuck with Chosa Dei! Not a whole lot I can do about it, is there? Except feel helpless." I sighed, backhanding sweat-sticky hair from forehead. "I didn't want the hustapha to cast the sand in the first place. . . ."

Her voice was rusty. "Because you knew what you might see?"

"I just—didn't." I shrugged. "I didn't have much chance to think about the future when I was a Salset chula. Slaves learn not to think about much at all, except staying alive." I hitched shoulders again in a half-shrug, disliking the topic. "I'd just as soon find out what my future holds when I'm in the middle of it."

Del nodded absently. Then smiled a little, going back to something seemingly inconsequential, because it was a thing she *could* grasp, banishing helplessness. "Then—we stay together. And nothing I do and say now will alter anything."

"Oh, it might. It could. It would." I spread my hands, laughing feebly in frustration. "Do you see, Delilah? There is no knowing the truth, because the truth is everchanging. The moment one truth becomes another, the old truth becomes a lie."

Del wiped away the dampness stippling her upper lip. "I don't understand you. You're not the man I knew."

I forced a grin. "Don't you take credit for that? Isn't it what a woman wants?"

She spat a Northern curse. "I don't know what to say. You have twisted me all up."

"Me," I said, with feeling. Then, before she could stop me, I closed my hand on Boreal's blade. "I am not Chosa Dei. A piece of him is in me, but most of

me is *me*." I paused. "Could Chosa Dei do this without swallowing her up? Without swallowing you?"

She gazed down at the hand upon the blade. At flesh-colored forearms, fuzzed with fine, sunbronzed hair, and normal fingernails.

"I know her name," I said. "She's mine, if I want her. If I were Chosa Dei."

"And me?" she asked. "Am I yours, if you want me?"

Slowly, I shook my head. "I'd never make that choice for you. You've taught me better than that."

A long moment passed. Then, "Let go, Tiger." When I did, she sheathed the sword.

I sat down on our bedding, glad that was over. Too much aqivi for wits confused by new and complex truths. "What *I* want to know is, how did you drink so much aqivi without passing out?"

Del smiled. "Part of training on Staal-Ysta."

"Training. In drinking?"

She knelt, crossed legs, leaned against the wall. "It is believed liquor makes sword-dancers careless; I have told you that often."

"Yes. Very often. Go on."

"Therefore it is a lesson we must learn *before* we risk ourselves."

"What?"

"We are made to drink through the night. Then again through the next day."

"All night—and all *day?*"

"Yes."

"Hoolies, you must have been sick!"

"That is the point."

"To make you sick?"

"To make us so sick we have no desire to drink again."

"But—you drank. Tonight."

"Drunkenness destroys balance."

"That's *one* of the things."

"So we are made drunk. Several times each year of our training, to increase our tolerance. So that should we drink too much, we do not lose the dance."

I thought about it. Twisted as it was, it made a kind of sense. "I've been drinking a lot of years . . . what about *my* tolerance?"

"Mine was perfected through discipline. Control. Yours—is merely *yours,* and subject to certain weaknesses in self-control."

"Northern pompousness." I thought about it some more. "So all that business about being able to drink more than me . . ." I let it trail off.

"I can," Del said softly.

I smiled, smug. "But I can *piss* farther."

She froze, and then she thawed. "I will forfeit that victory."

"Good." I stood up. "Now why don't you get some sleep while I go check on the horses?"

"I can go with you."

I smiled. "I know you're not drunk, bascha. But I *did* hit you pretty hard, and I'm betting your head hurts."

She put her hand to her jaw. "It does. I wasn't expecting that." Brows slanted downward. "I should repay you for it."

"You will," I declared. "With your tongue, if not your fist." I smiled, blunting it. "Get some sleep, bascha." I headed toward the curtain. "Oh—one more thing . . ."

Del lifted brows.

"What in hoolies possessed you to challenge that Punja-mite?"

"Which one?"

"The rich one. The one who wanted to buy you."

"Oh. Him." She scowled. "He made me very angry."

I eyed her suspiciously. "You were enjoying yourself."

Del grinned. "Yes."

"Go to sleep." I turned.

"Tiger?"

I paused, turned back. "What?"

Del's eyes were steady. "If you drew a binding circle to keep Chosa Dei in, why did you not leave your sword?"

"My sword?" And then I understood. "I could have."

"And Chosa would have been trapped."

I nodded.

Del frowned blackly. "Is that not what we're trying to do? Find a way to keep him trapped?"

I nodded again. "There *is* a way. I found it. My *jivatma* is the key."

Blue eyes blazed. Her words were carefully measured, as was her emphasis. "Then why not simply *do* it and be *done* with this foolishness?"

"Because," I answered simply.

"Because? Because *what?*"

I smiled sadly. "I'd have to stay in the circle."

"You—?"

"He's *in me,* bascha. There's more to do now than discharge a sword—there's also *me* to discharge."

Del's face went white. "Oh, hoolies . . ." she murmured.

"I thought you might see it my way." I turned back and went out of the room.

Twenty-seven

I didn't go to check on the horses. I went to see the old man.

Mehmet's aketni had set up camp in what had become the caravan quarter. Originally it had been a sprawling bazaar, in the days when Quumi was bustling, and caravans had encamped outside the city. But as Quumi's strength and presence faded, borjuni took to preying on caravans and travelers outside the walls. The bazaar, slowly deserted as Quumi died, altered purpose. Now it housed small caravans on the way to Harquhal and the North.

The sunbleached, dome-canopied wagons were easy to find, even in starlight and the crescent moon's dim luminescence. I made my way across the dust-layered, open-air bazaar and went looking for the hustapha's wagon.

In his typical uncanny way, the old man was waiting for me.

Or else he was simply awake, and made it look that way.

He was alone, seated on the ground on his cushion at the back of his wagon. Dun-colored danjacs, dyed silver and saffron by pale light, were hobbled a distance away, whuffling and snuffling in dust as they lipped up grain and fodder. Immense, tapered ears flicked this way and that; frazzled tails snapped a warning to inquisitive insects.

Bright black eyes glittered as I came to stand before him. "Did you see this?" I asked. "Me coming here?"

He smiled, stretching wide the wrinkled lips accustomed to folding unimpeded upon a toothless mouth.

I knelt down, drew my knife, drew patterns in the packed dirt of the bazaar. Not words; I can't read or write. Not even runes, though I have some understanding of those. Nor symbols, either, denoting water, or blessing, or warning.

Just—lines. Some straight, some curving, some with intersections. And then I put away my knife and looked at the old man.

For some time he didn't even look at the drawings. He just stared at me, into my eyes, as if he read my mind. I knew he couldn't do that—well, maybe he could; but a sandcaster usually only reads sand—so I assumed he was looking for something else. Some sort of sign. A confirmation. Maybe acknowledgment. But I didn't know what to give him, or even if I could.

At last he looked at my drawings. He studied them a long moment, moving eyes only as he followed the lines. Then he leaned down, wheezing, and slapped the flat of his fragile, palsied hand into the middle. It left a cloudy, fuzzy-edged print that obscured most of the patterns. Then he took his hand away and drew a line across his brow.

Which told me a whole lot of nothing.

Or maybe a lot of *something;* the gesture in his aketni referred to the jhihadi.

I drew in an exquisitely deep breath, filling my head with air. "*Am* I the jhihadi?"

He stared back at me: an old, shriveled man with a streak of grit across his forehead.

"If I am," I persisted, "what in hoolies do I do? I'm a *sword-dancer,* not a holy man . . . not a messiah with the ability to change sand to grass!" I paused, arrested, thinking about alternate possibilities. And feeling silly for it. "Or—is it supposed to be changed to *glass?"*

Black eyes glittered. In accented Desert he told me his aketni comported itself solely in expectation of Iskandar's prophecy coming true.

Ah, yes. Iskandar. The so-called jhihadi who got himself kicked in the head, and died before he could do any of the miraculous things he said he'd do.

Of course, *before* he died he also said he'd come back, one way or another. Apparently, if Jamail—in his Oracle guise—was correct, it didn't necessarily mean Iskandar *himself* would be back, but someone assuming his role.

I had no plans to assume *anyone's* role, thank you very much.

Without warning, consciousness flickered. Memories bubbled haphazardly to the surface of my awareness: alien, eerie, *sideways* memories painting pictures of a land as yet lush and green and fertile. I recognized it with effort, blotting out my own far different version: Chosa's recollections of the South before the disagreement with his brother.

Thanks to Chosa, I "recalled" very well Shaka Obre declaring he would find a way to restore it—he would find some*one* to restore it—no matter what Chosa did.

And it was possible he had, in Iskandar the jhihadi. No one knew much about him, except the city was named after him, and his own horse kicked him in the head—which is enough to get most messiahs remembered, irrespective of holiness. So Iskandar the man might not have *been* a man, not as we reckon men.

After all, no one really knows how magic works, where it comes from, or how it can be controlled. Not entirely. Not *absolutely*. They just borrow *pieces* of it, and hope they do it right.

Which meant, odd as it sounds, Iskandar might have been a construct, an aspect of Shaka's magic, meant to restore the South by changing the sand to grass.

Construct. A man *Made* for something, as Chosa Dei Made things. It seemed entirely possible Shaka Obre could Make things, too, even men—

I stood up abruptly, shaken to the marrow. A whole new possibility unfolded itself before me. And I didn't like it one bit.

"No," I declared.

The hustapha sat on his cushion, grit glittering on his brow.

"No," I repeated, with every bit of determination in my Chosa-remade body.

The old man shrugged, renouncing his intention to tell me anything.

Or was it he didn't know?

Breath came faster. "I'm a man," I said urgently. "A *man* man, not a construct. Not a conjured *thing*—"

Mehmet came around the wagon and stopped, staring at me in mild surprise, which altered quickly enough as he took in the tableau. His expression reproached me for taxing the old man.

"What *is* a jhihadi?" I asked Mehmet intently. "Messiah?—or magicked man conjured by a wizard for reasons of his own?"

He was scandalized. "The jhihadi is the most holy of all!"

"Not 'the' jhihadi—*a* jhihadi," I clarified in something approaching desperation. It hurt to breathe through the constriction of chest and throat. "Do you know where one comes from?"

Mehmet shrugged. "Does it matter? A past is not necessary—only the present and future. What he *does* is important, not what he *is*."

I swallowed painfully. Then turned on my heel and strode rapidly away from them both.

Away from the possibility—no, the *im*possibility—I didn't want to acknowledge.

I broke one of the most important rules a sword-dancer can ever have beaten into his brain—and body—by tongue-lashing, wooden practice swords, *and* real blades.

That is: not to be so distracted by your thoughts, no matter how chaotic, that you neglect to take note of your surroundings.

Especially if those surroundings decide for some unknown reason to become hostile.

Which my surroundings did.

To my pronounced—and painful—regret.

I never even made it out of the bazaar into the sidestreets, alleys, and passageways. Not completely, at any rate; I got about halfway, just on the verge of trading open space for the confinement of warrenlike streets, when a whole army of men converged upon me.

Well, maybe not an army. It just felt like one.

Maybe half.

Usually, when you get ambushed in a city, it's by one or two—or three or four—opportunistic thieves who want your money. If they're that open about everything, they arrive one by one like gathering

wolves, trying to intimidate by numbers and attitude.
It works with a lot of people. But with a man trained
as a sword-dancer, such tactics serve only to give him
the time to unsheathe his blade. And once there's a
weapon in the hands of a trained, skilled sword-
dancer, there's not a whole hoolies of a lot the attack-
ers can do. Because usually one of them loses a hand,
an arm—maybe even a head, if he insists—and the
others generally decide they have something better to
do.

Usually. But these friendly folk were not thieves. At
least, I don't think they were. They didn't use thieflike
tactics. They just *descended,* en masse, swarming over
me all at once. I wound up smack on my back in the
middle of the street, spitting sand, dung, blood, and
cursing.

Lying *on* my sheathed sword, I might add.

Hoolies, how embarrassing.

Once I was there, arms and legs spread-eagled, they
were actually rather restrained. A few kicks, a couple
of snatches, pinches, rabbit punches; no more.

Until someone quietly reminded them I was neither
predictable nor to be trusted, and that if they lost me,
none of them would survive. That *he* would have them
killed, if I didn't do it myself.

Which did a good job of convincing them they ought
not to waste any more time, and then someone
whacked me in the side of the head with something
very hard.

I woke up in the dimness, swearing, aware my kidneys were killing me. And my head, but that was
nothing new. The kidneys, though; that's pretty cold-
blooded. Also effective: a man doesn't feel much like
struggling when every move tells him it'll hurt like

hoolies, and make him piss blood the next couple of days.

Inside. A room of some kind. It was dry, musty, and dusty, stinking of rats and insects and stale urine. I seemed to be near a wall or some sort of partition, because I sensed a blockage behind me. I lay on my right hip and shoulder, bundled up like a rug merchant's wares. From behind me came a dim, nacreous glow. Sickly yellow-green. It illuminated very little, but I caught a glimpse of something—or some*one*—across the room, hidden in deeper shadows.

I stopped swearing when I realized I wasn't alone, and when I discovered it was rather difficult to make any sound at all, because something very taut and painful was looped around my throat. Wrists were tied behind me, and a length of something—wire? rope?—ran from them to the binding around my ankles. An excessively *short* length; my legs were bent up so that heels nearly touched buttocks. It was highly uncomfortable.

Which didn't make me very confident about the situation.

"Sandtiger."

So much for wondering if they—or he—knew who I was. On one hand, it made me feel like this had been done for a reason. On the other, it made me feel like I was in more trouble than just a random, if violent, robbery.

Especially since I heard the few coppers in my pouch rattle as I shifted, testing bonds.

"Sandtiger."

I stilled. The back of my neck itched, and forearms. My belly felt queasy.

"Do me a favor?" I asked. "Give us a little more light, so I can see what party I've been invited to."

Nothing. And then the voice asking, with a trace of mild amusement, if I was *sure* I wanted light. "Because if you see me, will you not then have to be killed?"

A cultured, authoritative voice; the kind that appears ineffective, until you demand proof of strength. The slight accent was of the Border country, with a twist of something else. It sounded vaguely familiar, but I couldn't place it.

I expelled a breathy, cynical grunt. "Hoolies, you'll kill me regardless—if *that's* what this is all about. If it isn't, you don't really care one way or another." I worked my wrists a little, found no give at all. If anything, the binding tightened.

Silence. And then light.

I swore in spite of the loop around my throat.

"Precisely," he agreed. "Now, shall we discuss once more what kind of payment you would like for the Northern woman?"

I told him what he could do with himself.

"I intend to," he said mildly. "I'm quite depraved, you know. It's part of my reputation. Umir the Ruthless, they call me."

I gritted teeth. "Is that why you want Del?"

"Is that her name?"

I swore again. This time at myself.

"No." The light came from a crude clay lamp set into a window sill. He stood in front of it, which threw him mostly into silhouette and limited its effectiveness, but the pale glow from behind me balanced the illumination and allowed me to see the characteristic dark Southron face with high-arched nose, sharp cheekbones, thin lips and deep sockets, but the eyes in them were an unusual pale gray. Borderer, I decided, in view of the accent. Rings and studded belt

glinted. "I want—*Del*—for the very reasons I gave
you before: I collect differences."

"What in hoolies is *that* supposed to mean?"

He gestured. "Some people collect gemstones, golden
ornaments, horses, women, men, rugs, silks . . ." Again
the smooth gesture illustrative of the obvious. "I collect many different things. I collect things that interest
me by their very different*ness*."

"So you want her."

"She is a remarkably beautiful woman, in a very
dangerous, deadly sort of way. Most women—
Southron women—are soft, accommodating things, all
tears and giggles—depending on their moods, which
are innumerable. She is most decidedly *not* soft. She
is hard. She is sharp. She is edged, like steel. Like
glass." His smile was faint in the thick shadows. "So
keenly honed she would part the flesh with no man
the wiser, and let him bleed to death at her feet, smiling all the while."

"As she'll part yours," I promised. "She's a *sword-
dancer,* borjuni . . . a fully trained, *jivatma*-bonded
sword-dancer. Do you have any idea what that means?"

"It means I want her more than ever." He smiled.
"And I'm not a borjuni. I'm a tanzeer."

"In *Quumi?*"

He shrugged. "With proper management, Quumi
could become profitable again. But it has only lately
come into my possession. I have annexed it to my
domain." He pointed northerly. "Harquhal."

"Harquhal is *yours?*" I frowned. "Harquhal hasn't
belonged to a tanzeer for years. It's a border town—
a *Borderer* town. You can't just walk in there and
take it over."

"It's when people believe you can't that you *can*."
He made a sharp gesture. "But we're not here to dis-

cuss annexations. We're not here to discuss anything, really—I just thought you might like to know that even as we speak, my men are abducting the woman for me."

I tried to break the bindings and succeeded only in nearly choking myself into unconsciousness. Shaking with anger, I subsided. "So much for offering to *buy* her."

"I pride myself on being a judge of men. When I learned who you were, I knew it was unlikely you would give in. *You* have something of a reputation, Sandtiger . . . there is talk that imprisonment in Aladar's goldmine changed you." He paused. "And the woman."

"How?" I spat. "Are you trying to say *I'm* soft, like the Southron women?"

"To the contrary—although some undoubtly *would* argue that; but then, they have no idea what motivates a man." He smoothed the rich silk-shot fabric of his nubby, slubbed burnous, rings glittering. "Those who understand men—or understand *you*—say the mine and the woman have made you more focused. More deadly than ever. Before, you cared mostly for self-gratification . . . now that life and freedom mean so much more to you—now that there is the woman—you are not so lackadaisical."

"Lackadaisical?" It was about the last word I'd choose to characterize myself.

"Men who are nomads—or once were—drift with the Punja, Sandtiger. Where they go matters little, so long as there is a job, or women, or wine." He smiled. "You were blessed with unusual size, strength and quickness, and a great natural ability . . . why should a man so talented waste his strength unnecessarily? No, he merely flicks the insect aside instead of squashing it, because he knows he *can* . . . and that if he should choose to squash it, his will be the quickest foot any insect has ever known."

He stopped speaking. I stared at him, unsettled by his summation. By his ability to judge so easily, and speak with such certainty.

I lay unmoving, cognizant of bindings. "Let her alone."

"No." He moved a single step closer. "Do you understand what I have just said? You are a man who cannot be bought. An anomaly, Sandtiger—a different kind of sword-dancer, whose whole lifestyle *is* to be bought. Slavery of a different sort."

I bit back anger, putting up a calm front. "So, am I to join your collection, too?"

"No. Sword-dancers are a copper a dozen . . . admittedly, *you* might be worth more than that, but not so much that you're worthy of my collection. No," he said thoughtfully, "were I to add a sword-dancer, it would be Abbu Bensir."

I blurted it without thinking. "Abbu!"

"I want the most unique, Sandtiger. That is the *point*. You are very good—seventh-level, I believe?— but Abbu is . . . well, Abbu is Abbu. Abbu *Bensir*."

I know. I know. It was stupid to feel even remotely jealous, in view of the circumstances. But it grated. It *rankled*. Because while it's bad enough to be trussed up and dumped in a stinkhole because you're inconvenient, being told you're not worth as much as your chief rival makes it even worse.

I scowled blackly. "Ever heard of Chosa Dei?"

He smiled faintly, brows lifted in amused perplexion. "Chosa Dei is a Southron legend. Of course I have."

I grunted. "He collected things, too. Mostly magic, though."

The tanzeer laughed softly. "Then we are very alike, the legend and I. I have acquired a bit of magic lore over the years."

Magic *lore*, not magic itself. I thought the distinction important. "What happens next, tanzeer? Am I to be left here as rat food, or do you have something in mind?"

"What I have in mind is the woman." He smiled as my muscles instantly knotted against the bindings. "I would not try quite so hard to break free, Sandtiger. That is not rope imprisoning you, but magic."

I froze. "Magic?"

"Runelore, to be precise." He shrugged. "I have a grimoire."

"A grim-*what?*"

"Gri-moire," he enunciated. "A collection of magical spells and related enchantments. The *Book of Udre-Natha*, it is called. The Book of the Swallowed Soul." The tanzeer smiled. "My soul is quite intact, as yet . . . but certainly bartered." He reached inside his burnous and drew out something that glowed dull gray-brown in muted illumination. "This is but a sample, a fragment left over—do you see?" He spoke a single word under his breath, and the thing he held flared into life. It glowed a sickly yellow-green. "There. Runelore. The *Book of Udre-Natha* is full of such small magics, as well as larger." He came closer, bending slightly to dangle the length before my eyes. "Do you see the runes? Hundreds of them, all woven together into a single strand of knotted, unbreakable binding, stronger than rope, or wire. That is what imprisons you, Sandtiger. At throat, wrists, ankles."

He gestured. "Skill or no skill, sword or no sword, even you cannot break free of *magic*."

Transfixed, I stared at the abbreviated length dangling from his fingers. Dim, pulsing light; runes knotted together to form a bizarre, living rope thick around as a woman's smallest finger.

He tucked the runes away. "I would not struggle too much," he warned. "Part of runelore, once set to bind, is to constrain such attempts. If you fight too heartily, the loop around your throat could quite easily strangle you. And I would hate to have that happen."

"Why?" I asked rustily. "What use am I to you?"

"Not to me. To Sabra."

Every muscle froze.

"*I* don't want you," he said, "but she does. And since I am not averse to making a profit, I'm pleased to be able to rid myself of you while also earning coin—*and* Sabra's gratitude. One never knows when such gratitude can come in handy."

"She's a woman," I said, looking for an edge. "You'll deal with a woman tanzeer?"

"I'll deal with anyone I must to secure the things I want." He shrugged. "I am a pragmatist, Sandtiger . . . for now, Sabra rules her father's domain, but that will change. It always does, eventually." He shook out the folds of his heavy sleeves. "By now they should have the woman—Del?" He nodded. "So I take my leave." He turned to the lamp, blew it out. The nacreous glow of binding runes cast sickly light upon his stark, shadowed face. "Sabra should arrive from Iskandar in a day or two. Until then, you'll have to make shift where you can. And if you think to shout for help, recall you are in my domain. I have promised the people I will restore her to her former glory—and

I have *also* told them they are not to meddle in my affairs."

I lurched, then stiffened as rune-bindings tightened. "*Wait—*"

He moved to the door and put his hand upon the latch. "I am not a murderer, borjuni, or rapist. I acquire things to *admire* them. It may please you to know I have no intention of harming the woman."

It was something. But as he shut the door and latched it, I wondered if he lied.

Lied about *everything*.

Twenty-eight

No light, save for the ghostly glow of rune-bindings. I lay in pallid darkness, bathed by sickly shadows, and wondered how far I could test the bonds without strangling myself. Umir the Ruthless had been clever; by also running the single length of rune-rope through loops at wrists and ankles, he made certain any sort of testing would tighten the noose snugging my throat.

Hoolies take him.

Then, again, I reflected, he seemed to think his soul was already compromised by his ownership of the *Book of Udre-Natha*, or whatever the hoolies it was.

I scowled into darkness. By refusing to think about magic most of my adult life, it seemed I'd missed out on a lot of knowledge and forgone conclusions. It seemed the South was *riddled* with magical items, grim-whatevers, would-be sorcerers, afreets . . . ah, hoolies, I don't care what they say, it's all tricks and nonsense.

Except Umir's "nonsense" was doing a fine job of keeping me out of action.

I lay very still and did a meticulous examination of my physical condition. My kidneys still ached unremittingly, and undoubtedly would for a day or two; a few

bruises here and there, abrasions; a couple of painful
gouges; a sore lump on the side of my head.

And a cramping discontent across my spine that told
me something else: they'd left me my sword. Still
sheathed and hooked to harness, which I still wore.

A question occurred: Why?

Then again, why not? Without my arms free, the
sword did me no good. And for all I knew, Sabra had
requested its presence as pointedly as my own.

And also something else: What if someone had *tried*
to take my sword, and Samiel had repulsed him?

If you didn't know his name, he could be downright
testy. It was a *jitvatma's* first line of defense; the second being its ability to do incredible, magical things.

Magic.

I chewed the inside of my cheek thoughtfully.
Hadn't I used magic the day before, to repair injured
knee, and restore arms and fingernails?

Hadn't I bent Chosa Dei—well, a *piece* of him—to
my will?

I shivered. The binding tightened at throat, on
wrists, on ankles.

I lay in the dust-smeared darkness and sweated
stickily, trying to swallow without giving the noose a
reason to snug itself any tighter. Trying to figure a
way of undoing Umir's magic.

Trying not to think of what they were doing to Del,
who—drunk or not—had swallowed much too much
aqivi, and received a tap on the jaw from a none-too-
gentle fist.

I slept, and woke up with a jerk that snugged the
noose a step tighter. Now it was *really* uncomfortable.
I cocked my head back, trying to put slack into the
tautness; rapped my skull against the upstanding hilt

of my sword and swore, hissing the oath in disgust, despair, desperation.

"Stupid . . ." I muttered hoarsely. "Your shodo would hold you up to ridicule—"

But I broke it off. I didn't really want to think about my shodo right about now. Twelve years dead, he still exerted a powerful influence over my behavior. Much as I hated to admit it. Much as I got sloppy and depended on size, strength, quickness and natural ability to win my dances, instead of the precise techniques my shodo had labored seven years to teach me.

Just as Umir had said.

Ah, hoolies. Might as well give it a try.

Shut my eyes. Thought about magic. And power. And need.

Thought about Del, and how if I didn't get loose Umir might bind her up in rune-ropes and haul her off to a lair every bit as impregnable as Dragon Mountain, and tuck her away behind wards I couldn't break no matter *how* much magic I summoned, because he had a grim-something.

Thought about me, left to lie here in a stinking, rat-infested, dusty, musty, dry-rotted room with no breathable air to speak of, and certainly no food or water, or even a way of relieving myself—

(—which would hurt too much, anyway, because someone—or several someones—had planted feet in the small of my back, somewhere in the general vicinity of my kidneys—)

—until Aladar's vengeful daughter arrived from Iskandar by way of Harquhal, and hauled *me* off to a lair every bit as impregnable as . . .

Ah, *hoolies*.

"Magic," I muttered grimly, "and let's be quick about it."

But quickness is not something that goes very well with magic. Especially if you have a renegade sorcerer—well, a *piece* of him—stuck inside you somewhere.

And the rest of him in your sword.

Thought about runes, and sickly light, and undoing all the knots.

Umir had taken the last bit of rune-rope from inside his burnous. It had been nothingness, a stringy patch of darkness. Until he spoke a single word.

What in hoolies had he said?

I thought about it. Hard. Until my head ached along with everything else, and sweat stung my eyes, and the cramps in neck, arms, and legs made me seriously consider moving even against my better judgment, because if I didn't move soon, the pain would become unbearable.

Umir the Ruthless. Who'd said Sabra might arrive in a couple of *days*.

Who'd said he didn't really want to kill me. But who had undoubtedly known that I'd be dead inside of two days anyway, because a combination of the slackness of sleep and the spasms of muscular cramps would cause me to move, and the bindings to constrict.

Until I choked to death.

Which meant that unless I myself engineered it—as soon as possible—I'd be dead of "natural causes" before Sabra arrived to collect me.

Magic. I shut my eyes and thought about it, willing myself to relax.

And fell asleep.

I came to with a jerk, gagging, and spat out a word. *The* word, recalling how the syllables fit together, and how Umir had pronounced them. A tongue-tangling, gnarled word, like the unruly spine of the stud when he humps and hops and squeals. But I knew it, and I said it—

And nothing happened.

Ah, hoo—

No. Something *did* happen: the glow brightened.

Not what I had in mind.

I tried again, altering intonation.

Nothing.

Yet again. Only this time, the pressure *increased*.

"*No*—" Desperately, I pressed my skull more fiercely against the sword, trying to escape the tautness. Spine arched, legs cramped, buttocks tightened. Kidneys blared discontent.

"*Un*do . . ." I gagged. "—not—do . . . *un*do—"

I summoned the word again, saw its shape inside my head, tried one more time.

This time I said it backward.

Light winked out. The pressure didn't slacken, but it didn't tighten, either.

For now, that was enough.

I said the word—*backward*—again.

Nothing.

"Undo—" I muttered. And thought about knots untying.

Nothing.

Swearing, I concentrated. Visualized rune-bindings I couldn't see, had never seen, except for a brief glimpse in Umir's hand.

Dangling from his fingers: a tangle of glowing runes, like a four-plaited Salset rein.

Memory wandered nearer.

—*think*—

Had it. Saw the lines, the patterns, the knots.

Thought about my *own* lines and patterns and knots;
the welts graven in flesh, slicing whitely through two-
day stubble; the intersections I'd carved into sand and
dust before the old hustapha; the interlaced layers of
knot on knot: double, triple, quadruple, wrapped twice
and thrice, then knotted again, then braided; then
joined by one and two and three and four—

Displaced by my panting, a gout of dust blew up into
my face. Irritated eyes teared. Runnels channeled
cheeks, reminding me of Mehmet's face when first I'd
seen him, dust- and sand-caked, thirsty, exhausted;
Mehmet, whose aketni harbored a hustapha, a sandcaster, who cast the sands for me and called me a jhihadi—

Or had he?

A ripple swarmed over my flesh. At least the runes
didn't tighten in immediate response, but it still didn't
feel *good*.

Flesh tingled. Every inch itched. And I couldn't do a
thing.

"—don't think—about that—"

But I did. Because a warping chill wracked my limbs,
setting my joints to aching. Weirdly, it reminded me of
the North, wrapped in winter's breath.

Nausea invaded my belly.

Hoolies, not *now!*

I swore against the ground. I sweated, then shivered
convulsively, in the two-faced touch of fever.

Now is not the *time*—

A sour belch worked its way up from the unhappy
contents of my belly.

What I need *now* is magic, not this—

Magic.

Which always made me sick.

Hoolies, maybe it *was* working!

With renewed determination—and a still discontented belly—I returned with increased vigor to my attempts at dispelling Umir's bindings.

I panted. Sweated. Ground teeth. Thought about runes: Southron, Northern, Borderer. Thought about knots untied, unlaced, undone.

Thought of everything *backward*.

Slackness.

Eyes popped open. Breath was thunderous in my ears. I thrust myself upright, chest heaving. Ash slipped free of neck, of wrists, of ankles. I brayed a hoarse laugh of triumph that combined unexpectedly with a throttled belch, then doubled over and fell sideways, sucking air and dirt and blood.

Ah, hoolies. I hate magic. It makes me *feel* bad.

Cramps eventually subsided to a manageable level. I lay there panting a moment longer, drying in the darkness, then pressed myself up again.

Del.

Oh, bascha. Give me a chance—I'm coming.

I got up, staggered to the door, wrenched it open crookedly on sun-rotted leather hinges.

And fell through into the dawn.

Twenty-nine

I stumbled into the shadow-curtained room, rebounded from the doorframe when I misjudged its nearness, and rousted Akbar's nephew. "Where is she? Where did they take her? Which way did they go?"

The nephew gaped, duly rousted.

One-handed—the other was full of sword—I caught a knot of cloth beneath his chin and jerked him off his pillow. "I said, *where is she?*"

"The woman?" he managed.

"No, I mean the *mare*." I let go of his nightrobe. "There were men here earlier—"

He tugged at his twisted attire. "Yes, but—"

"Which direction did they go?"

"Toward the North gate, but—"

"Did they hurt her?"

"No—but—"

"Harquhal," I muttered intently. "They'd take her to Harquhal—unless there's somewhere else—"

The voice came from the doorway. "Where in hoolies have you been?"

I jumped, spun, stared. "What are you doing *here?*"

Stalemate. Del knitted brows. Lovely pale brows,

276

set obliquely in a flawless, familiar forehead—unmarred by all save bad temper.

But never mind that. "I mean—" I frowned back. Then, rather lamely, feeling more than a little foolish, "Didn't they come for you?"

Boreal gleamed in her hands. "Those men? Yes."

"But . . ." I sat down—no, *collapsed*—on the edge of Akbar's nephew's bed. "I don't understand."

"They came," Del clarified. "Happily, I wasn't in the room. I was in the stable, looking for you."

Uh-oh. "For me?"

"Yes. The last thing you said to me was you were going to check on the horses." The scowl deepened; pointed reproach. "When you didn't come back, I went to look for you." She shrugged. "I heard them come. I stayed where I was. In the stall, with the stud." She scrutinized me. "You look worse now than you did two days ago."

I felt worse, too. Then, it was head and knee. Now it was everything else. "I *thought*," I began, with great dignity, "that I would rescue you."

"I'm fine." Then her expression softened. "Thank you for the thought."

Akbar's nephew stirred. "May I go back to sleep now?"

"Oh." I stood up, rubbed numbly at filthy cheek, then tried to arrange my back so my kidneys didn't hurt. Well, didn't hurt so *bad*. "We'd better get out of here."

Del stepped aside as I made my way by her into the common room, then followed. "Are you so sure they'll be back? They came here once and didn't find what they wanted. Sometimes a room already searched makes the best hiding place."

"They'll be back." I fought my way through tables,

kicking stools aside grumpily, and headed for our room. "I have the feeling Umir won't give up."

"Who?"

"Umir. The Ruthless. The man who wanted to buy you."

"Him?"

"Now he wants to steal you." I yanked cloth out of the way and leaned against our doorsill. "Do I seem real to you?"

Brows shot up. "What?"

"Never mind." I waved a limp hand. "Just—get our things. I'll see about the horses."

"Our things are *with* the horses." Del studied me. "After those men left, I packed and readied them."

"Readied—?"

"Saddled, bridled . . . with pouches already in place." Her expression was exquisitely bland, as if she didn't want to insult me but knew any comment would. "With all the botas filled."

I must look *really* bad.

"Well, then . . ." I straightened up, winced. "I guess we should leave."

Blandness was replaced with the faintest trace of dry concern. "You do not appear to be in condition to go anywhere."

"It never stopped me before." Grinding teeth, I pressed a hand against my spine. "Let's go, bascha. Sabra's on her way, and Umir will be back."

We repaired to the stable with due haste and brought the mare and the stud out, whereupon the stud took to lashing his tail and peeling back his lip. A shrill, imperative whinny—meant to impress the mare—pierced the pale new light. *And* my right ear, much too close to the stud's mouth. Horses can be loud.

I whopped him on the nose. "Not now, lackwit . . ."

Del swung up on her mare, assembling folds in the slack burnous. Boreal's hilt above her shoulder glinted in the dawn. "If you are in such a hurry . . ."

"I'm coming. I'm *com*—oh, hoolies, horse, did you have to do that?" I wiped a glob of slobbery slime from the filthy ruin of my left cheek. "The mare goes," I declared, "as soon as we reach a settlement that has a *gelding* for sale." I planted my left foot in the brass stirrup, catching hold of the stud's sparse mane—I keep it clipped—and dragged myself upward. To the detriment of my kidneys. "They went out the main gate, which means we should try the other one." I turned the stud and headed him around the corner of the cantina. "Umir doesn't know where we're going, and since I know he knows *we* know Sabra is after us, Julah is the last place he'd expect us to go."

"Won't he have dispatched men to the other gate?"

"The walls are falling down, in case you hadn't noticed. We'll look for one of the breeches." We rounded the cantina into the street proper. "I don't think—"

But what I didn't think never got said. A man stepped out of fading darkness and caught hold of my rein, pulling the stud up short. "I challenge you," he declared, "to formal combat in the circle."

"Nezbet," I gritted, "we don't have *time* for this."

"Shodo's Challenge," he clarified. "Or will you once again plead injury in place of cowardice?"

Del took a stab at it. "Just kill him, Tiger."

"*Shodo's Challenge,*" Nezbet hissed, still gripping the rein.

"Later," I suggested. "Right now we're sort of busy—"

"Tiger." Del's voice, stirred from equanamity into something more intense. "Others are coming."

"Umir's men? No." I answered it almost as soon as it was asked because I saw the others.

"Sword-dancers," Nezbet said. "Osman. Mahoudin. Hasaan. Second- and third-level. Honorable men, all." He smiled. "Will you say no before *them,* Sand-tiger the Coward?"

I tossed the free rein to Del. "Hold him," I said. "This won't take very long."

Surprise flickered in Nezbet's dark eyes. Then pride, and sudden pleasure. Lastly, recognition: he'd finally gotten his dance with the South's greatest swordsman.

Unless, like Umir the Ruthless, he tacked that title on Abbu.

I stripped out of my burnous, suppressing a wince of pain from kidneys, and draped it across my saddle. "Let's go," I said briefly. "We're burning daylight, here."

Nezbet let go of the rein. "Do you mean it?"

I bared even teeth. "Shodo's Challenge, is it not? To put me in my place?" I waved a commanding hand. "Hurry up and draw the circle."

Brows arched. "But *you* are the Challenged. *You* have the right—"

I spread fingers across my heart, inclining head. "I give the honor to you. Just *draw* the thing, Nezbet!"

"—isn't right," he muttered, but stepped away from me into the street to begin the proper circle.

I glanced down the street at the three approaching sword-dancers. Looked the other way. Fidgeted with a buckle on my harness. Glanced at the trio again. Finally looked at Del. "Maybe you should just go on. I can catch up."

"No."

"It's *you* Umir wants, not me. If you hang around just for this—"

"I'm staying." Del smiled. "You need someone to hold your horse."

I sighed. Bent to untie and unlace sandals. "Waste of time," I muttered. "Stupid would-be panjandrum . . ." I jerked the sandals off. "Ought to know better than to turn this into a challenge . . . stupid Punjamite should have been taught never to make it personal." I unhooked arms from my harness, sliding free of straps. "Thrice-cursed son of a goat—who does he think he is?"

Del, from atop her mare, with amused curiosity, "Do you ever hear yourself?"

"Hear myself? Of course I hear myself. I'm not deaf. How could I *not* hear myself?"

The smile blossomed, unrestrained. "Then perhaps one day you should *listen*."

"Don't have the time," I growled. Glared back into the street. "Is that thing finished *yet*?"

Nezbet straightened. Showed me white teeth against a dark Southron face. "Step into the circle."

"About time." I unsheathed, dumped the harness on top of the sandals and strode out into the street. Saw from the edge of my eye Nezbet's three witnesses range themselves against the cantina wall. *My* witness, on horseback, jabbed a sandal into the stud's nose to remind him of his manners. I reflected, belatedly, I might have put him somewhere else. He *was* a stud, after all, and the mare was a mare. "All right, Nezbet." I stopped at the circle. "Shodo's Challenge, you say."

"Yes." He continued smiling.

"Death-dance," I told him, then stepped into the circle.

Nezbet lost his smile. "*Death*-dance!"

I stood in the precise center of the circle, the Chosa Dei-infested blade a diagonal slash across my chest from hip to shoulder. "You drew the circle. I choose the dance."

"But—" He broke off, realizing his blunder.

"See?" I smiled, lifting brows guilelessly. "If you had *learned* from the shodo, you'd have known better than to fall for that trick."

"This was not to be to the death," he hissed, dark color ebbing to gray. "I was hired to find you, *defeat* you—bring you back to Sabra!"

"Plans go awry." I beckoned with a triple snap of fingers. "Step into the circle."

The edges began to fray. "This isn't the way it's supposed to *be!*"

I hunched an idle shoulder. "Life often isn't, Nezbet. But then third-level sword-dancers *know* that already."

Elegant nostrils pinched. He flicked a white-rimmed glance at Osman, Mahoudin, and Hasaan slouched against the cantina. Then looked back at me. "You said—" Splotchy color stained his face. "You said—any man may refuse a dance."

"I said it. It's true. But generally the man who refuses is the chall-*enged,* not the challeng-*er;* it would be pointless—and somewhat foolish—if the challenger withdrew after begging for the dance." I shrugged again. "And a Shodo's Challenge, accepted, can never be renounced, or the skill level is lost, along with all the honor. Especially before witnesses." I flicked the blade in new light. "A man such as yourself—*third-*

level, no less!—would never do such a thing. It would besmirch his honor to even contemplate it."

Nezbet was gray. "I may renounce the terms."

"I don't think so." I squinted past him at the trio. "But if you like, you can put it before your friends. They might be talked into lying for your sake."

"Lying!"

"The circle codes," I mentioned, "say something about other sword-dancers bearing witness against a man who reneges on a proper challenge."

"But—" Nezbet ground teeth. "You *want* me to renounce it!"

"I don't care *what* you do." I lowered the sword a notch. "I'm a little busy, Nezbet—would you please make up your mind?"

Jaw muscles flexed violently. Then he tore off his burnous, ripped thongs loose on his sandals, jerked arms out of his harness. And stepped into the circle.

"Better," I commended, and put my sword down in the middle.

It surprised Nezbet. Some of the tension and desperation drained from eyes and body. "I thought—" But he didn't finish. Smiling faintly, he set his sword next to mine.

"Who's arbiter?" I asked. "Which of your friendly trio?"

He was, abruptly, magnanimous. "Let the woman do it."

"Del," I called.

Nezbet and I retreated directly opposite one another to the perimeter of the circle. We would run, scoop up sword, commence. A true Southron challenge, with footspeed part of the dance.

"Prepare," she said calmly.

Nezbet stared at me. He was swift, young, and

agile, vibrant with life, prepared to spring and snatch up the sword. He knew he could beat me. *Knew* he could beat me. I was old. Big. Slow.

And my knee could not have healed since our last confrontation.

Stupid Punja-mite.

Nezbet smiled.

"Dance," Del said.

Thirty

I wanted nothing more than to teach the boy a long, lazy lesson, beginning with sheer power and ending with endurance. But I didn't have the time.

So instead, I settled for speed.

He gaped inelegantly as I snatched up Samiel, hooked the tip beneath Nezbet's blade, and sent it sailing out of the circle before he could even reach it. Hands closed on sand. I pinned the left with a sword-tip, lending it just enough weight to sting.

I leaned down over the boy, who knelt out of awkward deference to the steel biting into his hand. "The woman beat you," I hissed. "What makes you think *I* can't?"

Nezbet called me a name.

The sword tip pricked more deeply. "That isn't very nice. Where'd you learn that kind of language?"

So of course he repeated it.

I lifted the tip from his hand, traced a steel path up a bare arm, tapped him repeatedly under the chin to add emphasis to each word. "Not nice at all."

"Chula," he spat. "Everyone knows the truth."

"*Do* they, now?" I rested the blade on his left ear.

"Can an earless man still hear gossip?" Now to the mouth. "Can a *tongueless* man repeat it?"

Black eyes glittered. "Jhihadi-killer. You have no honor left."

"No, I suppose I wouldn't—if it were true I'd killed the jhihadi. But we've had this discussion before, and I don't care to repeat myself." I took the sword away, indicated his. "There it is, Nezbet. Fetch it back, if you like . . . the dance has hardly begun."

A trickle of blood smeared the back of his left hand as he rose. "You would allow—?"

"I'm polite," I said lightly. "Jhihadi-killer or no, I remember the seven years I spent with my shodo, and all the lessons learned."

Stiffened jaw flexed. "You will say I have forfeited if I step out of the circle."

"Not if I give you permission. That's in the codes, too."

Nezbet jerked around to face the trio in the shade. "You hear him!" he called. "He permits me to retrieve my sword without forfeiting!"

Stupid, stupid Nezbet. Have you no sense at all? Have you no idea of what personal dignity and self-control are all about?

Stupid me for asking.

I put down my sword once again and went bare-handed to my side of the circle. My kidneys hurt like hoolies, I needed to eat something, and I wanted very badly to find a nightpot.

But first things first.

Nezbet came back with his sword, then paused just inside as he saw my relinquished blade. "But—again? To run?"

It wasn't required. We'd begun. It was most definitely out of place, but not disallowable.

"There." I pointed. "That was a bad start for you. Why not try again?"

He stared at me for a long moment, unable to read my intentions. Then, frowning, Nezbet slowly set his sword next to mine. Retreated to his side of the circle.

"Dance," Del said.

This time he reached his sword and actually picked it up. But by the time he did, I was waiting for him. Samiel's tip teased his throat.

I tongue-clucked sympathy. "Sorry, Nezbet. You must have slipped in the sand." I bent and put down my sword. "Let's try one more time."

One of Nezbet's friends stirred against the cantina wall. Osman, or Mahoudin, or Hasaan; I didn't know which. "Kill him," he suggested.

"I think he's trying," I said.

The other flashed a grin. "No, Sandtiger. I mean you should kill *him*."

"Ah." I looked at Nezbet. "I believe they're getting bored."

Nezbet, who had *not* put down his sword, lunged directly at me. Thereby forfeiting any shred of honor, but I don't think honor—or even victory—was on his mind anymore.

Now he wanted to kill.

The steel sang, arcing out of the rising sun. A black slash of blade, silhouetted against whitening light. I sidestepped slightly, caught the wrist and broke it, then hooked Nezbet's ankle and sat him on his rump.

Meanwhile catching his sword before it hit the sand.

I gazed down pitilessly on the stupid Punja-mite. "I hate repeating myself, but this time I think I will." I bent down close. "You're too stupid to kill."

Nezbet, shaking, was mute. And about time, too.

"Where is she?" I asked. "How far behind?"

The boy still said nothing. Tears of shock and humiliation welled in dark eyes.

"Where is she?" I repeated.

"Coming," he muttered. "She and all her men."

"How far behind?"

He shrugged. "A day, maybe. She rides like a man."

No time to waste. I fetched my own sword, then stepped out of the profaned circle and walked over to his friends. Osman. Mahoudin. Hasaan. Or maybe the other order. "Which of you is next?"

Three faces were very still. Then one of them smiled.

I tossed him Nezbet's sword. "Which one are you?"

"Mahoudin. Third-level." He handed the blade to the young sword-dancer next to him. *All* of them were young. "You do me honor, Sandtiger. But I have learned the lesson: any man may refuse a dance."

I looked at the next. "You?"

In silence, he shook his head.

"You." The third and final man.

"Hasaan," he said simply. "And the price is not enough."

"Oh?" I lifted brows. "Any price is enough if there is a level to be attained."

Hasaan demurred. "Death is not the level I aspire to."

"Hoolies, boy, I'm not about to *kill* you! How can you spread word of my deeds if your guts are all over the ground?"

White teeth shone briefly. "May the sun shine on your head."

"It is." I glanced up, judged the time, angled a shoulder away. "Another time, then. When the price is worth the risk."

Mahoudin briefly spread fingers against his heart. "You should have killed him. He's lost his sword, and honor—the circle is closed to him. What is there left to live for?"

I paused. "The chance to learn some sense."

The second—Osman?—shook his head. "You've made him borjuni. Better to have killed him."

"Nezbet made himself." I turned and walked away, heading for Delilah.

Behind me, three quiet voices, intended to be private: "Big," one of them murmured. "Strong," from another. Followed by the third, "*Fast* for a man so old."

You can't win for losing.

Riding. Again. Hurting, again. And Del noticed it.

"What's the matter?" She reined the mare a sideways step from the stud. "You look sort of—gray."

"Need to—stop—" I gritted.

Del pulled up at once. "Why didn't you say something?"

"Because—we needed—to *go*—"

"That was hours ago." She watched me in concern as I bent in half over the stud's neck. "What's *wrong?*"

"I just—need to get down . . . for a bit . . . something I should do—" I slid out of the saddle, managed to find the ground, hung onto the stud. "Walking, at the moment, is not my idea of entertainment . . . do you mind?"

Del stared blankly.

"Then watch," I muttered. "Right now, I don't much care."

"What do you—*oh.*"

Oh, indeed. I hung onto the stud and got my business done, swearing all the while. The results were as expected, with kidneys as sore as mine.

Once decent, I dragged myself back into the saddle. Del heard the creaking, the swearing, and turned back to face me. "What did they do to you?"

"Generally beat me up." I pressed a hand into my back. "Someone had big feet."

"We should find a place to stop and rest. At once."

I grunted. "We're in the middle of the Punja."

"There are oases, are there not? And settlements? And wells?"

I squinted. "No settlement close by. But water's not the problem. That can wait until tomorrow evening. Right now, we can't stop." I set the stud moving. "I don't trust Umir."

Del followed, clucking to the mare. "Surely he will not come so far. For me? So far into the Punja?"

"I got the feeling Umir would go anywhere he needed to, to *acquire* whatever he wants." I glanced at her. "You don't see yourself the way others do. You are—different. And that's what he collects."

"No one sees himself the way others do. You don't."

"No," I agreed sourly. "And not as Osman and Hasaan and Mahoudin do either, apparently."

Del was blank. "What do you mean?"

"Nothing." I slanted her a glance. "How do *you* see me?"

"Me?"

Echoing myself: "I don't mean the mare."

Del glared. Then it faded, replaced by thoughtfulness. "I see the underparts."

"The *what?*"

"Underparts." She chewed a lip, thinking, brows tangled together. "The things not on top."

I laughed, and scrubbed at my face. "I forget some-times—you are Northern, after all . . . the language is not the same."

"I am reminded of that, myself, when *you* some-times talk."

So bland. I nodded acknowledgment of the point. "So, what is this underpart you see? The things not on top."

"The man inside the skin."

Something cold tapped a fingernail against my spine. It nearly made me squirm. "What about the *outside?*"

Del frowned. "What do you mean?"

"Do I look—" I paused, "—different?"

"Of course."

Colder yet. "*How* different?"

"Not like anyone else.'"

"Del—"

"What do you think?" she asked indignantly. "You are taller than all Southroners, but not so tall as most Northerners. You are darker than me; than every Northerner, but not so dark as a *Southroner*. Your eyes are green, not blue or brown, or even the occa-sional gray. And you are brown-haired, not black-; *not* fair, either." She sighed. "Is this enough for you?"

"No."

She muttered in uplander. "Your nose, then."

"My *nose?*"

"It curves upside down."

"My nose is *upside down?*"

Expressions warred in her face as she fought for the best explanation. Finally she settled for example. "You have seen Abbu's nose."

"Abbu's has a notch in it. Abbu's was broken. Mine never was."

"But you can see what it was, Abbu's nose. And many others. All shaped like this." She hooked a finger downward, bowing the knuckle out.

I tested mine. "I don't have a hook."

"No. Yours is much straighter, though not as straight as some tribes I have seen. Yours is more like a Northerner's. And your cheeks are not so sharp, so arched." Del studied me. "We have discussed this before. You are both, and neither. There are things of the South in you, and also things of the North. Like a Borderer."

I nodded impatiently. "Do I look *real* to you?"

"Real!" She frowned. "You asked that before."

"Just—do I look real?"

Pale brows arched. "Do you mean to ask, are you the man of my dreams?"

"No!" I glared. "Can't you be serious?"

"Not at the moment," she murmured, and burst out laughing.

Which only goes to prove you can't *talk* to a woman.

Camp, such as it was, was established with little fanfare: two blankets spread on the ground, wadded—in *her* case, folded—burnouses for pillows. Nothing at all for a fire: we lay on our blankets and chewed steadily at dried cumfa. Staring up at the stars.

"You meant it," she murmured.

"Sometimes." I lay very still. It was better not to move.

"Earlier. About seeming real."

"Just wondered."

"If you were real?"

I thought about it deeply, eventually dredging up an answer. "You wouldn't understand."

"I promise not to laugh."

"Oh, I don't know . . . I enjoy hearing you laugh."

"So long as it's not at you." Del smiled at the sky. "Sometimes, there is cause." She rolled toward me, settling her head into a spread hand on the end of a braced arm. "Do you not feel real?"

"My kidneys convince me I am."

"Then you have proof. Pain means you are real."

"But—" I frowned, chewing violently on the last bite of cumfa. "I don't know anything about me. I have no past."

The amusement died in her eyes. "You have too much of a past."

"I don't mean that. I mean I have no history. Only an upside down nose, and color like a brown burnous left too many years in the sun."

"So do most Borderers. Look at Rhashad: he has *red* hair."

"I don't look anything like Rhashad."

"Most Borderers do not look like one another. The dye lots are always mixed." Del smiled. "I don't mean to tease. But you do not strike me as the kind of man to *need* a past. You make your own of the future."

That cut too close to bone. "They said the jhihadi was—*is*—a man of many parts."

Del's gaze sharpened. She stopped chewing cumfa.

I scratched a patch of bruise. "Nobody knows much about Iskandar, either."

"He died."

I counted. "It's been eight days."

"Since?—oh." Del shrugged. "I think you will out-live Iskandar's ten days."

"Not if Sabra has anything to say about it. Or maybe Umir. The Ruthless."

"They must catch you, first."

"Umir caught me."

"And you got free." Del's brow wrinkled. "*How* did you get free? You have told me nothing."

I shrugged. "Nothing to tell."

"But they beat you, and you got free."

"I wouldn't have, if I hadn't used—" I stopped.

Del waited. And then realization sharpened her gaze. She pushed herself upright. "Magic," she finished.

I heaved a heavy sigh. "The sorriest day of my life was getting involved with magic."

"But it got you free of Umir. You just said so."

"It's also got me lugging around an infested sword. One I didn't want in the first place, but *now* . . ." I sighed again, very tired, letting it go. "Hoolies, it's not important."

Del lay down again. "You humiliated him."

"Who? Oh. Him." I sucked a tooth. "Nezbet got what he deserved."

"You might have beaten him fairly."

"I *did* beat him fairly! I gave him a chance to quit before we started, and *two* chances to give up. What did you want me to do—cut off his head, like you did Ajani's?"

Her tone was flat. "No. But—"

"But? Did you *want* me to kill him?"

Del said nothing.

"*Did* you?" I persisted.

She sighed. "It seems to me you left him injured and angry and humiliated. Some people, with nothing but that to think on, come to trouble you later. They make bad enemies."

"*Nezbet?*"

"You don't know he wouldn't."

I snickered. "With enemies like Nezbet, I'll live forever."

"I heard them. What they said. A borjuni. Why?"

"Why did I make him one? Or how did it come to be?"

"Both."

"I didn't make him one. It was his choice. And he *made* that choice by relinquishing his honor, according to the codes." I dug a cumfa string from between two teeth. "You know about codes. You know about honor."

"Yes."

"When a shodo-trained sword-dancer knowingly relinquishes honor merely to win, or kill, he relinquishes himself. He exiles himself from the circle." I shrugged. "He doesn't *have* to become a borjuni. But I don't know of a single sword-dancer who would be content to raise goats, or scratch a crop from the Southron desert."

"There are other things."

"Caravan guard, yes. But caravan-serais prefer to hire the real thing, not a dishonored man. They can't be certain of his allegiance—what if he *was* a borjuni, and leading them into a trap?" I shook my head. "There is no greater, truer freedom than being a sword-dancer. And no greater dishonor than breaking the codes. It follows you for life, mocking you every day. Until all you can think to do is become a borjuni, because none of them care. They just want you to be like them: to kill quickly and effortlessly."

"And you made Nezbet one."

"Nezbet is young. Nezbet came from somewhere. He *could* petition to reapprentice, starting all over again—but if he's smart, he'll go back where he came from and forget about the circle. He wasn't suited for it."

"Is that why you broke his wrist?"

"No. Well, maybe. Mostly, I did it because I knew
I didn't have another chance to give him. If he'd tried
one more time, he might have succeeded."

Del grunted. "No."

I smiled. "Misplaced faith."

"You are the best I have ever seen."

"Except for Abbu?"

Silence.

"Well?" I prodded.

"Abbu is—good."

"Umir says he's the best."

Del rolled onto her side. "Do you listen to the word
of a man who would steal a woman?"

"A man's morals—or lack of —don't affect his judgment of *sword*-dancing."

She muttered something in uplander.

"Of course, he hasn't *seen* me dance. Only heard
about me." I paused. "I think."

"Vanity," she murmured. "Vanity—and pride."

I was tired, and sleepy. I rolled onto my side carefully, showing her my back. "You've got your own
share of both."

No answer.

I drifted, sliding toward the edge.

Then she touched my back, tracing the line of my
spine with a single soothing finger. "Real," she said
softly. "Am I not proof of that?"

"You?" I asked sleepily.

"I am not an afreet. If you were not real, what then
could share your bed *except* an afreet?"

I smiled into darkness. "How do I know you're not?
Your say-so? A bit biased, *I* would say."

The finger departed my spine. Then prodded a sore
spot gently. "If I were an afreet, I'd have neither pride
nor vanity."

I grunted. "Then I guess we're both real."

Del turned onto a hip, bumping against me. "Go to sleep."

"Stop nattering, then."

The night was filled with silence.

Unless I snored, of course.

Del swears I do. But *I* never hear it.

Thirty-one

Inside me, something—*rustled*. It rummaged around in my mind, stirring up old memories, and replaced them with its own.

It was Shaka. Shaka's fault. He twisted childhood truths and made them over into falsehoods, because he was jealous of me. Of the things I had learned to do. The magic I could wield.

The things I had learned to Make.

It was all Shaka's fault.

And my task to put it right—

I sat up, choking, and spat out a clot of—something.

Beside me, Del roused also, levering up on an elbow. "Are you all right?"

Breathing steadied. The world righted itself.

I looked at her, scratching at the stubble I hated. "—'m all right. Just got something caught in my throat." I hacked, cleared it, spat. "Sorry."

She scrutinized the morning. "Dawn," she announced. "We may as well get up. As you would say: we are burning daylight."

"Not yet. The sun's not even up."

"Close enough." Del moved over, knelt in sand,

began folding her blanket. "We should be on our way."

"We should," I agreed. "But that means I have to move."

The answering smile was crooked. "Can you not heal yourself again? Restore all your aching bones?"

I snorted in derision, then thought about the suggestion. If there was a chance I *could* do such a thing. . . . "Tempting," I agreed thoughtfully. "You know—"

But it was gone.

Just—*gone*.

Something else was in its place. Not a thought; a *lack* of thought. A sort of absence of anything.

Except for Chosa, knocking at my door; rapping on my gate; tapping at my soul.

Do it. *Do* it.

Do it NOW.

Oh, hoolies, bascha . . . he's here. He's back—

I squinched my eyes shut and willed him away. Willed him to go, to leave me alone. After all, there was only a little piece of him inside me. Tucked away somewhere. I was much bigger, much stronger.

If I concentrated on what Del had said, maybe I could give him the slip. If I tried what she suggested—

No.

I vividly recalled the last time I'd done it. Something flared, promising much; something else waited impatiently. Wanting me to do it, because then he would have power.

My belly rolled. I shivered away from the image. "I—don't think so. I think I'd probably better leave well enough alone."

"But if you can *do* such a thing . . ." She shrugged, going about her business. "Imagine what kind of legend you could become if no matter how badly you were injured in the circle, you came back the next day as good as you were before."

"Imagine," I muttered, massaging a stiff shoulder. "Imagine what else they might say—maybe call me a sorcerer?" I shook my head. "No thanks. I've already got a magical sword. I don't need a magical *me*."

Del began packing saddle-pouches. "I only meant you look like you hurt this morning. I just thought, if there were a way—"

"I know. But I don't want to—" I left it at that, biting off the end of the sentence I'd meant to say: "—risk it." No need to tell Del I felt odd, disoriented, and somehow unbalanced. Let her think I just didn't want to do it, period. Somehow it seemed safer.

I got up very slowly, moving in sections, biting my lip on curses. I was bruised and stiff and sore from the ambush by Umir's men. Kidneys were afire. "Right now I just want to take things slowly, and get on our way." I made my way toward the stud, who would provide a measure of privacy.

Del had to be content with what I was willing to give her. *I* had to be content with knowing something more: that Chosa wasn't gone. Chosa wasn't quiet. Chosa was growing *impatient*.

I slung an arm across the stud's brown rump and leaned, shutting my eyes. The bruises would fade, I knew. The pain would diminish. The kidneys would remember what it was to do their task without producing blood. But Chosa would remain.

And continue trying, with brute force and intricate subtlety, to leech me of my will until I had none left, so he could claim the body.

If I used any more magic, I gave him the means to

succeed. Because every bit I summoned, no matter
the intention, gave *him* that much to play with.

Chosa Dei, collector—much like Umir the Ruthless—who gathered all kinds of magic so he could
"melt" it down and remake it in his image.

As he would remake me.

Del tapped the mare a step away from the stud.
"How much farther to the oasis?"

I glanced around, squinting. "Not much farther.
Two or three hours."

"And then Rusali tomorrow?"

"Depending on how hard we want to push the
horses." I scrubbed the back of a hand across my
forehead. "And how hard we want to push ourselves."

Del's brows knitted as she assessed my expression.
"Is it your kidneys?"

I scowled. "Kidneys are fine."

"You're lying."

"Yes, well . . ." I shifted in the saddle. "Nothing a
little rest won't cure."

Her frown deepened. "We could stop for a while."

"Can't afford to stop," I said brusquely. "Our best
bet is to keep on going as long as we can, and put as
much room between Umir and us as we can."

"Yes, but—"

"Just *ride*," I snapped irritably. "We're wasting
time even discussing it."

Del offered no reply. She just shook up her reins
and rode on.

Time—blurred. I sat atop the stud, who pulled at
reins in irritation: he wanted to go after the mare, but
I was holding him back.

I didn't know why.

Del, ahead, twisted in the saddle to glance back. Frowned. "What's the matter?"

I wanted to tell her "nothing." But it wasn't the proper answer.

"Tiger?"

I just sat there, shivering.

Del turned the mare, heading her back toward me. Her tone sharpened abruptly. "Are you all right?"

No. I felt—thick. Heavy. My skin felt stretched and tight.

Inwardly, I asked it: *Is that you, Chosa?*

Inwardly, Chosa giggled.

Oh, hoolies. The sun hurt my eyes.

Del reined in the mare before the stud could quite reach her. Her assessment was intense. "What's wrong?"

Something cold ran down my spine. *Let her go*, Chosa suggested. *You don't need HER.*

"I don't—" I shook my head. "Nothing. Just—tired."

She swore between her teeth. "Do you think I am blind? Your color is terrible. You're sort of a greenish-gray, in between all the bruises."

Let her go, Chosa said. *Right now, I only want you.*

I wondered if maybe I should. He'd been very clear about wanting Del before, to collect the magic in her sword as well as Del herself. I knew it was safer if she was somewhere else, where he couldn't hurt her.

But how do I tell *her* that?

Del's voice was unrelenting. "There is a way, Tiger. You could call on the magic again."

No, bascha. I don't dare.

"It's *stupid* to ignore the chance to heal yourself. Why turn your back on a gift?" The tone grew more pointed. "And if you don't, you'll never make it across the Punja."

I gritted teeth. "I *said* I'm just tired. Sore. It'll pass, Del. I've had worse."

"Then why are you sitting here?"

I managed a lopsided grin. "It seemed the easiest thing to do."

Her jaw tightened. "I don't believe you. Not a bit."

"Too bad for you," I jeered.

Eyes flickered. Mouth tightened. "If you wish to be so foolish . . . very well. But if you need to stop, say so. The oasis is not so far."

I shivered. I felt—*swollen*. "Then let's go on."

Let her go, Chosa said. *I'm beginning to lose my patience.*

I tapped heels to the stud and let him go on with the mare.

Mistake, Chosa whispered. *I don't like mistakes.*

I shivered. But I kept riding.

Del's legs approached. Stopped before me. I saw them at knee level. It hurt too much to look up from where I sat slumped on the blanket.

"How much longer?" she asked tautly. A dropped bota slapped sand by the hand braced to support my arm, braced to support me. "It has been two days since the dance with Nezbet, three since Umir's attack, and you are worse."

Much worse. "I don't know," I mumbled.

Frustration and fear made her strident. "You can't even ride, Tiger! How are we to escape the threat you say is coming if you can't even ride?"

I tilted my head back, setting my jaw against the pain. "What in hoolies do you want me to do? Pray?

It'll pass, Del—I just got beat up worse than I thought. It'll pass."

Deep inside, Chosa gloated.

"Will it?" She squatted. Her face was a travesty, stretched tight and pale and thin, but the words were brutal. "The bruises are worsening—you are black and blue and swollen, because you are bleeding under the skin. And from the *inside,* also—do you think I haven't seen it when you spit?"

"So maybe a rib broke loose. . . ." I gathered myself, shifted. "Look, bascha—"

"*You* look!" she retorted. "If it goes on like this, you could die. Is that what you want? To fulfill Iskandar's fate, so everyone knows you really *are* the jhihadi?"

"I just need some time to heal. All this running . . ." I let it go, summoning the strength to stand. "All right—just give me a moment."

Del's voice was glacial, as it is when she is very angry—or very frightened. "You are still passing blood."

I stood exquisitely still, giving my body no reason to protest. "Because someone—or several someones— kicked and punched me in the kidneys," I rasped. "What in hoolies do you expect?"

"I have seen a man die from that."

I stopped testing things. "What?"

"I have seen a man die from it."

Anger flared, burning away what little strength remained. "There's *nothing I can do!*"

"You can tend to yourself," she said. "You have the magic—*use* it!"

It was all I could do to answer. "I told you why I won't."

"No, you didn't. You just said you won't. Nothing

more." Del stood up stiffly. Her face was tight and pale. "I think you've given up. I think you *want* to die."

I wavered on my feet. "Oh, in the name of—"

"So you can die as the jhihadi, and be better than Abbu that way."

"What?"

Her mouth was rigid. "He's only a sword-dancer. *You* are the jhihadi."

No, no, bascha—it's because I feel so bad.

But why tell her that?

"Del—"

"If you can't beat him in the circle, you will beat him in your death."

I managed a laugh. "You're sandsick."

"Am I?"

"Do you really think I want to *die* to prove myself better?"

"More," she said bitterly. "To prove yourself *more.*"

"Sandsick," I muttered. Hoolies, couldn't the woman see I just needed to rest? To lie down again, and sleep, and *rest,* and let the body recover?

Let her go, Chosa said. *For now, I only need you. She will come later.*

It was easier to give in. "Go on," I croaked. "If you feel that strongly . . . look, I need to rest. Go on to the oasis. I can catch up later."

Clearly, it surprised her. "I don't want that. I want us *both*—"

"Go on. You. Go on."

"The oasis isn't much farther. You can reach it, *then* rest."

"Go on without me. I'll catch up."

The line of her shoulders was impossibly taut. "If you would simply use the magic . . ." She gritted teeth. "You only refuse because you hate it so much. Because you won't admit you need more than yourself."

I laughed once. Sat down very carefully. Tented my knees and rested my brow against them. "You don't understand at all—you have no idea what kind of toll magic takes—"

Self-control frayed. "It makes you sick," she snapped. "So? Too much aqivi does the same, but that does not dissuade you."

I mumbled something against my thighs.

Del swore. I heard her walk smartly through the sand, pause—muttering—then come back again. "I *will* go," she declared. Part threat. Part plea. But also a familiar conviction I knew better than to dismiss.

I dragged my head up. Something deep inside me flared from apathy into fear.

Del's face was cold as ice. Blue eyes glittered. She spat it out all at once, almost sing-song, acquiring determination with every syllable. "You have given me leave, though I take it anyway. And so I say this: If you will do nothing—if you make no attempt to *try*—then I will not stay here to see it. The death of the jhihadi will have no witnesses. And so his body will be consumed by the Punja until only bones are left, and they will be scoured in time, and carried away, and scattered unto dust . . . until there is nothing left. No jhihadi. No sword-dancer. And nothing at all of Tiger."

Stung, I applied a rather uncomplimentary term to her.

"Yes," Del agreed, and marched away to the mare.

I watched her go. I watched her saddle the mare; split the botas, leaving me half; then mount. She reined the mare up short. "I will be at the oasis until dawn. If you are not there by then, I go on."

She didn't mean it. I knew she didn't mean it.

Del's face twisted briefly. Then she spun the mare and left.

I watched Del *go*.

"Hoolies," I croaked, "she *meant* it."

Sand drifted in her passage, dusting me with grit.

Dull anger flared anew. "She's only doing this to make me come after her."

Of course she was. She'd tried everything else.

Anger died to ash. No one—and nothing—answered. Inside me, Chosa was silent.

There is a time to set pride aside. I sighed deeply, nodding. "All right, bascha . . . I'm coming." I pressed myself to my knees, prepared to try for my feet.

The world turned upside down, spilling me like meal.

Fear punched into my belly: what if I *couldn't* reach her?

"Wait—" I rasped. "Del—don't go *yet*—"

But Del, meaning well, was already gone.

Chosa Dei was not.

Fear faded. Replacing it was a dull, colorless surprise, that Chosa could do so much when I wasn't even looking.

"Punja-mite," I croaked.

It occurred to me to wonder, as I sprawled across the blanket, if Shaka Obre's construct was coming apart at the seams. Unraveling from inside out, because Chosa was cutting into pieces the fabric of my begetting.

"Iskandar," I muttered. "Is this how it happened with you?"

*   *   *

Hands. They invaded burnous, belt, unbuckling and stripping away. A hand lingered on my rib cage, then withdrew.

"Dead," a man said.

"Or dying," said another.

Then a voice I knew. "Take the horse and the sword, and any coin he might have. Leave the rest for Sabra. I don't care about him. I just want the woman."

Tentatively: "He is—the Sandtiger."

Umir, impatient: "What do I care about that? He's not worthy of my collection."

No. Abbu was.

Hands again. The belt was yanked from under me, leaving me bare from chest to dhoti. Coppers rattled briefly; someone cursed. If I could have, I would have smiled: a nearly empty pouch. Small pickings from the legend.

Sound: movement. A hand at my throat, grasping sandtiger claws. "Leave that," Umir ordered. "We want to make certain Sabra knows who he was."

"There is his face," someone said. "The scars . . ."

"Vermin may eat his face—and the *rest* of him— before Sabra arrives. Leave the necklet. Abbu Bensir himself may choose to make it a keepsake."

Abbu? Abbu—with Sabra?

"Water." Another voice.

"Put it on the horse. We'll take it all." Umir strode away. "Waste no more time recalling legends. His is finished now, and I want the woman."

I heard the stud snort. Then the urgent, rumbling nicker that wasn't greeting, but warning. Southron voices called out. Then the stud screamed. Then a man did.

Ah. Good boy.

Voices, gabbling about the stud. He had crushed a man's head.

"Leave him," Umir snapped. "You won't get close to him now."

Someone by me, bending. He picked up the harness, the scabbard. Paused. Through sealed lids, I could see it: The man looking upon it. The legendary sword. His hand so very close—why not unsheathe the blade and see what the balance is like? The *Sandtiger's* sword—

He screamed. Long and loud and horrified, as the magic ate into his bones.

Stupid Punja-mite.

Gabbling again, all around me. The man still screamed.

"Kill him," Umir said. "I will not have such noise."

In a moment, the screaming stopped.

Silence. A gathering of others as they contemplated the sword.

"Pick it up," Umir ordered.

One man protested that it was a magicked blade, and no one knew the spell.

"Pick it up," Umir repeated. "Use something to shield yourself—here, use the blanket."

They ripped it from under me, spilling limbs and head awry. Stupid Punja-mite. A *blanket* against Samiel?

A second man shrieked, called on his (deaf) god, then fell into sobbing. Dispassionately, Umir the Ruthless ordered him killed, too, because he did not like the noise.

"Leave it," he said curtly. "Magicked blade it may be, but I won't lose the woman. If no one can pick it up, it will be here when we return."

"But—what if Sabra herself—?"

Umir laughed. "Let us hope she tries. A woman has no business attempting to rule in a man's stead."

Retreat. Horses remounted. Men riding off.

I lay slack-limbed on the sand and wondered if it was worth it.

Maybe *I* wasn't. But Del was worth everything.

The merest breath of sound hissed through dry, unmoving lips. "Chosa?" I whispered.

Inside me, something rustled. Then flared into life, gibbering exaltation: the battle had been won.

Now there was the war.

"Ah, hoolies," I mumbled, "I *really* don't want to do this."

Thirty-two

I hunched beside the sword: obscene, unintended obeisance. But my bones were so brittle I expected them to shatter and crumble into dust even inside my living flesh.

Mottled, discolored flesh, but living nonetheless.

I stretched out a hand. Fingers trembled. The nails were bluish again; the forearms streaky black, tinged with violet, outlined luridly with traceries of yellow. What had begun as normal—if painful—bruising had spread to swallow me whole. The skin was puffy and squishy, swollen by leaking fluid.

Hoolies, I was a mess. No wonder Del got mad.

Because she was scared, too.

Pain centered in the small of my back. Fire burned brilliantly, climbing the length of my spine, then out along each of the ribs to curve around my chest and meet at the breastbone, where more pain lived. My whole body was a pyre.

Time to put it out.

The sword lay bare in the sand. I was very grateful; had Umir's man dropped it *in* its sheath, someone could have picked it up and carried it away. The blanket was no shield—nor anything else so plain—but the runes worked into the leather muted the weapon's bite. While sheathed in my harness, touching only the straps or scabbard, anyone could steal it.

"—song—" I croaked. "Hoolies, I hate singing—"

I wavered, nearly fell. I'd made no promises to Chosa—wouldn't keep them anyway—and he knew it well. He was taking no chances. By summoning the healing, I opened the door for him. And he would try to snatch it and tear it away from the wall, rushing in to fill the room that doubled as my body.

I didn't like the risk. I didn't like it at all.

But Umir was after *Del*.

I summoned my little song. Croaked it into the day. Reached down and caught the sword, then dragged it into my lap.

—circle, Tiger. Don't forget the circle—

Inside me, Chosa stirred.

He'd wanted me to forget.

On knees and one hand, I swung-dragged the tip of the sword in a ragged circle, taking care to seal the ends together. There could be no break, no crack in the drawn line, or Chosa would find and use it.

Circle. I hunched within the confines, cradling the sword, and sang my little song.

What a waste of—

Power reached out and caught me. It shook me from head to toe, rattling every bone, then threw me down again.

Belly climbed up my gullet. Chosa, crawling out?

"—sick—" I gulped. "—worse than aqivi—"

Every bone was wracked, twisting in sockets, pulling free of tendons.

"—wait—"

Blood broke from my nose.

"I take it back—" I mumbled. "—don't want it after
all—"

Power dug into my hair and jerked my head up
straight. I have a tough scalp, but this was too much.

"—s-ss*stop*—"

The sword glowed dully black. Inside me, Chosa
answered.

I panted. Labored to swallow. Twitched from Chosa's touch, sensing his invasion. Tried to shut it—
him—off, to deny him entrance.

But trying to deny Chosa also denied the magic.

Power had no patience. I'd sent it an invitation, and
it was bringing friends.

"I *take it back*—" I shouted. "Forget I said anyth—"

Power bent very low and looked into my eyes, as if
to judge the truth. As if to judge *me*.

"I'm just—a sword-dancer. . . ."

Power disagreed. It dangled me from its hand, as
Umir had dangled the runes.

Blood ran down my chin. I lacked the strength to
wipe it away; to do anything but breathe.

Hoolies, what have I done? What have I unleashed?

So much for the binding circle.

But it was meant to keep Chosa *in*, not keep Power
out.

And who would even try?

"I just—need—to be better . . . to go—and help
Delilah—"

The little piece of Chosa played hop-rock with my
heartbeat. It waxed and waned, like the moon.

The spasm wracked my body. Power shook me
again. Then released my hair.

The sword spilled from lax hands and out of elbow
crooks. I fell on top of it.

The edge snicked into one arm, shaving hair from

flesh. All I could do was laugh, stirring dust and sand with my breath.

Then the laughter died.

Because Chosa was very angry.

Chosa would take his revenge, one way or another.

I lay in the sand, on the sword. Wondering what in hoolies I was.

Wondering what I could *do*.

And what Chosa Dei would try.

Oasis. Near dusk, with the sun painting everything orange. Palm trees in sharp silhouette sprouted haphazardly, dangling beards and dates. Below, around the water, ranged Umir and his men.

One body lay on the ground, with a fallen sword nearby. I wondered if Del had killed him; or Umir, for his noise.

She stood on foot, and braced, with naked blade in her hands. Blood ran down the steel, regulated by runes, carried off the hilt before it could stain her hands. Although some would argue the stain was on her soul.

Umir, I realized, was hampered by his greed, as well as his upbringing. He wanted her unscathed, unharmed, for addition to his collection. No matter how unique her vocation, she *was* a woman, and he a Southroner. He certainly hadn't reckoned on Del herself taking steps to refuse him so violently.

It was almost laughable. But nobody was laughing.

I reined up quietly before anyone noticed me, putting Umir and his men between Del and me. They outnumbered us, but we had the major advantage. Umir wanted her whole. Del and I were not so picky with regard to Umir's men.

She looked past them. Saw me. Didn't so much as

flick an eyelash. Returned her attention to Umir before anyone even noticed.

I began to smile, anticipating the surprise, the overwhelming shock . . then the stud took a hand in the game by whinnying imperatively to the mare, who answered with shrill welcome.

"Hoolies," I muttered, disgusted, and yanked the sword free of sheath as Umir and company whirled, swordblades glinting in sunset.

Mouths dropped open, gaping. Widened eyes displayed whites. Someone muttered a prayer to the god of apparitions.

Umir the Ruthless just scowled.

A flutter of pleasure tautened my belly. I leaned forward with grave deliberation, perfectly at ease; perfectly prepared. "Someone," I said lightly, "has my belt and my money. Care to give them back?"

"Kill him," Umir ordered.

Nobody moved a muscle. Until one man did just barely, dropping belt and pouch.

I grinned. I knew very well what I looked like: me. *Me* me, which all on its own can be rather threatening, since I have practiced for many years. The legend in the flesh—firm, swift, *dangerous* flesh—not the puffy, mottled, discolored body Umir's men had discovered. "Dead, am I?" I asked. "*Near* dead, maybe? Or maybe neither one, merely the deviser of a trap—or of great and powerful magic."

And for once I wasn't lying.

Well, half, maybe. It had never been a trap, but why tell them that?

Umir's men stirred. But no one obeyed his repeated order to kill me. Who could kill a man who was already dead?

I waggled the naked blade. "Anyone else care to take my sword? I think he's still hungry."

"Fools," Umir snapped. "He's a man like any of you. Don't let him goad you—*kill* him!"

"Go home," I said softly, "before I lose my temper."

Umir's men went home. Or *some*where; nonetheless, they all departed, making ward-signs against great magic. Leaving Umir by himself.

I walked the stud up to him, slowly and purposefully. Flicked a glance at Del. Then pinned Umir with a stare. "You made three mistakes," I explained. "First, you bound me with magic, and challenged me to escape. Second, you left me for dead, which I consider an insult. You wouldn't do that to *Abbu*."

Umir, eloquently unruffled, folded his hands in wide, gem-weighted sleeves. "What is the third?"

I pointed with the blade. "You discounted *her*."

He didn't even look. "Perhaps I underestimated you. Perhaps you *are* better than Abbu Bensir, and perhaps I *should* reconsider."

I grinned. "That's better." A glance at Del. "Do you want to kill him?"

She hunched a shoulder. "I've killed one man today. Another would be surfeit."

I nodded as she bent to clean her blade on the dead man's burnous. "Then I will tend to it."

Umir paled, but only slightly. "I could have killed you twice. I left you the chance to escape . . . and both times you succeeded."

"And I'll leave *you* a chance." I sheathed the sword with a snap, jumped off the stud, approached Umir the Ruthless. "Your hands," I said gently.

Thin lips smiled. "You must take what you will have."

"All right." I caught his wrists, squeezed; hands spasmed rigidly as he gasped, and stabbed out of the heavy sleeves. Still squeezing, I made him sit. Then shut the wrists in one large hand, drew my knife with the other, nicked him to free the blood.

Umir grayed. "Do you mean me to *bleed* to death?"

"I don't mean you to do anything, except sit here." I shot the knife home again, then carefully smeared blood all over both wrists. "Nice bracelets," I commented. "Now, a little piece of advice . . ."

Umir's lips were pale. "What do you—?" He winced.

Del came over. She stood next to me and watched, one hand gripping her sword. I heard her indrawn breath.

"There." I released his wrists. Both were bound tightly by thick, twined ropes of rune-wrought blood, red-black in the setting sun. "Now, for that advice . . ." I leaned down close to Umir. *"Never annoy a man whose magic is greater than yours."*

Thirty-three

"Come on," I said to Del. "No need to stay here."

She stared after me as I turned back to the stud. I swung up smoothly, gathered reins, saw the tension in her shoulders; the questions in her eyes. But she asked none of them, because she knew better: you do not put even a small weapon into the hands of the enemy. She simply sheathed her newly-cleaned blade and went to her own mount.

Umir's mouth opened. "You're leaving?"

I shrugged as the stud danced, wanting to go to the mare. "No reason to stay. I don't like the company."

"But—" He lifted his blood-bound hands. "What about this?"

"Good color on you." I angled the stud southerly, discussing matters through reins. "You ought to make it a habit."

"You can't *leave* me here!"

"Of course I can. You have water, don't you?— right there in the basin. Binding your hands doesn't mean you can't drink. As for food, well . . ." I shrugged, bunching the stud under me. "Guess you'll just have to wait for Sabra."

"But—" He broke it off.

I took a deeper seat in the saddle and stilled the stud deftly, leaning forward toward Umir. "Unless you've lied. Unless she isn't coming at all."

Indecision warped his features. Then grimness settled. "She's coming," he said flatly. "From Iskandar to Julah. She will have left Quumi by now."

"Good. She can feed you when she gets here." The stud danced again as I gave him rein and glanced at Del. "You ready?"

Mutely, she nodded.

"Good. Then let's ride. We're burning the last little bit of daylight." But even as Del rode off, I reined the stud back once more. He didn't like it a bit, snorting and tossing his head. "Umir," I said quietly, "I wouldn't struggle too much. Those runes won't strangle you, but they might cut off your hands."

Umir sat very still.

I turned the stud loose and went after Del, laughing into the stud-born wind.

The amusement was short-lived. Del, as expected, did not allow me to get very far before taxing me with questions. The trouble was, she had too many, even for *her* mouth; she started out fine, but ended up in a Northern tangle.

"Start over," I suggested.

Del stared at me hard, teeth clenched. "*You* start," she ordered.

"I didn't die." I arched eyebrows at her expression. "I did what you wanted me to, so why are you complaining?"

Teeth remained clenched. "Because you might have done it *before*."

"Before what? Umir's arrival? Hoolies, it worked out very well. Now his men are hightailing it back to Quumi telling tales of a Sandtiger fetch . . . should add something to the legend, and save us a bit of hide."

"How?"

"Some would-be captors may decide not to try their luck."

She thought about it. "But you felt it was necessary to drive me away—"

"No." The humor died. "I felt it necessary to give nothing to Chosa Dei. *That* is why I refused to summon the magic again."

She stared angrily, weighing the truth. Assessing my expression; the sincerity of my tone. Her expression eventually softened, but doubt remained paramount. "But you *did* summon it."

"Yes. But not for me."

"If it was such a risk, as you say, then why—?" She let it die. Realization blanched her pale as her hair, plaited off her face. "But not for you," she said numbly.

I did not pursue that topic. "As for why I wanted us to leave Umir where he was, and in such haste, it's because I don't know how long in hoolies those rune-ropes will last. For all I know, he's already loose."

Brows lanced down. "How did you do that? How did you make them? What did you do to him?"

"Borrowed a little trick from Chosa Dei."

Del jerked the mare to a halt. She is not ordinarily heavy-handed, and the mare has a soft mouth. Gape-mouthed, the mare stopped, dark eyes rolling. I also reined in the stud. "What have you done?" Del asked. Her eyes searched my face. "What have you done to yourself?"

I shrugged.

Pupils spread in blue eyes, altering them to black. She studied everything in my face with avid intensity.

Then some of the tension faded. Now she looked for something else; for a different kind of truth. "Umir's men didn't kill you because they thought you were dead already. That's why you scared them off."

I shrugged again. "Close enough."

It clearly unsettled her. "Did you fail to come after me because of pride? Or because you *couldn't?*"

I grinned. "Close enough." But I wasn't as good as I'd hoped. Blood drained from her face. The look in her eye scared me. "I wouldn't have—*died,*" I told her hastily. "Not from Chosa's devising. *Umir's* men might have killed me, but Chosa wouldn't have. He wants the body too much."

Her voice was oddly toneless. "If he had won, you wouldn't be Tiger anymore."

I twisted shoulders. "Probably not."

Del swallowed tightly. "I left you to force your hand."

"I know that."

"I thought you would come."

"I know that, too."

"But you might have died, anyway . . . because you *couldn't* come." Del's expression was despairing. "What have I done to you?"

"Nothing." I tapped heels to the stud. "It's done, Del. None of this matters because I'm all healed and I'm still me."

"Are you?"

I arched a single brow. "I'll prove it to you later."

She didn't smile at the suggestive tone. "Tiger—"

I sighed. "I just learned a couple of tricks."

"Did *he?*" she demanded as I rode by the mare. "Did Chosa learn tricks, too?"

I shook my head, jerking the stud's back around as he looked for the mare. "He already knows them all."

*   *   *

It was a cool, soft night, and we treated it as such. I lay on my back, contemplating the stars and moon, slack-limbed in satiation. I was bare except for the dhoti, the dampness of exertion drying slowly on my body. I felt wondrously relaxed, gazing sleepily at the sky, but Del was wide awake. I never have understood how a woman, thoroughly satisfied, wants to discuss the state of the world, while I'd just as soon let the world drift right on by, taking me with it.

Her thigh was stuck to mine, as was a shoulder blade angled slightly against my chest. Del unstuck us both by rolling onto a hip, dragging her burnous to drape across exquisitely long, bare legs, as well as the hips and taut rump above them. Pale hair was loose and tousled: silver beacon in the darkness.

"What are you thinking about?"

Hoolies. They always ask.

I contemplated lying. But Del was not overly romantic—not like most other women—and the truth would not disturb her. "About Abbu."

She stiffened. "Abbu Bensir? *Now?*"

Maybe she wanted less truth after all. "Just—never mind."

But she went slack again. One hand touched my chest and began counting scars. It was a habit of hers, to which I never objected, because her touch felt good. "You want to beat him *so* badly."

"Didn't used to." I pillowed my head on one bent arm. "Well, that's not entirely true—I've *always* wanted to beat him—but it never mattered so much before."

"And now it does, because of what Umir said?"

"Umir says whatever he thinks will get him what he

wants." I scowled faintly, considering. "I think it has more to do with Sabra."

"Why? You know nothing about her."

"I know something. I know she's a woman tanzeer, and she's managed to hold her place."

"It won't last. You've said so."

"It won't. But if Abbu is riding with her, after telling us he wasn't . . ." I freed a pale ribbon of hair as it tangled in my necklet. "He is not the kind to lie."

Del shrugged, still counting scars. "Perhaps he changed his mind later. Perhaps Sabra convinced him."

"Nor is he the kind to be won by a woman's blandishments."

"You don't know that. Have you ever slept with him?"

I grunted. "Do I seem like the kind?"

"One should not judge." Del's voice was languorous. "I only mean that many men will do many things, depending on a bedding."

"You sound uncommonly knowledgeable."

"*You* know better than that."

"I only know what you've told me."

She considered getting testy but discarded it out of apathy. "I say again, men can be persuaded of many different things."

"I never thought of Abbu as a man to be bought by a bedding." I paused. "Nor *myself*, I might add."

"I have too little coin." Del shifted closer. "If she is a beautiful woman, he may have been persuaded to take up her cause. Or for the other reason."

"What other reason?"

"The chance to dance against you. He wanted it in Iskandar, before the stud kicked you in the head."

I smiled. "Maybe he weighs himself against my reputation."

"As you do against his?"

I shrugged. "Maybe."

"*Yes.*"

I gave in. "Yes."

"Well, I think this will be settled between you one day. Perhaps not for years, but one day." Her fingers found and stilled on the fist-deep, fibrous fissure carved below the short ribs on the left side of my chest. I could barely feel the pressure through the whorls of scar tissue. "I'm sorry," she whispered.

She said it every time. Meant it every time. And every time recalled how she'd very nearly killed me, in the circle on Staal-Ysta.

"Could have been worse," I said. "Could have been—*lower*—" I rolled over and atop her, crooking a leg across her hips, "—and then we'd *both* be sorry."

Del's laugh is smoke. It curled its way around me and drifted into the night.

When I am with this woman, the doubts all spill away. Because even if I am *not* real, at least I have this much.

Thirty-four

Ice, all around. Wreaths of it, riming rocks, glittering in saffron sunlight; in the warmth of a Southron day—

Wait, I said to myself. Ice? In the South?

Even deep in sleep, I knew better than that.

Which, of course, woke me up.

Del rolled over as I pushed myself upright and scowled fiercely into morning. A hand through tousled hair did nothing to rid myself of the afterimage, nor did a violent rubbing of squinting, sleep-begummed eyes. The impression was very clear: ice, in the South.

"Must be sandsick," I muttered, and reached for the nearest bota.

Del yawned, stretched, squinched up her face against pale new sunlight, peering at me one-eyed. "Why?"

I shrugged, sucking water.

The other blue eye came open. "I don't necessarily disagree, but I am curious as to why *you* would say so."

I swallowed and lowered the bota. "One need not explain one's dreams if one does not desire it."

"Ah." She put out a hand for the bota. "Unless one is the jhihadi."

"Jhihadis don't need to explain themselves, either. Jhihadis just—are."

"Like the Sandtiger."

"Yet more proof." I stripped aside blankets, stood up. I felt amazingly good for a man taken to task by a certain unspecified power, and later left for dead in the midst of the Punja. I felt *intensely* good—

And then recalled how I'd been healed, or remade, or whatever you want to call it.

Which meant the *real* me was just as battered and bruised, and no younger than before.

Or whatever me I was.

Scowling, I looked down at Del. "How was I last night?"

Pale brows shot up. Del blinked feigned astonishment at me. I realized her interpretation of the question, in view of the intimacy we'd shared, was not to be unexpected.

I rephrased it, waving a hand. "Not that. I don't need reassurances about *that*. I just meant . . ." I trailed off. "I'm not doing this very well."

Del, somewhat bemused, slid a foot into one sandal and began lacing the cross-garter thongs to her knees. "What are you trying to say? Or ask? Or—whatever?"

"Did I seem—*real*—to you?"

A number of expressions took turns upon her face. Amusement, curiosity, bafflement; also a flicker of uncertainty. At last, as she looked up at me, an unfamiliar tranquillity, as if she knew how much her answer meant, and was pleased to be utterly honest. "Indisputably."

I didn't let up; not yet. "You never doubted for once it was me?"

She stopped knotting sandal laces. "*Should* I have?"

"No. I don't think so. I mean, I felt like me to *me*."

I scratched viciously at stubble. "Never mind. I just—never mind."

"Tiger." Del finished the knot and smiled up at me. Fair hair curtained shoulders. "You were as you always are. I have no complaints. I doubt Elamain would, either . . . or any of the other thousands of women who've shared a night with you."

No, Elamain had never had any complaints, before she nearly got me castrated. Neither had any of the other women (not *thousands;* Del exaggerated), but I wasn't really concerned about them. What concerned me was that Del might—or might not—see any kind of *difference* in me. Anything that might indicate I was something of Shaka Obre, with a bit of Chosa, as well.

I felt like the same old me. But the same old me was—who?

"Sandsick," I muttered again, and went off to water the dirt.

Del's purposefully idle tone drifted in my wake. "And men say *women* are fanciful."

Which is because they are.

But I was a bit too busy to explain it to her.

Rusali was much as we'd left it, which was a year or so before. A typical Southron town. A typical *Punja* town in a typical Punja domain—except when we'd left it, its tanzeer was newly dead because a Northern sword-dancer had killed him in order to requench a *jivatma*.

Not Del. Theron. Who'd come hunting her for the death of the *an-kaidin* Baldur, whom Del had killed to blood her blade.

In hindsight, the explanation for both of them sounded similar. But Del's situation had been different. Theron had *re*quenched against all Northern taboos, in order to gain an edge. Lahamu, Rusali's tanzeer, dabbled a bit in magic, and had some experience with sword-dancing techniques. Theron decided to requench in order to have a better chance against Del in the circle, because by requenching in Lahamu he gained the Southron style, which she didn't know.

He'd nearly beaten her, too, but I'd figured out something was wrong and forcibly pulled Del from the circle. Ordinarily it would have forfeited the dance to Theron, but Del had quickly realized what he'd done. Theron's transgression made the dance invalid, except I'd decided, on my own, to teach him a lesson.

And I had. I'd killed him.

Meanwhile discovering just what it was to wield a *jivatma*, when one knows its name.

Ah, yes. Theron. Brother to Telek, son to old Stigand; both of whom, on Staal-Ysta, had conspired first to exile Del, then to kill us both by playing one against the other in the deadliest dance of all, because each of us wanted—*needed*—to win: Del, to gain a year with her daughter; me to win back my freedom from an oath-sworn, binding service Del had tricked me into.

Hoolies, so much had happened. Look at us *now*.

Look at *me* now.

Then again, don't. You might see something neither one of us likes.

Rusali. Empty of Lahamu, but also now of Alric, transplanted Northern sword-dancer, and Lena, his Southron wife, and all their mixed-blood girls.

We rode through the haphazard outskirts and into the city proper. Del was strangely bemused. "What?" I asked.

"Remembering," she answered. "We barely knew each other then . . . look at us now."

It echoed my own thought. Glumly, I said, "Now we know too much."

She smiled. "Sometimes."

"Then, again, there's a lot I don't know about you—and a lot you don't know about me."

That earned me a sidelong glance. "That may be— but there's a lot about you that *you* don't know."

I grunted. "I know enough."

"Then why do you keep asking me if I think you're real?"

I reined the stud around an overturned basket spilling refuse into the narrow, dusty street. "Don't you ever wonder if *you're* not real?"

"No."

I ducked a low-hanging awning, bumping left knee against Del's right as the narrowing of the street squeezed us closer together. "You never once wondered if maybe you weren't some sort of—construct?"

"Construct?"

I groped for the best explanation. "A conjured person. A *magicked* person, created by sorcery for a particular purpose." Like changing the sand to grass?

Del frowned. "No. Why would I?"

I tried to figure out the easiest way of explaining, without really explaining. "Didn't you think, when you realized how good you could be with the sword, that maybe you were something out of the ordinary?"

Del smiled faintly. "My kinfolk *always* told me I was out of the ordinary."

I scowled. "That's not what I mean. I mean—when you knew, in your heart, you were better than everybody. Did you think there might be a reason?"

Brows quirked upward. "Better than *every*body?"

"Well, not me. That hasn't been established."

She laughed softly. "No, I never wondered. When

I was young, and my brothers and uncles and father began to teach me weaponry, it was simply something to do. Everyone else did it. My mother had the great good sense not to forbid me the chance, and the other women had the great good sense not to criticize my mother for that. And when, on Staal-Ysta, I knew I could be *this* good—well . . ." The tone died out. When it resumed, the inflection had altered from idle recollection to grim acknowledgment. "By then, I merely wanted to be as good as was required to do what I had to do, in order to destroy Ajani. I did not think again on anything else, nor to question the good fortune that gifted me with the skill."

"Oh," I said at last.

"So no, I never wondered if I was a—construct?" She waited for my nod. "I have always been what I am. What I was required to be."

I said nothing. It had never occurred to me, either, until I squatted before the old hustapha and thought, for the first time, that all the natter about jhihadis and sand and grass might have some foundation in fact.

I shivered uneasily. Felt the weight of *jivatma* across my back, and the sorcerer it housed.

We took a room in a small, mostly empty inn whose proprietor was so glad for the custom that he gave us his very best. Which didn't mean much, really, but at least the bed was longer. For once my heels hit the end of the frame, instead of hanging over the edge.

Del knelt on the packed dirt floor and sorted out botas, untangling thongs from saddle-pouch buckles. "We can't stay long."

"Overnight." I loosened a knot in one of my sandal laces. "We can pick up provisions now, or wait until morning."

"I'll go now. You can bathe first." She rose, settling pouches beside me on the bed. "Assuming you *want* to bathe."

"And *I* assume, by your tone of voice, you think I should."

Del smiled. "Yes." And walked toward the curtain door.

"Where are you going?"

Elaborate clarity: "To buy provisions; I said so."

"We can do that together."

She shrugged. "No need. I'll be back by the time you're done, and use your water."

All in all I thought it somewhat odd. While Del was perfectly capable of provisioning us on her own, we usually did it together simply to make things easier. But I saw no reason to protest. Maybe she needed time to herself; women are like that.

Especially when they spend money.

My turn to shrug. "All right. If I'm not in here, I'll be in the common room."

"Sucking down aqivi; where else?" Del pulled aside the tattered fabric curtaining the door and was gone.

I ordered a bath brought in; the proprietor acquiesced by rolling in a warped half-cask, then lugging in buckets of water. Not many; not enough. But it was better than nothing. There were bathhouses in Rusali, but with them there's no telling how many bodies the water's washed. At least this way Del got mine, and me she already knew.

Not enough soap, either, but I made do, and left enough for Del. Then I took my freshly washed self into the common room, where I ordered aqivi, and spent some time drinking it.

Del eventually came back bearing burdens, nodded at me, then disappeared into our room. I contemplated wandering in to witness her bath, then decided she might not get bathed at all, in view of what sometimes happened when she was bare of clothes and wet, and stayed where I was. Drinking.

The aqivi ran out. I didn't order more. I went in to see what in hoolies was taking Del so long.

She sat with her back to me, swathed in a hooded burnous. I opened my mouth to ask her what in hoolies she was doing, when she turned, startled, and stared wide-eyed.

Struck dumb, I stared back. We neither of us moved.

All I saw were blue eyes. The bluest, brightest eyes. They were her same old eyes, with the same old color and clarity, but everything else was different.

I managed at last to speak. "What have you done to yourself?"

Her answer was very forceful, as if she tried to convince herself as well as me. "Made myself someone else."

I moved, finally. Stopped beside the bed. Put out a tentative hand and pushed the hood from head to shoulders. "All of it?"

Del arched a dyed-black eyebrow. "Blonde *and* black hair would make me even more obvious than I already was."

"But—I like you blonde."

She scowled. "It will wash out."

"What about this?" I touched one darkened cheek.

"That, too." A black-haired, dark-skinned Del, glowering, was oddly different from the usual fairer version, even with the same expression. "Do I look very Southron?"

"Not with *those* eyes."

She put a hand up, then let it drop back. "I'm a Borderer."

"Hah."

"You will say so, of course."

I studied her. Formerly white-blonde hair, sun-bleached, was now a dull black, still wet and slick. Darkened eyebrows were more pronounced, harshening her expression, and she'd even tipped eyelashes. The skin was a uniform brown several shades lighter than Southron color, not so far from my own—except she lacked the coppery tint.

I frowned. Stepped back. Chewed a lip as I considered.

I felt—odd. I had never before seen her as anyone but herself: pale-haired, blue-eyed Delilah, shaped by a cooler sun. She had been Northern from the outset, indisputably foreign, and all the more striking for the difference. But now she was, in color, more Southron than anything else; now looking much like other women, Del lost much of the distinctiveness that attracted every male eye. She was still strikingly beautiful, but in a much different way. In an oddly *familiar* way, since coloring as much as bone and flesh affects a woman's appearance.

Comparing the old Del to the new one underscored how men felt when the familiar became something else. Something more tantalizing.

Was this how Umir felt? Attracted to differences?

She was still remarkably beautiful. Skin stain and hair dye could not erase the clarity of her features, the flawlessness of the bones, nor the subtle self-awareness and elegant physical power that set her apart from others.

The dye was very bad. The skin stain muddy. But

underneath the dulled exterior lay the gleam of glorious steel.

"Why?" I asked.

She lifted her chin. "I am a Southron woman—a *Borderer* woman—being escorted to Julah by a hired sword."

I squinted a little. "Why?"

"Because no one is *looking* for that; why do you think?"

"Oh, and am *I* supposed to dye my hair, too?"

She shrugged. "You don't have to. It's *me* who stands out."

I nodded thoughtfully. "Didn't we discuss the fact I'm not exactly unknown in these parts? That there are certain physical differences that also set *me* apart?"

"They will ask for you, of course . . . but they will also ask for a fair-haired Northern bascha who carries—and uses—a sword." Del didn't smile. "Not a proper Borderer woman who buys a sword-dancer for protection, instead of wielding a *jivatma*."

"And you think that will throw them off."

"Either that, or we must split up."

"No." I didn't even waste a moment considering it. "It's true they'll ask for the Northern bascha . . . this might confuse them a little. But only a very little."

"If it earns us the freedom to reach Julah without being molested—and wherever else we must go—it will have served its purpose."

I smiled faintly, still assessing a black-haired, dark-skinned Del. "Is this your way of testing my—interest?"

"No," she answered dryly. "As *interested* as you are—and as often—I think I could be bald."

I grunted disagreement. "Bald women don't excite me."

Del was speculative. "You could shave your head."

Aghast: "What *for?*"

"To see if bald men excite *me.*"

"Close your eyes," I suggested firmly. "And then you can just *pretend.*"

Del's smile was still Del's smile, in spite of dye and stain.

So was my response.

Thirty-five

I was cold, cold as ice . . . cold as stone in Northern mountains wracked by a Northern wind. The air was sharp as a knife, bathing bare flesh in rippling pimples of protest. I shivered, wrapped myself more tightly in the threadbare coverlet—

—and realized I was awake, in the South, and sweating because of the warmth.

I threw back the coverlet, cursing sleepily, and realized the bed was empty of Del.

I cracked eyelids and saw her across the room, sitting against the wall opposite the bed. Just—sitting. And staring at her naked sword, which she held before her face in a level, horizontal bar. It was an unusual posture, particularly for someone sitting in an otherwise relaxed position. She wasn't singing for one of her little rituals. Wasn't honing the steel. Just staring. From my angle, the sword blade blocked her eyes. I saw a chin, a mouth, a nose, and the upper part of her forehead.

I hitched myself up on one elbow. "What are you doing?"

"Looking at my reflection." Del lowered the blade to rest across her thighs. One hand touched dyed

black hair, now dry and lusterless. Her gaze was fixed
and unwavering, centered somewhere other than here.
It was an eerie, unfocused expression. The hand fell
away from hair, landed slackly on tunicked thighs.
"Do you know what I have done?"

Awareness sharpened. "What do you mean? The
dye? I thought you said it would wash out."

Del stared blindly at me. "What I have done," she
murmured. And then slumped against the wall with
the sword across her knees. Her face was an odd mixture of realization and relief; weary recognition and a
transcendent discovery she clearly was uncertain could
bring her any peace. She closed her eyes, shivered
once, then laughed softly to herself. Murmuring something in uplander incomprehensible to me.

I sat up, swinging legs over the edge of the bed,
planting bare feet on packed dirt. "Del—"

Blue eyes opened and stared back. "It's done," she
said intently. "Don't you see?"

"What's done?"

She laughed out loud. Cut it off. Then laughed
again, half choked, splaying both hands against her
face in a peculiarly vulnerable, feminine gesture.
"Ajani," she said through her fingers.

I blinked. "That was almost two weeks ago. Are
you only just *now* realizing he's dead?"

Glazed blue eyes stared fixedly at me over stained
fingertips. "Dead," she echoed. And then tears welled
up without warning and Del began to laugh.

Awash with helplessness, I stared warily back at
her. That she cried out of something other than sad-
ness was obvious, because it didn't warp her features
with grief. She just laughed, and cried, and eventually
cradled a sword against her breasts as a woman does
a child.

"Done," she said huskily, when the laughter died away. "My song is truly ended."

Tears still stained her face, muddying her efforts at making herself Southron. But at the moment that appeared to be the least of her concerns. "Bascha—"

"I had not allowed myself to think about it," she said. "Do you see? There was no time. There were people after us—"

"They still are."

"—and never any time to think—"

"Not much more now; we ought to get moving."

"—nor any time to consider what I must vanquish *now*."

That stopped me. "Vanquish?" Oh, hoolies, what now?

Del smiled sadly. "Me."

I gazed blankly back at her.

"You asked me so many times, Tiger . . . and each time I gave you no answer, putting off the consideration for another time."

"Del—"

"Don't you see? I have finally come to myself. I know what I have done . . . but not what I will *do*." She smiled crookedly. "You said it would come to this. I chose not to listen."

It was not, I decided, the proper time to rub it in. Instead, I pointed her to another topic infinitely more important. "At the moment we're sort of in the middle of something else."

The diversion didn't work. "All those years," she said reflectively. "I gave him all those years, with nothing left for myself."

I waited, deciding she didn't need my comments.

"He took from me everything I knew in the space of one morning—kinfolk, lifestyle, virginity. With steel and flesh alike he shredded me inside and out—" She leaned her head into one rigid, splay-fingered hand, knotting dull black hair. "And do you know what I did?"

"Escaped," I said quietly. "Collected blood-debt for your kinfolk, according to Northern custom."

Del smiled. Such a sad, despairing smile, cognizant of accomplishment as well as recognition of what the task had required. "More," she said hollowly. "And I gave it to him willingly, all those years on Staal-Ysta, and the others spent searching for him. *I* gave it to him—Ajani did not insist. He did not *require* it." She leaned her head against the wall, combing black hair with darkened fingers. "I did what most people, even men, might have refused to do, or given up along the way when the doing became too demanding."

"You honored the oaths you swore."

"Oaths," she said wearily, "oaths can warp a soul."

I gazed steadily back. "But oaths are what we live by. Oaths are food and water when the belly cramps on emptiness and the mouth is dry as bone."

Del looked at me. "Eloquent," she murmured. And then, somberly, "We both of us have known too much of that. And allowed our oaths to consume us."

I sat very still. She spoke of herself, but of more; of me, also, putting faith into oaths meant to get me through the night, or through the day beyond. A chula makes his own future when the truth is too bleak to face.

"It's over," I said. "Ajani is dead. And if you waste your breath on regrets—"

"No." She cut me off. "No, no regrets—that much I do not acknowledge . . . I have sung my song as I meant to, and the task is at last accomplished. Honor is satisfied . . ." Briefly, a glorious smile. "But I am only just realizing—now, *this moment*—that I am truly free at last. Woman or man, I am completely free for the first time since I was born to be whatever I choose, instead of having it chosen for me."

"No," I said quietly. "As long as you stay with me while there is a price upon my head, you are free of nothing."

She sat against the wall holding the sword that had been sweet deliverance as well as harsh taskmaster. And then she smiled, and reached for the harness, and put the sword away. "That choice was made long ago."

"Was it?"

"Oh, yes. When you came with me to Staal-Ysta. When, in my obsession, I made the man into coin to be bartered to the *voca*."

I shrugged. "You had your reasons."

"Wrong ones," she said, "as you were at pains to tell me." She rose, began to gather up pouches and collect scattered gear. "After all you gave to me, in the midst of my personal song, do you think I could leave you?"

"You," I said clearly, "are eminently capable of doing anything you please."

Del laughed. "That is the best kind of freedom."

"And the kind you couldn't know if you hadn't killed Ajani."

She paused. Turned to look at me. "Are you making excuses for me?"

I shrugged negligently. "If I started doing that, I'd have no time for anything else."

"Hah," Del retorted. But accepted the bone with grace. She, as well as I, is uncomfortable with truths when they border on the soul.

*　　*　　*

The problem arose when I suggested it was a good idea if I kept Del's sword with me.

"Why?" she asked sharply.

"Because you said it yourself: you're a Borderer woman who's hired a sword-dancer to escort her to Julah."

"That doesn't mean you need to carry my *jivatma*."

"It means someone other than *you* should; who in hoolies else is there?"

We stood outside in the morning sunlight, saddled horses at hand, pouches secured. All that wanted doing was us to mount and ride—only Del wasn't about to.

"No," she declared.

I glared. "You don't trust me."

"I trust you. I don't trust your sword."

"It's *my* sword . . . don't you think I can control it?"

"No."

I bit back an expletive, kicked out at a stone, sucked teeth violently as I stared at the ground, the horses, the horizon; at everything but Del. Finally I nodded tightly. "Then you may as well wash out the dye and the stain."

"Why?"

"Because you toting around that sword will draw all sorts of attention, regardless of your color."

"I'll carry it on my horse," she said. "Here—I'll wrap it in a blanket, tie it onto the saddle . . . no one will know what it is."

I watched her strip a rolled blanket off the mare, spread it on the ground, then place harnessed *jivatma* in its folds. She tucked ends, rolled up the blanket, tied the bundle onto the back of her saddle.

"Can't get at it," I observed.

"You're supposed to protect me."

"And when have you ever allowed it?"

Del's smile was fleeting: white teeth flashed in a muddy face. "Then I guess we'll both have to learn something new."

I grunted. "Guess so." And climbed up onto the stud.

The Punja thinned as we neared the Southron Mountains jutting up beyond Julah. The sand was now pocked with the rib cage of the South's skeleton, the knobs of a spine all broken and crumbly and dark. Wispy vegetation broke through to wave spindly stems, and spiky, twisted sword-trees began to march against the horizon, interspersed with tigerclaw brush. Even the smell began to change, from the acrid dust-and-sand of the Punja to the bitter tang of vegetation and the metallic taste of porous smokerock, lighter by far than it looked. The colors, too, were different. Instead of the pale, crystalline sands in shades of ivory, saffron and silver, there were deeper, richer hues: umber, sienna, tawny gold, mixed with the raisin-black of crumbly smokerock and the olive-ash of vegetation. It made the world seem cooler, even if it wasn't.

"So," Del said, "what do we do once we reach Julah?"

I didn't answer at once.

She waited, glanced over, lifted brows. "Well?"

"I don't know," I muttered.

"You—don't know?" She slowed the mare a pace. "I thought you said we had to go to Julah."

"We do."

"But . . ." She frowned. "Do you have a reason? Or was this arbitrary?"

"It's where we're supposed to go."

"Is Shaka Obre somewhere in Julah?"

"I don't know."

She let a long moment go by. "I do not mean to criticize—"

"Yes, you do."

"—but if we are to go into the dragon's maw once again, don't you think there should be a purpose?"

"There is a purpose." I slapped at a bothersome fly trying to feast upon the stud's neck. "The purpose is to find Shaka Obre."

"But you don't know—"

"I will." Definitively.

"How do you know you'll know?"

"I just will."

"Tiger—"

"Don't ask why, Del. I don't have an answer. I— just know this is what we have to do."

"In spite of the danger."

"Maybe *because* of the danger; how should I know?"

"You don't think it's odd that you've brought us down here with no certainty of our task?"

"I think everything's odd, bascha. I think everything we've done in the past two years is odd. I don't even know why we've done it, or are *still* doing it . . . I just know we have to." I paused. "*I* have to."

She digested that a moment. "Is this all part of the sandcasting the old hustapha did?"

"Partly." I left it at that.

"What else?"

"You wouldn't understand."

"I might."

"No, you wouldn't."

"How do you know?"

"I just—know."

"Like you 'just know' we should go to Julah."

I scowled. "You don't have to."

Del gritted teeth. "That's not the point. I'm here, am I not? I just want to know what we may be facing. Is that so bad? Is it not appropriate? I am a sword-dancer, after all—"

"Del, just let it go. I can't give you the answers you want. All I can say is we're supposed to go to Julah."

"And where after that?"

"How in hoolies should *I* know?"

"Ah," Del murmured.

Which contented neither of us, but was the best I could do.

Dark, ragged rock, all chewed and twisted and jagged, glittering with ice. Cold air bathed bare flesh; fogged a rune-scribed jivatma; flowed through the narrow throat into the mouth beyond and wisped away into warmer breath. Not the dragon near Ysaa-den, but an older, smaller place, all twisted and curdled and fissured: dark hollowness rimed with frost—

"Tiger?"

I twitched in the saddle. "What?"

"Are you all right?"

"I'm just thinking. Isn't that allowed?"

She arched a single blackened brow. "Forgive me my intrusion. But it is nearing sunset, and I thought perhaps we should stop for the night."

I waved a hand. "Fine."

Del scrutinized me. "You've been awfully quiet the last few hours."

"I *said* I was thinking."

She sighed, aimed the mare in a diagonal line toward a cluster of tigerclaw brush, said nothing more.

Disgruntled by my own snappishness and Del's questions, I followed. Dropped off the stud and began to undo buckles and thongs.

Stopped. Stared blankly at my hands: wide-palmed, scar-pocked hands, showing the wear and tear of slavery as well as sword-dancer calluses. But as I stared the scars faded, the palms grew narrow, the flesh a darker brown. Even the fingers were changed: longer and narrower, with a sinewy elegance.

"Tiger?"

I glanced up. I knew it was Del, but I couldn't see her. I saw the land instead: a lush, green-swathed land, undulant with hills.

—*I will unmake what you have made, to show you that I can*—

"Tiger." Del snagged the mare's reins into tigerclaw brush and took a step toward me. "Are you all right?"

—*I will destroy its lush fertility and render it into hoolies, just to prove I CAN*—

Del's hand was on my arm. "Ti—"

—*I will change the grass to sand*—

I twitched at her touch, then shuddered. Stepped away, shaking my head, and rubbed at the place she had touched me. My hands were my own again, with no trace of what I'd seen.

No trace of what I'd heard.

Del's blue eyes, in a dark face, were avidly compelling. "Where do we go?" she asked. "Where is Shaka Obre?"

Without thought, I pointed.

She turned. Stared. Glanced back at me, measuring my mood. "You're sure?"

"Yes—*no.*" I frowned. Slowly lowered my hand. "When you asked, I knew. But now—" I shook my head to shed disorientation. "It's gone. I have no idea what I meant."

"You pointed that way, toward the mountains beyond Julah."

I shrugged. "I don't know, bascha. It's gone."

She chewed at a lip. "Perhaps . . ." She let it go, then sighed. "Perhaps you should ask Chosa Dei."

"Chosa Dei has had entirely too much to say of late, thank you. I'd just as soon keep it that way."

"But he would know. He is the one who imprisoned Shaka Obre." Her expression altered. "Is that how you know we must go to Julah? Because of him?"

Unsettled, I hunched shoulders. "Some things I just—sense."

Pensively, she nodded. "There is that part of him in you—"

I turned back to the stud, undoing buckles again. "For the moment, he's being quiet."

"Is he?"

"He isn't trying to unmake me, if that's what you mean. I'd know about that." I pulled down pouches and saddle, stepping away from the sweat-drenched stud to set things damp-side up to dry in the sun. "I promise: I'll let you know."

"Do," Del said pointedly, and turned back to her mare.

I sat bolt upright in the middle of the night, then thrust myself up and ran two stumbling steps before I stopped, swearing, and scrubbed sweat from my face. As expected, Del was awake also. Waiting.

I turned back, blew out a deep breath of disgust and self-contempt, walked back to the blankets. Stood aimlessly in the sand, feeling its coolness between my toes. Saw the gleam of Del's *jivatma:* three feet of naked steel.

I waved a hand. "No."

After a moment, she put it away. And waited.

I squatted. Picked up a chunk of smokerock. Flipped it into darkness and excavated for more. "Cold," I said finally. "Cold—and closed *in*."

"Is it Chosa's memories?"

"And mine. They're all tangled, layered one on top of another. I saw Aladar's mine. And Dragon Mountain. And some place I don't know, but I know that I *should* know it."

"Chosa," she murmured grimly.

I shivered, moved to sit on the blanket, drew the burnous over bare legs. "You know what happened to me. You saw. When Aladar threw me in the mine."

"I know."

I tasted bitterness. "It doesn't go away."

"Someday it will."

"It was bad enough when we were with the Cantéada, in their canyon caves . . ." I shivered. "Dragon Mountain wasn't much better, but at least Chosa made me think about something else. Once he had you, I didn't think of it at all. I just knew I had to kill him."

Her hand settled on my right leg, smoothing burnous and flesh. "What was it tonight?"

"A cold, small place. Funnels and tunnels and pockets . . ." I frowned. "And I was *in* it."

"Well, perhaps it was just a dream. A nightmare."

"I don't dream anymore."

It startled her. "What?"

"I don't dream anymore. I haven't for a few weeks."

"What do you mean? Everyone dreams. You did before."

I shrugged. "It's not the same. What I see are *memories* now, not dreams. Over and over again. Shaka and Chosa, but Chosa's always blurred. As if—" I broke it of with the flop of a hand.

"As if you and he are one?"

I grimaced. "Not quite. Chosa's still Chosa, and I'm still me. But the memories are tangled. I see mine, and I see his—and sometimes I can't tell the difference."

Del's hand tightened on my leg. "It will end. It will be over. We will find Shaka and discharge the sword as well as your memories."

"Maybe," I said grimly. "But if we purge me of Chosa, how much of me goes, too?"

Thirty-six

Beyond reared the mountains: raisin-black, dusty indigo, tumbled croppings of dark smokerock. Before them clustered Julah, a crude, ragged encampment of lopsided hovels—

No.

Julah?

Julah was a *city,* a full-fledged domain city, rich from mines and slave-trade.

I blinked. Frowned. Rubbed eyes. Glowered at the city again, as the Chosa-memory and mine traded places. This time it *was* a city.

Del's tone was grim. "I hoped never to come here again."

"No more than I," I agreed, recalling our subterfuge. Del, chained like a slave, with a collar around her neck, walking behind the stud.

It had been the only way. I took her to a known slaver, saying I wanted to breed her, and that I needed a Northern male; he, in turn, had sent me to the tanzeer's agent, who had agreed she deserved a proper partner. It had been designed to flush out her brother, stolen five years before and sold on the slaveblock; in the end, it had gone wrong, putting her in Aladar's hands and me in Aladar's mine.

We'd both of us escaped. But Del had killed the tanzeer, and now his daughter ruled in his place with vengeance on her mind.

Julah was a warren of close-built dwellings toppling one against the other, if you looked from certain angles. Narrow streets were choked with stalls, wares, livestock, refuse, turning passages into bazaars. The Merchant's Market proper was in the middle of the city, but bargains were best had in shaded corners tucked away from the heat of the day, and the rituals of the Market. Julah smelled of wealth, but stank of the means to gain it. The city was the largest slave market in the South, thanks to dead Aladar, whose mines ate living people and vomited bodies.

I'd nearly been one of them.

We rode through the variegation of midday, blocks of shadow and sunlight falling in angled, sharp-edged slants across adobe dwellings huddling one against another, laddering packed dirt streets. Awnings drooped over windows and doors, all deep-cut against the glare; one could tell how prosperous the family by the condition of awnings and paint. Bright, fresh-sewn awnings and clean pale-painted adobe boasted a successful family. Those of lesser luck trusted to the sun not to rot through fabric too quickly. And if the luck was truly poor, there were no awnings at all.

We wound our way through the outskirts into the crowded inner city, regimented by thick block buildings and the narrow streets cutting skeins in all directions. Dark-eyed children ran everywhere, chattering and shrieking, ducking beneath the stud's head, and the mare's; goats and fowl and cats and dogs added to the racket.

"What do we do?" Del asked over the noise.

"What we always do. Find a cantina with rooms, rent one, have a drink or two while sitting in the *shade*." I smiled. "I'd also suggest a bath, but it would wash out your Borderer blood."

Del shrugged. "I have more dye and stain."

The stud sidled over toward the mare, swished a lifted tail, opened his mouth to bite until I reminded him *I* was in charge and reined him away again. "We forgot to trade the mare in on a gelding in Rusali."

"She's not so bad."

"We'll get rid of her here."

"Or you could get rid of the stud."

That did not deserve an answer. "We can cut through this alley here and head for Fouad's cantina," I suggested, pointing the way. "It's a clean, decent place, well up to your standards—" I grinned. "And Fouad knows me."

Del arched a darkened brow. "In our present circumstances, I'm not certain that's wise."

"Fouad's a *friend*, bascha, from the old days . . . besides, I doubt anyone down here knows about our troubles. Too far from Iskandar."

"They *will* know, once Sabra returns."

"We're ahead of her."

"For how much longer? She was a day behind us, Nezbet said—"

"Umir said two."

Del shrugged. "Either way, we have little time. We would do better to conduct our business quickly. . . ." She slid a sidelong glance at me as we slanted mounts across the road toward the narrow alley I'd indicated. "If you know what business there is to conduct."

"Chosa knows," I said grimly. "He knows all too well."

Del looked uneasy. "I wish we knew what to do. What it will take to discharge the sword."

"*And* me."

"And you." She guided the mare around a pile of crudely-woven rugs piled in rolls against the wall. "Your sword is Northern-made, using Northern rituals, blessed by Northern gods—I can only hope Shaka Obre understands we mean him no dishonor."

"We don't even know if he's still alive."

She sounded a bit annoyed. "Then you can ask that of Chosa, when you ask him where to go."

I grinned. "A lot of people in this world can *tell* me where to go. But it isn't to Shaka Obre."

Del's mouth tightened. "Where is this cantina?"

"Right up ahead. See the purple awning?"

Del looked. "It *is* purple. And the bricks are painted yellow."

"Fouad likes color."

Del's silence was eloquent.

"You just don't appreciate the finer things in life, bascha. Here. Fouad has boys to take mounts—you can hand the mare off."

I reined in, jumped down, waited for the swarm of dark-eyed Southron boys all clamoring for the job of taking the horses to livery. The streets were much too narrow and choked to add anything more, and so Fouad had begun the practice of hiring boys to stable mounts at the end of the block, between two dwellings.

They came, as expected. Brown-skinned, black-haired boys wearing thin tunics and gauze dhotis, with brown, callused bare feet. They all vied for the job, promising better care than the next boy could give.

I chose a likely looking hand, set the reins into it.

"Bring the pouches back," I said. "We'll be taking a room."

"Yes, lord," the boy said. He was nearly identical to all the others.

"He can be testy," I warned.

"Yes, lord."

It was all I could get out of him. I gave him a copper, watched Del abstractedly select a boy for her mare, and grinned when she finally turned toward me, wading through the boys. "Isn't it nice to see helpful, ambitious children?"

Del grunted. "*Isn't* it?"

"It keeps them out of trouble."

She had tucked the blanketed sword bundle beneath one arm, unwilling to part with Boreal. "Is your friend to be trusted?"

"Fouad knows everyone, and he knows what everyone's done. If he sold out his friends, he'd be dead already." I gestured toward the deep-cut, open doorway. "I'll get us a room. If you want to sleep first, go ahead; I'm going to sit down in the shade for a bit and relax with aqivi and food."

Del shrugged, passing by. "I'm hungry, too."

Indoors, it was cool, cavernous, shady. I sighed, stripped off harness, found the perfect table near the door, and hooked out a chair. "Fouad!" I shouted gustily. "Aqivi, mutton, cheese!"

As expected, Fouad came out of his back room and threw open welcoming arms. "Sandtiger!" he cried. "They said you were dead!"

Del, pausing, looked meaningfully at me.

I ignored her. "Do I look dead to you?"

The Southroner laughed. "I didn't think it was true. They *always* say you're dead."

I shrugged, settling back against the wall as Del

acquired a stool. "Hazards of the profession. One of these days I suppose it *will* be true, but not for a long time."

Fouad stopped by the table. He was short, small-boned, friendly, with gray streaking black hair. He wore a vivid yellow burnous and a scarlet underrobe. Dark eyes glittered avidly as he smiled down at Del. "And is this the Northern bascha?"

Del did her best not to give the game away. But Fouad wasn't buying it. He grinned as she explained she was a Borderer who had hired the Sandtiger for escort. And he nodded, agreed politely, then shot a bright-eyed glance at me full of amusement and understanding as he moved away to fill my order.

"It's not working," I mentioned. "I just thought you should know."

Her mouth hooked sideways. "You might have chosen a cantina where the proprietor doesn't know you." She paused. "If such a place exists."

I sighed noisily. "Right now, I'm content. You may as well relax, too. By morning I'll know what to do, so we may as well enjoy the rest of the afternoon."

She'd hooked elbows on the table, but now sat more upright. "By morning?"

I glanced around the room, marking a few men here and there, dicing, drinking, talking. Glumly, I murmured, "You may have the right idea. About asking Chosa. It's time I gave him his chance to punish his brother."

"That's what you'll tell him?"

I snorted. "Let's just say I'll let him know I won't oppose him. I don't think Chosa can ignore the chance to punish Shaka, so he'll have to tell me where he is."

Her brow puckered. "Just like that?"

Some of the amusement faded. "Nothing to do with

Chosa is 'just like that.' Given a choice, I'd never talk to him again—but in order to *get* that choice, I *have* to talk to him." I scowled gloomily. "Let's talk about something else."

Fouad arrived with aqivi, mutton, cheese, and set everything down on the table. "Bascha," he said respectfully, "may the sun shine on your head."

Del smiled faintly. "And on yours, Fouad."

Content with that, he left. I poured us both full cups—accepting no protests from Del—and pushed hers across the table. "Watch the accent," I suggested.

"I'm a Borderer," she murmured. "Borderers *have* accents."

"Border accents, yes. Yours is uplander."

"They won't know the difference, down here."

"Fouad does. But Fouad doesn't matter." I lifted the pewter cup. "To the end of a quest, and to a future of adventure."

Del's mouth crimped a little, but she tapped her cup against mine. "The quest is hardly ended, and the adventure is growing old."

"Oh, now, let's not be down in the mouth about it. Look at all we've accomplished."

Del sipped, nodding. "Indeed, look. We are both of us panjandrums—but I'm not so certain it's good."

I drank half a cup, then grinned. "Neither of us is the sort to do anything without stirring up attention. It's the kind of people we are."

Del swallowed more aqivi, then set the cup down. "And shall we alter our habits when your sword is finally free of its inhabitant?"

"I don't know. Should we?"

She leaned forward on one elbow, cupping chin in hand. "Short of changing the sand to grass, there is nothing you can do to convince anyone of the truth:

that you are the jhihadi. If indeed that *is* the truth."
She sat back, sighing, picking dyed hair out of her
eyes. "Will we always be running away?"

"Not always." I shrugged. "You accomplished your
goal. Ajani's dead, and now you have another future.
I still have to accomplish *my* goal, and then I'll decide
mine."

"The 'threefold future,' " she quoted.

Uneasily, I stirred on my stool. "Let's worry about
that later. Right now I just want to eat a little, drink
a lot, and sleep in a decent bed." I glanced up idly as
a man halted by the table, standing behind Del. I was
accustomed to them staring at her, poking companions
with eloquent elbows, or stopping to get a closer look.
But this man stared at *me*.

He said something. Don't ask me what; it was
incomprehensible. Clearly it wasn't any kind of
Southron; just as clearly neither was he. He was too
big, too broad, too light-eyed, with hair a russet-
brown shade close to mine. I shrugged my ignorance
of his tongue as Del turned to look up at the man.
Her idle scrutiny sharpened.

He stopped speaking, seeing my blank expression.
Frowning faintly, he switched to heavily accented
Southron. "Forgive me," he said briefly. "I mistook
you for Skandic." He spread eloquent hands, smiling
inoffensive apology, then took himself out of the door.

"Whoever *he* is," I murmured, lifting my cup again

Del, pensive, stared after the man. Then the pen-
siveness faded as she turned back to me. "Do you
know him?"

"No. Or Skandic either, whoever he is."

Del sipped aqivi. "I thought he looked a little like
you."

"Who? Him?" I glanced at the doorway, empty of foreigner. "I don't think so."

Del shrugged. "A little. The same height, the same kind of bone, the same kind of coloring. . . ."

I stared again at the doorway, sluggish interest rising. "You really think he looked like me?"

"Maybe it's just that he doesn't look Southron." She smiled faintly. "Or maybe it's just that I have grown accustomed to looking at you."

I grunted. Then chewed at a lip, considering. I glanced yet again at the doorway.

Del smiled, seeing my indecision as well as the temptation. She lifted her pewter cup. "Go ask," she suggested. "Go find him and ask. You don't know. I do not suggest he is kin, but if you resemble this Skandic, this man might know something of the people you came from."

I tensed to rise, relaxed. "No. I don't think so."

She regarded me over the cup. "You don't know anything about your history," she said quietly. "Sula's dead. You may never have another chance. And he *does* look like you. As much as Alric looks like me."

Something pinched my belly. There was merit in what she proposed, but— "This is silly."

Del shrugged. "Better to ask than to wonder."

I chewed my lip again, undecided.

"Go," she said firmly. "I'll wait here for our things."

"This is *stupid*," I muttered, pushing back the stool. But I went out of Fouad's cantina wondering if Del could be right.

Wondering if, in my heart, I wanted her to be.

Thirty-seven

I paused outside the cantina, peering in either direction. The twisty street was crowded, keeping its own secrets. I hesitated, muttered an epithet, started to turn back. Then I saw the horseboys squatting against the building, waiting for the next customer.

I pulled a copper out of my pouch. Four boys arrived instantly. "Big man," I said. "A lot like me. He came out a moment ago."

One boy pointed immediately: to the right. Three other faces fell. I flipped the boy the copper with a quick word of thanks and went after the big foreigner Del thought looked like me.

I felt—odd. I had spent most of my life despairing of ever knowing anything about myself except for what I had won in the circle, or stolen from the dreams I'd dreamed as a child, chula to the Salset. But two or three weeks before there had been a chance, a slight chance, that I could learn the truth. That chance had died with Sula, who said she didn't know. I had castigated myself for even hoping, charging myself with the task of setting such hopes aside.

But hopes die hard, even in adulthood.

Now there was another chance. It was almost nonexistent, but worth a question or two. Julah was the first domain and city of any size beyond the Southron Mountains if you came up from the ocean-sea; it was not impossible that the stranger who looked like me could be from a neighboring land, coming inland from the seaport city, Haziz.

Yet I wondered. There were enough Borderers, mostly halfbloods, who resembled me. Cross big-boned, fair-haired Northerners with smaller, darker Southroners, and people like me result.

Still.

"Stupid," I muttered, making my way through the throng. "You'll never find him in the city, and even if you do, chances are he can't tell you anything. Just because he mistook you for someone else . . ."

Hope flared, then died, tempered by caution and contempt.

"Stupid," I repeated. And stumbled into a one-eyed man standing guard over a basket of melons.

I apologized for my clumsiness, patted him once on the arm, then turned to continue my search. And realized, as I turned, my limbs felt sluggish and cold.

I stopped. Sweated. Shivered. Blinked as vision blurred.

Chosa?

No. He didn't work this way. Chosa was not so subtle. Besides, I'd grown accustomed to anticipating his attempts to exert more power. This was not one of them.

Then what—?

Hoolies, the *aqivi*—which both of us had drunk.

I swore, swung around, staggered three steps and fell to one knee as numb legs failed. Pulled myself up and staggered again, tripping over a cat as it ran between a dozing danjac's legs. The danjac woke up as I fell against its ribs, grabbing handfuls of scraggly mane to hold myself upright.

A female. She shifted, turned her head, spat a glob of pungent cud. It landed on my thigh, but by then I didn't care. By then I wanted my sword, Chosa Dei or no.

I slapped weakly at the danjac's mouth as she bared teeth in my direction, trying to unsheath the *jivatma* with a hand nearly dead on the end of my arm. I staggered as the danjac turned her hip out from under me, but caught my balance spread-legged as the sword at last came free.

"Bascha—" I mumbled. "Hoolies, Del—it's a trap—"

Eyes. They stared, shocked and fearful and wary: a man in obvious straits swayed off-balance in the street, holding a black-charred blade with perilous control. I didn't really blame them. Sword-dancer or no, at the moment I was a danger to anyone who came near. Even if I didn't mean it.

"—bascha—" But even my mouth was numb.

Vision wheeled. The street fell out from under me; hip and elbow dug dirt. I managed, as I landed, to thrust the sword to arm's length, so I wouldn't cut myself.

Up. Blade chimed dully as I dragged it along the ground, thrusting myself to unsteady knees. Everyone hugged the walls, or went in and shut their doors.

Except for the men with swords, all swathed in dark burnouses rippling as they walked out of shadows into sunlight.

So. Now I would know.

To my knowledge, I have never employed a sword in any method save the one for which it was intended.

But now I did. I dug the tip into the ground, leaned my weight upon it, levered myself to my feet.

The men stopped approaching.

I smiled. Laughed a little. Heaved the sword upright into position and balanced very delicately with feet spread too far apart. If someone spat, I'd fall down. But a reputation comes in handy.

That, and Samiel.

The danjac was still beside me, whuffling discontent. Then a dark-clad, quick-moving body slipped beneath the belly, came up from under it with a knife; smoothly and efficiently sliced into the softer flesh of the underside of my forearm.

I dropped the sword, of course. Which was exactly what he intended.

And then he dropped *me* with a hook of agile ankle around one of my wobbly ones.

I landed painfully, flat on my back, banging a lolling head against hard-packed dirt. I bit my lip, swallowed blood; felt more flowing out of my arm.

But only for a moment. Everything went numb.

He gestured to the others. They came, putting away their swords. One man moved closer, then leaned forward to inspect me. I saw, through fading vision, the notched Southron nose. Heard, in thundering ears, the familiar broken voice.

"Why is it," Abbu began, "that every time I see you, you're wallowing in the dirt?"

Weakly, I spat blood. "So much for your oaths."

Dark brows rose. "But I have honored my oath. With Sabra as my witness."

Sabra. I looked. No woman. Only men, in Southron silks and turbans.

And then I saw her. The small, quick body which

had slid beneath a danjac to cut the sword from me. The one I'd thought was a man.

She stripped the sandshield from the lower half of her face, letting the cloth hang free to dangle from the turban. I saw the small, dark face, infinitely Southron; the black, expressive eyes, infinitely elated; the dusky flush of her cheeks and the parted curve of a lovely mouth. Infinitely *aroused*.

Sabra knelt. She was tiny, slender, sloe-eyed: an exquisite Southron beauty. Mutely she reached for my wounded arm, closing fingers around the flesh. Blood still flowed freely, staining her palm. She let go of my arm, stared intently at her bloodied hand, then looked into my eyes.

Her voice was very soft. "I gave the woman to Umir."

I twitched once. It was all I could manage. "Hoolies take you," I croaked, "and your broken-nosed bed-partner, too."

The bloodied hand flashed out and caught me full across the face, leaving sticky residue. Vision winked.

Went out.

—a fissure in the ground . . . a cracked opening that splits the ground apart, all blackened and curled awry like a mouth opened to scream. Inside, something glitters, ablaze like Punja crystals, only it isn't Punja crystals, but something else instead. Something white and bright and cold—

Deep inside me, Chosa rustled.

The mountains are familiar, tumbled ruins of sorcerous warfare; brother pitched against brother in a waste of strength and power. Shaka Obre means to protect, but Chosa Dei is determined to destroy whatever he can.

The warfare escalates until even the land protests, rising up to defy them both. Flesh falls away, but it isn't flesh of man; the flesh is the flesh of the land. Grasslands peel away, leaving bare rock and wasted earth.

Inside me, Chosa laughed.

"I can unmake it all, merely to make it again—"

The mountains tremble, and fall, forming new chains of peaks and hillocks.

Chosa raises his arms. The words he chants are strange, unknown even to Shaka. Meadows become a desert. A necklace of freshwater lakes becomes an ocean of sand.

Shaka Obre screams, to see his creation destroyed.

His brother merely laughs. "I TOLD you I could do it!"

"Then I'll hurt YOU!" Shaka shouts.

Deep inside the mountains, the last bastion of Shaka's making is warded against permanent summer, and the unyielding eye of the sun.

"I'll show YOU!" Shaka mutters.

But by then it is too late. Chosa has made a prison.

"Begone!" Chosa shouts, and points imperatively to the nearest hunch-shouldered mountain.

A rent appears in it: gaping mouth curls awry. Deep inside, it glitters.

"Go there," Chosa commands. "Go there and live your life without sun or sand or stars."

"Go THERE!" Shaka points: north, away from himself. A thin ruby haze issues from his fingers and encapsulates Chosa Dei. "There!" Shaka repeats. "Inside his own new-made mountain—"

And Shaka Obre is gone, sucked through the gaping mouth into the fastness inside the mountain, a necklet of pockets and hollows riddling the new-made mountain.

"You see?" Chosa says. "You don't have the proper magic."

And then he also is gone, escorted by brilliant wards to the far fastness of the new north, so different from the south.

That once was a single land, lush and green and fertile.

I twitched, then slackened again. Saw the patterns and whorls and grids, and the hustapha's gnarled hand slapping flat against spit-dampened sand.

Inside me, Chosa stirred.

Lines drawn in the sand—

The hand thrust itself into my groin and closed. I bucked, tried to shout; realized I was gagged. Realized I was stretched spine-down on a splintery wooden bench in a small, slant-shadowed room that boasted a single slot of a window, with arms and legs pulled taut to the floor, chained to rings. All I wore was a dhoti; little shield against Sabra's hand. I twisted away as best I could even as she laughed.

"Do you want to keep them?" she asked. And squeezed a little harder. "What should I do with you, to repay you for his death?"

I could make no answer through the gag. It was leather, once dampened, now dried into painful stiffness. There was more in my mouth: a hard, smooth roundness that threatened to make me retch.

Sabra let go. Black eyes were pitiless. "I could do much worse."

Undoubtedly she could. Undoubtedly she would.

Del. With Umir.

Sabra laughed as I tensed. Iron rattled dully, sweeping me back to Aladar's mine. Sweat bathed my face. This was Aladar's daughter.

"I had a brother," she said lightly. "He would have inherited. But when he was nine—and I was ten—I had him murdered. It was done with perfect skill, and no one ever knew. But none of the harem girls ever bore a boy again . . . or else they gave them away, so no more accidents would occur."

She had put off the black burnous and turban and wore a long-sleeved, calf-length white linen tunic instead, draped over baggy carnelian trousers. Tiny feet were leather-shod; the toes were tipped in gold. Sleek black hair hung unbound to her knees, rippling as she moved. On the bench, I tensed.

She was dusky Southron perfection, exquisite elegance. No wasted motion. No wasted thought. A lock of hair brushed my ribs, then slid downward toward abdomen. I nearly choked on the gag.

"He expected to live longer," she said. "He expected to have other sons. But all he had were girls, and I the oldest of all. The others were unworthy."

A small hand touched the fissure Del's sword had left in my ribs. Paused. Traced the scar, much as Del herself had so many times before. But the gesture now was obscene. I wanted to spit at her.

Reflectively, Sabra said, "You must be hard to kill."

I swallowed convulsively. Then wished I hadn't, as the gag tickled my throat.

Wished I had my sword.

My—sword?

Sabra's hand lingered, still tracing the scar. Then drifted to the others, including the ones on my face. "*Very* hard to kill."

What had happened to Samiel? I recalled with clarity what had become of Umir's men when they had

tried to touch him before. Had Sabra left the *jivatma*
lying in the street?

"I hated him," she said. "I was glad you killed him.
But I can't tell anyone that. There are appearances
. . . I should thank you, but I can't. It would be a
weakness. I dare not afford a weakness. I am a woman
tanzeer—the men would pull me down. They would
rape me to death." The hand moved away from my
face to my ribs once more, finger-walked each one,
then crawled to the edge of my dhoti. Nails stirred
coppery hair, slipping beneath the leather. "Would
you rape me, Sandtiger?

Is that what Abbu did?

Small teeth were displayed oh so briefly. "Should I
castrate you, so you can't?"

Hoolies, the woman was sandsick.

Fingers found the thong drawstring. "He bought
you for me, you know. That silly Esnat of Sasqaat.
He wanted to impress me, so I would consider his
suit. So I would marry him." Quietly, Sabra laughed.
"As if I would marry a man when I have a domain of
my own."

The memory awoke. Esnat of Sasqaat, Hashi's heir,
hiring me to dance so he could impress a woman.
He'd told me her name: Sabra. But I hadn't known
her, then. I'd known nothing at all about her.

Esnat, you don't want her. The woman would eat
you alive.

Sabra undid the thong, loosened it. Yanked the
dhoti aside, unheeding of my flinch. "It would interest
Abbu," she said thoughtfully, "to see how you
compare."

Hoolies, she *was* sandsick!

Sabra laughed softly. "In the *circle*, you fool; is this
all you think about? Like every other man?" She

flipped the dhoti back over my loins contemptuously. "Men are predictable. Umir. Abbu. You. Even my own father. They think with this, instead of with their heads. It is so *easy* to make a man do whatever I want him to do . . . when one doesn't care about these—" she touched genitals once more "—or *these*—" now she caressed her own breasts "—it's so easy to get what you want. Because you have no stake in the flesh." Black eyes shone brightly. "Sleeping with a man is such a small matter. But it binds him more certainly than anything else could—and then he does what I tell him."

I wondered about Abbu.

Sabra thrust fingers into her hair and scooped it back from her face, unconsiously seductive for a woman who didn't care what a man's response might be. Or maybe she knew, and *did* care; the woman was unpredictable, even as she claimed men otherwise.

She let the hair fall, sheeting down her back. "I don't care about the jhihadi," she continued calmly. "He meant nothing to me, nor his Oracle. But it was useful, that death. And the Oracle's. It inflamed all the tribes and made you easier prey." She smiled, stroking her bottom lip with a long fingernail. "Once my people killed the Oracle, they whispered it came of you and the woman, using blackest sorcery. So the Oracle couldn't unmask you; you destroyed him to keep him from it. So now you are hated for that, too." Sabra laughed throatily. "Clever, am I not? It made them all angrier. It made it all very easy."

The Oracle. Dead. Del's brother. Dead again?

"Jhihadi-killer," she said. "Murderer of my father."

I had killed neither man. But now it didn't matter.

Sabra shrugged. Silken hair rippled. "Eventually, I would have had him assassinated so I could have the domain. You saved me some trouble. If I could reward you, I would. But there are appearances." She tossed a curtain of hair behind a slender shoulder. "Rest the night, Sandtiger. In the morning you will dance."

Sweat trickled from temples.

She moved close again, dragging fingernails across my bare chest. Beneath it, flesh rippled. It wasn't from desire, but increasing trepidation. The woman unsettled me. "Abbu wants you," she told me. "He said he always has. When I asked him what he wanted as payment for his assistance, he said he wanted the dance. The final dance, he said. The true and binding test of the shodo's training."

A tiny spark lighted. Abbu and I were rivals, but never enemies.

"I agreed," Sabra said. "But there must be *provisions*."

The newborn spark went out.

Aladar's daughter left.

Thirty-eight

Near dawn, men came. One of them was Abbu Bensir, who had put off his sword. He waited silently just inside the door as the others unlocked the manacles, took away the gag, bound up the crusted knife slice in my right arm, left me food and drink.

They departed, closing the door. Abbu remained behind, leaning against the wall. He wore a bronze-brown burnous, a weave of heavyweight silk and linen that shone oddly metallic, even in poor illumination. It was far better than his usual garb, which was generally understated; I knew it had to be Sabra.

Light from the narrow slot of a window slanted across the room. He shifted out of its path so he wouldn't have to squint. "For the dance," he said, nodding toward the food.

I sat on the splintery bench, retying the dhoti thong, and didn't say a word.

"She has your sword, too. I told her what it was . . . she wanted it, of course. So she had Umir bring Del. The bascha didn't like it much, but she sheathed it for us. She said something about it was better for us to have it than some innocent child in the street."

I made no answer.

The husky voice was calm. "You know it has to be settled, one way or another."

I flexed the forearm, tightening and relaxing a fist to test flesh and muscle. The wound stung, as expected, but the bleeding had stopped, and the binding would protect it. It wouldn't interfere.

"It's how legends are made, Sandtiger. You know that. To all the young sword-dancers, it's what you *are*."

I lifted my head finally and looked at him directly. My voice croaked from disuse; my mouth hurt from the gag. "Does it matter so much to you?"

Abbu's shoulders moved in a shrug beneath the burnous. "What is there, save the legend? It's what people buy when they hire a sword-dancer. The man, the skill, *the legend*."

"You could have asked," I told him. "We could have had our own private dance, just the two of us, and settled it once and for all. No need for all of this."

He smiled, creasing a Southron face nearly ten years older than my own. Light glinted briefly on threads of silver in dark hair. Older, harder, wiser. Legend in the flesh, much more so than I. "What benefit in asking, Sandtiger? I meant to once, and found you beset by what Del claimed was Chosa Dei. Could I ask then?" He made a dismissive gesture. "And when you were recovered, you had no time for a true dance, according to the codes. There was Sabra, and all the others, hunting the murderer. And I knew you would never stop, never enter a circle against me, unless I forced your hand."

Dim light shadowed his features. I saw the steady, pale brown eyes, the seamed scar bisecting his chin, the quiet readiness. He was and had always been

something I was not: a man secure in himself. A man
so good at what he did it colored all his life.

In the circle, I was as good. Possibly even better,
though we couldn't know that yet. But I was not and
had never been secure within myself.

I just didn't tell anyone.

Abbu waited in silence. That he respected me, I
knew: he had put off his sword. I thought it unnecessary. I had been chained all night. As quick as he was,
I could attempt very little before he could counter me.

I looked into his face and saw banked expectancy.

Belly tautened abruptly "It was *you*," I declared.
"She was a day, two days behind. And then suddenly
she was here, waiting at Fouad's."

He grinned. "There is a disadvantage to being a
legend, Sandtiger. People begin to expect things.
When we realized you and Del had left Quumi, I told
Sabra—and Umir, once we met up with him at the
oasis—that you were bound for Julah. I didn't know
why, but I knew where. It's where you always go:
Fouad's. So I suggested they double up on mounts
and water and beat you here to Julah, so the trap
could be laid."

I recalled Fouad's unfeigned friendliness, his courtesy toward Del. "Fouad?"

Abbu hitched a shoulder. "You have no idea how
determined Sabra is. She is—not like other women.
What Sabra wants, she gets. Julah is her domain; she
is free to do as she likes, and *to* any person who happens to strike her fancy: man, woman, child. You
know what Aladar was like—I heard what he did to
you. The daughter is worse. The daughter is—different. Fouad would have been a fool to refuse her."

"What happens to Del?"

He shrugged. "She's Umir's, now. He'll do whatever he likes."

I sought something in his face. He had known, admired, desired Del. "Doesn't that bother you?"

Abbu Bensir laughed his husky, broken laugh. "Have you no faith in the bascha? Umir underestimates her—I know better. He beds boys, not women . . . and he wants merely to *collect* her. Collectors cherish their icons." He shifted against the wall, rubbing absently at the notched bridge of his nose. "Del is hardly helpless. I doubt he'll keep her long."

"Which brings us back to me." I picked up the cup of water, drank.

"It's simple, Tiger. We dance."

I nodded thoughtfully as I lowered the cup. "Sabra mentioned certain *provisions*."

Something jumped briefly in the flesh beneath one brown eye. "She promised me the dance. I didn't ask for provisions, merely the chance to settle it according to the codes. Nothing more than that."

I grunted. "Sabra may have other ideas."

"Sabra is ruthless," he agreed. "Far more ruthless than Umir, but—"

"But you trust her."

His mouth thinned. He pushed himself from the wall and walked to me, then around me, peering briefly out the slit serving as window. I heard his step behind me; the rasp of his broken voice, distinct and oddly tight. Each word was emphasized, and very deliberate: "Listen to me."

I didn't say a word.

Silence. Then, very quietly, with infinite clarity: "Sabra needs to show her power to all the male tanzeers, as well as the men of her domain. To prove herself. To hold them all with whatever means it takes, because she is a *woman*. She will do whatever she has to do. Left to her own desires, she might have had you flayed alive—have you ever seen that done?" He didn't wait for me to answer. "A man trained by our shodo, a seventh-level sword-dancer, deserves to die in the circle."

"Don't do me any favors." I set the cup down. "Once, we might have settled this in a circle where death was not required."

"Once," Abbu agreed. "In Iskandar . . . but a horse interfered. And also in the Punja, but then Chosa Dei interfered. And now it's much too late." Steps gritted again as he came around to face me. No more amusement. No more quiet goading. He was perfectly serious. "It will be quick, and clean, and painless. It will be an honorable death."

The words rose unbidden. "*You're* sure of yourself."

The flesh at the edges of eyes creased. He didn't—quite—smile. "I admire your bravado. But be sensible, Sandtiger . . . I am *Abbu Bensir*—"

Very quietly, I told Abbu Bensir where to go. Also when, how fast, and in what condition.

The recoil was faint, but present. And then he did smile. "Steel, this time. No more wooden blades."

I looked at the scar in this throat. "I nearly killed you then. I was seventeen years old, utterly lacking in skill . . . it's twenty years later, Abbu. And you're that many years older. Slower. Stiffer. *Older*."

"Wiser," Abbu said softly. "And the Sandtiger is not so young as *he* once was."

No. And he'd also spent a muzzy-headed night chained to a splintery bench, thinking about Delilah.

I looked again at his throat. "Funny thing, Abbu— I never thought you were the kind for revenge."

The tone snapped sharply. "Don't confuse me with Sabra."

I looked at him more alertly.

"This isn't for revenge. What do I care about that? What do I care about *you?*" He angled a shoulder toward the door. "I just want to dance."

I sought another edge. "Is she that good in bed?"

Abbu swung back, laughing. "Old trick, Sandtiger."

I shrugged. "At least it's a reason."

"She is—inventive. Uninhibited. But a woman, all the same, much like any other." He gestured. "I gave you my reason. I dance for the joy, the *challenge* . . . do you realize how long it's been since I danced with a worthy opponent?"

Sourly, I said, "I'd just as soon not."

"Too late." He turned, moved toward the door, looked back. "There is one more thing."

I waited.

Brown eyes glittered in sunlight. "I *am* older, even as you say . . . and growing older daily. There is in me now a desire to leave behind something of myself, if I am to leave the world. A name, if nothing else." The husky tone took on a quality I'd never heard in Abbu: intense, decided virulence. "Old men are flaccid in spirit, dying drunk in a filthy cantina, losing wits to huva dreams, or pissing in their beds. I'd rather die in the circle. I'd rather die honorably." He put his hand on the latch. "And if it's meant to happen, I'd just as soon have the Sandtiger do it than some Punjamite of a boy who caught me on a bad day."

I stared blankly at the door as it shut slowly behind him, latch falling into place. I wanted to call him a fool. But I thought about what he'd said. Applied it to myself. And realized he was right.

I'd sooner have Abbu kill me now than Nezbet do it later.

Of course, given a choice. . . .

Without any further ado, I ate the food they'd left and finished off the water. Then got up from the bench, stretched, and began to loosen up.

Abbu Bensir. At last.

The smallest flicker of anticipation lit a bonfire in my belly.

Thirty-nine

Dead Aladar's impressive palace was very much as I recalled it: white-painted adobe; tiled, elegant archways; palm and citrus trees planted for shade, and looks. Even the stableyard boasted layers of cream and copper gravel.

I was barefoot. The gravel was small and fine, but gravel nonetheless; I scowled faintly, assessing footing, thinking ahead to the dance. As yet the day was still cool, which meant the footing would also be cool, but I preferred packed sand or dirt to a circle drawn in gravel.

The stableyard was filled with spectators, except for the circle and a narrow perimeter around it. They stood against walls, squatted in gravel, sat upon benches and stools, dependent upon their status. All men, of course. Most, I assumed, were guards or mercenaries Sabra had hired to maintain a hold on Julah; the richly-dressed men were merchants and the politicians of the city, who would fight to snatch it away; others were trained sword-dancers who'd come down from Iskandar. I knew many of the latter, by name or by face. As one they stared at me, as I stood flanked by a knot of guards, and then at Abbu Bensir as he came out of the airy, elegant palace into the bright stableyard.

It was, I thought, silly. So much fanfare for a dance. But it was Sabra's idea, of course: she intended to see me killed before a multitude of witnesses, so no doubt could be attached to her part in the matter. What she meant was plain: she alone had caught the Sandtiger, killer of father, jhihadi, and Oracle, when *all others* had failed; see now as she meted out justice!

Hoolies, what a farce.

I wore only brief dhoti and necklet, naked of sandals, burnous, harness. It's the usual attire for a man entering a circle; extra clothing can foul the dance. Many of the sword-dancers had seen me dance before in identical garb, but none had seen me dance properly since coming back from the North.

Except, of course, for Abbu. He was unsurprised. But I saw and heard the reaction as everyone else saw the hideous scar left by Del's *jivatma*.

Yet something else for the legend. I found it a little amusing.

As I waited in my knot of guards, Abbu quietly stripped out of burnous, harness, sandals. Like me, he wore a dhoti; unlike me, there was no necklet, nor a fist-sized, lumpy fissure eaten out of still-living flesh. He was a spare, sinewy man several years beyond forty, seamed by knicks and slices gone pale pink or white with age. He was Southron, and therefore smaller, but Abbu Bensir lost nothing at all by boasting less bulk; nothing at all by giving up height to a lower distribution of weight.

Surreptitiously, I sucked in a substantial breath that lifted and spread ribs, giving me room to breathe, then released it slowly and evenly. I yawned once, twice; shook out arms and hands; felt the tingle in thighs and groin. Felt the rippled, ticklish clenching deep in my belly that always presaged a dance.

Umir the Ruthless had named me a gut-level dancer, a man whose quickness, power, and skill had never truly been tested to prove or disprove the legend. This time, I knew, was different. This time I would find out *exactly* what—and who—I was.

I thought of Sula. I thought of Del. I thought of the nameless mother who had birthed me in the sands, then left me there to die. All those years ago: thirty-six, thirty-seven, thirty-eight.

Hoolies, who cares?

It was *Abbu Bensir* I faced.

It began as a ripple. Then a quiet murmur. And at last a splitting of bodies: Sabra, Aladar's daughter, came out of her father's magnificent palace. With her came white-clad eunuchs carrying cushions, fans, gauzy screens quickly erected to shade her from the sun as she settled upon piled cushions. She wore vivid, bloody crimson: tunic, trousers, turban, and the palest wisp of modesty veil weighted with tiny gold tassels. Leather slippers were also red; the tissue-thin soles were glossy gold with freshly gravel-torn foil. It was, I decided wryly, Sabra's way of proving her wealth *and* her disdain for poorer people, even the rich ones gathered here.

She lifted a small, graceful hand, and everyone fell silent. Her voice rang throughout the courtyard, carrying even into corners. She knew how to pitch it properly. "Honored guests, today I bring you the justice of a powerful yet humble new tanzeer as personified in the circle, the South's greatest tradition. Let there be no question as to who the dancers are: Abbu Bensir, whom you know, and also the Sandtiger."

I sighed and cocked a hip as a murmuring filled the stableyard. This might take a while.

"Abbu Bensir," she repeated, "who is accorded the honor of being the South's greatest sword-dancer, trained by the most honorable and most revered shodo of Alimat, where only the best of the best are privileged to be trained."

Everyone knew that.

"And the Sandtiger, also trained at Alimat and was taught by the same shodo, but who repudiated the training, his honor, and codes by turning to basest infamy. He murdered three men: my father, Aladar, former tanzeer of Julah—" Her voice broke artfully a moment, then she recovered a perfect composure, "—and also the jhihadi, long promised to the South by prophecy and legend as the man who would save us all by changing the sand grass."

"Or maybe *glass*," I muttered.

"And lastly, the man who by blackest sorcery murdered the Oracle, the one sent to all of us to prepare the way for the jhihadi, so we could honor and welcome him."

"Anything else?" I murmured.

Sabra placed a hand across her heart, inclining her head modestly. "I am only a woman, and unworthy . . . but I have done this thing. For Julah, and all of the South—I *give you retribution for the deaths of three whom we loved!*"

Hoolies, what a performance.

"And so," she said quietly, "today I bring you justice. Today I bring you a dance that will never again be equaled. A dance to the death. A true and binding dance shaped of true and binding oaths, as taught at Alimat. All of the codes shall hold. The traditions shall be honored."

"It might be fairer," I shouted, "if somebody gave me a sword!"

It did what I expected: broke Sabra's hold; shocked merchants and politicians; made the sword-dancers laugh. The tension she worked to build was abruptly dissipated.

She didn't like it one bit.

"Here!" Sabra snapped, and one of her guardsmen muscled me over to her cushions. Black eyes were livid, but red-painted lips smiled sweetly behind the sheer red veil. "A sword?" she inquired. "But of course there will be a sword. A very special sword." Sabra snapped her fingers. "Surely you will know it. It is all a part of the legend."

For a moment, a moment only, I thought it was to be Samiel. And then, as quickly, I knew better than to hope it. Sabra was not stupid. If she had known nothing about *jivatmas* before setting out after me, Abbu would have told her by now. He knew enough about them to respect and be wary of them. He had seen Del's, and he'd also seen mine. Abbu knew better.

So, not Samiel, full of Chosa and Southron magic. Brief hope died.

A eunuch came forward bearing an oblong purple cushion. Displayed upon it was a sword, a Southron sword. A very familiar sword: shodo-blessed, blued-steel blade, with beadwire-wrapped hilt.

Strength, like sand, ran out. *"Where did you get this sword?"*

"You were careless," she said, "and heedless of the legend. Which makes it all the sweeter." Her eyes dwelled avidly on my face, weighing my expression. What she saw pleased her; Sabra smiled, and laughed.

Maliciously, she whispered, "I restore what has been lost, to make the legend complete."

I gritted teeth tightly. "It broke," I hissed curtly. "Singlestroke *broke*."

"And so you discarded it." Sabra shrugged. "The halves were found, and recognized. I had them brought to me, and repaired. So I could restore it to you."

"Hoolies, woman—you're *sandsick*. Steel once broken . . ." But I let it go, seeing the glint in black eyes. She knew. As well as I. As well as anyone, though she took no pains to tell them.

Steel once broken will always break again. No matter how skillful the mending.

Which, of course, is what she wanted.

Sabra gestured expansively, showing small white teeth. "Take it, Sandtiger. So the legend is whole again."

I was getting downright sick of hearing myself called a legend. First Abbu, now Sabra. I was a sworddancer, nothing more. A good one, I'll admit; I'll even say I'm great (which I've been known to do anyway) . . . but real legends are usually dead. And I wasn't. Yet.

I put out a hand. The cushion was snatched away.

"Ah!" Sabra laughed and coyly touched her breast. "So I am reminded . . . there are the oaths to be sworn, first!" She gestured to Abbu, raising her voice so all could hear again. "Will you come forward? All must be witnessed. All must be done properly, according to the honor codes of Alimat. Both of you must be bound into a blessed circle."

I wondered sourly how much she'd already known. How much Abbu had told her.

Sabra laughed again as Abbu came forward. "*Still*

I forget—how like a woman!" Another graceful gesture. "I have special guests. There—do you see?"

We looked, of course, as she meant us to. Directly
across the circle another sunshade affair was erected,
cushions laid out carefully as eunuchs gathered with
fans. Umir the Ruthless stood there. By his side was
a hooded woman well-swathed in Southron silk.

Singlestroke. And Del. What more could I ask for?

Freedom for both of us.

Hoolies, what a mess.

Umir brought her forward to the edge of the circle.
Close enough for me to see her wrists were bound
before her. Close enough for me to see her face and
the expression upon it. Clearly she was unhurt; just
as clearly she was annoyed. But she lacked *jivatma*
and freedom, even as I did. And as we each of us
gazed at each other, seeking truth behind mutual
masks, we knew there was no way out.

Umir had worked his own brand of magic. She wore
white samite, the costly Southron silk that only tanzeers could wear, because all else were forbidden save
by a tanzeer's permission. Plain, unadorned samite,
too bright in the light of the sun; a hooded, loose-
fitting burnous that grazed the tops of bare toes, neither belted nor fastened. It hung open from hood to
hem in heavy, unmoving folds.

Umir smiled at me. "Subdued, is she not? As is her
attire?"

I scowled, thinking him foolish.

"I prefer simplicity in all things; in the things I show
to the world. Surface understatement can be *so* effective . . . but underneath that surface, the complexion
is much different. In people—*and* in attire." He put
a hand on Del's shoulder, sinking fingers into samite.

"This burnous is a part of my collection, worth the price of three domains. Worthy of *her*, I think."

Umir caught cloth abruptly and pulled the burnous open with a skilled flourish, draping it inside out across his left arm like a cloth merchant showing off wares. The severe white burnous was abruptly something else; something incredibly *more*: a lurid Southron sunset awash in morning light. All the yellows, and the oranges; all the lurid reds—and everything in between—of a simoom-birthed sunset boiling out of the Punja's horizon bloomed against costly samite, and an even costlier woman.

Umir spread a hand across the brilliant lining. "Beads," he whispered softly. "Hundreds and hundreds of beads, colored glass and gold and brass . . . and feathers, *all the feathers*, from a hundred thousand birds not even known to the South . . ." He smiled fatuously, caressing the sunset lining gently as a man caresses a woman's breast. Beads glittered, rattled. Delicate feathers fluttered. "Worth three domains," he repeated. "And now a woman to wear it."

Deftly, Umir slipped the hood. It, too, was lined with beads of glass, and myriad vivid feathers. But I didn't care about that. Now her face was naked for everyone to see. Behind me, I heard the rustle; the murmur of Southron men looking upon a Northern woman.

She was blonde once again, and the skin was honey-fair. She wore white also beneath the burnous: a Northern-style tunic of soft-worked, pristine suede cut to mid-thigh. Legs and feet were bare, emphasizing her pronounced, powerful grace as well as Umir's victory; no Southron man ever saw so much of a woman—or displayed her so blatantly—unless he slept with that woman, or paid money for her.

Del did not smile. She didn't so much as blink. But then, she didn't have to. She was, in the sunlight, daylight to Sabra's night. Steel to Sabra's silk. And everyone there knew it, including Aladar's daughter.

Especially Aladar's daughter.

A small but worthy revenge.

Forty

Sabra stood in a welter of cushions beneath a gauzy sunscreen. "You will swear," she declared, leaving no room for question. "Swear the oaths of Alimat, that you will honor all the codes as your shodo taught you to."

I slanted a sidelong look at Abbu, standing next to me. "Don't you just love these people who think they know everything?"

One corner of his mouth twitched, which told me a thing or two. He might be in Sabra's pay as well as in her bed, but he didn't necessarily approve of her overacting.

Sabra's black eyes glittered. "I know what I know." She put out a slim, beckoning hand. A small, short-bladed knife was set into her palm. "*Elaii-ali-ma,*" she said coolly, "as I've taken pains to learn."

My amusement dropped away. A second more intent glance at Abbu showed me companion consternation in the faint frown and tautening mouth. I assumed he'd taught her the things she knew about Alimat and oaths. But what she touched on now was a private, personal thing only rarely ever addressed once the ritual was done, and then very obliquely.

She spoke now for the two of us, quietly and with conviction. "I am Aladar's daughter in all things, save one: I am alive. One day I will die, by assassin or murderer if I do not take certain measures, but for now I am alive. For now I am *tanzeer,* irrespective of gender. Aladar's power is mine—" She paused, marking our attentiveness; satisfied, she continued, "—as are all his resources, including certain scrolls extolling the virtues of many things, and spelling out the magic necessary to accomplish every goal." Behind the sheer crimson veil with its weight of golden tassels her young face was coolly tranquil, frightening in itself. "That magic, that power, is knowledge. Because of the scrolls and my father's prescience, I have that in abundance . . . and so the power is mine. I choose to wield it now to put order into your lives."

Abbu shifted weight slightly. "Sabra—"

Black eyes blazed abruptly. "You will be silent, Abbu Bensir. We have begun *elaii-ali-ma.*"

I stirred in defense, shaking my head. "Only the shodo—"

"In this, I *am* the shodo."

Abbu and I exchanged a look. Then Sabra made a gesture. Massive eunuchs with knives in their hands stepped up behind us both, impressing upon us—even in silence—that we should mind our manners.

Clearly, Abbu's role had altered. He didn't look very happy. But then, neither was I.

If Abbu grew *very* unhappy . . . anticipation fluttered. The two greatest sword-dancers should quench even Aladar's daughter, who was, I thought grimly, becoming more of a threat with every passing moment.

Not stupid, Aladar's girl. And very dangerous.

"Elaii-ali-ma," she repeated, "is required to seal the

circle against outside profanation. To seal the dancers inside, until the dance is done."

"We know what it is," I muttered.

Abbu nodded agreement. "Let's get on with it."

"Then give me your blood," she ordered.

I displayed my cloth-wrapped forearm. "Already gave my share."

"Then this will take little effort." She gestured sharply, and two eunuchs grabbed my arm. One of them tore the bandage free and bared the five-inch slice Sabra had put there herself.

Before I could protest, the little knife flashed out. I swore as it cut in at an angle across the crusted slice. Fresh blood welled. Sabra dipped fingers into it, then dabbed three dots onto Abbu's forehead. "By the honor of your shodo; by the codes of Alimat: you will not step out of the circle until the dance is finished and one of you lies dead. If you revoke this, if you renounce your personal honor and the honor of your shodo, you are henceforth denied the grace of a shodo-blessed sword-dancer's circle, whether true or of your own making."

A muscle ticked in Abbu's jaw. "According to the codes, which I swore to live by thirty years ago before the shodo himself, I accept the dance. It shall be as you require, in accordance with all the oaths."

She nodded once, then put out a hand. Without the aid of eunuchs, Abbu bared his forearm and watched dispassionately as Sabra sliced into it. He bled less than I had, since he was lacking a prior wound. For myself, I still dripped sluggishly; Abbu's blood ran in a single runnel until Sabra put fingers in it.

Three dots on my brow, too, beneath the disheveled hair. "For you, the same," she declared. "Do you understand the oath?"

"I suppose I could say no—" But I broke it off abruptly, no longer disposed to humor her in any fashion. "There is one little thing. You mentioned certain *provisions.*"

"Ah." Sabra smiled. "You might call it incentive. I want the dance to be the best there has ever been, with neither man holding back out of old friendships and rivalries. Such things can hamper the effort." Black lashes lowered briefly, then she looked at Abbu Bensir. "You are to kill him," she said clearly, "as artistically as you can. I want it to last a *long* time. Cut him to bits, if you like . . . carve him apart like rarest meat—but do not waste my time with protestations of loyalty, or a personal need to be merciful by killing him with one stroke." Her tone went soft, languid. In another woman I'd have said it belonged in bed; I began to wonder if this meant as much to her, or perhaps even more. "I think you know me well enough now to realize what might happen if you don't do as I say."

She was dead serious. Abbu didn't even blink, but the line of his mouth went tight and pale. He didn't look at me, because I don't think he could. He had accepted the dance in accordance with his oaths. Regardless of Sabra's bloodthirsty designs upon it, he couldn't forsake the dance, or he would forsake everything he lived for. And Abbu wasn't the type.

I opened my mouth to comment, but Sabra was now staring at me. "Hear me," she said quietly. "I am vengeful and vindictive. I am everything they—and you—have said of me; do you think I'm unaware?" She gripped the knife in one hand, dark knuckles turning pale. "I don't *care* about you . . . not about *either* of you. Do you understand? I want this for myself, and I will have it *my way.*"

I stared back at her, offering nothing. She was in complete control, with the hirelings—and large, attentive eunuchs—to back her up.

She bared small teeth. "I could kill you out of hand, before every man here—and that woman; would that satisfy you?" When I gave her no answer, she went on without inflection. "Well, it does not satisfy me. I prefer a greater *effort.*" She held out the knife; one of the eunuchs took it from her. "Hear me, Sandtiger, as I tell you my provisions: Abbu Bensir is to kill you. But *you* are to kill him."

I nodded sagely. "That's the way a dance to the death *usually* works: each man tries to kill the other."

Sabra smiled coolly, unperturbed by my insolence. "If you kill him, I will free you."

I wanted to spit, but didn't; settled for laughing out loud. "I don't believe you for a moment! The entire *point* of this dance is to execute me."

"Is it?" She shook out a fold in her veil. "No, I think not. It's merely to *entertain* me—and to prove to all the others I am worthy of my station."

I gritted teeth so hard my jaw protested. "Then why—"

She laughed lustily in amusement, tossing her turbaned head. "You fool—I want a good dance. I want a dance of *passion:* two men within a circle, servicing one another with steel instead of with flesh." The amusement faded abruptly, replaced by avid intensity. "Kill him, and you go free. But if he fails to execute *you*, he shall be killed in your place. I will see to it myself."

"You said that already."

Sabra's eyes glinted. "If you fail to entertain me, if you prevaricate to goad me—*or* dally to conserve your

strength—I will stop this dance at once and do worse
than have you killed."

I laughed. "What is worse?"

"First, I will geld your horse."

It caught me completely off-guard. "My—horse?"

"Then I will castrate you—and throw you into the
mine." Sabra smiled complacency. "I have your horse.
I have your sword—even the magical sword—and also
I have you. I learned when I was a child men value
their maleness most of all, and that of living posses-
sions . . . you will lose yours if you fail to entertain
me sufficiently, and be left to die in the mine." A
tiny, malicious smile. "I believe you know the mine.
You *visited* it once before."

I tasted metal in my mouth. "Leave my horse
alone."

It was sufficient to make her laugh. And then the
laughter died. "You will accept the dance according
to the codes you swore to obey. You will uphold the
binding vows you made before your shodo."

Oh, hoolies, bascha—and you thought *your* codes
were tough!

I shrugged false negligence. "What else can I do?"

"Complete the ritual!" she snapped.

Hoolies, she *does* know it all. . . .

Once again I shrugged. Then said the words she
wanted so much, the words Abbu had said as they
applied to me, and knew the circle sealed.

Along with my future. But I don't know as that
mattered so much anymore; Abbu, given his way,
would make it very short.

Or excruciatingly long, depending on your viewpoint.

I bared my teeth at Sabra. "I'll see you in hoolies."

Sabra smiled back. "You'll see it before *I* do."

Forty-one

Sabra herself took Abbu's sword and Singlestroke out to the circle. Abbu and I both watched, but neither of us saw. We didn't have time for it.

I had loosened up as best I could in the room before being brought out into the courtyard. It wasn't enough after a night spent chained up with no food or water until morning, but I'd done what I could. Overall, I was physically prepared: my once-sore knee was sound, the scar tissue was stretched, shoulders and thighs were loose. And although I didn't like gravel much, it wouldn't bother me; the soles of a sword-dancer's feet are always toughened from years of dancing barefoot.

I felt pretty good, save for the nagging sting of the freshly reopened slice in my forearm and the smaller cut Sabra had added. But I'd forget all about them once the dance began. You can't afford to think about anything save the dance itself once you've been set into motion.

I glanced sidelong at Abbu. His eyes were very clear, his expression perfectly calm, betraying no concern with what was about to happen. The Southron body was in good proportion, and the flesh was taut, lacking the telltale signs of liquor or huva abuse. He was older, but still exceedingly fit, with no excess weight or softness or dullness. I knew better than to hope he wasn't as prepared; Abbu Bensir had not lived this long—or defeated so many men—by being lazy about preparation.

But he *was* older. Older than me, of course, but also *old;* at least for a sword-dancer. It had to be in his mind. And although he'd said more than once I'd changed over the last couple of years; that the North had altered intensity and fitness, a glance at me now would dispel that. (And he had more than glanced, though he'd been very casual about it.) Between my getting sharper from being on the run, and the assistance of Chosa Dei in restoring a battered body, I was hardly a poor opponent. And I was a *younger* one.

I smiled. Shook out long, muscled arms; flopped big hands. Laughed a little, very softly, as I briefly worked broad shoulders, tweaking thick neck from side to side. "Should be interesting," I murmured. "Too bad we didn't get a chance to lay a wager."

"I did," he retorted. "I'll let you guess which way I bet."

I snickered. "Wise money goes on me."

"Not with that sword."

"I don't need a sword."

He smiled grimly. "Do you plan to dance with your tongue?"

"I outweigh you by nearly one hundred pounds."

Abbu nodded sagely. "Should slow you down."

"Never has before."

He watched blood-colored, silken Sabra kneel to lay out his sword. "I'm as fit as I ever was."

"*I'm* as fit as I was at seventeen years old, when I shattered your guard and nearly crushed your throat—

does it still hurt? Or ever bother your breathing?—
except now I'm a little older, a little wiser—" I
paused, "—and a whole lot *better*."

Abbu made no answer.

I drew in a breath, laughing softly. "Who does she
think she is—ordering *us* to entertain her? Hoolies,
Abbu—we've done nothing *but* entertain for—what?—
fifty years between us?" I snickered again. "I figure
we ought to be pretty flashy for—oh, two engagements?—and then we'll begin to dance." I paused.
"*Dance* dance, I mean . . . the kind from which legends are made."

Abbu's gaze was steady as he looked at me. "He
told me one day it would come to this."

"Who?"

"The shodo. At Alimat, one day. When I watched
a clumsy chula pretend to be a man."

I laughed outright. "Save the games, Abbu. It's not
your style—and anyway, you already told me you
were one of the first to suggest I might be better than
good."

He shrugged. "You are. But so am I. I am Abbu
Bensir." Very slowly, he smiled. "I am the legend
against which others measure themselves. Even
Sandtigers."

Politely, I disagreed. "You're old," I said gently.
"Old men are slower than young ones, and prone to
make mistakes once tired limbs begin to fail. You're
a legend, all right . . . but the light of that legend
usually begins to dim along with an old man's vision."

Abbu's mouth tightened.

Before he could respond, I jumped in again. "I'm
glad you helped her out so much, telling her all our
secrets regarding oaths, and whatnot. Another kind of
dance—the *normal* sort of dance—would have been

much too boring. At least this way we get a chance to show Sabra—and everyone else—just what kind of men we are." I shrugged. "After all, how many sword-dancers can brag about being trained at Alimat? How many of us actually swore the proper oaths?" I nodded. "All that secrecy serves no purpose . . . after all, there's no sense in trying to live up to a single shodo's expectations. Who cares?" I shrugged. "It's a good thing you brought it all out into the open."

The Southron face darkened. "I said *nothing*—"

But Sabra's return cut him off. "Go to the circle," she snapped curtly, and sat down upon her cushions.

Abbu gazed blankly at her, still too bound up in what I'd said, and the need to tell me the truth. "Wait—"

"No." She pointed. "Waste no more time."

"Sabra—"

"*Go*," she hissed, "or I'll have you carried out there!"

Laughing quietly, I turned and walked out to the circle. I stopped this side, letting Abbu walk all the way around, still thinking about what I'd said. I wanted him to think about it as long as he could. A fractured concentration can come in very handy—so long as it isn't yours.

I nodded. Assumed stance, arms hanging slack at my sides. I focused eyes, ears, body, narrowing *my* concentration to just one thing: the opening maneuver. I knew the parameters of the circle, the placement of Sabra's cushions, the positions of eunuchs and onlookers. Had already judged how fast I could run in gravel, how many steps to the swords, how soon I could scoop mine up.

Poised, I waited in stillness, quietly gathering strength

and the sheer physical power that had served me so many years. If she wanted entertainment—

I laughed without making a sound.

Hoolies, what a farce. A single initial parry between Abbu Bensir and me would offer more entertainment than she had a right to see.

I nodded again, still smiling. Focused on the sword. Refused to look beyond Abbu to Del, who stood across from me in the shade of Umir's sunshade. I saw the blur of blinding samite, but didn't look at it. Instead, I thought about the dance. Thought about Abbu. Thought about the move I'd made so many years before, that had nearly crushed his throat.

Sabra's voice: "Prepare!"

I grinned across at Abbu. "Did you teach her that, too?"

"Dance!" Sabra shouted.

I was already moving.

But so was Abbu.

A true circle for a true dance—as this one was—is fifteen paces in diameter. That means a man can cross one in fifteen strides; seven and a half, to the center. But there's one thing a lot of Southron sword-dancers forget, when they dance against me: my legs are longer than theirs.

Abbu, as expected, took seven and a half strides to the center of the circle. I took five.

I tore the sword from the ground. "Entertain us," I said, and laughed to see his face.

Singlestroke lay in the gravel. I had taken *his* sword.

"Not only younger," I taunted, "but also *smarter* than you. Not to mention faster—"

He snatched up Singlestroke: a sword is a sword, and no weapon is disdained. I let him grip the beadwire hilt; watched his expression alter; marked the shift in posture. The shock of seeing the sword had faded. Singlestroke had been "dead" to me for too long. Now he was merely a chance for me to upset the dance.

"Two engagements," I said. "Then all hoolies breaks loose."

Abbu didn't flick an eyelash. He just came in with Singlestroke.

He was good. *Very* good; I sucked in breath, ducked away, twisted his steel off my own. This was just the beginning—what would happen at the end?

Gravel hissed and chattered. Abbu drove me back, straight back, teasing me with steel. I caught the blows, turned them; threw steel back at him. His deftness and speed was incredible.

Back— I thought. Almost—

Blade scraped blade. Quillons caught, hung up, broke free as we wrenched them apart. All around us people murmured.

Almost— I thought. Two more steps—

I let him drive me back. Then countered his pattern, responded with my own.

"That's enough," I said.

Abbu's eyes flickered.

I grinned. Laughed. Stared straight at the scar that punched a hole in the flesh of his throat, then rotated a hip, shifted stance, lifted elbows and twisted wrists, giving him what he expected. What he had recalled so many times, in the darkness of his dreams; the memory of the maneuver that had nearly ended his life.

Let him remember it all.

Let him make himself ready.

Let him prepare the defense; consider the proper riposte—

Then take it away from him—from *them*—by purposely breaking the pattern.

By purposely breaking the sword.

By purposely breaking the oaths.

Exactly eight paces—my legs are much longer than theirs—and I was out of the circle.

I was *in* Sabra's shade, marking quickness as she sprang up. Judging how far she could get. Hearing her garbled call for guards as she tripped over cushions and silks.

Then Sabra was in my arms.

But I didn't intend to kiss her.

Forty-two

I knocked the turban off her head, sank a fist into thick black hair, and yanked her head back roughly to expose the fragile throat. Then settled my left arm across it, pressing a hard-muscled wrist into the taut-stretched windpipe.

One throttled outcry escaped her, and then she clawed at my arms. I shut off her breath easily with a slight increase in pressure. "Your choice," I told her.

She wavered, sagged minutely, then allowed slackened arms to drop back to her side.

"Better." I looked out into the courtyard, noting opened mouths and staring eyes, as well as stiffened postures. Saw Abbu still standing in the circle, broken Singlestroke in one hand; saw Umir across the way with a white-clad woman next to him, poised to move; saw—and felt—the tension in Sabra's hirelings as they considered options. "Five things," I said clearly. "Two horses immediately—and one of them better be mine . . . two Northern swords—leave them sheathed, if you please . . . and one Northern bascha." I looked across at Umir. "Cut her loose *now*."

For a long moment no one did anything. And then

398

Abbu threw down Singlestroke. His own sword lay in gravel just outside the circle, where I had dropped it on my way to Sabra. I didn't need steel. I wanted my hands upon her.

The chime of steel on gravel released everyone. They began to stir, to mutter; Umir cut Del's wrists free, and she moved away quickly. Someone came up from a stable block with the stud and Del's mare. Someone else approached me with two Northern *jivatmas*. Sheathed, as requested.

"On the horses," I said.

It was done. Del moved to mare, mounted, hooked arms through harness straps. Loose sleeves fouled on leather and buckles, but she jerked the fabric loose, yanking it into place even as Umir blurted a protest. Then she reached down and took the reins to the stud, turning him broadside to me.

I smiled. "Your turn," I said to Sabra.

She was perfectly rigid, barely breathing, trembling with tension and anger. I could feel it through crimson silk; in the rigidity of her neck; in the minute curving of stiffened fingers.

"Elaii-ali-ma!" I shouted. "Every single sword-dancer here knows what that means!"

Abbu's face was ashen. "Do *you?*"

"Three days," I told him. "It's in the honor codes: you all owe me three days."

"Those of us who are sworn, yes—"

"Doesn't matter," I told him. "I'm taking Sabra with me. That ought to make the others think twice."

Slowly he shook his head. "Such a fool, Sandtiger."

I smiled over Sabra's head. "One thing I have learned is that in order to stay alive, one must make sacrifices."

"This?"

"This," I confirmed. "Do what you have to do. Everything's different now . . . I can't afford to care."

Abbu thrust a fist into the air. *"Elaii-ali-ma!"* he shouted. "The oaths of honor are broken! There is no more Sandtiger among us, to enter the true circle in the name of Alimat! *Elaii-ali-ma!"*

Those who were sword-dancers echoed the cry. Then all, led by Abbu, turned their backs on me.

"Now," I rasped to Sabra, and walked her across the gravel to the restive, waiting stud.

Del, strangely white-faced, pulled him up short so he couldn't sidestep. A glance showed me she appeared to be unhurt, as did the stud. Then I turned my attention back to Sabra, still rigid in my arms.

"Time to go," I told her. Sabra opened her mouth. I immediately made a fist and chopped her just under the jaw, snapping her head back. It would hold her for a while.

She sagged. I scooped her up, threw her facedown across the front of the saddle, clambered up behind her. Grabbed a handful of raven hair and jerked her head up, displaying the slack face. "Not dead," I told her eunuchs. "But she will be soon enough if anyone follows us."

I dropped her head back down. She was dead weight across the saddle, arms and legs dangling. I pressed one hand into the small of her back, caught up the reins with the other, and nodded at Del.

She swung the mare and left at a trot. I followed at the same pace, hearing gravel hiss beneath hooves.

Hearing also the echoing cry that had filled the entire courtyard: *"Elaii-ali-ma!"*

We wasted no time. Our long-trot through narrow streets scattered passersby and earned us curses, but that was the least of our worries. All I wanted to do was get out of Julah as soon as possible; as far from Sabra's hirelings as we could, before they at last roused into action.

Del dropped back. "Where?"

"Up into the mountains."

She studied my face. "Are you all right?"

"I will be, once we're out of here."

She nodded, slackened rein, fell back behind the stud as we wound our way through canyons of adobe dwellings and ramshackle shelters built out of city refuse.

We left the inner city for the outer, where the streets were a little wider and less clogged. Now I tapped the stud out of a trot into a lope, guiding him through the crooks as I pressed Sabra one-handed down into the saddle and the stud's withers. It was not the most comfortable way I'd ever ridden, but I'd been left with little choice. I'd sincerely doubted Sabra was the kind of woman to do as I told her, even in the face of threats; she'd have spat in my eye and dared me to kill her. Since I didn't really want to do that, it was easier just to knock her out and carry her away.

"This way," I said, and reined the stud into an alley that led us through looming shadows to daylight again. "Keep riding," I said over the clatter of hooves. "Straight up into the mountains."

"How long are we going to keep her?"

"Not much longer. I have a plan for her." I patted Sabra's rump. "She's going to buy us safe passage to the place we need to go."

Del twisted in the saddle. "*Where* do we need to go?"

"Don't worry about it, bascha. I know what I'm doing."

Fair brow creased a little. "I've learned to be concerned whenever you say that."

I grinned, oddly content. "I see Umir made you bathe."

Del grinned back. "I see Sabra didn't bother."

Which was enough for the time being; things were normal again.

Up. Out of sandy hardpan into real dirt and webby grass, sprawling in clusters across the ground. Catclaw, tigerclaw, scrubby greasewood trees; beanpods dropped from feathertrees scattered pebbled ground. We chipped and gouged earth as we climbed, negotiating clinking rectangles of shale, and gray-green granite rubble.

Up. Over hillocks and shoulders and elbow bends out onto jagged escarpments, then in against sharp-cut walls. We left behind the first flank and went over across the second. Shale and granite were interspersed with smokerock, crumbling beneath shod hooves.

"How much farther?" Del asked. "There is no trail—do we keep climbing?"

"Keep climbing. We'll rid ourselves of Sabra any old time, then head higher."

"What are you going to do with her?"

"You'll see."

Del said nothing as the mare worked her way up the mountain. Both horses stumbled, staggered, splayed legs; slid back, recovered, climbed. Beneath me the stud heaved himself upward, head dropped and rump bunching. Shoulders strained, driving legs down through loose footing to firmer ground beneath. He grunted rhythmically.

Sabra's slack body slipped to one side. I caught a handful of hair and crimson silk, dragged her up, balanced her more securely.

"Is she dead?" Del asked.

"No. What good would a body do us?"

"What good does she do us at all?"

"Be patient. You'll see. As a matter of fact . . . wait a moment. Pull up." I halted the stud, tore strips of tough silk from Sabra's tunic, tied her wrists together. "No sense in making it easier." Then I prodded the stud out. "All right. Keep climbing."

It wasn't much farther before Sabra roused. She came to with a jerk and a twitch, then arched her back as she tried to counterbalance her head-down posture.

I patted her on the rump. "Careful now, tanzeer—or I'll dump you on your head."

Loose hair sheathed her face. Her words were muffled, but not the tone of voice. "Stop this horse. Untie me. Let me *go*."

I chuckled. "Not a chance."

She twisted mightily. I caught handfuls of hair and cloth before she went over. "Let me *go*," she repeated.

I stopped the stud. Tipped her off backward. Silk hooked and tore. Bound hands caught on the harness and hilt. Strung up, she dangled against the stud. Toes barely scraped the ground.

"If you insist . . ." I grabbed hair, pulled her upright, unhooked trapped wrists and dropped her to the ground. Legs buckled and she sat, crying out at the impact. "Now," I said calmly, "perhaps you'd rather walk."

She spat out a string of rather foul expletives, all

designed to make me blush. Except I don't blush easily. Then she stopped swearing and began speaking more clearly, if with no less conviction.

"You broke them. You *broke* them. You made a mockery of the oaths and honor codes."

"I did what I needed to do."

"Now you'll *die!*" she shrieked. "Do you think I don't know? Do you think I don't know *how?*" Sabra laughed stridently, tossing hair out of her face. "They'll forgo paying dances to kill you, all of those sword-dancers . . . you're meat to them now. They'll kill you first chance they get—"

"Elaii-ali-ma." I nodded. "I know all about it, Sabra."

"You're not a sword-dancer anymore. You have no honor. You broke the codes. You repudiated your shodo, and the honor of Alimat. Do you think I don't *know?*"

Wearily, I sighed. "I don't care what you know."

"You're a borjuni!" she spat. "Sandtiger the borjuni . . . how will you live *now?* How will you find work? No one will hire you . . . no one will ask you to dance. You're nothing but a borjuni, and you'll live by borjuni rules!"

"I'll live by my *own* rules."

"Tiger." It was Del. "We have company."

I glanced up. Nodded. "I wondered what took them so long."

Sabra, still sitting in shale and smokerock, twisted her head to look behind us. She saw what we saw: four leather-kilted Vashni warriors wearing human fingerbone necklets, mounted on small dark horses.

She scrambled up and moved close to the stud. "Vashni," she hissed. "Do you know what you've done?"

"Pretty much. It's the one reason I came up here."

"*Vashni,* you fool! They'll kill us all!"

"They won't kill any of us. Well . . . I suppose they might kill you, if you don't do what they want." I dug a rigid toe into her spine and prodded her off the stud. "Don't crowd him, Sabra. He might take a bite of your face."

Del sat quietly. Equally quietly, she asked, "Do you know what you're doing?"

I grinned. "Pretty much."

"Oh, good," Del muttered. "I guess I need not worry."

"Not yet." I reached down, caught a handful of shiny black hair, pulled Sabra up short. "This is Julah's tanzeer."

The four warriors sat impassively on their horses. Bare-chested save for the pectorals; also bare-legged. Dark skin was greased. Black hair was oiled smooth and slicked into single fur-bound plaits.

I smiled at the warriors. "This is *Aladar's* daughter."

Dark eyes glittered. Single-file, four men rode down the mountain. Sabra called me names.

"It's not my fault," I told her. "Blame your father. He double-crossed them in the treaty, and then he snatched a few young Vashni and put them to work in the mine. Vashni don't take kindly to that sort of bad manners . . . I wonder what they'll do to you."

She exercised her tongue a little more, until the four warriors pulled up close by. Then she fell silent, twisting wrists against silk bonds. Brilliant crimson finery was torn, soiled, befouled. Tangled hair obscured half of her face. The paint on her lips had smeared. She was altogether a mess.

"Sabra," I told them. "Aladar's daughter, now tanzeer in his place. Any business you have with Julah can be tended by this woman."

They ignored Sabra completely, concentrating on me. Del earned a quick assessment, being a woman and obviously foreign, but me they measured more closely. Then one of them made a gesture, and put a finger on his cheek. "You are the Sandtiger."

I nodded.

"You and that woman came here before, looking for a not-Vashni boy, one of Aladar's slaves."

"That woman" said nothing, but I sensed her sharpened awareness. Again, I nodded. "He remained with the Vashni," I said. "It was his own choice."

The warrior flicked a glance at Del, marking fair hair, blue eyes, the sword. He made another quick gesture I didn't understand, but his fellow warriors did. The three rode down slowly to Del and surrounded her, cutting her off from me. I stiffened in the saddle, aware of sudden tension, but the leader's eyes forbade me to move.

Each of the three warriors reached out and touched Del's shoulder. One touch only, then a half-hidden sign. Without saying a word, they reined back and turned their horses, rejoining the fourth warrior.

He nodded. "Bloodkin to the Oracle; may the sun shine on your head."

The common Southron blessing sounded incongruous coming from a Vashni. But it put me at ease. If they respected Del, they weren't about to kill us.

"Jamail," she said. "Is he with you again?"

Something pinched the pit of my belly. I recalled with sick realization that Del hadn't been present when Sabra had told me her men had killed Jamail.

"Bascha—"

But the Vashni overrode me. "The Oracle is dead."

Del, shocked, opened her mouth. Shut it. Shock was transformed to acknowledgment; her mouth to a grim, tight line. The flesh at her eyes was pinched. "Then I will have to sing his song, when I am free to do so."

"I'm sorry," I said quietly. "I meant to tell you myself."

"What is this?" Sabra asked. "Grief for a worthless fool? Did you *believe* all that nonsense about Oracles and jhihadis?"

I shrugged. "Doesn't matter anymore, does it?"

The Vashni looked at me. "Will you kill Aladar's daughter as you killed Aladar?"

I grinned. "I thought I'd let the Vashni have her, as recompense for the warriors Aladar stole."

Del spoke before they could say anything. She was, at long last, making sure everyone got it right. "Tiger didn't kill Aladar," she said clearly. "*I* did."

"You!" Sabra tried to wrench her hair free of my grasp. She failed, then gave it up, transfixed by new information. "*You* killed my father?"

"Recompense," Del spat. "For Tiger. For my brother. For all the others." Cold eyes glittered. "Your father deserved to die. I was grateful for the chance to see the color of his guts."

Sabra was rigid. "You," she whispered. "You—*not* him."

"No," I agreed. "But she just beat me to it. He wasn't a popular man."

Sabra stared at Del. "You," she repeated.

Then she reached up and clasped the grip of my sword, trying to tear it down from the saddle.

Forty-three

The stud spooked violently, lurching sideways. I swore, grabbed rein and harness; felt Sabra's frenzied jerking. The harness came free of the saddle.

"*Hoo—*" I lunged, leaned, grabbed hold; felt the stud bunch, then cut loose with a buck that nearly lost me my seat. As it was, my position was more than a little precarious.

Sabra was shouting. Both hands were locked on the hilt, tugging it free of sheath. I hung onto harness, tugging back, but the stud's violence distracted me. He stumbled, staggered, nearly fell. I was halfway out of the saddle, trying to jerk the harness and sheath away from Sabra. Sabra jerked back.

Overbalanced, I came off. One foot caught briefly in brass stirrup, then pulled free as the stud leaped aside and I twisted in mid-fall. I landed hard, one leg bunched under me, then threw myself full-length and flopped belly-down as Sabra dragged at the harness, trying to jerk it out of my hands.

I called her a nasty name, but she wasn't listening. By then she had the sword halfway out of the sheath.

"Tiger!" It was Del. I saw the glint of Boreal as she unsheathed the *jivatma*.

"Kill her—" I said hoarsely. "Don't let her get the sword."

But Sabra *had* the sword.

I pushed up, dove, caught silk. Felt the bite of steel in flesh as the tip dragged across one forearm. I reached to grab for the hilt; to peel her hands away. "Sabra—Sabra *don't* . . . you don't know what it is."

But Sabra didn't care.

"Get away!" Del shouted. "Tiger—you're too close."

"Hoolies, she's got the *jivatma*—"

Something inside me flared. Chosa Dei, scenting power, swarmed out of the dark little corner he'd used as a place to live, biding his time patiently. Now the time had come.

Sabra screamed. She scrambled through loose shale and tumbling smokerock, kicking dirt and debris and stone as she tried now to escape the sword a moment before she'd wanted so badly. Wet blackness ran up the blade, darkening twisted runes, then danced along the quillons and began to tickle the grip. Began to caress her fingers.

"Let it go—" I rasped. "Sabra—let it *go*—"

But Sabra didn't. Or couldn't.

A convulsion cramped my body. I tied up, spasmed, retched; blurted a grunt against the pain.

Sabra kept on screaming.

Hoolies, shut her up—

Blackness charred her fingers. Reached her wrists. Then, sensing unrestricted opportunity, engulfed her entire body.

The screaming abruptly stopped.

Within me, Chosa moved. No more tentative testing. No more anticipation. He went straight for the heart, and squeezed.

Sabra's mouth hung open, but made no sound. She

sat upright, clutching the sword. Rocking back and forth, with black eyes stretched so wide the whites showed all around them.

Chosa Dei was in her. Part of him, at least. The rest was still in me.

Sabra's features began to soften. The skin began to droop. The nose slid sideways as the mouth slackened to shapelessness. A keening moan bubbled from her throat.

She bled from nose and ears. The hands on the sword swelled until the flesh split like a melon. Chosa Dei had filled her utterly, and found she wasn't enough.

Breath came in heaves and gusts: sucked in, then held, then expelled. I crawled across the ground and reached for Aladar's daughter. Caught the quillons in one hand, both tiny wrists in the other. "Let her go," I grated. "There isn't enough of her!"

The Chosa in me lunged the length of my arms, trying to pour himself into Sabra, whom he saw as a means to escape. I felt him swarm into the quillons, up the grip, then to her fingertips.

I wrenched her hands loose. "No," I said hoarsely. "I said there wasn't enough!"

"Let him go!" Del shouted. "Let him go into her!"

"She'll die—she'll *die* . . . and he'll be loose. Do you really want him loose?"

"Better than in you!"

Nice sentiment, bascha.

Then Chosa came surging back. The tiny body was clearly unsuitable; I offered much better. Bigger. Stronger. *Alive.*

At least, for the moment.

"Tiger—let go of the sword!"

In leaps and bounds, he came, flowing out of

Sabra's body. I scrambled backward, thrusting the sword away, but realized I'd left it too late. The blade was black again, but so were my hands. Even as I swore, the blackness invaded forearms and climbed up to elbows.

"Drive him back!" Del shouted. "You've done it before—*do it again*—"

Legs flailed impotently as I scrambled to get up. My right knee failed. Belly knotted itself, then spewed out its contents. I grasped the hilt and clenched it in both hands, straining to force him back.

It would be so easy if I simply let him have me.

I lunged up onto my knees and hoisted the sword into the air. Brought it down against shale and granite, splintering dark smokerock.

Again and again and again. Steel rang a protest.

"Go back—" I husked, "—*go back*—"

Tried to focus myself. Tried to beat Chosa Dei back as I methodically beat the steel against the hard flesh of Southron mountains.

"go back—"

"*go back*—"

"GO BACK—"

Del's voice, strident: "Stop . . . Tiger, *stop*—"

"—go back—go back—go back—"

"Tiger—no more!"

"—back—" I gasped. "*Go back*—"

A litany. A chant. The kind learned at Alimat, to focus concentration.

In the North, they sang. In the South, we don't.

"Tiger—*let go*—"

"Go. Back," I commanded.

Someone hit me over the head.

"I'm sorry," Del whispered.

But I didn't care anymore.

*   *   *

I came to in grave discomfort, aware of constant movement, and blood pounding in my head. "What have you done to me?"

Del rode ahead on the mare, leading the stud. "Tied you onto your horse."

That part I could tell. "Hoolies, bascha—you might have let me ride *normally,* instead of throwing me over the saddle like a piece of meat!"

"It's what you did to Sabra."

I shifted. Swore. I was exceedingly uncomfortable, sprawled belly-down across the saddle just as Sabra had. Wrists and ankles were tied to stirrups. "Do you mind if we stop?" I croaked.

"We don't have any time."

"Time for what? What are you talking about? Del— what in hoolies do you mean?"

"Shaka Obre," she said.

"Shaka—" My belly cramped. "Del, for pity's sake—"

"It's for your own good."

"*How* is it for my own good?"

"Look at your hands," she said.

I looked. Saw the pallid, hairless flesh, all flaky and scaly. The crumbling, discolored fingernails. "Not again," I muttered.

"They told me where to go."

"*Who* did? What are you talking about?"

"The Vashni. They told me how to get there. So that's where we're going."

"Told you how to get *where?* What are you talking about?"

"Shaka Obre."

I spasmed. "You *know* where he is?"

"I told you: they told me."

"How do the Vashni know where Shaka Obre is? And why tell *you?*"

She twisted in the saddle and looked back at me. Her face was very white. "They know because they have always known; it's never been a secret among the Vashni. But no one ever cared, and no one bothered to ask. They told *me* because I am the Oracle's sister. They also told me because you are Chosa Dei—or so they believe." She shrugged. "I am to take you there, to imprison you in the mountain."

"Imprison me!" I flailed. "But I'm *not* Chosa Dei. I'm *me*. Didn't you tell them that?"

"You didn't see what happened. They did, and they're superstitious."

I gritted teeth, trying to keep from shouting. "I didn't see it—I was *in* it."

"I'm sorry," she said. "It was the only way they would let me take you. Otherwise they meant to kill you on the spot . . . I explained why we needed to find Shaka Obre, and they agreed to let me take you."

"You could untie me *now*. There aren't any Vashni around."

"They said they'd watch, to make sure I got you there safely." She paused. "Also myself."

"So you're just going to *leave* me this way?"

"They said they'd be *watching*, Tiger."

"Do they really know where he is?"

"They said they did. They gave me directions." She was quiet a moment, letting the mare climb. "They said they took Jamail there once."

It chilled me. "Jamail."

"He'd been having dreams. Since he had no tongue, he couldn't explain anything." She shrugged. "They took him to Shaka Obre. When he came back, he could speak. He had no tongue, but he could speak."

"How?"

"I don't know. But you said you heard him talk in Iskandar."

"Yes, but . . ." I was fascinated. "How could that happen?"

The mare climbed steadily. So did the stud. "The Vashni said Shaka Obre caused him to speak again so he could carry word of the jhihadi throughout the South. To prepare the way." Del looked back at me. "If Shaka can do that, surely he can discharge your sword."

"We had better hope so." I frowned. "Was it you who hit me?"

"I had to. You were trying to break your sword."

"I was?"

"And it would have made things worse. Chosa was already back in the *jivatma*—but you just kept banging the blade into the mountainside, trying to break it. If you had, it would have freed Chosa."

I frowned. "I don't remember that part."

"At that point, I doubt you remembered your name." Del reined the mare around a tumble of boulders. "So I hit you with my sword hilt."

"Thank you very much."

"And now I'm taking you to Shaka Obre, where you can discharge your sword."

"And me."

"And you."

"But can't we do this with me riding *upright?*"

Del's tone was flat. "I don't want to take a chance with the part of Chosa that's in you."

"Hoolies, bascha—I'm not Chosa, if that's what you mean."

"Not now, maybe."

"Del—"

She interrupted. "You don't understand. The Vashni told me. The closer we get to Shaka, the stronger Chosa becomes."

That shut me up.

I hung slackly over the saddle and contemplated my state. Blackened nails, dead skin . . . a bruised knee (*again*) . . . general discomfort. I felt sick and cold and tired. I needed some aqivi. I needed a hot bath. I needed a healthy body that hosted no part of Chosa.

"Hoolies," I muttered wearily. "When will this all be over?"

"Soon," Del answered.

It made me feel no better.

Forty-four

Del took one look at my face. "Are you all right?"

I cleared my throat pointedly, rubbing wrists with elaborate attention. "It's what happens when you're forced to ride slung across your own saddle on your own horse."

"No, it's not," she retorted. "But if that's your answer, you must be all right." Lines creased her brow when I didn't respond. "Are you *really* all right?"

"No," I answered truthfully. "You want me to go *in* there, don't you?"

"There" was the mouth I'd seen inside my head as I lay chained in Sabra's palace. The blackened, peeled-away opening; a hole leading into the mountain.

Del and I had left the horses down below, in a sandy, level area with a little bit of grazing, if you like Southron drygrass. We'd climbed up a little ways because Del said it was what we were supposed to do; now we stood facing a hole. The hole I'd seen in my mind, all mixed up with Chosa's memories of what he'd done to his brother. Like it or not, Shaka Obre was near.

Or what was left of him.

Del slid a step, flung out arms, caught her balance.

"This is where Shaka's supposed to be. They said it looked just like this: all broken, choppy smokerock, gaping open like a mouth. See? There are the lips— and just inside it looks like teeth."

A ripple tickled my spine. "I don't like it, bascha."

"It starts out small, then opens up," she persisted. "They've all been inside the first chamber."

I ignored the pinching in my belly. "The *first* chamber?"

She shrugged. "They didn't go any farther."

"But *we're* supposed to, right?"

Another shrug. "If we're to find Shaka Obre, we'll have to do what we must."

I sucked in a deep breath, held it, blew it out gustily. Scratched at a prickling scalp. "It's a lot like the mine."

"Aladar's—? *Oh.*" Now she understood. "Do you want me to go first?"

"No, I don't want you to go first. I don't want *either* of us to go."

"Then I guess we'd better leave." Del turned on her heel, slid down a step, then began to pick her way laboriously down the slope.

"*Del*—"

She stopped. Looked back. "Your choice," she said. "You're the one with a piece of Chosa trapped inside."

I kicked a rock aside. "I went into the Canteada hidey-holes. And into Dragon Mountain—where I rescued you. If you'll just give me a *moment*, I'll go in here, too."

She climbed back up the slope, slipping and sliding through rolling pebbles and crumbling smokerock. "If you want—"

"Never *mind,* Del." I ducked my head way down and squeezed my way through into the first chamber, scraping past the "lips."

The "mouth" was small. Very small. And very, very cold. I stopped just inside and felt the hairs rise on my neck. The ones on my arms tried to, too—except Chosa Dei had burned them away.

Deep inside me, something quivered. Trouble was, I couldn't tell if it was Chosa, or just my normal discomfort when faced with cave or tunnel.

"Tiger?" Del ducked through, blocking out the light. "Is this—it?"

I drew in a breath. "Seems to be." With two of us, it was cramped. I edged back toward the daylight as Del moved through. "So—now we've done it. I guess we can go . . ."

"This can't be *it,*" she murmured, looking around. "One little two-person cave?"

"I'm cold. It's dark. We're done."

"Wait." She put a hand on my arm. "It *is* very cold."

"I said that. Let's go."

"But why? This is the South. Why should it feel like the North?"

"It's confused, maybe." I edged away from the restraining hand. "There's nothing for us to do here—"

"Tiger, wait." She knelt, pressed a hand against the floor. "It's cold . . . cold and *damp.*"

"So?" I peered around impatiently. The chamber was little more than a privacy closet, with a low rock roof. If Del and I linked hands and stretched out either arm, we'd knock knuckles against both sides. "There *is* water in the South, bascha . . . or none of us would be here."

She moved her hand along the wall. The damp

stone was pocked with hollows and holes, falling away
into darkness. Del followed it to the back, then
blurted in surprise.

I stiffened. "What?"

"Move."

"Do what?"

"*Move.* You're in the light."

Reluctantly, I moved away from the opening. The
absence of my body allowed sunlight into the tiny
chamber. Then I saw what Del meant.

The first chamber was exactly that: the first. Cut
into the back wall, hidden in shadow when a body
blocked the opening, was a narrow passageway leading deeper into the mountain.

Hairs stirred on neck and in groin. "I don't think
so," I blurted.

Del, still kneeling in Umir's priceless burnous,
looked up at me in assessment. "How are you
feeling?"

"Pretty sick of all this."

"No. How are you *feeling?*"

I sighed, summoned a smile. "He's being very
quiet."

Del frowned. "We should be close to Shaka, and
the Vashni said Chosa would grow stronger. I wonder
why he's being so quiet."

"I don't. I'm just happy he is." I took a single step,
reached down to catch a sleeve. "Let's go, bascha."

She pulled sleeve—and arm—free. "I'm going deeper.
Stay or go, as you like . . . or maybe you'd rather
come with me."

"You don't know what's *in* there."

In muted light, she smiled. "Shaka Obre," she said.
And turned to go through the door.

In a moment, bright white samite was swallowed by
the darkness. So was Del.

"Oh, hoolies," I muttered. "Why does she always
do this?"

A muffled echo came back to me. "You'll have to
take off your harness. There isn't very much
headroom."

"Or much room inside *your* head."

But I didn't say it loudly. I just slipped free of
straps, wound them around the sheath, followed Del
into darkness.

Swearing all the while.

She was all hunched up when I made my way to
her, sitting on the rock floor with doubled up knees
jutting roofward. One arm cradled harness-wrapped
sheath and sword. The other was stretched out, picking at crevices cut into the walls.

"Ice," she said briefly.

"Ice?"

"Feel it yourself."

I sat down next to her, easing myself past out-
croppings that threatened to snatch at bare flesh. All
I wore was a dhoti, and no sandals, either. I sat for
only a moment, then shifted hastily to a squat. "Hoolies! It'll freeze my *gehetties* off!"

Del smiled. "Ice." She dug into a crevice, then
pulled her hand out and displayed fingertips.

I inspected. Touched. Ice, all right. Frowning, I
scraped my own share out of the crevice. It was gritty,
frozen hard. Not in the slightest mushy. "Like Punja
crystals—hard and sharp and glittery."

"Only this is real ice." Del rubbed fingertips together. "Like the ice-caves near Staal-Ysta."

"But this is the South."

She shrugged. "A sixth-month ago, I would have said there could be no such thing. But that same sixth-month ago, I'd have said there would be no need to find a Southron sorcerer in order to discharge a sword."

I grunted. "We don't seem to be doing much other than sitting here discussing ice."

"It *is* odd," she growled. "An ice-cave in the South?"

"So maybe it's a holdover from when there was no Southron desert, or Northern snowfields . . . maybe the world they made was nothing but a world, with no divisions at all." I shifted, rose carefully, rubbed at a stiffened neck. "Are we going on?"

Del got up, bent, kept going.

I stopped moving, because I had to. Held my posture, all bent over, with the wrapped sheath in one hand. Felt the uneven thumping in my chest.

I couldn't *breathe*.

"Bascha—"

Del was murmuring up ahead. She didn't know I'd stopped.

I shut my eyes. Gritted teeth. Scrubbed sweat off my face, and banged an elbow into rock. Swore beneath my breath, then set a hand against broken stone and tried to retain my senses.

He knew. Chosa *knew*.

I was light-headed. Dots filled my eyes, already straining to see. If I could see, and breathe—

"Tiger?" It echoed oddly from somewhere ahead. She'd realized I wasn't behind her. I heard scraping, a hissed invective; she came back to my side, rubbing the top of her head. "What's wrong?"

In choppy gasps, I expelled it. "He's here. Somewhere. Shaka."

She stopped rubbing her head, looking more alertly into my eyes. "Which way?"

"There's only—one way to go—unless we head out again—" I swallowed heavily. "Hard—to breathe—in here."

Frowning, she moved closer. "Can you go on?"

"Have to," I muttered.

She didn't say anything. Then put a hand on my arm. "I swear, I won't leave you again. What I did in the Punja was wrong. I left for the oasis because I thought it would make you follow—and I knew it wasn't far. Tiger—" Her face was strained. "I want you purged of Chosa, so you can be you again. But I don't want to hurt you. If this is too hard—"

"No." I sucked in a breath. "I've done harder things. It's just—everything. This place—Chosa . . . and Shaka. All the weight pressing down . . ." I scrubbed sweat from my face. "If I could *breathe* again . . ."

She touched my chest. "Slow down," she said softly. "We need be in no hurry."

Breathlessly, I nodded. Then motioned her to go on. "I'll be right behind."

Light glowed dimly. It glittered off bits of ice and leached shadows from crevices.

"Ahead," Del said.

I clutched the sheathed *jivatma,* dripping sweat as I moved. I wondered absently if the droplets would freeze to ice. My feet were so cold they ached, but I didn't say anything. Del was barefoot, too.

She stopped. White samite glowed. She turned her face back to shadow; to me. "It's a crack in the rock," she said. "Wide enough for a body . . . it runs up through the roof. There's light, and fresh air. Do you want to go through first?"

"You don't understand," I said thickly. "I'm not afraid, bascha—that passed some time ago. This is—different. This is—*power*."

She tensed. "Power?"

"Don't you feel it?"

"I feel . . . odd."

I nodded. "Power."

"Are you sick?"

"You mean—like usual?" I shrugged. "I'm so cold I can't tell."

She smiled. "Poor Tiger. At least I have Umir's burnous. I could share—"

I grunted. "Keep it. I'm not much for feathers and beads, no matter how much they cost."

"Do you want to go first?"

"Fine." I squeezed past her, moved into the narrow crack, stepped out into daylight.

And into Shaka Obre.

"*Hoo*lies—" I fell to my knees. Retched. Dropped harness and sheath and sword. "Oh, gods—*Del*—"

She was through. She took a step, then froze. Murmured something in awed uplander.

"—get out—" I gasped. "—got to—get *out*—"

Shaka Obre was everywhere.

Pressure flattened me. I tried to get up again, but my scrabbling earned me nothing. I lay sprawled belly-down with my cheek pressed into pale, gritty sand, while blazing ice crystals blinded me. Because I couldn't shut my eyes.

My guts knotted. Squeezed. My belly turned inside out.

"—*bascha*—"

Del didn't move.

It was nearly bright as day. It *was* day, inside; the place we had come into was open to the sky. But I couldn't look up to see it, because I couldn't move.

Fingers twitched. Hands spasmed. Toes dug fruitlessly.

"It's Shaka," Del breathed.

I knew that already.

"Shaka's *everywhere*."

I knew that, too.

"I can't see him, but he's here. I can feel all the power—" She sucked in an audible breath. "Is this what it's like to taste the magic?"

How in hoolies did *I* know? I was too busy trying to breathe to think about how things tasted.

Del knelt down next to me. "It's Chosa, isn't it?"

"Shaka," I gasped hoarsely. "He knows . . . he knows about Chosa—"

A hand was on my back. "Can you get up?"

"I'm too tired to try."

"Here." The hand closed on my shoulder, pressing against rigid flesh. "I'll help—"

It did help. I heaved myself up, managed to sit, then collapsed against the wall. The rock was very cold, but I was too limp to move. I drew up both knees and pressed an arm across my abdomen. My whole body wanted to cramp.

"We brought him here," I rasped. "Chosa—we brought him *here*."

"We had to," she said.

I rolled my skull against sharp rock. "We made a mistake. They'll tear me to bits, both of them . . . hoolies, it's a mistake . . ."

"Tiger." She touched a knee. "It had to be done. You couldn't spend the rest of your life fighting a sword. One day, you would have failed, and Chosa would have had you."

"He has me now. He has me now, and Shaka has *him*—" I grimaced. "Don't you see? One of them has to lose—and I'm caught in the middle."

The hand tightened. "I can't believe Shaka would put you at risk. He caused Jamail to speak."

"Then why not restore *me?*" I scraped myself off rock and sat fully upright, tipping my head back to stare up through the massive mountain chimney to the blue sky overhead. "Restore me, Shaka! So I can fight Chosa, too!"

The echo died away. Mutely, I looked at Del.

She rose. Went to the very center of the chimney. Tipped her head back and stared up, squinting against the glare. Sunlight bathed samite. She was white in the light of the day.

Her gaze came down. Frowning, she looked around. Assessed the wide-bottomed chimney. Then bent and scooped up pale sand, testing it in her hand before she let it fall back to the floor. "Punja sand," she said. "Fine, and full of crystals . . ." She looked around again. "This is a circle."

I grunted. "No. Just a natural chimney. See?" I pointed. "Just a part of the mountain."

"A circle," she said again, and paced to the far wall. "Six and one half," she murmured.

"See? It's not accurate. A proper one is fifteen." Some of the pressure and discomfort had passed. I heaved myself up, cursing, staggered to my fallen harness, but didn't pick it up. I was too busy watching Del.

She rounded the chimney, testing cracks and crannies with deft, questing fingers. "A proper *Southron* one is fifteen; my legs are longer than that."

I stared at her. Braced legs and tipped my head back again, looking up. Dizzy, I squinted. The chimney *looked* natural, but maybe it wasn't. Magic had put Shaka here. Magic, then, had made it.

It was, as Del said, a little more than fifteen paces in diameter, which made it a bit larger than a true circle. The bottom portion of the chimney was widest, curving smoothly into roundness. It was smokerock dark, but ice lined crevices and coated knobby protrusions, glittering in the light. The rounded chimney was striated by faceted ribs of stone spiraling toward the sky. It was hardly symmetrical, and it lacked a certain preciseness, being hacked out of sharp-angled rock. But the floor was properly sandy, and the circumference was round *enough*. One need only take up a sword and draw a formal circle.

Which I couldn't do anymore.

She dug into a crevice, judging its depth and width. Then withdrew her fingers. She stood very still, as if lost in thought.

"What are you doing?"

"I thought so," Del breathed, ignoring me altogether. "If he could be *lured* out . . ."

I looked at her more sharply. "Del—"

She shook her head. Lips were compressed. She squeezed eyelids together for a brief, tension-filled moment, then opened them again. The line of her jaw was grim. "How are you feeling?"

I countered dubiously. "How are *you* feeling?"

She looked through me, not at me. Murmured something beneath her breath in an uplander dialect I didn't know. She bit into her bottom lip, turned it white a moment, then let it go again. The blood flowed back.

"Done," she said softly.

"Bascha . . ." But I let it go. She wasn't listening. "Yes, I'm feeling better. Why?"

Del unsheathed her sword and tossed the harness and sheath against the wall. With deft preciseness, she set the blade tip into the sand and began to draw a circle. She spoke quietly to herself, never pausing an instant. When she joined the ends at the far side, across from the narrow crack, she lifted her *jivatma*.

"What are you doing?" I asked, for about the thousandth time.

Del stood very still. The light from above bathed her, setting hair and samite to glowing. Slowly the sword came up until it was in a familiar position: hilt at left hip, double-gripped; left elbow out for balance and dexterity; rune-scribed blade a diagonal slash lined up with her right shoulder, tipped outward slightly in precise, eloquent challenge.

"Take up your sword," she said.

I realized I stood very nearly in the middle of the circle Del had drawn. "Are you *sandsick?*"

"Take it up," she said.

I nearly laughed. "You yourself said we should never dance against one another with these swords. You always swore it was dangerous."

"It is." She didn't blink. "Take up your sword, Tiger. This is a true dance."

It was curt. "I can't."

"Yes, you can."

"*Elaii-ali-ma.* I broke all my oaths, bascha—I renounced my personal honor." Abruptly I was angry, because it hurt so much. "I thought it was plain enough. To *you* most of all."

"This dance has nothing whatsoever to do with any of that. Here, in this place, *elaii-ali-ma* is as nothing. This dance is the beginning. This dance is the ending."

Hairs stirred on the nape of my neck. "I don't like the sound of that."

Her tone was firm and sure. "Take up your sword, Sandtiger. We will settle it once and for all."

"You're sandsick," I whispered.

A wind hissed through the crack from the passageway beyond. It snatched tumbled fair hair and blew it back, baring the flawless face. Then rippled and caught the burnous, gusting beneath poised elbows. Heavy folds billowed, curled back; samite slapped ribbed walls. The full panoply of intricate sunset lining blazed forth within the chimney: all glass and brass and gold, and myriad brilliant feathers. Umir's costly burnous set the bastard circle alight, as well as the woman who wore it.

Ice glittered behind her, catching fire from sun and sword. "Dance with me, Chosa Dei. I stand proxy for your brother."

Forty-five

I scooped up the harness and sword. Then turned and stalked out of the circle—

Tried to stalk out of the circle. Something blasted me back at the boundary, flinging me back inside. I sprawled rather inelegantly, dumped flat on my back in the sand.

When the dust had settled and I could see again, let alone breathe, I sat up. Spat grit. Scowled at the crooked slot I had intended to enter on my way back out of the chimney, but obviously wasn't meant to.

"You can't," Del said. "We came through the wards when we entered, but clearly we can't go out again. At least—*you* can't."

I twisted my head to glare at her. "Chosa didn't set wards around a *circle*."

"No. I did that. Or rather, Shaka did." She shrugged. "Did you expect him to give Chosa leave to simply walk out again, while Shaka remains behind?"

"I didn't expect anything. Except maybe a little more *re*spect. And besides, how do we really know Shaka Obre's *here*, and that there are wards at all? I don't see anything."

"Not all power is visible. Weren't you the one telling me Shaka knew you were here, and that you knew *he* was here?"

Annoyed, I brushed sand off my chin. "I just don't see how you managed to ward the circle."

"I invoked Boreal. I think Shaka Obre is willing to use whatever avatar he can, since he obviously lacks a body. Just as Chosa does, which is why he wants you."

I grunted. "I'll reserve an opinion."

Del didn't answer. She just lowered her sword, stabbed it down into sand to sheathe it briefly, then stripped out of the burnous. She dropped it onto her harness into folds of Southron sunset, then pulled the sword out of the sand and stepped across the line.

Now two of us were bound. Me by wards and sword; Del by honor and oaths.

Barefoot, both of us, as was proper. I wore dhoti and necklet, Del wore Northern tunic. And each of us had a sword.

I stood up. Pulled Samiel free of sheath and tossed the harness aside. Turned to face Delilah. "The last time we did this, both of us nearly died."

Del smiled a little. "We were young and foolish then."

"*I'd* like to get older and wiser. But you may not give me a chance."

Del's voice was soft. "No more delays, Tiger. We came to discharge your *jivatma*. Let us purify the blade, so it may be free of taint."

"And me," I muttered.

"And you," she agreed.

I took two steps away, turned. "Then let's get it done!" I snapped, and brought Samiel into position without benefit of preparation.

It was an ugly beginning, lacking elegance or power.

We each of us tested the other, tapping blades, then disengaging; sliding steel across steel, then snatching respective blades away before the intimacy increased. It was slow, disjointed, amateurish; nothing of what we knew, save both of us were afraid.

We dug divots in the sand, kicking showerlets of glittering crystal. Blades clashed, fell away; tapped again for a brief moment before wrists turned them aside. Then Del, muttering something, began to sing a song.

I stiffened. "Wait—"

But Del didn't.

Hoolies, if she keys her sword . . . oh, bascha— don't do that. Because then the dance will be real . . . and I don't *want* it to be—I don't want to relive Staal-Ysta—

Del sang very softly. Silver blade took on the faint glow of palest salmon-silver.

Steel chimed, then screeched apart. I felt her pattern tighten; the increased power in the turn of wrists. Saw the tracery left in the air; an afterglow of *jivatma* forged and blessed in Northern rituals as binding as those I knew: the oaths of Alimat.

"Dance," Del hissed. "Come on, Chosa—*dance*—"

"Tiger," I said. "Tiger."

"Dance, Chosa. Or can't you?"

I snapped my blade against hers, felt the power in her counter, jerked mine away again. "Do you *want* to summon him?"

A faint trace of sweat sheened her face. "Come out and dance, Chosa. Or have you no power to do it? No skill to guide the sword? No grace to create the patterns?"

"He's not a sword-dancer, he's a *sorcerer*—"

"Sorcerers can dance. Chosa Dei remakes. Can't he

remake himself in your image? Can't he use your body as his? Can't he dance against a *woman?*"

"Hoolies, bashcha—" I hop-skipped, ducked a pattern, came up and caught blade with blade. Steel screamed. I broke her pattern easily, practically throwing her sword back at her from the force of my riposte. "What are you trying to do?"

"Dance," she said. "Just—dance. But I don't think Chosa can."

And Del began to sing again, coloring her blade.

Vision blurred. Overlaid with my own present memory was one of a past time. Of a sorcerer blasting sorcerer with power of such magnitude it could remake mountains.

Inside me, Chosa laughed.

"Don't *do* this!" I shouted.

Delilah's song increased. And Chosa, in me, heard it.

"Don't, bascha—" I choked, recognizing familiar cramps. Sweat ran down my chest to dampen the top of the dhoti. "Don't do this to me—don't make me *do* this—"

Her pattern grew intricate, tying up my own, then sliding out of the knot. I trapped her, twisted, banged the blades apart.

They met again almost at once, clanging within the chimney. If this was what she wanted—

Inside me, Chosa took notice.

Boreal glowed salmon-silver. With every knot and swoop, Del smeared color in the air. A glowing afterimage of runes and blade and power.

I was irritated. I hadn't wanted this dance. Hadn't wanted this confrontation. I had not even thought about it, because each time I began to I recalled the dance on Staal-Ysta, when Del and I had been matched through trickery and deceit. We each of us had danced then using every bit of skill, because so much—*too much*—was at stake. In the end, the dance had won, because so many years of training can thwart even the strongest of wills. You just *dance*, because you have to. Because the body won't let you stop, and pride won't let you give up.

We danced, Delilah and I. Teased one another with steel, flicking tips at noses and throats to promise we could do better, knowing we didn't dare. This was not a dance to the death, not as it had been for Abbu and me, but a dance to the *ending*, when Chosa would be defeated and the sword would be purified.

We sweated. Cursed. Danced. Taunted one another. Bit lips and spat blood. Dug deeper divots in crystalline sand, bracing muscled thighs and hips to translate power into arms. I exerted physical strength into the finesse of her patterns, beating her back with sheer power, until she darted in with quickness and grace and teased me into openings she was more than prepared to exploit.

Del slammed blade into blade, scraping edge against Northern runes. In the chimney, the noise was deafening, echoes increased fourfold.

I caught the blade with my own, twisting, and wrenched the steel apart, hissing invective at her for bringing us to this pass. I had long ago given up wondering, even a little, which of us was better. It simply didn't matter. Of course we *said* it did, merely to tease one another, but I knew in my heart of hearts we neither of us knew.

Del came at me, singing. Northern steel flashed in chimneyed sunlight, throwing slashes against ribbed walls. Clustered crystals of sand and ice glittered in cracks and crannies. The sun gazed down upon us, benificent arbiter.

Steelsong filled the chimney, spiraling upward along smokerock ribs. We hammered at one another, knowing each blow would be caught, and turned, and blunted. Because neither of us wanted to die. We simply wanted an ending: Del, to discharge the blade *and* me; me, to be free of the blackness of spirit that had nothing to do with Chosa, and everything to do with dishonor.

Elaii-ali-ma is what you make it, binding those who wish to be bound. And I had bound myself by completing the training and rituals, by accepting the oaths of blood before the legendary shodo of Alimat, knowing myself worthy in spite of my heritage. I had made something of myself, banishing the chula in the circle, giving birth to the Sandtiger.

And I had killed him also, by stepping out of Sabra's circle and shattering all my oaths.

Elaii-ali-ma. Making this the final circle.

"Dance," Del hissed, cleaving air, then stopping short to twist, and turn, and snap.

Such tiny, intricate patterns, requiring incredible skill as well as powerful, flexible wrists. I broke the patterns as best I could, slicing through salmon runeglow, then saw the blackened shimmer corruscate up my blade.

"No!" I jerked it aside, felt Del's blade slide by, licking through broken pattern to sting me across the forearm. Blood welled, dribbled.

Chosa was *awake*.

"Dance!" Del shouted, using my inattention to nick my arm again.

I stumbled back, then held my ground, beating away her hungry blade. Saw the blackness rising higher, splashing onto quillons, licking at fingers and grip.

I staggered. Nearly went down. My guts twisted inside out.

"Yes!" Del shouted. "Come out and dance, Chosa!"

The sorcerer, thus invited, surged out of his hidden corner. Ate his way through bones even as I cried out.

"Come out and dance," she hissed.

"Del—no—"

"It's Shaka Obre, Chosa. Do you remember him?"

I shook. Power ran down my arms to the blade. In my hands the sword was black; the sword was *entirely* black.

Without warning, I was empty.

I fell to one knee, struggled up. Blade met blade, held. Del cried out in extremity.

"Let go!" I cried hoarsely.

Boreal was abruptly extinguished, swallowed by Chosa's blackness.

"No!" I shouted. "Bascha—*let go!* Drop your sword! Don't let Chosa near it!"

Del didn't let go. Del didn't drop it.

Chosa Dei, who'd made it clear from the start he wanted sword *and* woman, swarmed up the steel toward flesh.

"Yes!" Del cried.

"Bascha—*let go*—"

She broke the final pattern, letting my blade slip through to slice across one wrist, and staggered to the edge of the circle. Blood ran from the wound, dripping onto crystalline sand. Where it dripped, smoke rose.

"Expunge—" she murmured dazedly.

"Drop it!" I shouted.

Blood fell onto the line she'd drawn in the sand.

Black Boreal trembled in Del's hand. "It's me, Shaka—" she whispered.

The line, and smoke, wisped away. Del staggered through, thrust Boreal into the ice-crusted crevice she had inspected so carefully . . . jammed the blade into the slot . . . jerked the hilt to the left so violently the steel snapped in two.

I dropped Samiel even as Del dropped Boreal. "Bascha—*no*—"

Chosa was free of the sword. Chosa was free of me. Chosa was free of everything except Shaka Obre.

Forty-six

Sand began to fly. It was scooped up from the floor, thrown piecemeal into the circle, then hurled against ribbed walls. Through slotted crack came a howling wind, buffeting flesh and rock. It wailed like a Northern banshee-storm, whistling across ice-rimed smoke-rock corrugated by Chosa's magic.

I spat, thrust up a shielding hand, fell to my knees as the blast howled into the circle. The dhoti was little protection; nearly every inch of me, bared, was painfully vulnerable to howling wind and stinging sand.

"Del!" She made no answer. For the sand, I couldn't see her. "Bascha—where are you?"

But the howling swallowed my words. I heard them myself, barely, only because I knew what they were.

My eyes were crusted shut. I hunched there in the circle, my back to the slotted crack, and felt ice and Punja crystals worrying at my spine.

In my mind's eye I saw where Del had been as she wedged Boreal into the crevice and snapped the blade in two. Slowly, meticulously, I made my way across the circle, then touched a taut-muscled leg.

"Del!"

"Tiger?" Hands caught me, hung on. "Tiger—I can't see!"

"Neither can I. Come on—*hang* on . . . we need to find Umir's burnous . . . ah, *here!*"

I dragged the priceless garment to us both, then huddled close to Del as I dragged it over shoulders and heads. It muffled the shrill keening and allowed us to open our eyes, peering out through a hooded opening.

"It's spinning," Del shouted over the noise. "The sand—it's *spinning!*"

"Dust demon," I said. "Whirlwind. It happens sometimes near the Punja . . . don't know why, but it does. They blow themselves out eventually, but *this* one—" I shook my head. "I don't think this is natural, and it's awfully big."

The shrill keening increased. Eerie sparkling lights crackled and snapped as spinning sand was sucked up chimney walls in a maelstrom of pressure, whistling along the ribs. Aching ears popped; I clapped both hands over them. Blood broke from my nose.

"It's them—" Del said. "It's Shaka Obre and Chosa Dei—"

"A minor argument, maybe?" I hunched in the burnous. "I don't care who it is—I just wish they'd stop." I blotted my nose in irritation. Pulled the burnous more tightly around one shoulder as the wind snatched at fabric, snapping it furiously.

"Look."

"I can't *see* anything, bascha!"

"Look," she repeated.

I looked, squinting and cursing. Saw sand, still flying; crystals still yanked upward through ribs and pockets and whorls, sucked out through the chimney hole glowing sunbright and fair far over our heads.

Something else was flying. Something orange, and red, and yellow, and all the colors in between. "What?" And then I began to laugh. Reached out and caught a feather. "Umir's burnous is shedding!"

Del's head came out of folds. "Is it? It *is!* Oh, Tiger, no—"

I just kept laughing.

"Tiger, all the workmanship—work*woman*ship, more like!" A yellow feather caught in Del's tangled hair. "All the care and effort . . ."

"Not as much care and effort as went into your *jivatma*." I stuck my head out farther. "The wind is dying down."

It was. The keening howl faded. The dust demon blew itself out. The floor was now of rock, ice-free, dark-brown smokerock, lacking even a grain of sand. The only things left in the chimney were Del and me and feathers.

And two Northern *jivatmas*, one of which was broken.

I pulled Del up from the floor, shrugging out of the molting burnous. "About Boreal—" I began.

Del clapped a hand over my mouth. "Listen!"

I listened. Peeled fingers away. "It's quiet."

"*Too* quiet."

"After all that howling, *anything* would seem too quiet."

"*Listen!*" she hissed.

A piece of rib cracked off and fell next to us, shattering on the floor. Followed by another.

"Out!" I blurted, shoving her toward the slot. "Hoolies, get *out* of here!" The ribbing of the chimney crumbled.

Del ran, ducked, twisted, sliding through the narrow slot. I started to follow, paused; looked back at my *jivatma*.

"Tiger!" She had a hand and tugged hard, scraping my right shoulder into an outcropping.

"Samiel—"

The chimney fell into itself, collapsing into bits and pieces of smokerock large enough to squash a horse.

"Tiger—come *on!*"

"Wait," I mumbled tonelessly, staring back into the chamber even as it collapsed. "Wait—I *saw* this—"

"Tiger! Don't waste your only chance!" She tugged again at my arm.

"But I *saw* this . . . it's part of the threefold future—"

"You also saw us die, or you, or me. Come *on*—"

The vision snapped. "All right. I'm coming, Del— let *go*—"

Del let go. Hunching, twisting, ducking, we scrambled through the passageway as the mountain around us remade itself. The chimney was gone, I knew, filled up with tumbled rubble. If we weren't quick about it, the rest of the place might fall down.

I banged elbows, knees; stubbed toes; smacked my head once or twice. But Del did much the same, so I didn't complain about it. We scrambled through the smokerock bowels and at last reached the chamber; burst out of the passageway into dim light; out of that into the day.

We did not, in our haste, take time to judge the footing. We simply ran, taking the shock into knees and ankles, steadying balance with stiffened arms and splayed hands, landing on rumps if we overbalanced. Cursing, spitting grit, sobbing for breath, we slid-scrambled down the mountainside, scraping rock and rubble and dirt.

The tumbling slide ended eventually, spilling us out onto the flat where we had left the horses. We landed, sucked air, twisted onto bellies, staring up at the ruined mountain.

Dust still hung in the air. A few feathers drifted down: red and yellow and orange.

We waited, holding breath. Dust—and feathers—settled. The day was bright, and quiet.

I flopped facedown in the dirt, sucking in great gulps of air, then heaving them out again. It dusted my face with grit, but I didn't care. I was alive to notice; there's something to be said for dirt.

Del patted my shoulder limply, then stretched out on her back. A lock of littered hair fell across my elbow. "Done," she croaked. "The *jivatma* is free of taint."

For a moment, too busy breathing, I didn't bother to answer. When I did, it was half-laugh, half-gasp. "—course, we can't *get* it, now—"

"But it's purified. It's clean." Del breathed noisily a moment. "And *you're* clean, too."

"Actually, I'm pretty filthy."

She slapped a shoulder weakly. "Clean of Chosa Dei."

I felt a little better. Managed to turn over; even to sit up, hooking elbows over knees. Peered out at the Southron day, picking grit off a bloodied lip. Then glanced sidelong at Del, still sprawled on her back, and laughed huskily.

"What?"

"You. There are feathers stuck to you." I picked one off, displayed it. "A filthy, sweaty sandhen all ready for the plucking."

Del sat up. "Where?"

"In your hair, mostly. Here." I unstuck another.

Muttering, she began to inspect her hair, yanking feathers out of tangles.

I twisted and looked back at the mountain, twitched prickling shoulders. "Shaka Obre and Chosa Dei . . ." Another prickle ran down my spine. "What do you think happened?"

"I think they blew themselves out, as you said dust demons do." Del glanced up, squinting against the brightness. "You are the one who is sensitive to magic. Tell me: are they there?"

I stared up at the hollow mountain. Waited for hair to rise, for belly to grow queasy. Nothing at all happened. I was dusty, tired, and sore, but I felt perfectly fine. "I don't think so."

"Where might they have gone?"

I shrugged. "Wherever magic goes when it has no home."

Del looked sharply at me. "Magic without a home . . ."

It sounded as odd to me, but it made a strange sort of sense. Then I frowned. Pointed. "Look way off there in the distance, along the horizon."

Del looked. "Lightning."

"It's not the right time of year. In the summer, every night, heat lightning lights up the sky, but that's not what that is."

She studied it more closely. "Do you think—?"

I shrugged. "I don't know. But they were both reduced to *essences* . . . maybe nothing more than the memory of power. And that's the end result: a crackle in the air and a flash of light now and then."

Del shivered. "Why did Chosa have a body in Dragon Mountain? Shaka didn't here."

"I don't know. But seeing how Chosa worked, luring villagers to the mountain to serve his own purposes, I imagine he *stole* a body. Shaka wouldn't do that."

Del looked at me. "Was this part of the threefold future?"

I smiled crookedly. "One of the futures I saw, all mixed up with the others. But it's hard to see it clearly when you're right in the middle of it . . . and then when Chosa's memories kept interfering with mine—" I shrugged. "I never knew which was which, or whose was whose. But from the looks of things, I'd predict our future is rather quiet." I reached out and caught a wrist as she dug idly in dirt. "Now. Why did you break Boreal?"

Del's brows knotted. "It was the only chance. And only that: a chance. I thought if Chosa were loosed behind the wards, even his own wards, Shaka might destroy him, or at least overpower him. But I knew as long as Chosa was in you, needing you so much, you wouldn't be able to break Samiel. So—that left Boreal." She shrugged defensively. "I wanted to lure him out, tease him into *my* sword during the dance . . . and then break her."

"But—your *jivatma*—"

Del dug a deeper hole. "I don't need her anymore. My song is finished. Now I start a new one."

"Bascha—"

"Leave it," she said softly.

I nodded, respecting her wishes. Then heaved myself to my feet, muttered as knees cracked, limped my way to the stud.

"So, old son, couldn't leave me yet." I patted a sweat-crusted shoulder. "Even in the midst of that, you waited here for me."

The stud shook his head and snorted, showering me with dampness.

"Thank you," I said gravely. "What happened to the mare?"

The stud didn't tell me, but I had a good idea. She'd probably broken her rein and headed down the mountain when the chimney collapsed, or when the howling began. We'd find her down below, waiting for a person. Horses are like that.

I patted the shoulder again. "We've sure been through some times. . . ." I rubbed a scraped shoulder. "Most, I'd like to forget."

"Tiger?" Del. "We have company."

I spun and looked up at her. "Where?"

She pointed. "There."

I moved around the stud, one arm across his rump, wishing I had a sword; *any* sword—then saw I wouldn't need one.

"Mehmet!" I blurted. "What are *you* doing here?"

Mehmet grinned. He wore dusty saffron burnous and equally dusty white turban. "Sandtiger," he said. "May the sun shine on your head."

I squinted very hard. "Am I sandsick? Or dead?"

"Neither. I am I, and here."

Frowning, I nodded. "That's something, I guess. But—*why* are you here?"

"The old hustapha is dead."

Which baffled me even more. "I—uh—I'm sorry. I mean—" I gestured helplessness. "He was a nice old man . . . I'm sorry."

"He was old, and his time was done." Mehmet climbed up the slope that lipped over onto the flat. "I have left the aketni below."

"You brought *them* here, too?"

"The hustapha said I must. It's here it all begins."

"What begins?"

He grinned. "You are to give me a message."

I touched my breastbone. *"Me?"*

Mehmet nodded. "The hustapha said: the jhihadi."

"But—" I stopped. Glanced upslope at Del, who continued picking feathers as if there was nothing else as important. Frowning, I looked back at Mehmet. "I have no message for you."

He was perfectly serene. "The hustapha cast the sand. He saw it would be this way. He sent us here to find you, so you could give us the message."

"I don't *have* a message—ah, hoolies, horse—do you have to do that here?"

The stud spread back legs and began to water the dirt. I moved quickly, avoiding the deluge; found myself stepping this way and that as he splattered. We stood on the lip of the slope—Mehmet, the stud, and I—and water runs downhill . . . so do other things.

"How much do you have?" I asked crossly, as the stud continued to flow.

"The message," Mehmet mentioned.

"I told you. I don't have any—" I stared at the urine as it ran down the slope. I watched the flow split, diminish; watched it channeled by dip and pocket; saw it diverted by bits of smokerock too big to dislodge on its own.

Patterns in the dirt. Channels and runnels and funnels. Lines filled, and overflowing; diverted in other directions.

"Water," I said blankly.

Mehmet waited politely.

"Water," I repeated. Then looked around intently, found the proper twig, bent down to draw in the dirt.

"Tiger." Del, from upslope. "What *are* you doing?"

I heard her come down, scraping dirt and pebbles as she moved. But I didn't give her an answer, too busy with the task. Consumed by the pattern.

She stopped next to me. Didn't say a word.

Eventually I looked up. Saw two pairs of eyes staring: one pair blue, one black.

I laughed up at them both. "Don't you understand?"

In unison: *"No."*

"Because you're both blind. We've *all* been blind." I stood up, tossing the twig aside. "Look at that. *Look* at that. What do you see?"

"Piss in dirt," Del said.

"I said you were blind. What else?"

"Lines."

"And piss *in* the lines. Don't you see?" I stared at them both intently. "All you have to do is put *water* in the lines. Only make the lines big. Make the lines deep. Put pullies at the cisterns. Dig channels in the dirt. There's water in the North—just bring it down from *there!*"

Del was astonished. "Bring water from the North?"

"Bit by bit. Divert the rivers, the streams . . . build patterns to bring it *here.*" I grinned, shrugging scraped shoulders. "And turn the sand to grass."

Mehmet fell to his knees. He spat into his hand, slapped it flat against the ground, then striped a line across his brow. "Jhihadi," he croaked.

I shrugged. "It's all a matter of viewpoint."

Del looked at me. Then she looked at the stud. Then picked another feather from her hair—this one was red—and blew it into the air. "I think you're sandsick," she said.

"Jhihadi," Mehmet repeated.

I grinned hugely at Del. "That wasn't so hard, after all."

She arched a skeptical brow. "If you are so wise, O jhihadi, tell us what we should do *now?*"

My grin died away. "We'll have to think of something."

Mehmet scrambled up. "Come with us!" he cried. "Come with the aketni. If we are to go North, to bring the water down—"

I put up a silencing hand. "Wait. First of all, it won't be that easy. You can't do it by yourselves. You'll need people. *Lots* of people. You'll need to dig more cisterns, find more water . . . build ditches to channel the water . . . but you'll mostly need to convince the tribes, tanzeers, and everyone else that this is the way to do it."

Mehmet nodded. "It begins with a single person. It has begun with the jhihadi. There will be more who believe."

Del was dubious. "It would take a very long time."

"We have time. And now we have a future." Mehmet touched his heart. "May the sun shine on your head."

"Second," I said, "we can't come with you. Del and I have a little—problem. We have to leave the South."

"Leave?" Del echoed.

I kept talking to Mehmet. "So we can't go with you."

Del wasn't finished. "Where are we going, then? We can't go to the North. Where are we supposed to go?"

I kept talking to Mehmet. "So you'll just have to take your aketni and do the best you can. Talk to some people. Go to other tribes. Tell them what I told you." I paused. "What the *jhihadi* said."

"Tiger—" Rather more insistently, "—where in hoolies do we go?"

I clapped Mehmet on the arm. "He wasn't such a bad old man. I'm glad I got to know him." I turned to the stud, untied him. "Give greeting to the aketni."

"Tiger!"

I climbed aboard the stud. "Are you coming? Have a stirrup."

Del stared up at me from the ground, hands on hips. "When you tell me where we're going."

"Right now, over-mountain. South to the ocean-sea. There's a city called Haziz." I reached down to catch a hand. "Come on up, bascha. We're burning daylight, here."

Forty-seven

In my line of work, I've seen all kinds of women. Some beautiful. Some ugly. Some just plain in between. But when *she* walked into the hot, dusty cantina and slipped the hood of her white burnous, I knew nothing I'd ever seen could touch her.

Everyone else in the common room stopped talking. Stopped moving. They all just stared.

The vision in the white burnous looked across the room directly at me with eyes as blue as Northern lakes. *This* time, I knew what a Northern lake was.

I stretched legs. Grinned. Sighed in appreciation as she crossed the cantina to my table. "I sold the mare," she said. "I have booked passage on a ship. And laid in provisions." She looked at the plump botas piled on the table. "I will let you bring the aqivi."

"I'd planned on it." I stood up, hooked thongs over shoulders, motioned for her to precede me out of the cantina. "Where are we going?"

"To the ship."

"No—I mean, where are we *sailing?*"

"Oh." Del made her way through the throng of fisherfolk. "You said you didn't care."

"I don't *care* . . . I was just curious."

"The only ship sailing tomorrow is one bound for a place called Skandi."

"Where?"

"Skandi."

"Never heard of it."

"Neither have I."

I bumped shoulders with a man, apologized, moved around a crippled woman. "Skandi?"

"Yes."

"The *word* sounds familiar." I took two long steps, caught up and fell in next to her. "Isn't that what the man called me in Julah? The one you said looked like me?"

"He said Skand*ic*. He asked if you were Skandic." Del stopped and looked at me. "We thought he meant a person . . . do you suppose he meant a *place?* That he thought you were from his homeland?"

I stared back at her a long moment, examining possibilities. There were too many to consider, so I gave up. Shrugged. "Oh, well. I guess we'll find out, if it's where we're going anyway." I peered over her shoulder to the docks and the mass of sail. "Is that our ship?"

She looked. "No. The one next to it."

I scowled, chewing a lip. I wasn't sure about any of this.

"Come on," she said. "It will be all right."

At sundown, we stood side by side on the dock, contemplating our future as it floated in black water. Del's voice was muted. "Are we doing the right thing?"

I shrugged. "I don't know. Seems like we don't have much choice."

She sighed. "I suppose not."

I summoned false gaiety. "Besides, think of all the places we'll see. People we'll meet. Adventures we'll have."

She looked sidelong at me. "It's the last one *you're* interested in."

I put a hand on my heart. "That hurts my feelings," I told her. "You just *assume* things about me without giving me the benefit of doubt."

Del snickered. "I know better."

Having gotten that far out of nerves, we fell into uneasy silence. The ship was tied up at the dock, creaking and rocking and rubbing. A tongue of wood connected it to the dock, waiting for dawn; for Del and me to climb it to the ship.

I scratched idly at my cheek, rubbing a blackened thumbnail against claw marks. "Look at it this way— it'll be a chance to start over."

"You won't like it," she declared.

I arched an imperious brow. "How do *you* know?"

"I know. You've been 'the Sandtiger' for too long— how will you deal with anonymity?"

"Ano-what?"

Del smiled. "No one knowing who you are."

"Oh, hoolies, who cares about that? I've been a panjandrum and a jhihadi. Neither one got me much, except to make me a target." And now a borjuni, but I didn't say that.

Del looked into my face, then gripped my elbow a moment. "I'm sorry, Tiger. I wish it might have been different."

I shrugged dismissively. "The aqivi's been spilled . . . and anyway, it was my choice. No one stuck a knife in my back and *told* me to break the circle. I did it on my own. And no one can deny it didn't do the trick."

She looked away. "No."

"And besides—" I broke it off.

She waited. Then, gently, "What?"

"This isn't—*home*. Not anymore. It's not the same, the South . . ." Something occurred. "Or maybe it *is,* and I can't live with it anymore. I just know that when we came down from the North, before Iskandar, I felt good. I was home. And then Iskandar happened, and the old hustapha and his sandcasting, and then Abbu and Sabra and everything else. . . ." I sighed. "I'm no messiah. I just had an *idea*. Maybe it'll work, and maybe it won't, this channeling of the water—but that's all it is. An idea. Anyone could have had it. It just happened to be me." I shrugged. "And now it's over. The jhihadi isn't anything special, or holy . . . just a beat-up, battered sword-dancer who no longer can enter a true circle—" I cut it off abruptly, staring at the creaking ship for a long, intense moment. Until the topic was bearable. "Besides, you lost more," I told her finally. "You lost Jamail again."

Her jaw tautened. "Yes."

"And also a *jivatma*."

She ducked it. "So did you."

I shook my head. "You know that sword never meant as much to me as yours did to you. You *know* that, bascha."

She gazed blindly at the ship. Didn't say a word. Just turned and walked away.

I let her go without protest, because sometimes it's for the best.

In the darkness, in the silence, I heard the indrawn breath. It caught itself, soft and fleeting: a self-stifled, private moment. She'd turned as I lay sleeping, so we touched at rumps and shoulders.

I twisted, turned over. Snaked an arm beneath her loose one and scooped her against my chest, hugging powerfully.

"It's stupid," she whispered.

"No."

"It's only a *sword*."

"That's not what you're crying about."

She gulped a choked laugh. "*What,* then? I sang my song for Jamail; that part is done. That part I understand. I've given him his passing." She swallowed noisily. "Why do I cry for the sword?"

"I told you: you aren't. Not for Boreal. You're crying for *Delilah* . . . for the loss of what you knew." I shifted a trifle closer, stroking a lock of hair from her face. "All your oaths are complete. Your vows are executed. Your songs have all been sung."

"I don't understand."

"You're crying for Delilah, because you don't know who she is."

In poignant vulnerability, she hitched a single shoulder. "I'm just—me."

"You don't know what that is. Trust me, bascha— I've felt that way myself."

"But . . ." She thought about it. "Who am I, then?"

I spoke gently into her ear. "An honorable woman."

Half-sob, half-laugh. "What is *that* worth in the place we're going?"

"I don't know. Something. We'll let them decide a price."

"Them," she murmured reflectively. Then, very softly, "It's all I've been for *seven years* of my life. A vengeful, obsessed woman, bent on killing men. Now all those men are dead. All the blood is spilled. What honor is there in that?"

"The honor is in the oaths, and your commitment to them."

Del twisted abruptly, turning to face me. I could see the shine of her eyes. "What about you?"

I shrugged easily. "It never meant the same to me. That sword—or the honor."

"Don't lie." Vehemently. "I know you better than that."

I smiled. "Maybe. But if honor meant as much to me as it does to you, I'd never have broken my oaths."

"And you'd be dead."

I grinned into her face, all of inches from my own. "You're *that* certain Abbu would have won?"

She didn't answer at first. Then, "That's not fair."

"Of course it's fair. If you really think he'd have won, you can tell me."

Silence. Then, "No, I can't."

"*Do* you think he'd have won?"

"See?"

"Do you?"

Del laughed. "We'll never know, will we?"

"*That's* not fair."

"Life often isn't." She lay quietly a long moment. "She was everything I was. My blooding-blade. *Everything*. She was my talisman, my surety . . . as long as I had Boreal, I could be anyone. I could survive the worst."

"You'll survive the worst now, no matter what happens."

Del sighed. "I don't know."

I poked her in the breastbone. "You sound just like a woman."

She stiffened. "What does *that* mean?"

"Nothing. I just wanted to get a rise."

She relaxed. The teasing had done its job. "We'll need to buy swords."

"Tomorrow. When we get a chance, we'll have new ones made. *Properly* made; none of this Northern fol-de-rol that sucks souls out of people into steel. I want an old-fashioned sword, like Singlestroke was."

She touched my cheek, stroking scars. "I'm sorry about him, too."

I shrugged away the sorrow. "He was dead already."

Her tone was as empty. "So was Jamail."

I kissed her on the forehead. "Go to sleep, bascha. Tomorrow we set sail for the rest of our lives."

She was very still a moment. "I hope you don't get seasick."

I snorted. "Save the sentiment for yourself."

Epilogue

We sailed at first light. Neither of us was sick, unless you count the discomfort of second thoughts. Standing at the rail, we watched Haziz fall away. Our past fall away. Doubts riddled us, but neither of us would admit it. Not that easily. Not to one another.

Del raked back hair and locked it behind ears. Then clutched the rail again, white-knuckled. Her eyes watched avidly as the rim of known land dropped below the horizon.

Helpfully, I suggested, "You could jump overboard. I can't, of course, because I don't know how to swim. But you could swim back to Haziz. We're not that far."

"Far enough," she mourned. Then shifted against the rail, leaning a hip into mine. "We're doing the right thing."

"I answered that already."

"It wasn't a question. It was a statement."

"Didn't sound like it." I turned my back to the water, hooking elbows over the rail. Changed the topic on purpose. "Why don't we get married?"

Del gaped. *What?*

"Get married." I shrugged idly, watching her expression sidelong. "We might as well."

"Next you'll want a family!"

I laughed. "I don't think we have to go that far."

Del's expression was a mixture of bafflement and curiosity. "Why do you want to get married?"

I waited a moment, purposefully abstracted. "What?—oh. I don't know." I shrugged. "It was just a passing fancy. It passed."

Del was very quiet. She still leaned against the rail, but no longer touched me. "I never thought about it. Not since I went to Staal-Ysta. Marriage?" She shook her head. "I am not the kind."

What had begun merely as a method of distracting her from our uneasy departure suddenly took on a new complexion. Even if I wasn't serious, Del was. And now I was curious. "Why not?"

"There is too much expected."

I challenged her. "No more than what we have."

She mulled that over, lines creasing her brow. "I just . . . I don't think so. Not for me. I had not thought to swear *that* oath. Not with you."

Unexpectedly, it stung. Now it was *personal*. "Why not? I'm not good enough?"

"That isn't what I mean."

"Or is it just that you're afraid of making any sort of commitment?"

Del sighed. "No."

"Then why not? What's wrong with the idea?"

"I'm not ready."

"No. What you mean is, you just don't want to grow up."

"That has nothing to do with it!"

"Of course it does."

She scrubbed a hand across her face, muttering in uplander.

"See?" I prodded.

Del took her hand away from her face. "It is not that I think you unworthy, or that I don't care. It is only I'm not ready."

"That's just an excuse. You'd rather make no commitment so that if things ever get tough, you can just walk out of the hyort."

Del gazed at me speculatively. "We're not in the South anymore. There wouldn't be a hyort."

"You're avoiding the subject."

"No." She laughed, shaking her head. "Ask me again later, when I have recovered myself."

It didn't matter anymore that I'd never intended the topic—or the question—to be serious. "Oh, *I* see. It was a stupid idea. Is that it?"

"Not stupid. Odd."

Odd? I scowled fiercely. "You don't fool me. You just want the aqivi without having to pay for it."

Del studied me expressionlessly. Her tone was exquisitely bland. "Believe me, I pay."

I couldn't hold onto the irritation. Laughing, I gestured surrender with both hands raised. "All right. I give up. It was a stupid idea. How silly of *any* man to want something he can count on. Someone to come home to."

As expected, she was ablaze instantly. "Come home to? Is that what you think I'll be? Someone to 'come *home* to'?" She pressed herself off the rail. "You know me better than that. I am not a docile Southron woman staying home to cook kheshi and mutton, emptying your slops bucket when you are sick from too much aqivi. I will be a companion walking *beside* you every step of the way, or even running or riding; stitching your wounds and tending your fevers, when you are foolish enough to get hurt. I will shirk no part of my duty, nor lay down my sword for you. And if *that* is not wife enough, then I want no part of you; nor should you want it of me!"

Waves slapped at the ship. After a moment, I nodded. "That should be enough."

"Then be content with it!"

I grinned. "Oh, bascha, I am. I just wanted to hear it from you."

Hot-eyed, she glared. "And are you satisfied, then, that I have spewed so much tripe?"

I laughed out loud. Hooked an arm around her neck. "You spew prettier tripe than anyone I know."

Unmollified: *"Hunh."*

I squinted beyond her, pointing with the arm slung over her shoulder. "Look at the sun on the water. Like sunglare off the Punja."

After a moment, she laughed. An odd, throttled laugh of rueful discovery. "You meant none of it!"

"None of what?"

"Getting married!"

I laughed. "I'm not the marrying kind."

Del's expression was exquisite: a blend of concern, relief, contemplation. "I feel odd."

"Why odd? Aren't you glad? You're not cut out for it any more than I am."

"Am I not?"

"You *said* you weren't! You've told me several times, at various dramatic moments in various dramatic ways over the past couple of years—including a few moments ago—that you were not suited to marriage. I didn't think you'd changed your mind quite *that* quickly, woman or no." I paused. "Why do you feel odd?"

"I think I feel *happy*."

"Happy? That we're not getting married?"

"That we don't have to. That there are no expectations. That we are what we are."

"Oh." I wasn't sure I understood exactly what she meant, but didn't feel like pursuing it any longer. Instead, I held her very close, setting my temple against hers as sea-salted wind ruffled our hair. Like Del, I felt happy. "We're free, bascha. Both of us. For the first time in a very long time."

"Free?"

"Of songs and oaths. Free of blood-born swords. Freed of who we *were;* to become whatever—and whoever—we choose." I sighed, feeling younger, and much relieved. "I think we'll like it, bascha . . . everything will be different."

Deep below in the hold, the stud rang a hoof off wood.

Muttering disgust, I buried my face in her hair. "Maybe not *everything*."

Delilah, laughing, hugged me, as we sailed into the sunrise.

DAW

An Exciting New Fantasy Talent!

Mickey Zucker Reichert

THE BIFROST GUARDIANS

☐ **GODSLAYER: Book 1**   (UE2372—$3.95)

Snatched from the midst of a Vietnam battlefield, Al Larson is hurled through time and space into the body of an elvish warrior to stand against Loki in the combat with Chaos.

☐ **SHADOW CLIMBER: Book 2**   (UE2284—$3.50)

Here is the unforgettable tale of the thief-hero Taziar Shadow Climber and his quest for vengeance against his father's slayer. Together with the barbarian lord Moonbear, he will face all comers in a world where death waits one swordstroke or evil enchantment away!

☐ **DRAGONRANK MASTER: Book 3**   (UE2366—$4.50)

United at last, the characters from *Godslayer* and those from *Shadow Climber* join in a climactic conflict between the forces of Chaos and Order, forced to fight their way from the legendary world of elves, gods, and magic to the bloody battlefields of Vietnam, and back again.

☐ **SHADOW'S REALM: Book 4**   (UE2419—$4.50)

They had killed the Chaos Dragon, and, in so doing, released a force against which all their spells and swords might prove useless—a primal power which now sought to destroy them—and their entire world.